UNDYING MERCENARIES
Steel World
Dust World
Tech World
Machine World
Death World
Home World

STAR FORCE SERIES
Swarm
Extinction
Rebellion
Conquest
Battle Station
Empire
Annihilation
Storm Assault
The Dead Sun
Outcast
Exile
Gauntlet

LOST COLONIES TRILOGY
Battle Cruiser
Dreadnought
Star Carrier

Visit BVLarson.com for more information.

Rebel Fleet

(Rebel Fleet Series #1)
by
B. V. Larson

Copyright © 2016 by the author.

This book is a work of fiction. Names, characters, places and incidents are either products of the author's imagination or used fictitiously. Any resemblance to actual events, locales or persons, living or dead, is entirely coincidental. All rights reserved. No part of this publication can be reproduced or transmitted in any form or by any means, without permission in writing from the author.

ISBN-13: 978-1519012661
BISAC: Fiction / Science Fiction / Military

= 1 =

The first time I witnessed a stellar flux it was midnight, the moment when Tuesday was about to become Wednesday.

I was sitting at a bar on the tropical island of Maui at the time. The bar was called TJ's, and it bordered on being a dive. It was a local hangout, not a fancy tourist place. The crowd was muted most of the time, and there was no pounding music to drown out the crash of the surf that was about two hundred steps to my right. I liked it that way.

"Whoa!" Jason gasped.

"What...?" I asked.

"Leo, do you *see* that?" he demanded.

Jason was a bronzed-skin guy who haunted TJ's as a regular. He was about five years younger than I was, and he'd become my friend over the last month or two.

Turning to him, I followed his gaze. He wasn't looking up at the sky, but rather at the waves. Frowning, I stared at a bubbling spot. There was a light source down there, something which made the foaming water glow green and white. The rest of the ocean was inky black all around it.

"That *is* weird," I agreed. "Could one of your Hawaiian lava vents be blowing its nose down there?"

"We don't have stuff like that on this side of the island."

I took him at his word. Being a drifter from the mainland, I'd spent the last two months here, but I was far from an expert on natural events of this kind.

When I looked back at Jason, his eyes were wider than before. He was looking up at the sky now.

"Don't tell me..." I said, following his gaze again.

We stared at the sky together. What we saw drove us to leave our drinks behind and walk out onto the open sands.

The stars could be seen clearly—but there was something unnatural about them. I was a Colorado native from the Rockies, and I'd often been treated to gorgeous starry nights. But this celestial event was definitely out of the ordinary.

For about a minute, the stars did an odd, wavering dance. Then a nebula appeared between Earth and the Milky Way. I'd learned the term "nebula" only recently from news reports. Apparently, it was what you called clouds of dust and gas that hung between the stars. Usually, they were the result of stars that had blown themselves up in nova explosions—but there weren't any dying stars in our stellar neighborhood.

"Don't take your eyes off it," Jason said. "It won't last. I watched vids on the net—it never lasts long. The glowy stuff appears for a while then vanishes again."

I didn't argue with him. I didn't even tell him the proper name for the glowy stuff. Instead, I just gaped up at the sky alongside him, figuring it was a once-in-a-lifetime opportunity to witness a mysterious natural event.

"Are we going to die, Leo?" Jason asked me suddenly. "Is that what this means?"

"Uh... I hope not."

"What do you think is out there in the water?" he asked a moment later, looking at the light in the sea again.

Jason was young, slightly drunk, and impetuous under the best of circumstances. I'd teamed up with him over the last month or two as he seemed to be even better than I was at finding piecemeal jobs and getting laid at bars like this one. It was the kind of life I'd embraced after leaving my Navy career behind me.

"Hey..." I said. "Kim's watching us. She's got a friend with her tonight. Let's—"

But I was talking to Jason's back. He headed right back into the bar, which was open to the sandy beach, and curled an arm around Kim's friend.

Kim didn't like Jason much. She didn't seem to like me, either. Lord knew we'd given it our best, but we'd both already struck out with her.

But a young man like me is always on the lookout for new opportunities. After all, "no" and "never" were two entirely different words. Smiling, I joined the three of them.

"Are you guys going out there?" Kim asked me immediately. The look on her face was a mixture of worry and curiosity.

"We sure are," Jason said. "Come on!"

As a group, we headed out across the sands. How could we not investigate? Over the last three months, there'd been numerous accounts of the stars turning into glowing dust-fields for a time, then smoothing back over and showing our familiar bright pinpoints of light again. As far as I knew, there hadn't been any reports of splash-downs of debris—but that might have just changed.

"This could be highly dangerous," Kim said.

"You always worry," Kim's friend said.

"What's your name?" I asked the new girl.

"This is Gwen," Jason said giving me a hard look.

I caught on immediately. He was claiming Gwen. Hell, his arm was still lightly draped around her waist. That was moving pretty damned fast, even for Jason. They'd only met about ninety seconds ago.

Jason had always been fond of the blonde ones, but I liked Kim's straight black hair just fine. Taking a tip from my friend, I slipped my hand around Kim's back when we reached the water.

Kim gave me a funny look. "Are you drunk?"

"Not nearly," I said. "Look out there! It's still bubbling. What I think is weird is that light. Where's it coming from?"

She forgot about my hand and didn't shrug me off. She stepped closer to me, in fact, as we stared at the water.

From the bar, the underwater lights had looked like a small patch of ocean that was farting up bubbles. Up close, the strange effect had taken on a different character. Whatever was down there—it was pretty big.

"It can't be an animal," Gwen said. "Not even a whale would make that kind of gas release."

"I agree," I said. "Maybe a small plane went down—or a boat."

"How could we have missed that?" she asked.

Looking at her in surprise, I could tell right away she was a woman of substance. She sounded educated and possibly opinionated. It made sense, as she was Kim's friend. That didn't bode well for Jason.

"I don't know," I answered her, "but *something* has to be down there with its lights on. I don't think it's a natural lava vent."

"No…" Gwen said. "Not lava. It would be orange and steaming if it was."

"There's only one way to find out," Jason said, pulling off his shirt and handing it to Gwen.

"What are you doing?" she cried. "Hold on—you don't have to go out there! What if it's boiling hot or something?"

"If I feel heat, I'll swim right back."

He didn't invite me on his little adventure. He didn't even bother to look at me. His eyes were all over Gwen, and I knew he was putting on some kind of mating-dance display for her.

It was all instinctual, and I could tell it was working. She looked both worried and excited. She followed him a few steps until her feet were in the waves.

My eyes went to Kim. A man will do damned near anything to impress a girl, and I'm no exception, but my reading of Kim was less certain. She looked excited, but also upset. She'd crossed her arms. I guessed she was more of a worrier than a daredevil.

I took off my shirt and handed it to her, along with my cellphone. She looked at these items in surprise.

"You're really going out there too, Leo?" she asked me seriously. "I didn't figure you for a crazy."

I shrugged. "Someone has to pull Jason's ass out of there if a shark takes a bite out of him, or something."

She didn't argue. She didn't say anything. She just watched me closely as I splashed out into the surf.

Jason was already swimming smoothly, arm-over-arm, passing the breakers. I trotted out, soon finding myself wading, then swimming—but I didn't dive right in. Something told me not to.

As I got closer to the bright, foaming spot, what surprised me most was that the water *wasn't* hot. Quite the opposite. It was *cold*. Abnormally cold for Hawaii, even at night.

"Hey! Jason!" I called out.

He waved back at me over his shoulder. Then he dived directly into the bubbling region.

That was the last I saw of him. About a minute passed while I watched the sea with growing concern. Jason could swim like a dolphin, but this was the open ocean.

Getting closer to where he'd vanished, I began treading water. The cold grew worse, and I almost felt like shivering.

The bubbles and the green light were still churning. But overhead, the nebula that had appeared so mysteriously was fading away, turning back into brilliant individual stars again.

"JASON!" I shouted.

Nothing came back. The ocean was empty.

It occurred to me then that Jason might never come back. I steeled myself for what I had to do. In the military, we'd all sworn not to leave a man behind. I felt that old urge to risk my ass overcoming my better judgment once again.

Behind me, on the shoreline, I saw and heard the girls. They were thigh-deep now, about fifty yards or so behind me. They were shouting something, but the wind was up, and the waves were crashing all around. Their words were mangled into high-pitched noises.

It didn't matter. They were freaking out, that much was clear. They knew Jason had been under for too long.

After sucking in about seven deep breaths, I plunged into the icy water, heading down toward the source of that green-white light.

Usually the ocean at night is pitch-black, especially on a moonless night like this one. But I found I could see fairly well due to the gleaming rays coming up from the bottom.

It was bright down here—even brighter than it'd looked from the beach. I found myself squinting into a glare as I got closer.

There was an oval region about twenty feet down. Something was lying there on the bottom, bubbling furiously. The bubbles kept me from seeing the source of the activity.

The light reminded me of the brilliance produced by arc-welding. Could something metallic be burning? I knew from the Navy it was possible to weld underwater, but I could hardly think of a reason why something like that might be happening here.

Instead of going directly into the bubbles, I swam low and circled around. Maybe Jason had gotten himself fouled on something. If I could see him and drag him out…

Then I spotted him, and I knew right away he was in trouble. His limp body was being buffeted by the released gases, but it stayed stuck to the bottom. I swam hard toward him and grabbed onto his ankle.

He was *cold*. Ice-cold. His right hand was touching the base of the disturbance. He was touching the object that was emitting the bubbles. His hand had to be caught on something.

I could see the base of the object now, a black surface with holes that emitted bubbles and beams of bright light. I didn't stare into it for long, sensing it might burn my retinas.

Grabbing onto Jason as firmly as I could, I dug my heels into the seabed and pulled under his arms. He didn't budge. I ran my own hand down his trapped arm, and I was shocked to find that his arm was encased in a chunk of ice from the elbow down.

His entire right arm was crusted with it. The bubbling block had somehow frozen him to it, and I figured that if I touched it I'd be stuck down here too.

I didn't know if Jason was alive or dead, but I still had some air left in me. I'd been a good diver all my life, and I could swim for three minutes underwater if I had to.

Bunching up my muscles, I clasped my hands around his chest and heaved. My feet slid on the sandy bottom, and I almost touched the thing that had him.

I wished for a knife. If I'd had one, I would have hacked the ice, or even his wrist—but I hadn't brought any gear. I hadn't planned on any of this.

There wasn't time to swim back to the bar to get help. If Jason wasn't dead already, he'd be a goner for sure by the time I got back down here.

My body was running out of oxygen, but I got an idea then. Instead of just tugging, I wrenched his body from side to side, trying to get a chunk of that ice to break off.

I've always been a strong, broad-shouldered man. It only took a few seconds. Suddenly, he was free in my hands, floating.

Lungs burning, my blood pounding in my veins, I kicked hard off the bottom. Desperate for air, I pulled Jason up to the surface.

I had him with my arm across his chest, swimming with a side-stroke. Gasping and wanting to throw up, I dragged him toward the beach.

The girls came toward us, splashing and shrieking. They helped me drag him to the shore. People from the bar came out carrying lights.

"I called 9-1-1 even before you dove down," Gwen said. "I can't believe you got him out of there. What happened?"

"His hand was frozen—stuck to some kind of object on the bottom."

"Frozen?" she demanded. "How could that be?"

I didn't have any answers. We reached the sand, and I let Jason down. I began working on him, pumping his chest, turning his head to let the water out. I blew air into his lungs but not much went in. I put my hand behind his neck to prop him up and open an airway—

That was about when Kim started screaming. I didn't even look at her as I was too focused on getting Jason to breathe again.

"His hand..." she sobbed. "Where's his hand?"

That got my attention. I looked to see what she was talking about.

Jason's right hand was missing. It was a clean cut, as if it had been done by an axe.

But I knew what had happened. His hand had been frozen to that thing down there. When I'd broken him free, his wrist must have been brittle enough to snap.
What could be so damned cold?

=2=

Jason didn't make it. He'd been a good kid, and he'd taught me as much about the world as I'd taught him. But that was all over with now.

When the doctor came out and gave us the news, Gwen sobbed and ran out of the sliding glass doors. I couldn't blame her. She was a tourist who'd just met us. She'd had enough heartache for a Tuesday night in May, especially when she was supposed to be on vacation.

The doc, a guy named David Chang, shook his head sadly.

"A very strange case. His hand—you say it was frozen to some kind of underwater object?"

"That's right, doc," I answered. "I pulled him free of it."

"And your name is?" he asked.

"Leo Blake, sir."

He nodded vaguely. I could tell something was bothering him. That wasn't hard to understand. The whole situation was downright weird.

"You resuscitated him at the scene—that was well done. But he never regained consciousness, not even in the ambulance."

"Well…" Kim said sadly, "at least he didn't suffer."

Doctor Chang glanced at her then turned back to me. "There was an infection of some kind… We detected it in his blood-work. Was Jason sick recently?"

"No, not at all. He was as healthy as a horse. He raced out into that ocean, determined to find out what was down there."

Dr. Chang nodded, obviously troubled. "Well, I'm going to have to report this to the CDC, just to be sure. And I'm going to have to ask you to remain in the area... You still feel fine right now?"

A chill ran through me. Was this guy suggesting I might be some kind of plague-carrier?

"I'm fine," I said firmly.

"Good! Please come back in the morning. We'll be running tests all night on Jason, but as the last person to come into close contact with him, I'd like to test you, too."

"Great," I said unhappily.

I walked out of the hospital with Kim, but we realized we were stranded. Gwen had been driving, and she'd taken off.

"Nothing like a walk to freshen you up," I told Kim. "I'll take you back to your hotel."

We started down a gentle slope. Cars zoomed past. The night was warm, humid and breezy.

Kim seemed to be brooding, so I let her take her time. Finally, after we'd gone a few hundred yards, she gave me a funny look.

"Did you touch that thing?" she asked. "Down there in the water?"

"No," I said. "I saw what happened to Jason. I didn't want any part of it."

"I can understand that, but you *did* touch Jason."

"So did you," I pointed out.

She looked alarmed.

"You're right," she said. "When I carried him out of the water with you... His hand was already gone by then... He must have been bleeding... We wouldn't have seen that in the dark and the water. He could have infected—"

I laughed. "Come on, Kim," I said. "Stop worrying so much."

"I can't help it," she admitted.

"Look, if there's some kind of space-virus going around, it will take time to incubate. Isn't that how it works with any disease? You can't catch an illness instantly. It takes days."

"Yeah, that's how it normally works."

"Doctor Chang was just being cautious."

She sighed then, and her hand snaked out to catch mine. We held hands as we walked downhill to the line of brightly-lit hotels that were strung along the highway between the beach and the road.

I took her to her room, and we lingered at the door.

"That was really brave, what you did out there," she said.

"Not as brave as Jason who dove after some kind of fallen UFO."

She shook her head. "No, it was braver. He didn't know there was anything dangerous about it. You did."

There were holes in that argument, but I would be damned I was going to point them out. I smiled at her instead.

She looked me over thoughtfully. "Light brown hair, soft brown eyes, thick jaw… You have the body of an ape, but the face of an innocent. I bet you get away with a lot, don't you?"

"Uh…" I said.

"You want to come inside?" she asked. She was looking down as if suddenly shy. "There's no way I'm going to sleep tonight."

"Sure," I said brightly. I was tired, but a man has to take opportunities like this by the horns.

We made love over the next hour or so, in between soul-searching moments. Kim had never been so close to a death before, and it was hitting her hard. Seeing another person die always made you realize how fragile your own life was. She had been dreading a night of brooding insomnia and was more than a little interested in some intimacy—even with the likes of me.

When she finally passed out, I found I was the one who had trouble sleeping. I couldn't stop thinking about everything I'd seen tonight.

I felt like I had to tell someone official about it. Over several sleepless hours, I decided who that someone was going to be.

Slipping out from under Kim's sleeping form, I got out my cellphone and took it onto the balcony. Then I called Washington D. C.

One might think that phoning the capital in the middle of the night would be not only pointless but downright rude. The six hour time difference, however, made up for all that. It was mid-morning on the East Coast.

I tried to get my old commander on the line, but that failed. Rather than giving up, I called general information at the Pentagon.

The phone was answered by a bored clerk. After explaining what I wanted, I was pushed up the chain a notch. The second person was a woman who at least sounded like she knew what she was doing.

"Name?" she asked.

"Lieutenant Leo Blake, Navy Reservist."

I heard her tapping at a keyboard. "What can we do for you, Lieutenant?"

"Last night I was involved with a stellar flux event."

"Lt. Blake," the voice interrupted. "Thousands of people witness these events every week. They're thought to be natural phenomena that haven't yet been explained by science. Any hysteria is an unwarranted—"

"Look," I interrupted. "I'm not calling to whine at you. Something fell to Earth, I think, and I swam down to find it. Interacting with the object caused the death of a friend of mine."

The voice was quiet for a few seconds. "Blake, are you saying you had personal contact with an unknown object related to a local stellar flux?"

"I'm saying that, yes."

"Hold please."

Rolling my eyes tiredly, I did as the voice commanded. Talking to government types was bringing back all kinds of memories. I'd gone into the Navy thinking I would make a career of it, but I'd been newly married at the time. The marriage had failed, and my wife had left me. After that, I'd left my career behind.

Hawaii had supposedly been a way to relax for a time and gather my thoughts about the future. I'd rapidly turned into a beach-bum, but that hadn't been entirely a bad thing. Now, my old life was coming back to me.

The wait on hold lasted for nine minutes. That's the trouble with cellphones, they're really good at telling you just how much time you've wasted.

Finally the line crackled again. There were some beeps, and I thought I'd been dropped—but then a new voice spoke.

"This is Vice Admiral Shaw," the voice said.

I was immediately shocked into wakefulness. There were only two hundred and sixteen admirals of any variety in the U. S. Navy, the maximum allowed by law. As a result, they weren't exactly commonplace. The fact I'd managed to get one on the phone—well, that was a frigging miracle.

"Uh... sorry to disturb you, Admiral Shaw," I said. "I was just reporting in about an unusual encounter that I thought might—"

"Let me ask you some questions, Blake," Shaw said suddenly. "Did you touch the object you found?"

"No sir, not directly. I went down to rescue a friend who'd done so. His hand became frozen to the object, which was boiling like a witch's cauldron."

"Someone *else* came into contact with the object?" Shaw asked sharply.

"Yes sir—but he didn't make it. He died just a few hours ago."

"I see."

There was a pause, during which I had time to reflect upon how unsurprised the admiral seemed by all my statements. He hadn't asked for details about the bubbling or the light or the cold. He hadn't even seemed surprised to learn that the man who'd touched it had died.

I got the sense he was conferring with someone else, or maybe taking notes, so I waited. I'm an impatient man by nature, but I was willing to stay good and quiet for an admiral.

"Blake, why did you leave the Navy?" Shaw asked me suddenly.

"Um... Personal problems, sir."

"Oh yes, your wife. The dates coincide. I'm sorry for that upheaval in your private life, but your commitment to military service goes beyond such matters. You're a trained naval aviator, and that sort of investment is something we don't like to lose."

Frowning, I wasn't quite sure what to say. He sounded like a recruiter.

"I... I served out the terms of my contract, sir. And I'm still in the active reserves."

"That's correct. And as of right now, I'm reactivating you on an emergency basis. Your reactivation is effective immediately. You're not to speak to anyone else about this, understood?"

"Sweet Jesus!" I said in an uncontrolled reaction. "I mean—I'm sorry sir, but this is a shock. Uh... to answer your question, yes, I understand."

Shaw chuckled. "Welcome back to the Navy, Blake. Stay within ten miles of your current GPS coordinates—yes, we've triangulated your phone. I'll send someone local out from Pearl to pick you up."

My mind was whirling around like a bug in a toilet. I couldn't take it in all at once. What should I do? What should I say?

I couldn't argue with him about the legalities. I knew he could pull the strings to do this if he wanted to. Finally, a question occurred to me, and I opened my mouth to ask it.

"Sir, what *was* that thing I found down there? You must know."

There was no answer. My phone had fallen silent. At some point over the last few seconds, the admiral had disconnected. The bastard hadn't even said good-bye.

"Shit," I said, lowering my cellphone.

Staring out at the city, my eyes were drawn to the ocean beyond. It was inky black with tiny pinpoints of light moving over it here and there, marking the passage of local boats. Farther out to sea, bigger ships sailed by, and planes glimmered overhead. The dawn was coming soon, and already the eastern sky was brightening with pink, predawn light.

The world was going on as usual out there, but my life had just taken an abrupt and unexpected twist.

Inside my head, I asked myself over and over again: *Leo, what the hell possessed you to make that damned call?*

=3=

As I'd been ordered to stay put, I figured Kim's place would be as good as any to wait. It was sure better than the rented cot I had out on the highway.

I slid back into bed with Kim, but she wasn't asleep anymore.

"Who was that?" she asked. "Who were you talking to on the phone?"

"No one," I lied, because I'd just been ordered to do so.

She kicked me in the side, and I grunted unhappily.

"You're not getting away with that," she said. "Get out."

I looked at her with bleary eyes. I really needed some sleep.

"What? Why?" I demanded.

"Because I'm not putting up with you calling other women from my hotel room."

"That's not—"

She kicked me again. "Out," she said.

"Damn, girl…" I said, getting up with a groan.

I'd been kicked out of bed before, both literally and figuratively. I could have argued, but I knew it wasn't going to do me any good. Even if I managed to talk her into letting me stay, she wasn't going to let me get any rest.

"If you change your mind, call me," I said and left.

Almost staggering now, I made my way down to the beach. It was closer than the flophouse room which I'd been sharing with Jason. It was cleaner, too.

I found a chaise lounge out in front of one of the beachfront hotels. If you were lucky, you could catch a few hours on one before getting chased off.

Stealing a towel, I draped it over my face and began dozing on the beach. There were dangers involved in this kind of thing, but I was desperate. For one, you might get robbed. Also, more than once I'd gotten a ferocious sunburn by sleeping too many hours without sunscreen.

Deciding to take my chances, I fell into a hard sleep. My dreams were troubled, and they were cut short by a man wearing a frown and carrying a two-way radio.

"May I see your hotel card key, sir?" he asked me.

I looked around. It was about ten a.m., if I had to guess.

"I must have left it in the room," I said. "I'll go get it. My wife can let me back in."

He stared at me suspiciously as I hopped up and headed for the hotel's beach entrance. I needed to move quickly before he asked my name. If he pushed it, I would have just said the room was under some made-up name—but it was best not to start a chain of lies.

I left him watching my back and talking into his radio. If I'd looked homeless, he probably would have called the cops. But I'm gifted with the looks of a man who *should* be employed and successful. That simple fact had gotten me through troubles during my beach-bum life on multiple occasions.

When I got to the door of the hotel, I lucked out when one of the guests came out just as I arrived. I caught the door and slipped inside.

Heading straight to the restrooms off the lobby, I cleaned up as best I could. You'd be surprised how much a man can do with soap, water and a load of six-inch brown-paper towels.

After that, I joined the shuffling crowd at the complimentary breakfast. No one objected, and I ate like a king. I even went back for seconds.

Feeling refreshed, I exited the front of the building. The key to this sort of life was looking like you belonged wherever you were. The doorman let me out with a smile and a nod, as if he was expecting a tip. I could have told him the well was dry, but instead I nodded back.

"Could you call me a cab?" I asked. "I have to go to the hospital."

He frowned but complied without question. I appreciated that kind of service.

When I arrived at the hospital, I tossed the driver some of my slim supply of cash and walked into the emergency room. After requesting Doctor Chang, I was surprised by the answer.

"He's been... detained," the receptionist said. "But we were told to expect you. Please take a seat."

"Detained?" I asked. "You mean he's off-shift?"

"No, he works from midnight until mid-morning usually. But he left some time ago."

Getting a bad feeling, I nodded as if unsurprised. "The Navy guys picked him up, didn't they?"

She blinked at me then nodded.

"Two men?" I asked in a conversational tone.

"No, three. But only one of them was in uniform."

"I see. Well, I'll check back with you later."

"Hold on, I was supposed to call them."

She dug out a card, which I snatched from her surprised fingers.

"Sir? I need that card..."

I studied the number then handed it back to her.

She frowned at me sternly. "Are you some kind of criminal?" she demanded.

"No," I assured her. "No more than Dr. Chang was."

That seemed to click with her, and she lowered her voice, becoming more affable. "What's this all about, Mr. Blake?"

"Military experiments," I said. "I'm in the Navy."

"Ah..." she replied. "The flux event last night! That was *you* out there, wasn't it? Everyone's been talking about that poor kid you brought in."

Then I remembered Admiral Shaw's orders.

"I'm not supposed to talk about that."

"I see."

She was cold again, so I left her alone. Heading outside, I saw a car pull up. There were three men inside. One of them was in a Navy uniform.

These guys looked serious. The two in plainclothes wore particularly unpleasant expressions. They looked like spooks to me—CIA, or something like that.

I performed a sharp left turn and walked toward the road. I never looked back over my shoulder.

Behind me I heard them troop into the emergency room.

Something was up. Call it a bum's intuition, but I can always tell when security is looking for me. Right now, the back of my neck was all tingly.

Sure, I could have gone inside and demanded answers. But what if they'd arrested me on the spot? What if Admiral Shaw wasn't an admiral, but a spook of some kind instead?

The number one question in my mind concerned Dr. Chang. Why had they taken him away then returned without him? Where was he now? It wasn't going to take long for the chatty receptionist to tell them I'd just left. On instinct, I tried the first door I found that led back into the hospital. It was locked.

Trotting around the building to the back, I found another entrance near a dumpster. This door had been propped open. Why? Maybe the janitor wanted a fresh, morning breeze.

Slowing down to a walking pace again, I nonchalantly stepped into the place. Anyone eyeing me would know right off I didn't belong here. I was wearing swim trunks, an open shirt and sandals. It was a far cry from scrubs and lab coats.

Not even I could pull off walking through the back offices of the hospital. I was stopped by the first desk-jockey who popped out into the hallway.

"Sir? Can I help you?"

"You sure can," I told the pencil neck with squinty eyes and big round glasses. "I'm afraid I've lost my way. Could you show me to the main floor? I'm supposed to be visiting my mother."

"Ah, I see. Did you know visiting hours haven't started yet?"

"No—sorry. Could you point the way to the waiting room?"

The drone gave me a look, and I knew he was deciding whether or not to call security. I waited with confidence, and he smiled at last. My honest face was really paying off today.

"The main floor is that way," he said. He pointed then went back to his office. I headed in the indicated direction for a dozen paces but ducked into the first side passage I could find. After that, I ended up in a janitor's closet to avoid more prying eyes.

Janitors usually work at night, and the closet was nicer than others I've been in. I figured that if I sat in here a half hour or so, they'd probably give up and search somewhere else.

I had ample time to reflect upon the nature of my life-choices, and how they'd brought me to this low moment. But mostly, I kicked myself for calling Washington in the first place.

These dancing stars must have the government on edge. Whatever they were doing in response, it was apparently heavy-handed. Bureaucrats *hated* unexpected events, and watching the stars flicker on and off in the sky must have been near the top of their "undesirable" list.

I thought about calling or texting someone, but I knew my transmissions would be traced. So, I shut off my cell and took the extra step of unplugging the battery. I didn't want to take any chances.

Despite my best efforts, I heard a scuffle of footsteps outside my closet about forty minutes later.

"In here," said a voice.

I steeled myself. Somehow I'd failed. Maybe they'd played back security camera files or questioned a nosy worker. It could have been anything, and it really didn't matter what had gone wrong. They'd caught up to me.

Manufacturing a smile and snapping open the door, I stepped outside in their midst like I owned the place.

"Gentlemen," I said, "I've been waiting. Shall we go?"

They showed their teeth in anger. One of the plainclothes types, a brute with a crew-cut so tight it looked like it might bleed, jutted out his lower jaw. "You're coming with us, Blake."

"That's what I said—but can I call General Shaw, first?"

The brute looked confused for a second.

"That's *Admiral* Shaw, Lieutenant," the Navy man said. He was a black guy with a paunch, but he looked like he'd be tough in a fight. They all did.

I turned to the Navy man. He was a Commander, which meant he outranked me.

"Right... Of course, sir."

This exchange had given me a small amount of information. For one thing, Shaw was the man behind the scenes, pulling their strings. Apparently he really *was* an admiral—either that, or he was using that covering title with everyone. CIA stiffs often pretended to be officers in one service or another.

I eyed the Commander. He seemed real enough. As a Navy man, would he really harm a fellow sailor? I wasn't sure, but I felt certain I was going to find out.

=4=

They led me to the car I'd seen them drive up in. That had been damned near an hour ago, and I couldn't help but feel proud I'd kept them running around the hospital for that long. It wasn't even a large building.

The brute was in the backseat next to me. The Navy guy was in the front passenger seat, while the third man drove.

The driver was the smallest and the meanest looking of the bunch. He was as silent as a stone. He didn't even look in the rearview mirror at me when I tried to catch his eye.

"So," I said, "are you guys all stationed at Pearl?"

"I am," the Commander said.

"I didn't catch anyone's name," I prompted.

"That's because we didn't give you any names, fool," said the brute sitting next to me.

"Let's be civil," the Navy man said. "He's new."

"He doesn't act like it," the brute insisted. "He acts too smooth, like he knows the game already. That's it, isn't it? You've been tipped off, haven't you Blake?"

This series of statements baffled me, but I didn't let that show.

"Of course I know," I said, figuring they were more likely to talk openly if they thought I already understood what was happening. "Did you think this was all an accident?"

The brute lowered his already low brow. He turned in his seat and put his arm up on the headrest behind me. He stared at me intimidatingly. This was effective, but I pretended not to care.

"You're a pilot, aren't you?" he asked. "Flying pukes always think they're better than the rest of us."

"I didn't know you'd served," I said.

"Marines. Two tours back in—"

"Shut up," said the Commander from the front seat. "Don't you know when you're being pumped, you moron?"

The brute looked pissed, but he *did* shut up. I gave him a little smirk, hoping to get him talking again. His face reddened, and he balled up his fists, but he kept quiet.

I turned my attention to the Commander. He was obviously the man in charge.

"What happened to Doctor Chang?" I asked.

"That's none of your concern, Blake."

"Why? Did he fail the blood test?"

For some reason, this statement touched off a serious reaction. The brooding driver veered off the road, taking a violent turn onto a side street. As best I could tell, the road went nowhere. We were heading up the side of a mountain—which pretty much described what happened when you turned inland from the shoreline on any island in the Hawaiian chain.

It was farm country or some kind of nature preserve. Then again, as I pondered the mental map in my head, it might have been part of an airfield owned by the military. That didn't surprise me.

"What are you doing?" the Commander asked the driver.

The driver, who had been quiet all along, sneered at him.

"This is bullshit," he said. I was surprised to hear he had a lower-class British accent. "I'm done with it. We'll finish this and move on. Just like we agreed."

"Blake is a Navy man, and he hasn't taken the blood test yet," insisted the other. "This isn't officially sanctioned!"

"Piss off. In the end, it's all going to turn into a shit-show. We might as well start right now."

"Control your sym, Dalton!" the Navy guy ordered.

"Are you threatening me, Jones?"

By this time, I was becoming concerned. I had some names to go with their faces, but that wasn't making me any happier.

The many ideas I'd been entertaining about the nature of my near-term fate had been vanishing one by one. Quarantine? A term of imprisonment? A straight-out killing to hide a secret? None of these were fitting.

And what was a *sym*, anyway? Did I really want to know?

These men, I realized now, were no more on my side than I was on theirs. Only the Navy man seemed to have any kind of compassion.

Dalton drove like a madman. He took every turn at top speed, throwing us around. That gave me an idea.

The next time he took a left, I threw myself into the brute sitting next to me in the backseat.

"Get the fuck off me!"

"Sorry," I said, even as I quietly unbuckled his seatbelt.

He shoved me away violently, banging my head against the steel frame of the car.

I caught a lucky break then. Possibly, it was the only one I would get for this entire long day. While he was fumbling for his seatbelt, good old Dalton took another hard turn.

Reaching across the brute, I popped his door open and shoved him *hard*.

Up until that point, I hadn't displayed any kind of strength. Like I said, I'm a man with a powerful build. Still, I wouldn't have liked to arm-wrestle this marine, but then again, I might have surprised him.

As it turned out, I overdid it. The combination of Dalton's crazy driving, my hard shove and the lack of a seatbelt, launched that bastard right out of the car like he'd been fired from a cannon.

For a split-second, he seemed to hang out there in open space, still in a sitting position. He threw out his arms then vanished. I couldn't help taking a wincing glance behind the car as I watched him go into a tumble.

"Man overboard!" I shouted.

"You crazy fuck!" Dalton snarled. He slammed on the brakes as I'd expected him to do.

I recovered first and vaulted out of the car. My belt was already off, so I was able to get out of the vehicle before the others.

A gun barked three times. Ducking and turning, I decided to hug the car's trunk. I didn't have time to run off into the palm trees that lined the street.

Another gun fired, but it didn't seem to be in my direction. There was no sting, no sparks from the car or the asphalt.

What I saw when I took a peek over the trunk lid shocked me. Both men had guns out—but they weren't shooting at me. They were shooting at each other.

Jones was clutching his side, which was spouting blood. His uniform was wrecked. He sagged down against the car door with a look of shock on his face.

Dalton turned his grin, and his gun, toward me.

"Right," he said. "It's your turn, mate. You're whale-shit now. Isn't that what you Navy buggers say?"

I hugged the trunk of the car, skirting around it to avoid him. My plan was to get to the lieutenant commander's gun.

Dalton wasn't that stupid, unfortunately. Rather than chasing me around the bush—or in this case, the Ford—he moved around the front of the vehicle to stand over the dying man's body. He put one more round into him to make sure, and his victim slumped.

Laughing, he turned back to hunt for me. I was desperately trying to get to the driver's side door to see if he'd left the keys inside—he hadn't.

Dalton stepped close to look at me.

"Too bad," he said, aiming his gun at my face. "You, I was gaining respect for. These others were too straight. Too dumb to win in the end."

I had no idea what he was talking about, but when he tightened his grip on that pistol, I said the word every murder victim says at the end: "Wait!"

Boom!

I heard it, even though I shouldn't have.

Boom! Boom! Boom!

Dalton spun around and went down. My first thought was that he'd been nailed by the brute from the backseat, but that guy was nowhere in sight. We'd left him a quarter mile back down the road.

Then my head snapped around, and I saw Commander Jones.

He had his gun up again. I was surprised to see that he was alive. Maybe he'd faked his death, or maybe he'd gotten a second wind. I wasn't sure which it was, but he was the one who'd shot Dalton down.

I heard sirens in the distance. I walked around the car and moved to Jones. I squatted beside him. His eyes followed me, and his breath whistled from the holes in his lungs.

"Why'd you shoot your partner?" I asked him.

"I'm out of this contest," he wheezed, "but I wanted the winner to be Navy—like me. Don't be a dick, Blake."

"You guys are bat-shit crazy," I said, shaking my head, "I don't know what the hell is going on, but thanks for saving my ass, anyway."

He shook his head. "I haven't saved you from anything. I've cursed you. Remember: don't trust anyone. When they come, you'll find they don't die easy. You should cut out the heart, take off the head, or maybe burn them to be sure. Hell, feed the enemy to pigs and turn them into shit."

I squinted into the eyes of what I was now certain must be a madman.

"You've got to *run*," Jones told me. "Throw away your cell. Take this car and run. Don't look back. Try not to listen to your sym until you're sure you need it to stay alive. Sometimes... it lies to you."

"You're not making any sense," I said, "but I've got to take you back to the hospital." With a grunt, I put my hands under his armpits and tried to lift him into the passenger seat.

He surprised me by putting his gun in my face.

"No, Blake. Leave me, or I'll shoot you, so help me. Get the hell out of here."

Throwing up my hands, I shook my head. There was no pleasing some people. After taking the keys from Dalton, I climbed into the Ford. I started up the car and drove away at speed.

Looking back at that moment later, if I had it to do over again, I think would have turned around and run them all over several times.

Just to be sure.

=5=

The car wasn't something I could keep. Neither was my cellphone. But I figured I should make one last play before I ditched them both.

"Vice Admiral Shaw, please," I told the Pentagon switchboard at the Naval Intelligence office.

"There's no one listed under that name."

"This is Commander Jones on an unsecured line. I've got an emergency."

"Hold please."

I waited. I knew they were locating me, but I didn't care. Making random turns onto dusty back roads one after another, I crossed the island while I waited.

Finally, the line went live again.

"Your codename, please?" asked another voice.

"I don't have any codename. I want to talk to Shaw."

"There's no one here by that name."

"If Shaw wants to know what happened to his team, he should talk to me now. This is his last chance. I'm ditching everything in five minutes."

"Hold please."

Groaning, I did as I was told. About when I'd decided I'd had enough, the phone spoke to me again.

"This is Shaw. Who is this?"

"Lt. Leo Blake."

"Blake?" he asked, sounding surprised. "Where are you?"

"I'm driving the car your three goons loaned to me."

"They *loaned* it to you? Are you saying you've stolen government property? Blake, this is—"

"Cut the shit... uh, sir," I said. "Your men went crazy, and they tried to kill me—at least, I think that was their plan."

"Listen to me carefully," Shaw said. "You might have a disease which can affect the mind. I want you to return to the hospital. You were never tested properly. Everything will be explained when you get there."

I laughed. "Right. Like how you explained things to Doctor Chang? Why's he dead? What did he do that was so wrong?"

I was fishing for information, and he went quiet for a moment. Then, like every good sucker, he took the bait.

"Chang had the disease, too. It's very dangerous. You need to report back to the hospital immediately."

"I feel fine. What's this disease called? What are the symptoms?"

"It doesn't have a formal name yet. It's an infestation by a symbiotic organism. A parasite that affects the mind. Victims endure paranoia and violent tendencies. Hysterical strength and delusions take over in the advanced stages."

That rang true to me. Jones had talked about a "sym" and how it could make you crazy. The thought of having a parasite in my body made my skin crawl. But I didn't let any of this come through in my voice.

"Come to think of it," I said, "Dalton did foam at the mouth a little. Jones had to put him down like a dog."

Admiral Shaw suddenly became angry. "Where are my operatives, Blake? Give me a full report, that's an order."

"I don't even know if you're a real admiral," I said. "At the switchboard, they said there wasn't anyone in the building by that name. I'm thinking of going to the media with this entire story."

Shaw chuckled evilly. It was an unexpected reaction.

"Think you can take them all, is that it, boy?" he asked. "Go ahead and try. Paint your butt red and moon the bull. You'll be dead by noon tomorrow as they scramble over one another to get to you."

Thinking about the bloodlust in Dalton, I wondered if he could be right. In any case, it didn't sound encouraging. I decided to change tactics.

"I'm going to talk to you no matter who you are, Shaw, out of the goodness of my heart. The three men you sent after me are all dead—except maybe for the marine. He fell out of the car doing about seventy, so he might still be breathing."

"I don't believe it... You took them *all* out? That's astounding. Have you morphed in some way? Were you infected earlier than you let on?"

Morphed?

"Um... no," I said.

"This was all a setup, wasn't it?" Shaw went on, his voice rising. "You're a finalist playing for someone else, a predator preying on others by pretending you're weak!"

"Damn, more crazy talk about these killings like they're part of some kind of game. To answer your accusations, I'm not a player in your little contest. I don't even know the rules. I just got lucky and pulled a few fast moves. Jones gave me a break before he died, too. That's all it was."

"No," he said. "That's not true. If you've survived this long, you've got to be good, whether you know it or not."

"This conversation has to come to an end soon," I said. "I can't let you track me down."

He sighed heavily. "You've put me in a very bad position."

I rolled my eyes at that one. He wasn't the one running for his life, trapped on an island in the Pacific.

"Excuse me," I said, "but five people have died around me in the last twelve hours. I'm having trouble crying for you, Admiral."

"An insubordinate smart-ass as well... I'd read that in your file, but I had no idea it was this bad."

"Any last words before I hang up?" I asked.

"Yes. Stay alive. You're one of the last on our side—one of the last from our military, in any case. It's imperative that you stay alive for now."

"I'll do my damnedest, sir."

"When you get to a safe spot, call this number again. Use the codename 'Orion.' Have you got that?"

"Orion. Got it."

I hung up and threw the phone out the window. Then I did a U-turn and headed for a beach area I knew well. I ditched the car in a vacant lot filled with junk and walked away in my sandals.

By the time I'd walked a mile, I found myself in familiar territory. That was the good thing about living on an island. Pretty quickly, you got to know your way around. After all, Maui was less than forty miles long.

Distantly behind me, I heard sirens and the like. I was sure somebody was upset about all the carnage I'd left behind me.

Feeling a little shaky, I walked toward my former home. To be safe, I passed it along the beach side first.

The cops were already there. I kept walking along the shoreline, throwing rocks into the surf like I didn't even notice. I carefully avoided looking at the place, and I knew I could never go back there.

Damn. I was going to be hard-up without any money. My wallet was worse than useless now. If I used an ATM card, every red light in D. C. would begin blinking.

Hungrily, I thought about the hollow leg of my bed, where I'd stashed several hundred bucks. Shaking my head, I had to let it all go.

Walking down the beach with nothing but the clothes on my back, I began mentally listing the people of means in my life that I could contact.

The list was thin, but there were a few souls on it who might lend a hand. I spent the rest of the day hitting up every one of them, and I collected a grand total of one hundred and eighty-eight dollars. That wasn't a lot, especially in Hawaii.

Night fell at last, and it was a relief when it did. I knew it would be harder for them to find me in the dark. Besides that, I'd already gotten a sunburn despite having purloined a straw hat and a long-sleeved shirt. Even my toes in my sandals were stinging.

With a sigh, I headed back to the beachfront hotels. I knocked on Kim's door at about ten, even though I figured she might be out partying somewhere.

To my surprise she opened it, doubtlessly after checking me out through the lens of her peephole at length.

"What do you want?" she demanded.

"I'm hurting," I said. "I need help."

Kim looked me up and down.

"You're sunburned," she said at last.

"Yeah."

"Have you never heard of sunscreen?"

I shook my head, took off my hat, and held it in both my hands.

"I'm sorry," I said, staring down at my stolen hat. "Sorry to trouble you. I'll go now."

Slowly, I turned away, but she sighed and opened the door wider.

"Come on in."

Looking as sad as any dog that's ever been caught whizzing on the furniture, I stepped inside. She talked about Jason and the events of last night. We both agreed his death had been a shock. I told her nothing of having killed two or three assailants since then—I didn't think it would help my case.

Forty minutes later, she took me out to buy me a burger. I ate three, as I hadn't eaten all day long. It felt great to be doing something other than walking the streets.

Finally, knowing I needed help, I told her of the day's events. In my heavily edited version of the story, I'd escaped the men in the car without violence. I was merely a victim being chased across the island by merciless thugs.

"Can't you call your parents?" she asked me.

"Nope," I said. "I don't want to get them involved. What if these crazy people go after them, too?"

She stared at me in concern. "You came to *me*, though. You didn't have any problem dragging me into this mess."

"Admiral Shaw doesn't know about you. They don't know you might be infected with—whatever this is."

Kim licked her lips. I could see her worrying brain chewing the situation over. She didn't like the taste.

"What if they come after me? What am I supposed to do? Should I cut my trip short and run back to the mainland?"

Something in her tone made me look up from my second bag of fries. I could see her eyes were wide, fearful. She was freaking out a little.

"Just stay away from hospitals. They seem to find people that way."

"But what if I get sick?"

"Don't worry," I said. "I pulled Jason out of the water and gave him mouth-to-mouth, and I still feel good. You're not infected. You're fine."

"Maybe you've got some kind of natural resistance," she said, winding up that long dark hair of hers with a finger. "Maybe I'm the one that they're really looking for."

"Why would you think that?" I asked her.

She stared at me again for a time, then suddenly smiled.

"No reason," she said. "You must be tired, right? Let's go back to the hotel."

She paid the bill, and we left. I wanted to leave the tip, but I was just too damned poor. I felt kind of bad about that. I told myself that when this mess was all cleared up I would get a job and pay off my debts.

"This is the last week of your vacation, right?" I asked her.

"Yeah. But Gwen took off. She's flying back home tomorrow. Seeing Jason die—it was too much for her. I'm alone on the island."

"Thinking of going home too?"

"Maybe. Let's go have a drink. You look like you could use one."

We had several. They were strong, and by midnight, I was happy for the first time in twenty four hours. Arm-in-arm, we headed back to her place.

Kim wasn't as drunk as I was. She'd been nursing her drinks. She smiled vaguely as we collapsed on her bed.

I reached for her, and at first, she recoiled. But then, she slowly relented. We made love again. It felt great to be alive.

It had been a long day, and after we'd satisfied each other, I passed out. I didn't even take off my sandals. I was totally drained.

Just as I was beginning to dream, I heard a strange sound. Sort of a clank.

I opened one eye. There, standing over me with a wild look of fury on her face, was Kim. She had a long metal floor lamp in her hands, and she was holding it like a batter swinging for the fences. With a grunt, she swung the lamp's heavy base down at me.

Clearly, she wanted to bash my skull in.

=6=

In my short lifetime I've pissed off any number of women. I'd be the first to admit that. But until this very moment, none of them had actually attempted to murder me.

When Kim came at me with that lamp, I couldn't believe it. Rolling off the bed and onto the floor with a thump, I managed to avoid her first swing. Fortunately, she was no athlete—but her enthusiasm made up for that lack of physical power.

She turned, snarling, and lifted the lamp with both hands again. She held it over her head like some kind of medieval war hammer.

Scrambling to my feet, I jumped back, but there's only so much space to retreat in a hotel room.

She swung again, sweeping the air with a powerful blow. I dodged, and the base of the lamp took out the TV. It crashed into junk on the floor.

"Hold on, girl!" I shouted. "What's wrong? Was I that bad? I thought you enjoyed it!"

She didn't even seem to hear me. She lifted the lamp for a third try.

That was my chance, and I took it. I rushed in and pushed her onto the bed. She struggled with me, but I didn't expect it to be a contest. I thought she'd burst into tears and curl up and declare exactly what her problem was.

She did none of those things. Her eyes were determined. *Mean.*

I had to climb onto her and hold her wrists by force to keep from being injured. She was all claws and teeth, and she kept slamming her knees into my back. *Damn!* Those skinny limbs were stronger than they looked.

"What the hell is wrong with you, Kim?" I demanded, shouting into her face.

Panting through her bared teeth, she looked around with a crazed expression.

"He won't kill me," she said. "I'll kill him first. He won't kill me." She was almost chanting the words. It was as if she was talking to herself.

"Listen," I said. "I can see you're in a bad mood. I'm willing to leave, no hard feelings. Would that be okay?"

Her eyes focused on mine for a moment.

"No," she said. "Don't leave yet. I need to kill you."

At last, I was beginning to catch on.

"Kim, listen to me," I said. "I was wrong before. I think you *do* have the disease. Whatever it was that came down from space. Whatever Jason found on that bubbling rock at the bottom of the sea, must have infected you. You have to try to control yourself."

"No I don't. I have to kill you."

"Why?"

"Because you'll kill me if I don't."

"How do you know that? Who told you that?"

She looked around the room. "I don't know. Something did."

"It was the sym," I said, putting it all together in my head. "They call it a sym. Maybe it's some kind of symbiotic life form…?" I asked aloud. "Yes, it must be some kind of parasite in your mind."

"Why are you talking so much?" she demanded, her voice rising to a wail. "Why haven't you killed me yet?"

"I don't feel it—not like you. Not yet, anyway. I think maybe some people are better able to control it than others. There was this guy named Jones—"

She began struggling again.

"Stop that," I insisted, "you're bruising up your arms. Let's call a truce, okay?"

"No!"

I heard something then. Something from outside—something bad. It was a single squawk from a cop's radio. Then I heard footsteps coming from the walkway. We were on the third floor, overlooking the parking lot. The window was cracked open, and the curtains were fluttering slightly in the breeze.

"You called the cops?" I asked her. "Before you tried to kill me with a lamp?"

"In case you got the upper hand," she said. "Insurance."

"That's just great. You're going to jail. You know that, don't you?"

Kim laughed, and kneed me in the back again.

"Help!" she screamed. "Help me!"

"Oh, dammit," I said.

A hammering began at the hotel door.

I knew what I had to do, but I sure as hell didn't want to do it. I got up off Kim and walked toward the door. I took pains to turn my back on her as I reached for the doorknob.

Before I unlocked and opened it, I counted to three. It was hard to do.

One... two... three...

The hammering on the other side became intense. I was trying to time things right. I had to open that door just in time to have the officer see Kim, looking deranged, coming for my back.

It was a calculation. Lots of things could go wrong. She might not do anything, or she might manage to clock me before I could open the door. The cop might even believe her story. The situation didn't look good for me, and I knew I was going to have a hard time getting the cops on my side on this one.

Unfortunately, this was the only move I could think of pulling, so I took the chance.

On three, I yanked open the door and threw it wide. It was raining hard outside, and the man standing in the doorway was dripping wet. Behind him, the railing above the parking lot ran with beads of water.

Shock ran through me as I realized the man standing on the walkway outside wasn't a policeman. He was none other than the same marine I'd tossed out of a speeding car earlier today.

His suit was torn up, and he didn't look happy to see me at all. There was a pistol in his hand. He had it raised up even with my head. I shied away, but he fired without compunction.

For a split-second, I thought I was dead. In fact, I was sure of it. But the bullet sailed over my shoulder. It took out Kim instead. She'd been charging up behind me with that damned lamp again.

Shot right between the eyes, she fell back, flopping and bleeding on the thin brown carpet.

The killer looked at me and shook his head.

"You can't be a chicken if you want to survive," he said to me matter-of-factly. "When they get like that, you have to take them out. Even if it's a pretty girl."

My mouth hung open, and I stared at Kim. She was really dead on the floor. I couldn't believe it.

The marine wasn't done yet. He drew a long knife and walked to Kim's body. He chopped at her neck. I grappled with him, but he was strong. With two final quick strokes, the head was off.

"You crazy bastard! You killed her!" I said, unable to comprehend what I was looking at. It was too much.

"Damned straight I did. You can thank me later. Did you know it took me all frigging day to find you? I wanted to shoot you too—don't think I didn't. But Shaw's got some kind of hard-on for you. Now, are you coming with me, or are you going to stay here and take the blame for this mess?"

Stunned, I staggered out of the room after him. He waved at me with his pistol.

The enormity of what I'd just seen ate at my mind. I'd witnessed the murder of a nice girl who I'd liked. A woman I'd made love to twice—just hours ago. She might have been out of her mind, but she hadn't deserved death and mutilation.

I felt a blind rage begin to build inside my skull. It must have been shock over the murder that triggered it. But instead of rushing to attack the murderer, I came up with an instant plan.

"Cop!" I said, pointing down over the railing toward the street.

He fell for it. It was a believable enough development.

As he looked for the phantom police car, I stepped close and pinched a nerve in his blocky hand. Self-defense training had its benefits.

I snatched the falling pistol out of the air and brought it into line with his body, backing away.

He spun around to face me. It was then, I think, that he saw the murderous intent in my eyes. Oddly, he smiled when he recognized the expression.

"Ah…" he said. "So you *do* have a sym. They told me you were harmless, but I can see it, looking right at me out of your eyes."

"Tell me your name," I said with an animal voice that wasn't entirely my own.

"My friends call me Samson," he said. "But you're not my friend. You can call me—"

Before he got out another word, I shot him seven times in the chest. I would have fired more rounds, but the pistol was empty.

Then I threw his body over the railing onto some parked cars. A windshield shattered, and two car alarms began singing.

Too bad murder wasn't enough to stop a thing like Samson.

* * *

The stars exploded again after I killed Samson. I was on the run, out in the open, or I might have missed it.

It was the middle of the night, and the rain had finally stopped, but I had no way of knowing the exact time. I'd ditched my wallet, my cellphone, and everything else that might have identified me or connected me in some way with the heinous crimes of the day.

As I walked through a forested area, I came to a clearing and looked up. The sky had cleared and brightened. But it wasn't the light of the Moon I was seeing—it was much too bright for that.

The stars had come out from the behind the clouds, and they were moving. That stopped me in my tracks. The Moon was rising on the western horizon, but the light was coming from a glowing nebula that had appeared directly overhead. There was no missing this display. It was the granddaddy of all stellar flux events.

Scruffy clouds crawled across the face of it, but the luminous effect shined right through. I'd watched my share of vids on the internet and live broadcasts about the mysterious stellar flux. The revealed nebulae were usually a greenish yellow. They normally grew in an oval shape then receded some fifteen minutes later.

This time was different. The skies were blazing. The colors were magnificent—magenta, green, and with a stripe of glimmering blue down the center like the hot core of a living flame.

I moved out of the trees and walked around in an open field, gaping upward. Out on the highway, cars honked and slowed. People were hanging their heads out of their car windows. I heard a distant squeal of brakes and the crunch of metal smashing into metal.

I didn't bother to look. No one did. We were all fixated by the display overhead.

On TV, I'd heard guys in glasses and suits try to explain these strange events. There were theories about prismatic effects such as refracted glints of light coming to us from deep in the galaxy. Some thought the flux effect was caused by a wormhole. Others claimed a different form of space-time like a rip that temporarily allowed us to see the center of our galaxy. They postulated that perhaps the black hole suns that we suspected lurked at the core of the Milky Way were colliding.

It really didn't matter who was right. The stars hadn't been acting normally for some time now, that was for sure, and everyone on Earth knew it.

But tonight was different, not only because it was a bigger rip in the heavens than we'd ever seen before, but because something came through that rip to visit us.

The central slash of blue-white light flared brighter as I watched, and then something slid away from it. More shapes soon followed.

I could see long, sharp triangles of reflective silver. They had to be made of metal. Shaped like arrowheads, I watched them flash in, moving fast at first, then slowing down and joining a growing formation that hung together in the sky.

Seven, eight—thirteen. Each object appeared, moved into position, and hung there.

I squatted down in the wet, rippling grasses. I didn't bother seeking shelter. Where could I have gone? Earth appeared to be at the feet of an invading fleet of spacecraft—I had no doubt in my mind that's what I was seeing gather overhead. There was nowhere to hide.

It occurred to me, as the fleet continued to gather, that my Earth was like an island. A lonely scrap of land in a vast ocean. We were nothing more than monkeys in trees, beasts who'd long assumed the rest of our ocean was populated by nothing other than an infinite number of lifeless waves.

But we'd been wrong. There *were* other islands, after all. We could see them at night. We'd even had the hubris to give them silly names. Now, the creatures who'd apparently existed out there all along had come to visit our chunk of floating rock.

I sincerely hoped they would turn out to be friendly.

=7=

After what seemed like a long time, but was probably no more than fifteen minutes, the bright rip in the sky faded and closed.

The ships remained behind, however. There were thirty-one of them in all. I'd counted several times, until I'd gotten the same result three times in a row.

My mind wasn't happy. I was shivering, despite the fact the night was humid and warm. I felt a desperate urge to relieve myself, and I went ahead and did so.

All the while, I never stopped craning my neck around to look at the sky, eyes wide and rolling.

After the stellar flux had faded, I noticed one of the silver ships was growing in size. I realized it was descending. Silently, the wedge-like shape came rapidly closer to Earth.

There was no sign of a propulsion system. No running lights. Only the moonlight made it visible at all. The descending ship was a dark shadow with one edge of it reflecting the Moon, like the gleaming blade of a knife.

Seeing it come down got me to my feet. I started to run. Surprisingly, I ran like the wind. My lungs sucked in air. My feet pounded and splashed in puddles. My sandals were soon lost in the rocks, mud and plants, but I didn't care.

Twice, I took a tumble over something hard in the dark and sprang up again like a cat, bleeding and dirty, but I ran on anyway.

Instinctively, I headed for the water. I don't know why, but I'd come to think of the beaches and the warm ocean beyond them as a refuge over the last few months.

Cars honked as I blurred over the highway, but I didn't even look. They could have hit me, but I must have gotten lucky, like a deer that bolts over a road and makes it by chance to the other side.

When I reached the sands, which were still slightly warm from the heat of the day, I began formulating a rudimentary plan.

I'd swim out into the ocean. *Way* out there. Then I'd tread water and wait, going under as much as possible. Whatever this alien ship wanted to do to the island, it could do. With luck, I'd be skipped over. Hell, I was a good swimmer. I was familiar with the currents, and I could tread water until frigging Friday if I had to.

My feet splashed into the waves, and I began to feel a surge of well-being. Somehow, I felt sure that escape was just ahead.

The waves swelled and crashed over my knees, then my hips. They drowned out the sounds from the island behind me. People were driving around frantically, trying to get home, trying to find refuge, just like I was. There were wrecks strung all along the highway and the streets of Lahaina.

But the descending ship was closer than ever. It hung over the center of the island. I stopped wading into the sea to look back, feeling awe overtake my other emotions.

Drifting west and close to the surface now, the ship glided over the land. It was *huge*—at least a half-mile long. It was as if an aircraft carrier or a super-tanker had taken flight and now sought vengeance upon the land-dwellers who had dared to crawl like fleas over its decks.

I watched as it slowed and hovered, motionless. It was close to the ground, maybe a hundred yards above the West Maui Mountains and the forest preserve. The alien vessel sat low, almost touching that primitive region at the top of the island—one of the wettest places on Earth and averaging more than an inch of rain each day. What could it want with that dense jungle?

The pause didn't last long. I soon saw some activity under the ship. Tiny, brilliant stabs of light flashed like intermittent lightning.

The lights flashed again and again. I looked for matching explosions on the ground, but I didn't see any. What the hell were they doing?

After about a minute more, during which I breathed hard and stared with eyes like marbles, the ship began to move again. It turned ominously toward Lahaina.

Turning back to the ocean, I waded out into the surf. I'd seen enough. I didn't want anything to do with that ship. If people were dying back there, in their homes, hotels and cars, I knew that I couldn't save them.

When the water hit my chest, I dove in. The surf was rough, and I could feel the undertow snatching at me—but I didn't care. If I drowned tonight… well, that might be a mercy.

Swimming deep, I let the tide take me out to sea. I tried my best to avoid the coral, but I got a stinging cut or two. That would be bad in the morning—if there was one.

I became aware of two strange things several minutes later.

One was the simple fact that I was still swimming underwater, still holding my breath, and still not passing out. I was in shape and an experienced diver, but I'd never lasted so long without air before.

Two, there was a light shining down from above me. Green-white and bright, it refracted heavily in the moving ocean.

I knew that light. It was more familiar when seen through seawater. It was the same glare I'd seen the night Jason had died.

Looking up from my position under the water, I could see what had to be the ship. Why had it come out here after me? I didn't know, and I barely cared at the moment.

My lungs were beginning to starve for air. I had a choice to make. I could either swim up to the surface for a breath, facing whatever these invaders had in store for me, or I could stubbornly drown down here on the bottom of the sea.

A large part of me voted for drowning. It would be so much easier that way—but I couldn't do it. Kicking off the sandy bottom, I headed for the surface. Powerful strokes sent me surging out of the water. I gasped and shook my head, squinting up at the ship's broad, flat belly.

The light switched off. For a time, nothing happened.

"Well?" I screamed over the sound of the waves. "Get on with it!"

For several more long seconds, the ship and the sea were calm. The sounds of the waves were weird. They echoed off the belly of the vessel, making it sound like I was inside some kind of cavern.

Irritated and wary, I began to swim toward the shoreline.

Before I made it to the beach again, a different light began to shine. It was bluish, glimmering, and each time it pulsed it grew brighter.

This was it, then. They were going to fry me with some kind of laser. It all seemed anti-climactic.

Finally, the beam pulsed to a brilliant glare. In my last instant on Earth, I realized this must have been the lightning-strokes I'd been seeing up on the island.

I couldn't see anything other than the light and the sea. The glare was too much. Swimming in the direction I hoped led to the beach, I felt my foot touch sand for a bare second.

Then the beach, the sea, the sound of the wind, even the ship that loomed above me—all of it was gone.

=8=

When I was conscious of my surroundings again, I was lying on an uneven floor.

My eyes swiveled blearily. I tried to get up, but I couldn't.

The floor and every wall in the chamber around me looked like a honeycomb, built of endless, interlocking hexagons. Each hexagon was domed and about an inch across. I wasn't sure what kind of material they were made of, but it didn't look like metal to me.

A finger came into focus just then. Attached to that finger was a person. She was standing over me, working her nails on the walls, making them crumble.

I saw her face, and it took me a minute, but I recognized her at last. It was Gwen, the blonde girl I'd met on the beach at TJ's. I hadn't seen her since she'd run out of the hospital when Jason had died a few days back.

She didn't seem to be interested in me. Instead, she casually walked around the chamber poking at the walls. After a few minutes of this, she knelt beside me and peered into my eyes.

"You awake?" she asked.

I said something unintelligible. In response, she hit me. *Hard.* Harder than I'd ever been hit by a girl in my life. Not even my older sister could have packed a wallop like that when I was five and she was thirteen.

Stunned, I felt another blow strike me, then another. She was methodically beating my head in. Around about the fourth or fifth blow, I blanked out.

Sometime later, I woke up again. There was no way to know how long I'd been out, but I suspected it hadn't been long.

This time I was wiser and pissed off. I waited with my eyes barely cracked open, looking around. Gwen was picking at the walls again, coating her fingernails in white dust.

After a minute or so, she squatted down beside me. I almost winced, but I managed to control the reaction.

For reasons unknown, we both had on papery-thin sleeveless blue tunics and nothing else. No shoes, no underwear—nothing. I found this fact odd and interesting, but I was quite busy at the moment, pretending to be unconscious.

I noticed that Gwen had something in her hand, and I realized why her blows had hurt so much. It made me feel a little better to know she hadn't been hitting me with her fists. She wielded a metal tube, and her small hand gripped it tightly.

"You awake, Leo?" she asked softly.

I kept right on faking, but it was hard. Part of me wanted to fight back. I wanted to snarl at her and demand to know what the hell she was doing.

After a few seconds, she stood and went for the wall again. My hand shot out instantly, grabbed her ankle, and pulled her off her feet.

She went down with a squeal. I sprang to my feet, and we wrestled for the metal tube. She managed to touch me with it, and I learned immediately that it was capable of delivering a nasty shock. A snapping sound and buzz on my left arm made it go limp for a second.

But the struggle was uneven anyway. While she was still on the floor, I managed to wrestle away the tube.

Breathing hard and blinking in fear, she scooted away from me on her butt. She hugged up against the wall and cowered. She clearly expected a beating.

I shook my head. "What's wrong with you, Gwen? One minute you're sweet, and the next minute you're trying to kick my ass."

"I'm doing it for points," she said, in a tone that suggested I was an idiot.

"Points?"

"You don't get as many points for nailing the same target over and over again, but it still counts. So, are you going to put me down or not?"

A flash of memory went off in my head then—I had awakened before. Earlier I'd found myself here on the floor in this room and put on my papery clothes. Then, I'd been clubbed down from behind. Maybe the beatings and the shocks had driven me to forget the recent past...

My eyes narrowed, and I looked at Gwen. I thought about whacking her one for a second, I seriously did, but seeing the fear in her eyes made me lose heart.

"No," I said. "I'm not going to hit you."

She looked surprised and confused. She stood up warily and fled the room. I followed her and found myself in an open passageway. The walls were made of more honeycombs, but the deck was smooth, and it lit up with a reddish glow when our feet touched it. Her footsteps left a softly lingering trail of light behind her as she ran.

She didn't make it very far. An arm shot out from a side passage, and she was knocked flat.

Another figure stepped into view and began methodically whacking her with the same kind of metal tube she had used on me. Sparks flew as the blunt instrument made violent contact with her body.

Call me a fool, but I couldn't take that. I ran up and shoved the man away from her. I was shocked to recognize him: it was none other than Dr. Chang.

Gwen lay on the floor, looking lifeless.

"What the hell are you doing, man?" I demanded, grabbing his shoulders and shaking him.

He struggled to get away from me. His eyes were wild.

"A team?" he demanded. "You two have teamed up? You tricked me! Is a team even legal? I call it cheating!"

He swung his tube at me.

What could I do? I had no time to think of a way to get out of this fight. I beat the guy down. I wasn't proud to do it, but I didn't think I had any other choice. I was sure he wouldn't stop trying to nail me with his club until I was laid out on the floor like Gwen.

Pulling my blows, I let the shocking effect of the club do most of the work. He sagged down to the floor on his butt, the wall behind him smeared with blood.

He was still conscious, so I kicked his weapon away from him and checked on Gwen. She was barely breathing.

"You've got some explaining to do, doc," I told him. "…and so does she, actually."

"Why aren't you finishing it?" he asked. "What are you waiting for?"

"As long as you behave yourself, you'll be just fine." I replied.

"Ah," he said in sudden understanding. "You're not on her side at all. You just don't know the rules."

"Then why don't you explain them to me?"

"We all got here over the last hour or so. Captured from the islands," he said, clearly agitated. "At least, I think it's been an hour... Things started off friendly enough, with everyone finding each other and milling around, trying to figure out what's going on. But then a big man came into the central room and began handing out these clubs. He told us they held essentials inside—and they did. Each contained a smock and some food."

As he spoke, I knew I'd missed the relatively calm time he was describing. I'd awakened alone, put on my clothes, and was immediately attacked.

"How many people?" I asked. "How many are aboard?"

"I don't know."

"Was the big stranger some kind of alien?"

"No, he looked human. He was an older man who seemed comfortable being in command. He handed out the weapons and explained the situation. Then he walked away. I don't know where he went."

Chewing that over, I looked at Dr. Chang and asked one more question. "Why'd you start beating on each other?"

"Because of the rules," he said. "The stranger explained the rules. Each of us has only one way out: to beat down everyone else on the ship. If we don't win, we might make it if we get a higher score than the rest."

He had a glassy look to his eyes as he told me this. He wasn't all there. That could have been due to head trauma, but I wasn't sure.

"That doesn't make any sense at all," I told him. "Why hit each other?"

"Don't you get it? Whoever wins gets to go back to Earth. At least, that's what he said."

"And you guys all believed him?"

He shrugged. "It didn't matter if we all believed. Some people apparently did, and they began shocking each other and smashing skulls. I ran at first. Several others did, too. There was an awful fight in the central room."

"Where's that?"

He pointed the opposite direction down the passage. I looked that way. There were dark stains on the floor that resembled blood.

"You all just went crazy at once?" I asked. "It seems hard to believe."

"It's the sym," he said with certainty. "Symbiotic parasites. We all have them, living in our skulls. They're part biological and part nano-tech. They make us paranoid, violent. They also seem to enhance our physical strength and help us heal."

"Symbiotic parasites? The guys that chased me around down on Earth mentioned something about that. You've got one?"

"I've probably got millions of them in my bloodstream, actually. Feeding on me, changing my personality at times."

"How's that even possible?" I asked.

"There are precedents in nature," Dr. Chang said. "*Toxoplasma gondii*, for instance. It causes all kinds of neurological disorders in humans. But keep in mind this organism that people are calling a 'sym' isn't natural. It was designed purposefully to change our behavior and physiology."

A muffled scream came echoing down the passage from the central room. I stood up, having heard enough from the good doctor.

"I'm going to put a stop to this," I told him, hefting my club.

Dr. Chang grunted. "I don't know who won the big fight in the central room, but whoever they are, they might disagree. I think they're waiting in there, waiting for the rest of us to finish each other off."

I glanced at him. He was scheming too, watching to see what I would do. I could see it in his eyes.

"I don't plan to play their game," I told him. "At least, not the way the owners of this ship want me to."

"Don't you want to go back home?" he asked.

I shrugged. "Everyone's gone crazy back home. I need to figure out what's going on and put a stop to it. Besides, I don't trust them at all."

Dr. Chang's eyes narrowed. "I like the way you think. You still have your wits about you. Many of these people—they're no better than animals."

He had his club back in his hand. One end was splotched red. He slapped it into his hand, smearing his palm in the process.

Walking away from him, I headed for the central chamber he'd directed me toward.

It could be a trap. Part of my mind warned me not to go—but I kept walking. I was determined to keep my own ideas and plans in charge.

I felt surging emotions. Fear. Anger. A lust for blood... but I kept walking. For all I knew, all these feelings were coming from my sym. Maybe it didn't want me to enter the central chamber.

Well, that was just too damned bad.

There were bodies on the floor. About twenty of them. They were piled over one another. Some skulls were bashed in, and their lifeless eyes stared at me. Others were unconscious but still breathing.

Off to my right, I heard a sudden popping sound. I lifted my club as I whirled.

It was the man I knew as Dalton. He was slowly, loudly, clapping his hands together. It was a mocking applause, matching the smirk on his face.

"I should have known you'd show up," he sneered.

=9=

"I can't believe you survived," I said, breathing hard. My eyes swept the room looking for more enemies. "Jones shot you several times."

"True enough, that," he said. "Jones didn't make it this far this time, but I did. Don't you know that given time the syms can heal up anyone who isn't stone dead?"

"I don't know much about the syms."

"Right... Still pretending to be just another simple wanker, eh, Blake? That's not going to fly with me. Not now. You're going down."

"You think they'll let you off this ship if you beat me?" I asked. "That story is bullshit. My theory is that they're watching us fight for fun. Maybe this is a reality TV show for these aliens."

"They'll let us keep breathing, anyway," Dalton said. "That's how it works. Now how about you and I play the game?"

Then he attacked me. He was a trained fighter, I could tell that. He came at me swinging his club in wide loops. I almost stepped in under his guard after the club went by me—but I noticed something else that kept me from doing so.

He had his other hand down at his waist, gripping something. Another club? No, it wasn't big enough.

I danced away, refusing to take the bait. He pressed forward, stepping deftly over the bodies. He wasn't as big or strong as I was, but he was agile and confident.

"What have you got in your other hand?" I asked him.

He showed me a toothy grin then lifted the object. It took me a squinting second to recognize it. The weapon was a splintered length of gray-white bone as sharp as a dagger. It was fresh, too. He must have ripped it out of one of the bodies that lay at our feet.

"You're a sick fuck," I said.

He chuckled. "You're going to know just how right you are soon."

We circled, but there wasn't really anywhere to go. I had the option of running out of the chamber, fleeing off into the ship somewhere, but I didn't want to take that approach.

What about Gwen and Dr. Chang? If I hid, he would hunt them down and kill them eventually. I still held out hope that I could get people to come to their senses.

I was in no mood to kill anyone today, but I had to make my play. Instead of striking for Dalton's head or his ribs, I went for an easier target. I smashed my club at his club, purposefully driving it down onto his knuckles. Our hands were unprotected by a guard of any kind, leaving them vulnerable to that kind of strike.

Keening in pain, he dropped the club. I lifted my weapon high and brought it down on his skull, but not before he managed to dart in and stick me with his bone-dagger.

That's when I lost it. It was the pain that released the rage my sym was trying to foment in my mind. I smashed him four or five times more than was absolutely necessary.

Thirty seconds after the fight had started, he was sprawled out on the floor.

Pulling the bone shard out of my left side with a grunt of pain, I tossed it aside with plenty of hissing and cursing. After a few minutes of this, I limped out of the room toward the passage where I'd left Dr. Chang. My idea was to offer him protection in turn for whatever medical aid he could render.

The moment I stepped out of the chamber, the color of the floor and walls changed. The glowing nimbus that surrounded my feet went from red to green.

"Time!" boomed a voice. It seemed to come from everywhere at once. The walls were broadcasting this one simple word. "Time!"

"Drop your weapon, Blake," the voice called from the passageway. "This round is over."

I looked around and spotted the marine. He was standing over Dr. Chang's slumped body. Gwen lay there too, unmoving.

"Samson?" I asked in disbelief. "I just killed you last night!"

"Drop your weapon, Blake!" he repeated. Then he dropped his, and it clattered on the deck. "Drop it, or you'll forfeit the win."

"What win?"

"The first heat is over. You made the cut. Only five aboard did."

I suspected a trap, but I was confused. I calculated he was too far away to charge me.

"Why do you give a shit whether I win or not?" I asked.

He grinned, and it was then I noticed he wasn't one hundred percent healthy. He moved with pain. Could his body still be recovering from the bullets I'd pumped into him a few hours ago?

"I want you to make it to the next round," he said, "so I can beat you down personally. Nothing else matters to me right now. I missed my chance this time because you were so chicken-shit you evaded the ship until the last minute."

Seeing he'd dropped his club, I warily set mine on the floor as well. But I kept my eyes on him every second.

He relaxed fractionally, leaning back against the nearest wall. "That's better. I'm still hurting from your slugs. You hammered me up pretty good—the bullets almost made it through my vest."

"I should have shot you in the face," I told him.

He gave me a rumbling chuckle and made a kissing face at me as he leaned against the wall.

Following his example, I leaned up against a wall too.

"We're not in good shape for more of this," I said.

"Won't matter," he said. "We'll be patched up before next time."

Shaking my head, I mustered a smile. "I got Dalton."

He guffawed. "That little shit deserved it."

Nonchalantly, I moved to check out Dr. Chang. He looked dead to me, but it was hard to be sure. Dalton and Samson had looked dead, too.

Samson coughed, and that distraction was the moment I was looking for. I grabbed up Dr. Chang's club and swung it two-handed for the marine's face. This time, body armor or no, he was going down hard.

But my sneak-attack never landed. I did get the pleasure of seeing surprise register on Samson's features, but that was all.

My whole body filled with numbing pain from the electrical shock I'd just received. I'd been tased twice before in my life, and this sensation reminded me of that.

Slumping to the floor, I was helpless at Samson's feet. I could still hear and see, but I couldn't move. I fully expected him to rain blows down upon my skull.

But he didn't.

Another set of footsteps approached.

"That was a clear foul," a familiar voice said.

"Yeah, but he missed the rules session," Samson said. "Don't kick him out for this."

"The rules are the rules. We can't be soft."

"I know, but he didn't know what would happen."

"You told him not to attack."

"He probably thought it was a trick," Samson insisted. "I was his enemy. He had no reason to accept my authority. He struck first, just as I would have."

"That's true... hmm," the man said. "All right. I'll amend the logs. He's moving forward to the next round with you. Hope you're happy."

"Thank you, Admiral Shaw, thank you!" Samson said.

I heard the sound of heavy boots striking the metallic floor as they walked away.

Then Samson got down on his hands and knees. He peered into my staring eyes, and he grinned.

"You made it, buddy," he said sarcastically. "We're going to be best friends now!"

He laughed and jeered into my frozen face.

But I wasn't listening to him. I was thinking about the man in the boots. The man in charge. He was Vice Admiral Shaw to me—but who was he really?

=10=

Within a few minutes, I was able to move again. Shaw's voice boomed through the ship full of dead and wounded.

"Everyone who can walk must now move to their individual cell. Anyone not in their cells will be purged in five minutes. This is your only warning. Move!"

Struggling to get up, I found Samson was trotting away down the passage. I saw his feet slapping on blood, hair and leaving a trail on the deck. He certainly seemed to be in a hurry.

Where his feet struck the floor, the floor glimmered yellow now. Red had meant open combat. Green had meant enforced safety—what could yellow mean? Could it mean the environment itself was dangerous?

I didn't know, but I levered myself up and onto my feet. My side stung where Dalton had stabbed me, and my head was a swollen mass of lumps.

Figuring my cell must be the one I'd started out in, I stumbled to it and stepped inside. There'd never been a door on this chamber, but when I entered one appeared behind me, sealing me in. The floor beneath my bloody feet went green then. Apparently, this was my home sweet home.

Squatting in there, I rubbed my injuries. I checked the wound in my side, expecting to see a bloody mess. It wasn't pretty, but it was already healing. Could that be the work of my sym? The idea of something slithering inside my blood was upsetting.

After several minutes, I began to hear wild screams outside the door. I thought it was—yes, it had to be Gwen's voice.

"Gwen?" I called out.

"Leo? I'm hurt. I'm frying!" she could hardly get the words out between screams.

"Get up and find your cell!"

She screamed some more. I struggled with the wall where it had been open before. Could this be why she'd been picking at it earlier? Had she seen these doors open and shut?

I called out to her a few more times, but I didn't hear anything more. I didn't know if she made it or not. At last, it was quiet outside.

Then things changed. I thought I felt my cell move. I was sure of it. It felt like being in an elevator, like I was being shunted somewhere.

The feeling was an unpleasant one. I had no trust whatsoever concerning my captors. What could be their purpose? They might be doing all this just for their own entertainment. I wouldn't have put it past whoever had designed these cruel games.

The sensation of movement suddenly stopped. My club was in my hand, and I stood where the door should be. I was breathing hard, ready for anything—or so I thought.

Every few seconds, my eyes flicked down to the floor, checking the color. It was still green.

"There will be a rest period before the next phase," announced the walls. "Survivors of the first phase will be required to socialize and recuperate."

"Screw you, Shaw," I muttered to myself.

Thinking it over, I decided I hated Shaw most of all. Dalton was an evil prick, sure. Samson had shot Kim to death before my eyes and sawed her head off. But I hated Shaw even more because he was orchestrating this torture-session.

The doors vanished again. I'm using the term "door" loosely here. In reality, a section of the honey-combed wall simply melted away.

The passages I'd seen before were gone. Instead, there was an open area. All around it, cells were standing open. Five of them.

Warily, the inhabitants leaned out to look at one another. I recognized the faces. Dalton was to my left, eyes slitted, shoulders slumped. Samson was to my right. He filled the doorway of his cell.

The fourth door revealed a cautious face. One I hadn't expected to see again.

Gwen stood in the cell across from me. I wouldn't have seen her at all, except for the fact she couldn't hide in there. She was at the back of the space she'd been trapped within. Her eyes slid around wildly then fixated on me.

"Gwen?" I asked, incredulous. "How can you be...?"

"I did my damnedest," Samson said. "I really did. Shit."

"That bitch was dead on the floor!" Dalton declared, pointing at her. "She never should have made it to her cell! I swear it's a cheat!"

Gwen didn't speak. She licked her lips and eyed us with fear and savage determination. I felt sure she was planning our deaths—or how to trick us again.

My eyes went to the last door, but whoever was inside, they must have been hiding.

"She's tricky," Samson said, pointing at Gwen. "That must be it. Just like this asshole, Blake."

"Blake's not that smart," Dalton told him. "*You're* the problem. You're a complete prat. You're aware of that fact, aren't you? I can't make it any simpler, sorry."

The two snarled at one another and squared off.

"Guys," I said, pointing to the floor. "The deck is green. Let's get along for now."

Mumbling curses and threats, they stepped out into the open and nursed their injuries. In the middle of the floor, there was a large black object that looked like it was made of porous stone. A random pattern of holes covered the surface of it.

Dalton and Samson pushed their tubes into these holes. They fit perfectly, then the stone began to glow.

Several things occurred to me at that moment.

"You guys have done this before..." I said.

"What was your first clue, Blake?" Samson asked. "We washed out last time."

"You came back?"

"We were finalists. They came back for more recruits, and we must have still been on their lists."

"Recruits for what?"

"For their ships, professor," Dalton snorted. "What do think this is all about? We're trying out to be crewmen."

I stared at him. It had to be true. Why else would they heap such abuse upon us? Was I being subjected to tests of fitness? Just so I could fight for some kind of alien army? I didn't like the idea. I began immediately planning to lose the next round.

"What happens to those who lose badly?" I asked.

"They die—for real. The near winners, the ones that show promise and impress their syms, they get to keep on going. Sometimes, like this time, they might get several chances to come back and try again."

Samson shrugged. "It's like trying out for a team."

Dr. Chang finally appeared at the fifth door. He'd been pressed up against the wall, hiding and listening.

"I guess you aren't going to start clubbing one another," he said.

He stepped up to the central rock and shoved his metal tube into it. "Why are we doing this, exactly?"

"The tubes will fill," Samson said.

"With what?"

"Whatever we need," the big man answered with a shrug. "Whatever our sym tells the rock to put into it."

Figuring it couldn't hurt, I joined the circle.

"I wish for a tube full of hard bourbon," I said earnestly. "Tennessee whiskey, not the cheap stuff."

The others chuckled, and I thrust my tube into the slot. There was one more open spot. I looked back at Gwen.

She was still lingering in her cell, silently regarding us.

"I know you're a worrier, Gwen," I said. "And I don't blame you at all. But you were told to participate. I think it would be safest for you to join us."

She shrank back so I could hardly see her.

"The floor is still green," I said. "Take advantage of it."

The guys were watching her. We all were, except for Dr. Chang. He was examining his tube closely. "I think something is filling it. I don't see where it's coming from."

Gwen stepped out at last. She walked forward on feet that were almost silent. She didn't meet any of our eyes. She plunged her tube into the rock, and then she backed away like she thought it might explode or something.

The rock glowed green-white, and I realized that I knew that light. Next, it grew cold.

"That's what the rock did at the bottom of the sea," I said. "That must be when I got the sym."

The others looked at me then squinted in the silent glare coming from the rock. The light faded quickly.

Nothing special happened for about a minute after that. At last, Dalton lost patience. He drew his tube back out and opened a sliding compartment. Inside was a syringe.

He grunted with unhappiness. "What the bloody hell am I supposed to do with this?"

"Stick it in your ass," Samson suggested.

"I'm a physician," Dr. Chang said, "maybe I can be of help."

"Back off!" Dalton said. "Nobody is giving me a shot. I'll do it myself." He took the syringe out and plunged it into his arm. The thing morphed as he did so.

"Oh shit! Get it off!"

The syringe melted, shrinking, until it vanished.

"Where did it go?" Samson asked.

"It went inside me. It was a trick! That bastard Shaw... I think I've been poisoned."

"That seems unlikely," Dr. Chang said. "Their technology is way beyond ours."

"You think so?" Dalton snarled.

"Yes, clearly. What I think they did was present you with a normal-looking syringe in order to inform you as to appropriate usage—in this case, physical contact. Upon touching it with your flesh, it melted into your bloodstream."

"That's bullshit... but... I *can* feel it in me. Something's there. Makes me a little sick."

He looked a bit green. I opened my tube and found a roll of bandages inside. I wrapped them over my head as well as the puncture wound Dalton had given me. The injuries immediately began to feel better. Soon, the bandage disappeared.

Samson got a tube of liquid, which he drank. Dr. Chang found several medical instruments. He was happy about that. He wanted to examine the rest of us.

"Those instruments are for you, Doc," I told him. "Try them on yourself."

He did, and they melted away too. He complained about this. "Doesn't even make any sense."

"Maybe it does if you're an alien," said Gwen, "or a sym looking out of human eyes."

We all looked at her. She had taken her tube and retreated with it to stand in the doorway of her cell. I could tell now how she'd survived. She was more paranoid and sneaky than the rest of us combined.

"Open it," I told her.

At last, she did. She laughed. She pulled a lovely purple blossom out of the tube. It was a Hawaiian flower.

"I might as well make the aliens happy," she said, and put the flower in her hair. It immediately sank into her scalp, healing the lumps on her head.

She walked over to me and looked shy. "Sorry about trying to beat your brains out," she said.

"It's okay. That was your sym at work."

"I guess so—but at the time, I really, really wanted to kill you."

"I believe it. How about now?"

She shook her head no. "Hey, have you got any more of that bandage? My neck still hurts and my ribs are sore, too."

I looked at her side, where the papery cloth didn't cover. I caught quite an eyeful, as we were all almost naked.

"Um… I'm out of bandages," I said. "Hey, I'll catch you next time, OK?"

"Sure."

I had to smile. Was she being nice for real, or just to soften me up for the next round? It was hard to tell, but it was impossible not to respond to her positively. She was a lovely girl.

After we'd all retrieved our tubes and taken our medicine, the floor changed to yellow. I really did feel better, that was the strangest part. It was as if I'd slept a few nights and had several good meals. I was even able to open my right eye fully. It'd been swollen half shut up until now.

"What's next?" I asked.

"I don't know," Dr. Chang said, "but we'd better get back to our cells."

Gwen was already in hers, and the rest of us followed suit.

"What's happening?" I demanded of Samson and the others.

"I don't know," the big guy admitted. "We didn't get this far last time."

"Why not?"

"We hit each other right here," Dalton said. "Shaw said to socialize, remember? We broke the rules and hit each other while the floor was green."

"Yeah, *you* screwed it up," Samson said. "We got all healed and ready for more fun—but the next thing you know, we'd been dumped in the ocean."

"I would have killed you, meatball, if they'd have let me!"

"Wait," I said, interrupting the two. "You guys started in Hawaii last time around, right?"

"Nope," Samson said. "Jersey for me."

"And I'm from Manchester, U. K," Dalton said. "But the ship dropped us in the sea near Hawaii."

That made me frown. If I was kicked out of this ship for some kind of failure, where would it drop me?

"But I never saw any reports of a ship coming down to grab people before," I said. "Have you?"

"No," Dalton said. "This time was different. There were lots of big ships tonight, not just one small one. This time it seems like a bigger deal."

"I think it's the last time the aliens are coming," Samson said.

"How do you know that, shit-for-brains?"

They began arguing, and I wanted to ask them more questions now that I had them talking. I wanted to ask about Shaw—and a dozen other things—but there wasn't any more time.

The door to my cell materialized again, sealing me off from the others. The sensation of movement returned. My cell was sliding upward. Where would I come out next?

My heart began to pound, and it became hard to swallow. My club was in my hand, gripped tightly.

I was determined to get in at least one hard blow before I went down.

=11=

After a brief period of time, the doors vanished again. We were shocked to find ourselves face to face. The central chamber was gone. Our cells were gone. At least three of the four walls of each cell had vanished. We were all in a single large room looking at one another warily.

The floor was still green, or I had no doubt these people would've started smacking each other again.

"This round will be different," Shaw's voice said. "The group of five you're with is a team for this round. You'll be facing other teams. You're not to damage anyone on your own team—not even by accident. Instead, you must defeat all the others."

"Aw shit, I'm just *dying* to clock Leo!" Samson complained. He eyed the back of my head like he saw a target.

Shaw's voice continued explaining. "There will be a central rock formation. The team to take that rock and plant one member's tube at the top of the highest point for one hundred seconds, wins the heat. The rest will be eliminated."

"Okay," I said, turning to the others. "Listen up, I have a plan."

"Sod off!" Dalton said. "Shaw didn't make you leader."

"Do *you* have a plan to win, Dalton?" Dr. Chang asked.

"I do," Gwen said. "Why not do nothing? Why don't we hide and wait for someone else to take the rock?"

They looked at her like she was crazy.

"Winning doesn't help us," she said. "Let's lose and go back to Earth instead."

Dalton gave her a nasty laugh. "We thought the same thing when we went for each other last time," he said. "but it didn't work out. Every crazy rube on Earth will be gunning for you. You'll be killing and getting killed, same as up here. There's no way out of the game."

"Except, maybe, to win," Samson said. "At least, that's what we're hoping."

Gwen looked lost, but determined. "All right then. I'm willing to listen to Leo's plan."

"Okay Blake," Dalton said. "What do you have?"

"We advance to the bottom of the rock," I said, "but we don't charge up. We fight anyone who comes at us, that's it. When they hurt each other at the top, we charge all at once at the end. Hopefully, we'll have our five against two or three. Got it?"

"That's it?" Dalton said in disbelief. "I could have come up with that!"

"But you didn't," Samson pointed out.

"Shut up."

The floor flashed to yellow, which I knew by now meant we had to get the hell out of our cells. Next, one of the walls vanished, revealing what looked like some kind of rock garden.

There were boulders everywhere. Some were flat with canted surfaces. Others were rounded off on top. In the middle was a huge rock, much bigger than the rest. Our destination was obvious.

"Careful!" shouted Dr. Chang, pointing down. "The floor is blue, only the rocks are red!"

"What the hell does blue mean?" Samson asked.

"Why don't you go down there and find out?" Dalton suggested with a nasty chuckle.

Samson had one foot in the air. I yanked him back.

"Hop from rock to rock. No one touches the floor," I ordered.

This time, no one questioned my authority. As an ex-officer, it came to me naturally enough to give orders. This was the strangest form of boot-camp I'd ever heard of, but the dynamics of leadership hadn't changed.

Dalton led the way. Crouching, he hopped nimbly from rock to rock, sticking to the flat ones.

I followed with Samson and Dr. Chang behind me. Gwen brought up the rear.

We could see the other teams. There were five groups of five, all of us converging on the center.

It was immediately obvious they had plans of their own. Two groups raced straight for the mountain. A third hung back uncertainly, right where they'd started.

The fourth fell to quarreling among themselves. One was pitched off a rocky shelf onto the blue floor. I heard screams, but they were cut short.

"Man down!" chuckled Dalton. "Let's hope all these fools murder each other."

We followed our plan, moving to the base of the rock cautiously, taking our time. We didn't rush upward, but we got a front-row seat as the early-birds did.

There was a ferocious battle up there. At one point, I thought someone had thrown a club at us, but then the owner came crashing down past us. His neck was broken, but his eyes were still wide and alert. He rolled into the blue, and he fried there.

His body began to smoke in time. We watched with our lips curled in disgust.

"That's not right," Dalton said. "They aren't just shocking them."

"No," Samson agreed, "he's cooking down there."

The two teams that had met to do glorious battle at the top of the boulder now separated. Three members of one group were left victorious, while the last man of the losing team ran off. The flag was planted, and a stand-off began.

We stared expectantly at the other two teams. They looked back at us with equal hopefulness, but no one moved.

A big number appeared on the ceiling then, or rather, appeared to float a few feet from it. Ninety-nine, ninety-eight...

"It's a countdown!" Samson said, "We have to go for it now!"

"That's what the others want. Hold." I said.

"You're going to screw us, Blake," Dalton complained. "I always knew you were a cock-up waiting to happen."

"Hold," I said firmly.

The four-man team lost their cool first. They charged up the hill, howling. Maybe they'd realized this was their best chance. With only four people, they were weaker than the rest—except for the current king-of-the-hill group, which was down to three.

The battle was vicious. It was best of three vs. a mean group of four. The higher ground seemed to be helping the current kings, but that didn't—

"Behind us!" Gwen shouted.

The fifth group, who'd hung back right at the door to their collective cells, had circled around while we'd watched the battle for the center. They were springing from rock to rock, coming right at us from behind.

"Samson, take point!" I shouted.

Spotted, the enemy gave a wild battle cry. Their gaze had an animalistic quality. I suspected it was a glimmer of the rage coming from their syms. I don't think any of us would have been so aggressive without this constant goading from inside our minds. We went animal when threatened, shedding away thousands of years of civilized behavior and breeding.

My own team began to make guttural noises in response. I didn't know why the sym was less influential on my emotions—but it clearly was.

I flanked Samson on the right. Dalton moved to stand on the big man's left. Behind us were our weakest members, Gwen and Dr. Chang.

The enemy line came on hard, but seeing they were spotted, some of them fell behind the rest. Three met our line of three, and the fighting began.

Dalton darted in, quick as a cat, and struck a bigger man in the kneecap. The guy went down howling. He tried to grab at the rock, but Dalton beat at his fingers viciously, dislodging his grip.

Dalton's victim fell into a crack between two rocks and began an awful screeching as he burned down there.

Samson wrestled with his opponent, who came in close. Using his great strength, he threw the guy toward the pits.

Unfortunately, the guy slammed into Dalton, and they were knocked off the rock together.

My antagonist faced me next. He was a tall, lanky guy. He thrust with his club, trying to touch me with it. I knew the tip would numb my limbs, and he had a lot of reach on me, so I gave ground.

Gwen threw herself low and smashed the guy's toes with her club. I was impressed with her sudden rush of courage. My opponent stumbled, and I brained him. He fell unconscious.

Just like that, the enemy was broken. The last two had fled.

Looking for Dalton, I found Dr. Chang had made good use of his position in the back. He laid down, hugging the large flat rock we'd been battling over, and grabbed hold of Dalton's tunic. Using pain as a goad, Dalton had crawled hand over hand onto Chang's back. He was now resting on the flat rock, panting. His left leg was bloody and stiff, and both his feet were smoldering.

"We did it," I said.

Gwen shook her head. She pointed upslope.

The fight was still going up there, but it was about over. The three man team was down to two members, one of whom looked half-dead.

"Come on," I said. "Let's finish it."

We marched up there and faced the group at the top. When we got there, we were surprised to see another face we recognized.

"Jones?" Samson said. "I don't frigging believe it."

Commander Jones was up there, standing tall. He stared down at us like a true king. At his feet was an Asian guy who was pretty beat up, but was still moving.

The number on the ceiling had begun counting again, but it was down to thirty-three this time.

"Jones," I said, "I don't want to fight you. We outnumber you. Stand down."

"Negative, Blake," he said. "I'm your superior officer in the Navy. *You* back off."

We stared at one another for a few seconds. Finally, Samson rushed up.

"I'm not doing this shit again!" he roared.

Jones cracked his club on the big man's head and shoulders, shocking him, but Samson didn't go down. Instead, Samson jammed his stick into Jones face, and the officer was knocked from his perch.

Dalton and I swarmed up after Samson. We took the hill, and we let the others retreat. There was no need to hurt them further.

The clock ran out to zero, and the room went green at last.

We'd won the day... but how many more contests were there left to go?

=12=

We never saw what happened to the losing teams. They simply weren't there anymore after we were herded back into our group cell and allowed out again later. Our team, however, was permitted by our captors to stay together.

"None of this makes any sense," I told the others. "Why make us kill one another? If what they want is an army, why not simply shanghai all the decent candidates? Forcing us to eliminate each other just makes us hate our masters, and it seems so wasteful."

"Maybe they only want the best of us," Dr. Chang said. "I've been thinking about these contests—when my mind is fully my own, that is."

By now, we'd all realized that we were having episodes of paranoia. Sometimes these moments had clear causes, such as when someone was charging us and yelling. At other times, we were inexplicably overwhelmed by emotion, becoming the one initiating an assault.

I seemed to be the only member of my group that was able to contain these urges. Only rarely did I lose control. I didn't know why this was the case, it just was. Maybe it had something to do with my military training. Whatever the reason, I'd ended up becoming the team leader.

"I believe these aliens," Dr. Chang continued thoughtfully, "whoever they are, must want only vicious warriors to serve them."

"Hmm," I said. "I guess that fits. Do you think that's out of some kind of surreal sense of honor?"

"Either that, or there's a need for the most savage individuals, and no one else."

I didn't like the answer either way.

When the next chamber was revealed to us, we were all on edge. We were all hungry and dirty by now. Dalton's leg was in bad shape. Fortunately, we were allowed another respite.

The room had that same rock with the five slots. We approached it together and used our tubes without being told. When the rock stopped glowing, we withdrew them.

When we pulled the tubes back out, we found fresh rolled-up bundles of clothing and squeeze-tubes of what looked like water.

Dalton drank some of the fluid immediately and poured the rest on his damaged legs and feet. He hissed with pleasure.

"What's it taste like?" Samson asked.

"Rat piss," he replied with closed eyes. "But it's fixing my legs."

The rest of us applied the fluid to our injuries and drank some of it as well. It was salty and oily at the same time. Body-warm, it was unpleasant, but we drank it anyway. My head soon cleared as did everyone else's.

Gwen tried on her new clothing right away. She put it on over her ragged, torn-up tunic and only ripped off the old garment after she was covered by the new one. The rest of the team watched in mild disappointment.

Samson was remarkably less shy. He tore off his old clothing first and then pulled on the new suit. It looked a thousand times better.

The clothes were a darker blue than our tunics had been. The fabric was also much more substantial. There were epaulets with a single round button of metal on each shoulder.

"These look like uniforms… sort of," Samson said.

"Well, aren't you catching up nicely," Dalton sneered. "Didn't the doc just say we're soldiers in a slave army?"

"I'm pushing you into the next pit I see, you greasy, burned-up little slime-bag," Samson promised him.

Dalton shut up and glared at us while he cautiously kneaded at his newly healing legs.

Dr. Chang and I went next, dressing with curiosity. The cloth was thicker, tougher. It also covered more. The garment seemed to stretch and contract as I put it on, almost as if it was adjusting itself to my physique.

Once I had it on, the new uniform just felt good to wear. In spite of the boys' renewed sniping at each other, I hoped proper clothes would change their mood. Successfully working through the last trial together made it seem like we were coming into our own—ready for business.

"Hey!" Dalton complained. "Look at Blake, here. He's got a *gold* button on each shoulder. The rest of us have only silver buttons. Who put you in charge, Blake?"

I turned to face him, and we squared off. At that point, a large figure approached our group. It was Shaw.

"Where did *you* come from?" Dr. Chang asked.

"I have the keys to this place," he explained, "and an officer's rank. You see my shoulders?"

We looked at him. He was wearing a blue uniform, the same as ours, but there were gold triangles on his shoulder. I hadn't noticed that the first time Shaw had come around—but then I'd been lying stunned on the floor at that point.

"I'm not sure what you're getting out of this," I said to Shaw. "Why cooperate with these aliens?"

Shaw gave me a tight smile. He was a big man, about the same dimensions as Samson. I got the feeling that he could fight like Samson, too, even though he was older. His hair was gray at the temples, and there were deep lines in his face, but his eyes were the merciless color of steel.

"You're not merely *cooperating*," he said. "You've been given an honor. Earth has been invited to participate in the greatest event in a thousand years."

"What event?" Dr. Chang asked.

Shaw kept looking at me, as if Chang didn't exist.

"Congratulations. You are now members of the Rebel Fleet. Leo Blake, this is your team to lead. You have full responsibility for their actions. If they make an error—that error will be assigned to you. Do you understand, crewman?"

"In theory, yes," I said. "But I don't know the rules we must abide by, and none of us understand this Rebel Fleet you're talking about. For one thing, who are you rebelling against?"

"You'll learn quickly enough. Any infractions will be met with harsh punishment. That is the way of the Fleet."

"Okay..." I repeated. "May I ask some questions?"

"There is limited time and not much point to it, but I will allow it."

"How many more trials by combat will there be?"

His grim smile returned. "In a way, that is up to you. Advancement within the Fleet is largely based on defeating other members. Not killing them, mind you, but defeating them in duels."

"Duels? Fair, organized fights?"

"No..." Shaw replied thoughtfully. "Not always fair—rarely organized."

"Great," Dr. Chang said, "sounds like we're to be living on edge."

Shaw's cheek jumped. Without looking, his hand shot out to grab Dr. Chang around the throat. He began crushing that neck.

I could see the doctor's eyes bulge. He tried to get his club out, but he dropped it.

Samson growled and grappled with Shaw, trying to pull his fingers from Chang's throat. There was little effect. Shaw kept staring at me, as if waiting.

Things were getting out of hand. Dalton moved around behind Shaw, lifting his club. Gwen did the same.

"Hold!" I shouted at my crew. "Sir," I said, addressing Shaw. "I apologize for Dr. Chang's behavior. I'll punish him myself."

Shaw's face relaxed, and he nodded. He released Chang, who fell to the deck, wheezing.

"You have just learned about Fleet discipline," Shaw said. "Commit every such lesson to memory."

Then he left us. We circled around Chang. If there was one man we all liked, it was the doctor.

He didn't get up. He looked at us with pleading, desperate eyes.

"He can't breathe," Gwen said. "Shaw crushed his windpipe."

"I've never felt strength like that," Samson said. "Shaw's fingers were like iron."

Dr. Chang pointed at a soft spot at the top of his sternum. I knew what he wanted. "I need one of the squeeze bottles. Now!" I shouted.

Gwen quickly handed me her drinking bottle. I ripped the straw out of it and knelt beside Chang.

He was beginning to pass out. His eyes rolled up into his head. The man was turning blue, and I knew we didn't have much time. He wasn't getting enough oxygen.

"We need something sharp," I told them.

I heard a ripping sound.

"This?" Samson asked as he handed me his rank insignia. It had a sharp edge on the underside where it attached to the uniform.

I took it and stabbed Chang in the throat. He barely reacted to the pain. Stuffing the tube from the straw inside the bleeding hole, I heard air whistle as it passed through it.

About a minute later Chang regained full consciousness, although his throat still looked oddly folded inward and was purple with bruising.

"Did anyone else save their drink?" I asked the team.

Dalton handed his over, grumbling. I took it and spread it around Chang's throat. He was soon breathing more easily. Ten minutes later, he removed the tube himself, thanked us, and sat up.

"I was a dead man," he said. "Again... Thanks for your help."

"No problem," I said. "Let's remember, people, not to mouth off to those with higher ranks than ours. Shaw isn't what he seems. I doubt others will be either when we finally meet them."

For once, no one argued with me.

=13=

When our next destination was revealed, it gave us the biggest shock of all.

We'd learned to recognize the signs of a new challenge by now. Just before the door to our group cell vanished, the floor always shivered, changing from a safe green tone to a brighter yellow. That meant we were shortly going to be coerced into exiting our chamber.

Now that we'd become familiar with the routine, the simple fact that the floor colors had shifted gave everyone a surge of adrenaline. How quickly we could be conditioned! Every time the main door had faded away in the past, it had revealed a new surprise beyond. Violence and pain had invariably followed.

We gathered at the spot we knew the gap would appear. We gripped our clubs and flexed our muscles. Like a pack of growling dogs, we waited to learn the nature of our fate.

I had just enough time to reflect on how we five individuals had congealed into a team. The process hadn't been specifically suggested or ordered by anyone. We'd done it naturally, reflexively. For humans, banding together against a common foe was a survival instinct.

Less than twenty-four hours ago any one of us might have murdered the others. Despite this, we now thought of ourselves as a single force against whatever was on the far side of that door. Our most basic natures were on display, and this response, at least, had been positive so far.

The door faded at the exact moment we'd known it would. We thought we were ready for anything—but we were wrong.

When the wall vanished and revealed its secrets, we saw a chamber a hundred times larger than all those we'd seen before. The size of it was awe-inspiring.

The deck was normal metal. I noticed that first. There were no colors to guide us. The ceiling was made of that familiar honeycomb design, but it was so distant that it might as well have been the sky.

Sprawled out for what had to be a square mile or more, was a vast, multi-tiered deck. The place hummed with activity. Thousands of people in uniforms like ours worked in tight groups all over the ship.

Several things struck us right away, and as my team was a vocal one, they began speculating immediately.

"What are they working on?" demanded Dalton. "Are those plane-like crafts supposed to be spaceships?"

"They must be," Dr. Chang said. "Fighters, maybe? Leo, you've been on aircraft carriers. Is that what this is?"

"I think so," I said, nodding slowly. "It's huge, and those ships look more like horseshoe crabs than fighter jets, but this whole scene reminds me of an aircraft carrier below decks."

"Um, guys?" Gwen said. "The floor in our room is still yellow under our feet."

"Right," I said. "Let's move out."

Taking the lead, I stepped out into the open. Looking behind me, I saw what looked like an endless row of pods like the one we'd just exited. I noticed gaps between many of the pods that appeared to be blank regions of decking.

As we watched, the pod that we'd grown to feel safe within sealed itself again. Samson reached out to touch it, and there was a snapping sound.

He drew back his hand, cursing. "It shocked me!"

"That decking *was* yellow," Dr. Chang said.

"That's right, stupid," Dalton added unnecessarily.

We watched in concern as our pod sank into the deck. It vanished completely, leaving behind only smooth metal. We felt a sense of loss. Nothing bad had ever happened to us inside that small safe zone. We'd been allowed to rest, heal, and converse like normal humans inside those walls.

Turning away, we gazed with open-mouthed amazement at the hangar deck—for that's what I'd come to believe it was.

"What do we do, Leo?" Gwen asked, her voice almost a whisper.

"We wait for orders. Quit gawking. You don't want to look like a rookie."

The other teams had begun to take notice of us. It was hard not to. Every person on the deck seemed to know what they were doing—except for us.

A group paused in their work and pointed at us. From a distance, they looked a bit odd. As they climbed down from their small ship and walked toward us, that sense of wrongness increased dramatically.

"They're not human!" Dalton hissed out. "They're freaks!"

"They've got *tails*," Gwen said, "furry long tails like leopards or something."

"I see big teeth... small vestigial claws," Dr. Chang said. "Interesting. They appear to be humanoid, air-breathing... and clearly a predatory species."

"Maybe they'll tell us what we're supposed to do," Samson said hopefully.

"Or maybe they'll eat us," Dalton said. "Why don't you go and find out which it is, Samson?"

"Don't lift your clubs," I said. "Hold them, but don't swing them around or look threatening. Let's try to make friends."

The group of cat-people came closer than would normally be acceptable to humans without offering a greeting. Instead, they sniffed the air as if checking us out that way.

"Hello," I said. "Can we help you?"

The leader was a big male. The other four were all females. The big one was tall, about seven feet, if I had to guess. He might have been taller if he'd straightened up. They all had a sort of hunch to them, but I wasn't sure if that was the way they carried their spines naturally, or if they were lowering their heads on purpose.

The leader gave the air one last long sniff. He ended it with a snort that sent a wet gust in my direction.

"Monkeys?" he demanded at last. "They feed us more monkeys? What's wrong with Fleet Command?"

I saw his neck and lips move, but the voice I was hearing in spoken English wasn't coming out of his throat. Somehow, his language was being translated into one that we could understand.

I'd noted previously that this was happening around Shaw as well, and sometimes the words being spoken didn't match up to the translation. For example, Shaw's name sounded more like "Shu-ah" if you listened closely enough.

Were these translations occurring inside my head or through some kind of intermediate device? I didn't know, but I was glad we could at least talk to these creatures.

"We've survived the trials," I said to the cat-man. "We're the best crew from Earth."

"The best of Earth!" he laughed as if that were greatly ironic. The other cats surrounded us, laughing too. "You're mere rinds!" he boomed. "All bone and no meat. Dried-up, fly-blown and tasteless."

"Are you in command here?" I asked. "I don't see a triangle on your shoulder. I see one gold button, the same as I have."

His eyes narrowed. My comment seemed to have pissed him off, but I didn't care. He was already pissing me off plenty. I tried to reflect on my emotions, wondering if my responses were being goaded by my sym, or if his shitty attitude was the cause of the problem. I suspected it was a combination of both.

"You asked if you could help us," said the large cat-man. "The answer is 'yes.' Here, you may hold my tail."

Turning around, he lifted his yard-long tail. It was covered in coarse fur. The hairs were mostly black, with gold spots for highlight, just like the fuzz on his head.

I looked at his tail, frowning. I suspected this was some kind of insult. Glancing at Samson, I got an idea. I waved him forward and made a small tugging motion with my hand.

Samson stepped forward immediately. "I'll do it, Blake," he said.

With a wave and a smirk, I indicated that he could be my guest.

Samson grabbed the tail firmly in his massive hand. The female cats began giggling. That was when I was sure we'd been insulted.

"That feels *excellent*, monkey," the cat-man purred. "Be it known that you have served Ra-tikh well. Do not move now, I must relax in order to relieve myself."

Another round of twitters came from the females as the lengthy appendage began to convulse in a spasm.

Samson smiled dryly as he squeezed Ra-tikh's tail and pulled it hard. The cat-man began to turn around—but Samson didn't let him. He hung onto the tail with all his strength.

Ra-tikh growled. It was a terrifying sound that made the hairs on the back of my neck stand up. Somewhere, in my distant monkey-past, a creature like this one had torn up some of my relatives. My brain was certain of it.

But Samson didn't care. He kept his grip and grinned at Ra-tikh.

"You're right kitty-man," Samson said. "This does feel good."

Ra-tikh went berserk. He twisted around with startling flexibility, reaching for Samson's face.

My team had been through Hell together very recently. They didn't need any further goading. They all lifted their clubs to beat on that big skull, but I waved my fellows back.

Ra-tikh's teeth were bared, and his fangs revealed. They sank into Samson's hand, but he kept his grip anyway.

Intervening, I rammed my stick between those toothy jaws, prying them open a bit.

The females were growling now, and I could tell by their eyes they were about to attack us.

"Hold!" a newcomer boomed. It was none other than Shaw. He walked up to us and gave everyone a stern glare. "You were not instructed to harm one another!"

"All I did was hold his tail the way he asked," Samson said, his teeth gritted in pain. "Then this crazy pussycat turned around and bit me."

I could feel the big cat's hot breath on my hands as I drove the club into his throat a little further, causing him to choke.

"Ra-tikh," I said loudly. "I release you from captivity. Let go of him, Samson."

Samson did as I'd ordered, and Ra-tikh withdrew his long teeth from Samson's hand.

Our two groups separated slowly, backing away from one another. Shaw stepped between us, nodding. He made no further comment about the confrontation as he delivered fresh orders to my people.

"There will be one point awarded to both teams," he said.

"One point?" Ra-tikh complained. "That's hardly worth coming across the deck."

Shaw shrugged. "It wasn't much of a contest."

Ra-tikh and his crew retreated irritably. They cast frequent glares over their furry shoulders as they left.

"You're hereby assigned to the hangar deck," Shaw told the team. "The Fleet needs more crews. Every Rebel world must provide at least one crew. You've been chosen to serve here. Do not dishonor Earth."

He turned around, beckoning for us to follow. We did so warily, eyeing every group as we crossed the decking.

The other crews were, for the most part, humanoid as well. That was the term Dr. Chang had for them, anyway.

Every predatory species back on Earth seemed to be represented. Things with cruel, curved beaks like a bird of prey, as well as cats, wolves, bears and wet-skinned lizards. There were plenty of stranger varieties which were harder to describe.

"A question, Admiral Shaw," I said.

"Granted."

"Why is this ship full of aliens? Why so many *types* of aliens? Who gives the orders at the top?"

He paused and looked at me. "I thought that was clear. We are all related species. We were all seeded upon our worlds long ago. Your lot took on a certain cast to your features, but you're not primates native to Earth initially. Here on this ship—these are your people. We are all cousins."

In shock, we eyed the bustling teams.

"They're all humans?" Gwen asked in amazement.

"No. That's the name of your particular species from a group classified as primates. I'm saying that we're all related in a much larger sense. Collectively, we're called The Kher. We're wild Kher, however."

"Wild?" I asked. "As opposed to what?"

"Originally, the Imperials planted us on our home worlds. We're not quite sure how that happened, we might have escaped or been purposefully released into specific ecospheres. They've never bothered to tell us the truth. But in any case, only your distinct strain is comprised of human primates."

"You're blowing my mind, Shaw," Dalton said.

Dr. Chang began gesturing for attention, looking at me.

"Sir," I said, "can Dr. Chang ask a question?"

"Yes."

"Are *you* human?" Dr. Chang asked, his eyes narrowed to slits.

Shaw drew himself up to his full height.

"I'll try not to take that question as an insult. Your near-total ignorance has been taken into account on your behalf in this case—but don't push it."

He began rolling up his sleeve. There, under his blue uniform, we saw a row of scales that were embedded into the flesh of his arm. They looked like diamond-shaped brownish stamps.

That wasn't all. The way his arms moved—the bones, the muscles—they were all wrong. I could see that clearly now that his flesh had been revealed. He had an extra elbow about where a man's wrist would have been. He held his hands cocked slightly, and they could bend farther than ours could.

Then Shaw showed his teeth to all of us as we gaped at him. I wasn't certain if this display was a threat, a demonstration of amusement, or something else entirely.

=14=

We learned fast over the next two days because we had no choice. We were assigned a small spacecraft, called a heavy fighter. It was just like every other vessel that rested on skids on the hangar deck.

At first, we weren't even allowed to go aboard her. We were only allowed to clean the exterior and take tests every several hours proving we could identify the various ports, armament and latching mechanisms.

We didn't really have "days" aboard the carrier, which we learned was named *"Killer"* or something that translated that way. With so many different life-forms represented aboard, no one would have been able to agree on how long to work and how long we should be allowed to rest.

We also learned our syms did the translating when we interacted with others. The symbiotic life-forms inside us were artificial and served many purposes, including communicating at a distance. Rather than using a radio with a traditional headset, we used our syms to relay and transmit messages.

"Days" or "shifts" were about twelve hours long. Every six hours we were ordered back to our pods for rest. We always retired hungry and sore. After we were fed, we sprawled out on thin pads on the floor and slept. It was uncomfortable, but apparently the concept of a soft mattress was a rare one in this galaxy. Most of our fellow predators had never heard of the idea, and they scoffed at it when we tried to explain.

Inside our group's pod, smaller chambers had now appeared. We were able to sleep separately, and we were expected to relieve ourselves on the decks inside these tiny cubicles.

"This is gross," Gwen had repeatedly complained, even though the deck promptly absorbed all waste.

We soon got used to it. We had no choice.

"When do we get to fly this thing?" Dalton asked Shaw on the third "day" since gaining access to the hangar deck.

Shaw turned on Dalton slowly. We all thought he was going to smash him one, or maybe throttle the life out of his noisy throat the way he'd done with Dr. Chang. But he didn't.

"You're not yet ready," Shaw said. "But I have hopes that you will be by the time we reach the front."

We looked at one another in alarm. "The front? What front?"

He showed his teeth again. We'd learned this was usually a sign of amusement, but not always.

"Did you think *Killer* was built for something other than war?"

"No, but..." Dalton trailed off, disturbed.

"Sir," I said. "Who are we at war with? For that matter, what kind of organization are we?"

"As I've said, we are the Free Kher. We serve in the Rebel Fleet. The Empire is our enemy, and it rules between this star system and the rim of the galaxy. The Imperials will come for us, as they have always come, when this part of the galaxy is lit up by the Central Fires."

I had no idea what he was talking about, but I nodded briskly. "I see... so this 'front' is at the center of the galaxy, then?"

"No, of course not. It is in a nearby arm of the galaxy. A region known as the Orion Spur of the Cygnus Carina Arm. Don't they teach you primates anything about your local surroundings on Earth?"

"Surroundings? You mean as in what stars are nearby? Very little, sir."

He sighed and shook his head. "Pointless. This entire assignment is beyond pointless."

"What do you mean, sir?" I asked.

He shook his head. "Don't worry about it. We're going to enter the active region of the flux soon. If *Killer* doesn't scatter too badly as we approach the next beacon star, we'll be arriving at the Orion Front soon enough to satisfy your curiosity."

He left us cleaning the ship again, but Dalton threw down his smart-wipes in disgust.

"Bugger him!" he exclaimed. "This freak expects us to fight and die on this ship, but he won't tell us what his war is about?"

"Pick up that rag, Dalton," I ordered. "People are watching."

Ever since our early run-in with Ra-tikh and his crew, others had been considering taking us down. We looked harmless enough to be easy targets. If Samson hadn't managed to get hold of Ra-tikh's tail and make him look foolish, I'm certain other groups would have challenged us to combat by now.

That was the way things went on this ship. You gained status by deeds in battle or by abusing rival teams. If you wanted a better ship, you had to fight for it. There seemed to be few other methods of conflict resolution aboard *Killer*.

At the end of the "day" Shaw returned with another officer. This guy was squatty and mean-looking. If I had to choose, I'd say he reminded me of a two-legged walrus. He had whiskers as thick and straight as shoots of dry spaghetti poking out around yellowed tusks.

We'd long ago figured out that Shaw wasn't an Admiral. He was more like a Lieutenant. This walrus-guy had a diamond on his shoulders, meaning he was a commander.

The rank insignia were easy to figure out once you understood them. Our own circular button-shaped insignias showed we were of the lowest rank. A stick-like line indicated a person was an officer in training, while the lieutenants started off with triangles. If your emblem was silver you were junior, gold you were senior. A dull, coppery colored insignia was a punishment rank, indicating you were about to lose your status entirely.

It was Gwen who'd figured out that the geometric shapes were logically related to ranks. Basically, the more sides your shape had, the higher rank you were. Triangles were lieutenants, diamonds were commanders, and so on. Presumably, if we ever met a guy with octagons on his shoulder, we were looking at a high-level admiral.

"This is Commander Tand," Shaw said. "He's going to teach you how to service the interior of your heavy fighter."

We didn't come to attention or salute, but we did stand still when the new officer arrived. It was hard to know how to show respect in the Fleet. With so many creatures with varied physiques, there was no standardized way to greet a superior other than by appearing quiet and alert.

Shaw left, and Commander Tand touched his hand to the side of our fighter. It was a thrill to see it open. We'd seen other crews entering their ships, but we'd never been able to do more than imagine the interior of ours.

"You enter through contact here," he wheezed, locating the touch plate.

There were no windows or portholes on our fighter. Nevertheless, once we were inside, it looked as if we could see everything. At least forty percent of the hull was translucent. Anything not blocked directly by opaque equipment, served as a window.

The technology was fascinating. Gwen and Dr. Chang speculated on how it worked, but Tand glared at them until they shut up.

Commander Tand was short and wide. He never had to duck as he moved through the ship. Once all of us were inside the closed space with him, we were bathed in his unmistakable fleshy and alien scent. Somehow it made his presence more intimidating.

"Which of you is the pilot?" he questioned, whiskers twitching.

"I am," I said, and no one else argued with me. None of them had flown so much as a backyard drone before.

Tand glanced pointedly at the gold circle on my shoulders.

"You are in command, *and* you're the pilot?" he asked. "You have chosen to take two difficult roles at once—but that is your decision to make."

I shrugged. I hadn't known we'd had any such choices, but I didn't see an easy way out of it now. No one in my feisty little group could assume command of a military spacecraft. Samson was an ex-marine, but he didn't seem like officer material to anyone. Likewise, no one else could be easily trained to pilot her. It was all up to me.

Tand showed us around the small vessel. It was compact in the extreme. There were three small decks with low ceilings. There were very few spots where I could stand up straight, and all of those spots were in hatchways that connected one deck to another.

"In battle," Tand said, "you'll be floating much of the time."

"What about G-forces?" Dr. Chang asked. "I don't see any padding. There's only a simple harness attached to each of these metal seats."

"Observant," Tand said. "Some of the more primitive crews still don't understand such things even after significant hands-on exposure. Make this one your engineer, Blake."

"Consider it done. He's also the ship's medic."

Tand twitched his whiskers at me. Was that a smile? It was impossible to tell.

"Good enough," he said, "but if this ship is damaged enough to injure the occupants, you'll probably all be dead within seconds."

"Could you answer my question, Commander?" the doctor persisted. "What about the G-forces?"

Tand didn't take offense. "These fighters have anti-gravity systems. Otherwise, no being could survive the acceleration and spinning they're capable of in combat. Inside the vessel, no matter what it does, you'll all be floating."

"That does sound convenient," I admitted.

"It would be impossible to accommodate the differing mental and physical requirements for so many variants of the Kher otherwise."

"Commander," I asked him sometime later, as he showed us every compartment aboard and explained its function, "why are there crews here from so many different worlds? Wouldn't it be easier to recruit and train one planet full of the best of us?"

"That's not our Law. All must participate in the culling. All must resist our ancestors when they come. No one can sit back, making no sacrifice while others die in space."

His little speech was delivered with vehemence, and I believed it was from the heart. But I didn't find it comforting. Quite the opposite in fact.

"So…" I said. "We're expected to die?"

"Of course," he rasped. "We're all going to die on the Orion Front."

"That explains why everyone seems to be in a bad mood…" Dr. Chang reflected.

Tand looked around the group. "Do not despair! Your sacrifice will not be in vain. As always, when the Old Ones grow weary of their sport, when they sicken of the slaughter of worlds, they will retreat for another millennium—or at least, they will move on to abuse others on the far side of the galaxy."

My crew and I exchanged worried glances. There was no way to candy-up this revelation. Had we fought so hard, learned so much, only to die in a hopeless fight far from home?

Tand showed us around, but we received no instruction on weaponry or flight controls. Most of the lessons involved maintenance procedures. When he was finished, he addressed us again as a group.

"I heard that you pulled Ra-tikh's tail when he asked you to hold it," Tand said. "He will hate you forever for that insult, but it's very amusing." He chuckled then, making a sound like a small combustion engine.

"It is Ra-tikh that needs to be concerned about our anger," I said smoothly, knowing that was the proper response to make. No one on this carrier accepted weakness of any kind. We'd been reminded of that lesson in various ways every day.

Tand nodded, and he made no further comment. He left us inside the ship with orders to clean every crevice.

"This is a dead waste," Dalton said as he worked to remove unidentifiable stains from the steel seats.

"You got that right," Samson echoed. "I vote we find a way off this deathtrap."

They all looked at me thoughtfully.

"You're a pilot, Blake..." Dalton said suggestively.

"Oh right," I said, "I'm going to fire up these engines and blaze my way through one of these bulkheads. Don't hold your breath."

"Not now," Dalton said. "Not today. But when they teach us how to fly this thing... They have to let us out into space to do that, don't they?"

I nodded. "Sure guys. First chance we get, we'll head back to Hawaii."

That seemed to please Samson and Dalton. Gwen knew better, however. She came to me and cocked her head as she looked up at me.

"I didn't know you were a pilot," she said.

"I didn't tell people back on Earth."

"Why not? I've always thought pilots were kinda cool, even though I've never met one before." She said this with a gleam in her eye.

That made me smile. Seeing her face, looking up at me, I recalled happier times.

Only days ago, I'd been a beach bum with very little ambition. Now, I had a goal, but it was a grim one: staying alive.

=15=

The next day, they issued us weapons. This came as a welcome surprise.

Our sidearms looked like flashlights. Perhaps a foot in length, they ended in a bulbous metal tip.

"Hold out your weapons," Shaw ordered.

We were arrayed in front of our ship. We'd been allowed to name her, and Gwen had come up with the winning name: *Hammerhead*. The name had struck us all as fitting because the heavy fighter looked somewhat misshapen. Also, Hawaii had quite a few scalloped hammerhead sharks in her waters, and they were mean fish.

We clumsily drew our weapons and held them out. Shaw pointed to mine.

"This button on top fires the weapon," he said. "You direct the bulbous tip toward the enemy, and depress it."

With that, he stepped back and stopped talking.

"Um… is that it?" I asked.

"Yes. The weapons are simple to operate."

"How do we know if it's loaded?" Dalton asked, looking at his weapon from every angle.

"They are always loaded—at least until the charge is depleted."

We reacted with alarm. Everyone carefully moved their fingers away from the firing button.

"Wait a minute," Samson said. "I tried mine out the minute I got it. How come Dalton doesn't have a hole in his side?"

The feisty little man gave him a snarl. "You ass!" he said.

"They don't work onboard the carrier. Not unless an officer activates them for some reason. They only work when you've been deployed."

"How can you tell if they need a fresh charge?" Samson asked, pointing his weapon at Dalton and pushing the button again. The other man returned the favor angrily.

"If the firing button depresses and fails to come back up, it's out of charge. You'll find they'll give you about ninety shots before failing. When they are getting low, the button won't come up as far as it does when the weapon is full."

I nodded slowly. These were, quite possibly, the simplest sidearms I'd ever heard of anyone designing. One button literally did everything.

"How do they kill?" I asked.

"Cellular disruption. They have little effect on inorganic matter, but a living creature, even an armored one, will die of organ failure if you hit the right spots."

I glanced up at him. "I didn't think we'd be fighting in close. Why issue these at all? They seem like a pointless danger to crews."

"You think like an officer," Shaw said, "but you are wrong, and you will never be an officer!"

He said these final words quickly as he stared at me, challenging me with his eyes. I figured out he was putting me in my place, and I said nothing.

After a moment, Shaw continued. "Although we fight in space most of the time, we must also remove the enemy from their hunting grounds after sweeping the skies of their ships. These weapons serve well in such cases."

There was so much I didn't understand, but Shaw and the others grew angry when we asked too many questions in a row. In fact, almost everything made Shaw angry. I realized this was going to be a serious case of on-the-job training.

"You will be trained now in the use of these weapons," he continued. "The winning crew will be rewarded. Follow me."

We did as he ordered, tossing bewildered glances at one another. The winning crew? What did that mean? Target practice?

We should have known better. As we walked along the decking, we were joined by other crews led by officers. Ra-tikh and his group were among them.

We were taken to a central region of the hangar. A circular area lit up yellow. It looked to be about a hundred yards across. The circle encompassed us and four other crews.

Beyond that illuminated ring, a crowd grew. These were veteran spacers. Crews that already had their sidearms and darker blue uniforms, indicating they'd completed basic training.

"Stay within the circle," Shaw ordered.

He then backed out as did his peers.

"I've got a bad feeling about this," Gwen said. She held her disruptor in her hand with her thumb on the button.

"The weapons will be activated shortly," Shaw told us.

As he spoke, the floor lurched under our feet. I heard the sound of heavy hydraulics as the floor inside the lit circle lowered itself, turning the area into a pit.

"When the floor goes red, incapacitate all the other crews," Shaw called down to us.

"That wanker!" Dalton snarled. "I'll shoot him first!"

"It probably won't work," Dr. Chang said.

"Yes, save your fire for the enemy," I added.

"What are we supposed to do?" Samson asked me unhappily.

I could tell he didn't like his flashlight-weapon or this mosh-pit of death we were descending into. All around us, the other teams seemed just as disgruntled as we were.

Most of the teams were standing where they'd been placed, but not Ra-tikh's crew. He had them moving—toward us. As Ra-tikh's team approached us, members of the other teams shuffled out of his way, hissing and pointing their weapons at him. They squeezed the buttons again and again, but they'd yet to become active.

"Ra-tikh is going to try to take us out," I said. "Samson, when they give the word, throw yourself down on the ground.

The cats will try to nail you because you humiliated their alpha. We'll mow them down when they shoot low."

"What if they go for you first instead, Leo?" Gwen asked. "That kitty doesn't look at you with any love in his eye."

"You're right," I said, nodding. "Okay, we all drop and fire as many shots as we can when they get in close. Aim for the chest area. Let's do some organ damage!"

We didn't have long to wait. The floor went red seconds later, and the battle was on.

We threw ourselves flat. Dalton fired first. He did so from behind Samson, directly at Ra-tikh's group. They were both lying down, but Dalton was on his elbows, using Samson's body as a shield.

I sprawled and began firing as well. I found it hard to aim my weapon, however. I would have much preferred a pistol grip.

There was no flash of color or sizzle in the air. The guns made a loud singing sound and vibrated in our hands. Could they be sonic? I wasn't sure.

"Don't spam!" I shouted. "Aim those shots. We only have ninety each before we're out!"

Finally, one of the female cats spun around and stumbled. She got back up again, but remained off-balance.

"Focus fire! Put one down at a time!" I shouted.

We fired a series of carefully aimed shots at her. She went down and stayed there. I wondered if she was dead—it wouldn't have surprised me if our officers let us kill one another in this exercise.

"Ra-tikh next!" I ordered.

But almost as if they knew our plans, the remaining three females got in front of him, running interference.

We beamed them until another fell.

Our team took hits as well. "My eye! My eye!" Samson cried out, rolling around in pain, clutching his face. Dr. Chang moved to his side automatically.

"Get down, dammit!" I ordered him, but it was too late.

The doctor took a series of hits. With a stunned look on his face, he rolled away, foaming at the mouth and shivering.

Gwen crawled over to his body, but before I got a chance to tell her to get out of there, I noticed that she was using him as a shield. I couldn't argue with that strategy. She was a thinker, all right.

I took my first hits then. They stung like hot pokers. I felt a burning sensation, and my teeth ached at the same time. I figured it must have been the vibrations. Extremely powerful vibrations like ultrasonic beams were hitting us.

It was like being killed by a microwave. We howled and squinched up our faces. One of my teeth fell out, and my tongue swelled up so much I could hardly talk. I must have taken a hit in the mouth.

The cat team fared worse. They never made it to us.

We took Ra-tikh out last. He fell to all fours in the end, moving with alarming speed, despite the fact he was crawling. We beamed him until he slumped down, blinded and twitching. His eyes were red-rimmed and swollen so they bulged from the sockets.

"Okay," I said in a slurring voice. "Who have we got left?"

"Me," Dalton said.

"I'm still alive," Gwen said. "But my weapon is out."

I looked around the field. Two teams had been wiped out. Two others were hurt, but they were huddled in tiny fortresses built with their comrades bodies. These last two teams were still in the running.

"They should stop this," Gwen said. "Why train us for weeks then order us to kill each other?"

"I don't think anyone is really dead," I said. "These beams aren't penetrating chest cavities or skulls."

"That's right," Dalton hissed between clenched teeth. "They can do a number on your bollocks, though."

"We have to get fresher weapons," I said. "Only Ra-tikh's team moved much. They were knocked out early, and so their weapons must still have a charge in them."

"Are you crazy?" Gwen demanded. "We should just stay down."

"They haven't canceled this battle yet," I said. "If we don't grab those weapons out there, we're going to be fried by the team that does. Look, those last two teams over there are barely shooting at each other, and they aren't hitting anything either. They might be running out of ammo."

They both looked at me in pain, but Dalton nodded. "All right. Consider it done."

"We go together, three paces apart."

"Damn you guys," Gwen said, tears streaking her face. She had bruises and red welts all over.

"Let's go," I said.

Lurching to my feet, I set off in a stumbling run. I'd taken more damage than I'd thought. My legs still functioned well enough, but they felt like someone had taken a whip to them.

I passed by Ra-tikh without taking his weapon. He had used his disruptor quite a bit before going down. Running until I got a good disruptor with a fresh charge, I paid for it with a few light hits, but nothing that took me out.

It was then that I noticed the circle of decking around our arena was shrinking. The outer edge was blue about ten yards in from every direction. I crouched among two fallen female cats.

One of them looked at me weakly. She was still conscious, still breathing.

I knew I should use her as a shield, but I couldn't bring myself to do it—not while she was still conscious. Nodding to her, I staggered to my feet again.

"Let's charge the group on the left," I said to my team.

They looked at me in pain and horror, but we could all see the officers weren't going to let us get out of this without fighting. They were herding the teams closer now, refusing to let us hide among our fallen.

"They must know how many shots we've fired," Gwen said. "They must know we've still got live weapons."

"Ha!" shouted Dalton. "I just nailed one of those bastards up on the rim. See him dancing around up there?"

I glanced at him. "Don't screw us. We've almost won."

"You've got to be sneaky about it—that's all," he said. "I've got two disruptors. One, I'm firing at the enemy. The other is held low. I angled it up—"

"Come on, let's finish this," I said.

The blue ring ate up Samson behind us. I might have heard him groan in helpless agony, but it could have come from any one of the teams.

We advanced steadily, firing with our fresher weapons. In the end, the enemy stood up and charged. I recognized them—they were almost human, like Shaw, but that twist to the lower wrist gave them away.

We beamed them down and turned to face the last team—but it was already over. They'd been too injured, perhaps, to crawl away from the blue zone. They'd been consumed and shocked into submission.

A cheer went up from above us. It was a strange cheer, filled with honking, hooting and even a few barking sounds.

But we knew what it was, and we stood tall as the deck went green. Then the pit began rising up to rejoin the main deck far above.

=16=

We were allowed a full shift to recover from our injuries. God knows we needed it. We were bleeding internally, and at least half the eyeballs in my group had been blinded.

The healing efforts of the salves and liquids we applied in our private pod took longer than they ever had before. Only Dalton's burns in the rock pit had taken longer to disappear completely.

After our health had improved, Shaw came to see us in our group's pod.

"I can scarcely believe your crew won," he told us.

"I'll take that as a compliment, Lieutenant," I said, making a point of calling him by his proper rank. I was still annoyed that he'd passed himself off as an Admiral when we'd first spoken. Such thoughts brought up new questions for me. What else had Shaw lied about?

"You'll be expected to return to your duties at the start of the next shift," he said, ignoring our injuries. "Do you have any objections?"

"No objections, just questions, sir," I said. "Can you explain to me how you arranged to pick us up back on Earth? I mean, our governments must have been involved?"

"Since you have proven your dedication to the cause, this is a good time to reveal more information to you," he said. "Our legal requirement is to find recruits on every planet who are worthy of serving aboard our ships. We asked for Earth's cooperation, and your governments gave it to us."

"But *how* did you get Earth to cooperate?"

He shrugged dismissively. "We showed them recordings of the enemy fleets. They saw Earth may well not survive this event. That was enough."

It made sense to me, but I pressed for more. "When I called the Pentagon, they connected me to you directly. Were you on Earth or in space?"

"We gave them communications devices compatible with our ships. The largest governments of Earth were provided with them. If you'd called Moscow, Berlin or Washington— any of them would have connected you to me. They were involved long before you met up with one of our probes."

"What probe?"

"The stone carrying the symbiotics. I believe you said you found it underwater?"

"Yes, right," I said, remembering that night. "The bubbles and the light... why'd you make it attractive? To get someone to check it out?"

"Yes. The first test of many. The sym was designed to locate a brave, capable candidate. It found you because, among other things, you were a competent swimmer for a land-mammal. You were also a creature brave enough to risk his life when faced with the unknown."

I nodded slowly. "Right... The bubbling was just to get a curious fool's attention..."

"You were honored, not tricked!" Shaw barked.

"It seems like it was a little of both," I said. "But never mind about that. Did you know that a friend of mine reached that probe first, and he was killed by it?"

Shaw shrugged like he couldn't care less. "Another trial which you survived. The weak must be weeded out."

"Right... So the sym got into my bloodstream, and it tried to make me angry enough to find others who carried syms and kill them."

"Yes. We find it's easier to clear out the dead wood while candidates are on their home planet. Survivors are gathered several weeks after the process begins. Only the best of them can be used to form a crew."

"Samson said you really wanted me to be one of those survivors. He even shot Kim to keep her off me."

"That's right," Shaw admitted. "I was in charge of Earth's recruitment drive. Due to your primitive technological state, very few pilots were attracted by the probes. I wanted you to at least make the early cuts for this reason."

I glanced at Gwen, who was eyeing Samson in shock. Apparently, she hadn't known he'd killed Kim back on Earth.

"The female you mentioned," Shaw said, "what was her name?"

"Kim," I said.

"She was an accidental recruit. Normally, symbiotic hosts are too distracted to attempt mating. But you, Blake, you are an unusual case. You managed to pass on the sym infection to Kim sexually."

I cleared my throat.

"There was blood at the scene too," I said. "When our friend Jason died, we all touched him."

"Ah," Shaw said, nodding.

But Dalton was looking at me now. He eyed me and Gwen suspiciously. He'd been flirting with her steadily since we'd teamed up, but she'd always rebuffed him.

"So, you think you're a big player with the ladies, is that it, Blake?" he asked. "Nailing girls back on Earth and in space? Your kind never quits, do they?"

Then he turned to Gwen and gave her a sour up-down glance. "Don't think you're fooling anyone, Missy. I've seen you look at him. Disgusting!"

Gwen huffed and looked embarrassed. She walked out of ship, insulted. I gave Dalton a frown, but he only gave me an unapologetic shrug in return.

Shaw watched us. "The mating habits of Earthers are uncommon," he said. "Most wild Kher varieties have seasons. Your subspecies seems to mate at will."

"Yes, I guess that's true," I admitted. "But you still haven't told me how you managed to answer my call when I contacted the Pentagon."

"Your government was informed of our intentions. They did not object as they could see one of our carriers in high orbit, and they were frightened by it. They participated in the search for candidates by maintaining a fiction about the stellar flux."

"May I ask a question?" Dr. Chang asked warily.

"It seems that you already have," Shaw pointed out.

Dr. Chang cleared his throat. "What causes a stellar flux, exactly?"

"The flux effect is an opening in space," Shaw explained irritably. "Two points are briefly connected, and if there is no scatter, objects can come through. On Earth, when the luminescent cloud phenomenon occurred, you saw the point of origin of our probes. After they came through, the breach closed, and the skies returned to normal."

"So..." Dr. Chang said thoughtfully. "That means the probes and your ships must be from quite a distance away. Somewhere with a nebula and a bright star cluster."

"Correct. Now, however, I'm through with this interrogation."

He left, and we all looked after him thoughtfully.

All of us, that was, except for Samson. He thumped me on the back.

"Thanks a lot, Blake," he said. "That was not cool."

"What's wrong?"

"You told Gwen that I killed Kim! She's the only human woman on this ship. I've got no chance now."

Dalton produced a dirty laugh. "Yeah, right-o. Like she was going to warm your knob, anyway. No lady wants an animal as far down the chain as you. She might as well shag an ape. My advice is to get used to your hand—"

Samson reached for him, but he skittered away, flashing his teeth at us.

The two of them chased one another for a time. I heard a commotion shortly afterward, and I didn't feel the slightest temptation to intervene. Both of them deserved whatever they got from the other.

When they came back, Samson seemed oddly chastened. "Gwen, Leo," he said, "I want to say something."

He kept his eyes downcast while we listened.

"I'm sorry for killing your friend, Gwen. I wasn't in my right mind."

"I thought I killed you myself," I told him. "Twice."

Gwen's lip trembled, but she didn't break down. "I thought I killed you too, Leo. Good thing your head is so hard."

I looked around the group. "We were all in the grip of our syms," I said. "We have to forgive ourselves now, and each other. We can't hold grudges over what happened. We won't be able to function as a group if we do."

Then, I proceeded to make all of them apologize to one another. Everyone but Dalton sounded sincere.

"Sorry all," he said in a snotty tone.

It sounded almost as if he was sorry we were still alive, but I let it slide. It was probably the best I was going to get out of him.

After our moment of contrition, the group seemed a little more relaxed together.

"Dr. Chang," I said, moving to his side. "You seem thoughtful and quiet."

"I've been thinking about what Shaw said. I can see how it played out. Earth learned the truth, or at least some of the truth, and they promptly approved these abuses of their citizenry."

"I suppose it was a small price to pay to keep a possibly hostile fleet happy," I said. "But *I'm* not happy."

"You wish it was someone else who'd been drafted into this?"

"Don't you?"

He looked down and nodded.

"It's always that way when a real war comes along," I told him.

Gwen had come back into the room by then, and she looked at us both seriously. She crossed her arms under her breasts and frowned.

"This isn't our war," she said. "These aliens have no right to expect us to die for them against some other bunch of aliens we never heard of."

"You have a point," Dr. Chang said, "but then again, so do they. Perhaps we didn't know we were within their territory. I gather that Earth has been kept like a wild preserve for centuries. Now, they've decided we've grown up enough to participate in their organization like full-fledged members."

"They don't respect us. They came with warships. They bullied our governments with the threat of attack—implicitly, if not explicitly."

"Yes," Chang agreed, "that's probably true. But that's how empires always behave. They're our cousins, remember."

"Huh…" I said. "Cousins… I thought *we* were the savage ones. Most of these people are pure carnivores. They're mean—downright ruthless. I guess we were more civilized than we thought."

Dr. Chang chuckled. "I may not go that far. For the last few decades we've been relatively humane with one another, true. There are no more cannibals and relatively few genocides, but that state of affairs has been very brief in duration. Perhaps the Kher, these mean-spirited people, can give us insight into our true natures."

"What about his claim that we're all related?" Gwen asked in an accusatory tone. "Do you believe it?"

"Yes," Dr. Chang said. "These creatures have a physiology that's irrefutably similar to our own. Natural evolution would tend to produce creatures of far more variety."

"You expected something like a duck-billed platypus?" she asked.

"That would make more sense," Chang said. "Think of it, so many species are on this ship, all from different planets. Yet, they're all of similar size? We're almost all bipedal. Two eyes, one head. Why would such a common biological design evolve to dominance on a hundred worlds all at the same time? It's like rolling a thousand dice and coming up with all sixes."

Gwen shook her head. "The idea that we were seeded on Earth by some ancestor is a hard pill to swallow. I've never heard of such a theory."

"I would suspect biologists would be the least surprised," Chang said. "There are too many gaps in our evolutionary trail to make it complete. Take the eye, for example. There are no intermediary steps in the fossil record to—"

The floor went yellow then, and we all knew what that meant. I slammed my hands together, making a booming sound.

"All right nerds," I said, "back to work! Rest time is over."

As we marched back to *Hammerhead*, I thought about what I knew of human history. It was full of cruelty, unfair treatment and exploitation. It stood to reason that our distant cousins from the stars would be no less self-serving.

When we got to our heavy fighter, Commander Tand was standing in the hatchway waiting for us.

"There you are, slothful beings," he said. "Today is a critical day. Today, we're stepping up your training schedule. Everyone to their stations!"

We looked at one another then trooped past him and boarded *Hammerhead*.

"Is this because we won the contest?" Samson asked.

"Yes, exactly. Victory is always rewarded in the Fleet."

"What's our reward, exactly?" Gwen asked warily.

Commander Tand looked at her, and his whiskers bristled.

"Today, we fly this ship! Today, you shall become true spacers!"

=17=

I was shocked. Sure, I'd piloted plenty of aircraft, but thus far, I hadn't received a moment's worth of flight instruction on this beast.

"Sir…" I began, "do you really think we're ready?"

"Yes," he said, drawing out the final 'S' sound into a hiss of what I took to be happiness. "I've been *so* bored with all these crews. You primates have shown promise, but I honestly didn't expect you to be given this honor so soon. The CAG has stepped-up the master schedule significantly. Battle is coming, and our best crews must learn to fly!"

He seemed inordinately pleased about everything he'd said, but the rest of us were wide-eyed in alarm.

I wanted to ask him what he meant about a "master schedule" and why he thought it had been "stepped-up", but there wasn't time. He had us all humping around the ship, checking every reading and double-testing the seal on every hatch.

It was our pre-flight checklist. I knew it by heart already, but today, instead of finding it dull, my heart pounded in my chest.

Commander Tand climbed into the pilot's chair, and he had me take the co-pilot's seat. I wasn't disappointed at all to see him take over the primary controls.

"The flight controls are very simple," he said. "First, use your sym to access the virtual interface."

I did as he said and signaled when I was fully connected. The sym was able to superimpose graphics in three dimensions by overlaying my natural vision. It was disconcerting to see things that you knew logically weren't really there. Even more disturbing to me was the idea that my sym was interrupting the nerves connecting my eyeballs to my brain—but I'd gotten used to that idea over time, too.

"You start the engines with this icon here," Tand said, "then apply gentle touch-pressure to the contact points under your fingers. Notice how they'll follow your hand wherever it goes, so you'll be comfortable."

He did these things as I watched. Outside, the ship began to rumble. Crews scrambled away from us on the deck, but it didn't seem to send out a wave of exhaust and flame. Apparently, our propulsion system burned clean and was harmless to those moving around the hangar deck.

"Now," Tand said, "you must engage your sym up-link!"

I did as he ordered. My senses were instantly overlaid by new imagery. Not only could I see through *Hammerhead's* translucent hull, but I could see beyond the external hull of the carrier itself.

What a shock that was! We were in open space. Cranking my head around, I could see a blue orb with a smaller white one nearby. Could that be the Earth and the Moon? It had to be. Beyond that was a painfully bright yellow star.

"Is that our sun?" I asked. "We're still in our home system?"

"Yes, Blake. Now shut up. I must give you a week's instruction in three hours."

"But don't we have other pickups to make?" I asked. "Other planets to visit?"

"That's been dropped for now. Fleet Command has decided to put us in the field with only half our recruitment and training finished, thank the stars!"

I could tell he was dying to get out there and fight whatever enemy we were supposed to face. I didn't share his eagerness.

In my knowledge of military history, when a unit was deployed and sent to the front before its training was complete, that invariably meant the war was going badly.

"Pay attention!" Commander Tand demanded. "Your sym is providing you with enhanced perception. This is controlled by your mind as you interact as a single unit with your sym. You must master the new interface quickly."

Breathing hard, I nodded.

"You may 'look' around you in any direction," Tand explained. "Try to zoom in on your home planet now, please."

I looked in that direction and squinted my eyes. The Earth didn't get any closer.

"I can't see anything other than a small blue ball."

He grunted unhappily. "They told me you were a pilot."

"I am," I said, "but I've never used a control system like this. I've always used my actual eyeballs."

"Ah…" he said thoughtfully. "I see what the problem is. You're attempting to see the planet with your optical organs. You must work with your sym, and use your mind. *Will* yourself closer."

I tried it, and it worked. I zoomed in sickeningly fast. The vision of Earth swam and wavered. It was alarming to behold.

"Is this some kind of telepathy?" I asked.

"No, not at all. Your sym reads your neurological biochemistry. There's no magic involved."

"Fascinating…" I said, looking around and zooming at the Moon. I could see every crater, including the shadows of the darker side. "I've noticed my sym no longer tries to make me angry."

"Yes, that function has ceased to be useful. Now, it is learning your engrams, just as you're learning to control your relationship with it. In time, you'll find your perception enhanced dramatically while flying this fighter."

I believed him. Already, I could tell that space all around me was accessible. I turned away from the Sun and toward the outer planets. I looked for a bright spot, found Mars, and zoomed in again. The reddish-brown world swam into view. I could see the polar caps, and I laughed.

"I can see Mars!" I shouted to the others. "Honest to God, I can see Mars from here. Up close!"

"They're all glad for you," Tand assured me. "Now, pay attention. We must fly."

The ship's flight controls were almost as simple as the single button on my disruptor. Everything boiled down to pushing a few ethereal buttons, monitoring various instruments, and using my perception-enhancing sym-link to direct the ship.

Below *Hammerhead*, a hole had opened up in the deck of the carrier. We dropped through it. We fell down a long shaft full of flashing lights. After what seemed like a half-mile, we fell out of the bottom of *Killer* and hung in open space.

Looking around, I saw the big ship in detail. There were other fighters out here, maybe a hundred of them. They were performing maneuvers—dodging, firing at invisible targets, and skimming close to the mothership's hull on practice attack-runs.

"Now, we must turn on the anti-grav system," Tand said. "Do it manually."

I signaled Samson, who found the recessed button and pressed it. In an instant, we were all weightless.

Killer had artificial gravity, maintaining a pull that felt pretty close to one G. Out in open space, in order to tolerate being thrown about, we needed to ignore gravity completely.

"Take us to that rock over there," Tand ordered.

I looked around, following his perception. "You mean Mars?"

"Yes. Over there."

Shaking my head, I engaged the engines as he'd shown me. The ship bucked, but that was only registered with our senses visually. Inside the ship, we didn't feel a thing.

"Whoa, that's a weird sensation."

"You'll get used to it. Fly the ship. Increase power."

I goosed it. I'd been dying to find out what this baby could do, and I wasn't disappointed when I put the hammer down. We zoomed away from *Killer* with startling acceleration.

The fact that I couldn't feel the acceleration was both disconcerting and pleasing at the same time. The G-forces I'd just applied—hell, we might have all died without the anti-grav system.

"Keep going," Tand urged. "Full speed. We need to get out into open space to test our weapons for the first time."

He got no arguments from me. I was flying again. If you know anything about pilots, we're as happy as pigs in manure when we're cruising around off the ground. This ship was the most amazing thing I'd ever had the pleasure of flying.

When we were something like half-way to Mars, several million kilometers from *Killer*, Tand had me slow down and drift.

"When I'm not aboard, you'll have no one to tell you what to do—other than Fleet Command. They will not have time to hold your hand. You will only get general orders, such as attack target X, etc."

"I understand."

"No, I don't think that you do. You must train your crew. You must become as close to them as you are to the sym that lives in your blood. They will keep you alive. Your task, besides flight, will be to make tough, fast decisions."

I thought about that. Independent fighter command? That seemed crude, but with a zillion different kinds of aliens flying ships around, I guessed it made some kind of sense.

"Won't there be a squadron commander or something like that?"

"Yes," he said, "but it's our experience that new crews rarely listen well. They will swarm a designated target, but not with enough coordination to maintain a tight formation."

"I see... Show us how to use the weapons."

He began doing so, and we were both soon so absorbed that we didn't notice when Dalton drifted near.

He had a wrench in his hand. He squared himself behind Commander Tand's broad, leathery skull, feeling for leverage by hooking his legs on a bundle of pipes that ran over the deck. Before I had time to ask him what he was doing out of his seat, he slammed his wrench into Tand's bony head.

"Ha!" Dalton shouted. "I got him, guys!"

I disabled my sym and looked at him in disbelief. Tand was bleeding. He was out cold, slumped in his seat.

"Take over, Blake," Dalton said. "Fly us home to Earth. We're free at last!"

=18=

When I turned off my enhanced perception, I was instantly returned to the cramped quarters of *Hammerhead*. With a growl of frustration and disbelief, I threw a punch at Dalton. He dodged away and looked at me in shock.

"Okay, I get it," he said. "You like it here. They bought you off with flying a fighter again. Or maybe you've gone—"

"Shut up," I said. "Do you really think the Fleet will let us escape? They'll find us again. They've got to have some way of finding us by our syms. Did you even think of that?"

"Who cares?" Samson said, floating up from the mid-deck to the flight deck. "The Fleet is pulling out. They won't delay to hunt down one crew."

I looked at Tand. He had been a good officer. Shaw was a bastard—but Tand had been very focused and professional.

"What are we going to do with him?" I asked.

"I've got an idea…" Dalton said, pointing toward the airlock.

Becoming angry, I climbed out of my seat.

"This isn't our war, Leo," Gwen said, touching my arm. "You have to admit, this is the best chance we'll get."

"Yeah," I said, "yeah okay. It just took me by surprise. Everyone get to your stations—but leave Tand alone. We can leave him marooned on Earth for now."

They scrambled into their positions around the ship, bumping their heads into equipment because no one was used to null-G yet.

Remembering what Commander Tand had taught me to do, I first scanned for Earth. For a panicky instant, I couldn't find it. We were farther out than we had been the first time I'd seen our home world.

But then I spotted it, and I zoomed in.

"Everyone hang on to something," I said. "Applying thrust."

The ship bucked and swung around in a sickening loop. I closed my eyes to prevent a wave of vertigo, but my mind kept feeding me data. I could see it all.

We were heading toward Earth at a violent pace, accelerating steadily. How fast could this little ship go?

"*Hammerhead*," I heard a voice in my mind say. "This is traffic control. We've detected a protocol breach. You're about to leave the exercise zone."

My face screwed up into a grimace of worry. I didn't even know how to operate the com system. Experimentally, I tried simply talking to it.

"Traffic control," I said. "We've got a problem. We'll let you know when we've got it fixed."

This was nothing like the carefully coded back-and-forth exchange between Navy pilots on Earth, but I wasn't surprised. A hundred worlds probably had a hundred different communication protocols.

"*Hammerhead*, this is traffic control," the voice continued. "You've exited the safe zone. You're ordered to reduce your speed and alter course immediately."

"Working on it," I said confidently.

"Go faster!" Dalton hissed. "Get us home!"

I didn't even look at him. I was too busy trying to use my enhanced perception to scan local space.

Tand had hinted that detection systems like radar and lidar were inherent in the interface I was using. I only had to allow the computers to send that data to me, to let me *see* what was around our ship.

After another few seconds, I managed to enable the sensors. A mass of data flooded in, stunning my mind with moving diagrams and colorful shapes. All this was overlaid on a magnificent view of space around *Hammerhead*.

There were contacts. Lots of them. The big one had to be *Killer*. Far away, maybe a million kilometers off, were more big ships like ours. Each carrier was hanging in space at a great distance. Around them were swarms of tiny contacts, like bees circling a dozen hives.

As I grew more able to interpret the massed data, I saw that many of the closest spacecraft were converging on our position. We were passing another carrier, in fact, and its fighters looked like they were chasing us.

"It's no good," I told my crew. "We're surrounded. They'll start shooting soon. Even if they don't, they'll recapture us when we get to Earth—I don't even know if I can figure out how to land in an atmosphere without burning up."

I looked around the group.

"It's your call, Blake," Dr. Chang said. "We can't see like you are able to."

"You're a bloody coward," Dalton said. "That's all this is."

"I say go for it," Samson said. "We're all going to get killed in this crazy war, anyway."

My attention turned toward Gwen. "What do you think?"

She looked frightened. "I don't want to die right now under their guns. I'll take another week of life and hope for more."

I nodded and killed the ship's acceleration. Turning my attention aft, I was able to spot our carrier and focus on it. *Hammerhead* dutifully swung around and headed home.

"Everyone hang on," I said. "I'm going to kill the anti-gravity system."

"What?"

They scrambled to strap in. I killed the anti-grav and we were suddenly being torn apart by what registered to my sym as mild acceleration compared to what we'd been pulling before.

Handling the ship as gently as I could, I contacted *Killer* again.

"Traffic control," I said. "We have regained control of our spacecraft. There was an accident, and we've got an injury. We're heading for base. Please clear for an emergency landing."

"*Hammerhead*, switch over your manual controls to remote-enabled when you get within ten thousand kilometers. We'll take over from there."

All around us, I saw a cluster of thirty fighters imitating our maneuvering. They swung close, examining us curiously.

My crew stared out at them, able to see them with their naked eyes, they were so close.

"You weren't lying," Dalton said. "Do you really think they would have shot us down?"

"No army likes deserters," Samson said.

No one else spoke while we flew back to *Killer*. When we got close, I engaged the remote piloting option, and we were drawn up into the carrier.

Five minutes later, we opened the hatch. A dozen armed troops surrounded our fighter. They aimed their disruptors at us, and we put our hands on our heads. These weapons didn't look like much, but they weren't going to fire on low power this time.

An angry group of thumping creatures with bulging back muscles and skins like rhino-leather boarded *Hammerhead*. They marched us off the ship, took our sidearms, and shoved us into our group pod.

The pod sank into the deck. It had become a prison again. I had no idea what they were going to do with us. They hadn't even asked any questions.

But I didn't think they were happy about our attempt to go AWOL.

=19=

Shaw ran his eyes over a flimsy slip of screen-paper. These computers, which were like sheets of cloth, could display anything you desired. They were lightyears ahead of conventional tablets and notebooks back on Earth.

Lightweight, highly responsive and intuitive to use, screen-papers were everywhere aboard ship. We'd all been issued a personal unit as well when we'd qualified for flight training.

"You've all been reduced in status," Shaw said. "Your failure has lowered my rank as well, because I'm your immediate superior."

I saw his triangle was now silver. My crew had carried silver circles, now they were coppery, and mine was silver. What surprised me was they changed on their own. Apparently you didn't have to pin on new ones. They must be controlled remotely.

"Sir," I began, having worked out my lie ahead of time. "I accidently disabled the gravity controls. Commander Tand was knocked unconscious as a result and—"

Shaw threw up an irritated hand. "Save your lies. The investigation will be conclusive."

"Who will perform this investigation?" I asked.

"Commander Tand, of course."

Dalton made a pained face.

"I see..." I said. "That seems like an easy way to bring down a competitor, don't you think?"

"What are you talking about?" Shaw demanded.

"Officers gain rank by dueling or outperforming their superiors, right?"

"Of course. There is no other way."

"Ah, but there is," I said. "An opportunistic officer could claim another man's underlings were insubordinate. That way, the rival's score would suffer without requiring any direct conflict."

Shaw curled his lips back to show me an overabundance of teeth. "This is why I hate primates! You think like dishonorable dogs!"

I cocked my head to one side. "Then it's happened before? Good officers have been reduced in this way?"

"Yes, it has happened. Honest predators always lose against such tactics. Most of our top commanders are primates precisely *because* you're naturally underhanded!"

This was all news to me, and my mind was churning as to how to use this tidbit. I knew that I was considered by everyone aboard to be a sneaky primate. If they were going to prejudge me anyway, I figured I might as well own it.

"Listen, Shaw," I said. "There's no need for you to join in our punishment. I'll take full responsibility. I'm a new pilot, flying for the first time. The fault was mine."

He looked at me with narrowed eyes. "Don't you think I know that?" he demanded. "But your failure is my failure."

"It doesn't have to be. It's unreasonable to expect a perfect performance from a rookie pilot. Do all your pilots fly like experts their first time out in space?"

He shrugged and chuckled.

"No," he admitted. "Most of them fly like birds with a broken wing."

"Exactly," I said. "I can fly, but my mistake was due to natural distraction. I was overwhelmed by open space. Disoriented."

He looked at me suspiciously. "Why are you so willing to take all the blame?" he demanded.

"Because that's *my* path to honor."

He showed me his teeth again, but I could tell he was beginning to buy it. I only hoped there wasn't a log someplace recording the fact that I'd waited a full three minutes after Tand was knocked out to turn off the anti-grav.

"You'll learn your fate during the next work period," he said at last.

Then the pod doors shut, and we were locked in for the night.

We schemed all night long, just the way primates everywhere tended to do, apparently. When the pod doors opened again, we had our stories straight. Everyone's report would match down to the last detail.

But, as it turned out, none of that mattered. Commander Tand himself opened the pod at the start of the next shift, and he looked at us with baleful eyes.

"Here is my fine pack of failures," he said. "It took all I could do to prevent them from gassing your pod while you slept in it."

None of us had slept much, but we'd never thought it might be our last moments of life. We all stayed quiet and listened.

"Scoundrels, all of you," he said. "When that anti-grav system was accidentally disabled, you should have contacted traffic control immediately. Instead, you tried to fly back to Earth!"

I blinked three times before that sank in. When it did, I lowered my head in shame and mumbled an earnest apology.

"I'm sorry sir," I said. "I'd only learned how to fly *Hammerhead* minutes before the accident."

"That's what saved you," he said. "I emphasized the stepped-up training schedule. I explained that your home planet was probably the only landmark you knew in space. Still, it was a hard sell. Most of the upper officers are primates, you know."

"Is that right?" I asked, as if it was news to me.

"Yes, and like you, they're suspicious of the motives of others. Predators are always more direct. Your type—creatures that have always been the hunted as well as the hunters— you're always filled with guile, treacherous."

It was clear when he said these words that he believed there was nothing lower in the cosmos than a primate. Still, he was giving me more hope than ever. He spoke of these things as if they were foreign ideas that he'd recently learned about and didn't yet fully comprehend. I could barely believe my luck, but it sounded like the Commander was falling for it.

Over the last few weeks, I'd come to understand that even though everyone aboard was genetically related, we weren't all alike. We'd evolved on separate worlds for many generations. We'd taken on characteristics that were unique to our backgrounds and our personalities.

"As to punishment," Tand continued, "you'll not be allowed to board *Hammerhead* for two shifts!"

I had to will my face not to react in astonishment. We looked at one another, baffled. To these people, that was a punishment as it was a dishonor to be useless. To sit around without an assignment was humiliating.

To us, of course, it was a vacation.

"Um," I said, "what are we supposed to do in the meantime, sir?"

He made a sweeping gesture of dismissal. "Explore the ship. Sit in your pod and rot. Play with your genitals the way all primates seem to do. I don't care."

He left us with an air of grave disappointment, and we shared secret smiles.

"This has to be the best punishment duty I've ever pulled," Samson said. "You're some kind of genius, Leo."

"Thanks," I said, accepting the compliment at face-value.

"He's no genius," Dalton objected. "He just got lucky."

"He seems to do that a lot," Gwen pointed out.

She approached me while everyone watched, and she put her hands on my arm. "Hey, maybe we can take a look around together."

"Okay," I said, seizing the moment. "Let's go."

I left the others muttering in disappointment as I walked the decks. We were in mid-shift, and that was a good thing. Most of the crews were too busy with their ships to pester us. Many were starting their flight training just as we'd done a few days ago.

As we walked along, my eyes scanned the place desperately, looking for a spot where Gwen and I could be alone. She wasn't thinking that way at all, unfortunately.

"Hey, there's Dr. Chang," she said. "He's at the elevators to the reactor. You want to go down there? I want to see the cores with him."

I snaked an arm around her waist and pulled her to me. It had been weeks since I'd last been with a girl.

"I had another idea in mind," I said.

She pushed me away. "No way," she said. "I can't believe you're even thinking of *that*! Besides, there are a million people watching us."

"There's always somewhere to go."

Shaking her head, she retreated. I threw up my hands and sighed.

She relented long enough, looking me over thoughtfully, to give me a kiss on the cheek.

"Maybe someday," she said. "Just not today."

Then I watched her trot away to join Dr. Chang.

"Rejected?" asked a voice behind me.

I turned to see one of Ra-tikh's females. She was the one with the smallest ears and the biggest butt. I'd been checking out the cat-girls now and then. It was hard not to. The truth was, they had excellent body-shapes. I wasn't used to their faces yet, but the biggest contrast by far with any human girl was their coat of fine fur. They also had those long tails… which had begun to intrigue me.

"Who are you?" I finally asked her.

"I'm Ra-tikh's fourth."

"That's your name?" I asked incredulously. "What, are you ladies—his slaves or something?"

She grew instantly angry. "You know nothing of the people of Ral, yet you make crude and offensive jokes? I'm leaving!"

"Wait," I said. "I'm sorry. You're right. I don't know what I'm talking about. Tell me about yourself."

Pausing, she reconsidered then stepped closer to me.

"I'm Ra-tikh's fourth," she repeated, "but my name is Mia."

At least, "Mia" was what her name sounded like to me. But I could hear more guttural syllables underneath the translator's sound than I could ever hope to pronounce.

I looked into her big, remarkable golden eyes. I could certainly get used to them, I thought.

"Mia," I said. "That's nice. Show me around the ship, Mia."

"You order me? I'm not part of your crew. I'm not your—"

"Hold on," I said, putting up my hands.

That was another mistake. She put her hands up, claws out, in a gesture that matched my own as if we were going to fight.

I lowered my hands slowly. "I meant that as a request. Will you *please* show me around the ship? You've been here longer than I have."

She looked at me warily for a few seconds then suddenly warmed up again. I was getting the idea these cat-people were all touchy and moody. They could be friends one second and vicious enemies the next. In a way, it wasn't surprising. I'd petted more than one purring cat only to have it bite me a moment later.

"I'll honor your request," she said. "Walk with me."

We moved together down the central aisle between the fighters. Each sat in a dished-out region of the deck. Many were surrounded by their crews who climbed over them, working hard. As we passed, the crews looked us over in surprise.

"You make them stare," she said. "They know you've put down Ra-tikh twice. They all must know this."

"Uh... Yeah, sure. I bet they do."

I was lying of course. I doubted most of them knew who I was. But if a girl wanted to be impressed by me—even a cat-girl—I couldn't very well let that go to waste.

Mia led me farther away from her crew and mine with every step. When we were close to the recycling systems, she took my hand.

Her palm felt odd. It was a little leathery in the center and decidedly fuzzy around the edges. It was a warm, small hand. I took it in my larger grip and held on.

"Behind these tubes," she said, leading me into a dank area.

Some of the big tanks that surrounded us now were dripping. The steamy tanks warmed the air and left puddles on the deck.

When we found a private spot, she stopped me then went to look around in several directions.

"No one is here. No cameras—at least, none that I can see."

"Okay... that's good I guess."

She returned to me and turned around, aiming that shapely butt in my direction. I looked at it admiringly, but I was confused.

"Mia, why'd you bring me here?"

She looked at me over her shoulder like I was some kind of idiot. "You may hold my tail. Isn't that what you want? That's the signal your pheromones are sending."

"Uh... I still don't understand. Are you going to pee on me?"

Then she did one of those instant switch-things, changing gears from nice to nasty in less than a second.

"You insult me? You lead me on then refuse? I am humiliated. Can you hate Ra-tikh so much that you would do this?"

"No, no, hold on. Are you suggesting we have sex?"

"Of course! Is this not the way your people mate?"

I looked around. We *were* in a secluded place. She was still dressed, but I knew these uniforms could be pulled open in any number of ways. They'd been built so as to accommodate various physiologies.

Realizing I had a decision to make, I took a full two seconds to make it. That's a long time for a young guy who's been alone for weeks.

It wasn't the environment that was making me stop to think. To be honest, I wasn't so sure *how* I was expected to perform. Clearly, I hadn't thought this whole thing through. And what was Ra-Tikh going to do if he found out? I guess I was a bit thrown off.

I didn't know what I'd really expected. Sure, I'd been flirting with a girl-cat, but I hadn't expected her to be so direct.

What convinced me in the end was Mia's questioning face. She was, in a way, very innocent. She could tell that I wanted sex, and so did she. For her, that seemed to be enough.

I suspected my cautious reaction must have been very confusing for her. Apparently, she didn't understand that humans made a big deal out of mating. I realized just how complicated modern humans tend to make life's simplest experiences. Mia and her kind lived in the here and now, and they didn't understand why the monkey-types wanted to think about every angle.

"You're very appealing to me," I said. "But can we touch first? Kiss?"

"Kiss?" she asked.

I touched her gently, and I kissed her. She pulled back her head, eyes squinting in confusion. I think she was afraid I might bite her.

But after a moment, she came around. I taught her how to kiss. I hadn't done that since high school.

As she got used to my kisses, our touches became more urgent.

At last, she turned around again, pressing herself toward me. By that time I was ready for anything.

What was it like? It was hot—literally hot. Her body temperature was much higher than mine. It almost burned. But it felt great, like nothing I'd imagined. I could tell she was enjoying it too.

When we were both thoroughly satisfied, I was glad I hadn't chickened out.

=20=

After my rendezvous with Mia was over, I had time to ask her a few questions.

"Do you… do you mate like that with Ra-tikh?"

"Rarely," she said. "I'm his fourth, as I said. He does not favor me."

"And… is that why you wanted me?"

She looked at me seriously. "Yes. Partly. He insults me with his lack of attention. You have defeated him twice, injuring him badly the last time. I liked that," a slow smile spread over her face. She suddenly looked like she was hunting me with her eyes as her tongue darted out to lick her lips.

"I see. Is it only by chance that there's only one male in your group?"

"Yes, that was good luck. On our world, females outnumber males about nine to one. By the odds, there should be no males in our crew."

"Lucky bastards," I whistled.

"When I saw your only female spurn you," Mia continued, "I knew I had a chance." She sprang up, shook her tail and looked down at me happily. "Now, I will go to Ra-tikh and tell him he's been humiliated for a third time!"

"Whoa! Hold on girl!" I said. "Just a minute. I didn't do this to start a fresh war with your crew. I was hoping to make friends."

"Make friends?" she laughed. "By stealing a mate? That's absurd, and you are disappointing me. When a male steals a mate, he does it proudly after having bested another male."

"Yeah..." I said, scratching my head. "I get that. But I can't take you into my crew. Only five are allowed."

She crouched suddenly beside me. Her eyes were big and intense. I noticed her pupils had become slits. It was a little unnerving.

"Yes," she said, "an adjustment must be made. Kick out that female who refused you. I will replace her. Better yet, you could toss her into space the next time you fly your ship. It could be another accident."

Now, at long last, I was beginning to catch on. I hadn't quite understood why Mia was seducing me in such an insistent fashion.

Her standing in her own group was low. In my crew, she'd be the only female—or at least, that was her plan. That would make her powerful, the number one girl, instead of the fourth place finisher with the bottom rank.

My hesitation made her mad again.

"You lead your crew, do you not?" she demanded. "Decide: will you have me or that cold one who refuses you?"

"Uh..." I said, standing up. "It's not that simple. Look, this was real nice, but I—"

She slapped me. In truth, it was more than a slap. Her claws left four bloody lines on my cheek.

"Damn, girl!" I pressed a hand to my stinging face and gave her my undivided attention.

"You want to have both of us, don't you? Primates always have a scheme."

"It seems to me that you were doing your share of the scheming today."

That was the wrong thing to say. As a man, I'd always excelled at pissing off females, and Mia seemed to be no exception.

She turned to run off, but I reached for her—and grabbed her tail. How could I help it? There it was, right in my face. It was the only thing I could reach—like some kind of handle, almost.

She whirled again, her odd golden eyes blazing. I winced, fully expecting to get savaged.

"Is that it?" she asked. "You demand me again so soon? I don't know your people, but it is unusual for a male to become so quickly aroused a second time."

"Right…" I said uncertainly, but I recovered quickly enough. "You're just so beautiful," I offered brightly.

She smiled, and we did it again. My legs were shaking after that, but I felt good all over—except for my bloody cheek.

In the afterglow, I reflected on this strange situation. It might well be true that the descendants of the Kher were all related, but we certainly weren't a single people. We'd taken some pretty radical twists and turns down different evolutionary paths over the millennia. The ramifications were physical, emotional and hormonal, not just cultural. My mind was trying to grasp it all at once.

"I've come to a decision," Mia said when we separated. "You make me feel good. I will enjoy being with you from time to time. I still hope to make you give up on your female, who you are clearly in love with. I will watch, and I will wait."

She made this little speech proudly, almost as if it was some kind of ceremony. Maybe on her planet, that was how a girl stated her intentions to horn-in on a different family, or pride—or whatever.

"That's great," I said, not knowing how else to respond.

She stepped close to me very quickly and nuzzled into me. Her chin was tucked and her body was close and powerful, but sweet, as we embraced. She nipped my collarbone once without breaking the skin, while looking up at my eyes. Then she darted out of my reach before I could speak or grab that tail again.

Mia left me, and I let her go. She was happy, and I was happy, and that was the best possible outcome in this freaky situation.

Walking back to my own pod, I washed my face tenderly, wiping the dried blood from my cheek.

"What did you do to her, you goat?" asked Dalton.

I turned to see him wearing a dirty grin.

"Who?"

"The cat-girl. Half the ship watched you walk away with her. You shagged her, didn't you? Did she want it, or did she fight? Maybe a bit of both?"

He came closer and put a finger to my bloody cheek, laughing. I grabbed that finger and threatened to break it.

He struggled with me. "Let it go, mate!"

"What do you mean half the ship knows?"

He ripped his hand away from mine.

"They were all watching," he said. "We're all on the same carrier, my randy friend. Everyone knows when these things happen. I've been trying to catch something with a tail myself today. One of those bird-girls seems to like me. They're weird-looking, but I could get used to it."

Heaving a sigh, I turned back to patching up my wounds. I'd put the magic salve on them, but we were out.

I wondered what Gwen was going to say when she heard about this.

Less than an hour passed before Gwen returned with Dr. Chang from the reactor cores. She seemed animated.

"It was *amazing* down there!" she told me. "I asked to see the computers that control the whole thing, but they wouldn't let me near the touch-consoles. Hey... what happened to your face?"

From across the pod, Dalton hooted.

We glanced his way, then Gwen looked back at me. She frowned, and I looked guilty. I couldn't help it.

"I met up with some of Ra-tikh's crew," I confessed.

Gwen stepped closer, touching my cheek gently.

"Are those scratches?" she asked. "Did they attack you?"

Her reaction was going my way, but Dalton wasn't going to let such an opportunity pass. He swaggered up to us, grinning.

"You going to tell her how you beat old Ra-tikh again?" he asked me.

"One of the females attacked me," I told Gwen.

"Because he grabbed her tail!" Dalton said, laughing.

"What?" Gwen asked in confusion. "Did she urinate on you or something?"

"I bet he wanted that, too," Dalton said.

Having had enough, I stood up and threw a punch at him. He dodged, countered, but then I caught him with a left hook, and he fell to the ground. He rolled away and got up.

Gwen watched all this, and she began to catch on. Shaking her head, she walked up to me and stared into my face.

"You had *sex* with a cat?" she demanded.

"Yeah…" I said. "It was her idea, though."

Gwen was disgusted. "Eew! She has a tail and everything—how *could* you? Men are disgusting!"

She left the pod then, and I didn't go after her.

"That was great!" Dalton said. "The look on her face… priceless!"

I moved toward him again, and he ducked out the door. I could hear him laughing all the way down the passages.

Another voice spoke as soon as the place had quieted. It was Dr. Chang. I hadn't even remembered he was inside the pod with us.

He stepped out of his cubby and looked at me.

"Don't feel shame," he said. "These people—they're our genetic relatives. Like Neanderthals and Cro-Magnon. We're all brothers and sisters. I wouldn't be surprised if there was reproductive compatibility between some of the various races."

"What?"

"I mean that she might be able to have your child."

"Oh… That's just grand. Thanks for putting that special thought into my head, Doc."

"You're welcome."

* * *

Ra-tikh came to our fighter the next day. We'd finally rested up and served our "punishment" in the eyes of the officers.

Ra-tikh was not in a good mood. His women followed him at a safe distance. His fur was all standing up on his back like he was some kind of angry animal—which in a way, I supposed he was.

"Blake!" he called out. "I demand satisfaction!"

"What can I do for you, Ra-tikh?" I asked, stepping out of the fighter's undercarriage. I wiped my hands on a rag and tossed it down.

Behind me, my crew drew their disruptors, but I waved them back.

"You have humiliated my crew," Ra-tikh said.

"You talking about the battle in the pit? Or how about when Samson held your tail for you?"

He bared his teeth. His fangs glistened a gray-white.

"No. Those acts were fairly done. I'm talking about dishonor. You mated with a member of my crew."

I shrugged. "So? She's a free girl, not a slave."

"That doesn't matter!" he shouted. "You did it to embarrass me. We must fight a duel to the death. It is a matter of honor."

I considered that. I wasn't sure I could take him one on one. Probably, he was banking on that.

Around our ship's pit, a crowd had begun to gather. I saw Shaw among them. He had his big arms crossed over his bulging chest muscles. He didn't look happy, but he wasn't ordering us to go back to work, either.

Duels of honor between men of the same rank were allowed in the Rebel Fleet, I knew that. Apparently, Ra-tikh did too.

Thinking fast, I came up with a new approach.

"Where I come from," I said, "the challenged man gets to choose the weapons for a duel. I choose *Hammerhead*. You in your ship, me in mine."

Ra-tikh looked dismayed. His big mouth opened, but no sound came out of it. We both knew he was a rookie pilot with no similar experience to fall back on.

"Forget it, Blake," Shaw boomed from the crowd. "No dueling in fighters at your rank. The fighters are more valuable than your entire crew to us."

I shrugged. "All right then, I choose disruptors at one hundred paces."

"What's the point of that?" demanded Ra-tikh.

My smile was a confident one. "I know I'm better at aiming a disruptor than you are."

He glowered, thinking it over.

"Don't like that offer?" I asked. "I'll give you another one. We'll trade crewmembers. One of mine for one of yours."

Ra-tikh perked up. "That might be acceptable."

His gaze turned toward Gwen. He appraised her frankly. "I think that might be *quite* satisfactory.

"Lt. Shaw?" Gwen called out. "There's no way I'm going to go live with four cats! I'm allergic!"

"Your pod assignment is up to your crew-chief," Shaw said.

Gwen looked shocked. She came up to me angrily.

"You bastard," she hissed. "All this for sexual favors? You're no better than Ra-tikh."

"Ease down, Gwen," I said. Turning back to Ra-tikh, I gave him my best smile. "Do you agree to a trade?" I asked him.

"I do. Honor would be served."

I nodded slowly, walked over to Dalton, and put my arm around his shoulder.

"You like cat-girls?" I asked him.

He looked suspiciously at me at first, but then he brightened.

"I do indeed!" he said. "I could go that way!"

"The big kitty might kick your ass."

"I already get that from you."

I chuckled, and shoved him toward Ra-tikh.

"Here," I said. "You can have my fourth. Now, send one of yours to me."

The brawny cat looked shocked. He froze for a second then made a choking sound.

"You have a hair-ball, or something?" Dalton asked him.

"You give me this creature?" Ra-tikh demanded.

"Are you backing out of our deal?" I asked him. "You said honor would be satisfied by a trade of crewmembers. Choose or be dishonored."

Ra-tikh looked around the crowd in pain. There was no way out of this one. They'd all heard what he'd said. It was time to either put up or shut up.

"Very well," he said. "Take my fourth. I do not want her, she stinks of monkey!"

He pushed Mia toward me, and she slashed at his hand, but they parted ways with no further violence.

Mia sauntered over to my ship and slid her tail around my waist. She looked like she'd caught herself a mouse. Perhaps, in a way, she had.

Ra-tikh turned around and stalked away. Dalton ignored him. He was already chatting up the three remaining cat-girls, asking who was third in line.

The crowd melted away, disappointed. They'd been hoping for blood.

=21=

After the crew switch, just about everyone was happy—except for Ra-tikh and Gwen.

Ra-tikh was stuck with Dalton, so I could understand his displeasure. The guy had been annoying from the first moment I'd run into him back on Earth, and that had never changed.

Dalton himself, however, was in heaven. He couldn't thank me enough for the new arrangement. He'd managed to land a fuzzy girlfriend within hours, and as I'd expected, an extra male in the pride made all the females happier.

As far as Ra-tikh went, I could wish Dalton the best of luck on holding his own, but who was I kidding? I hoped he got his ass kicked.

In my own group, both Dr. Chang and Samson were naturally curious about the new girl. Gwen wasn't so thrilled. She stopped talking to me, and shut herself in her cubicle much of the time.

Me? I had the time of my life. Sure, it was weird at first, but Mia and I quickly adjusted. She learned what I liked, and I learned what she liked. There wasn't much mystery. She let me know instantly if she didn't like what I was doing.

"Are you concerned about Samson?" she asked me a week after she'd joined the crew.

"What about him?"

"Is he lonely?"

I looked at her, suspecting she was getting an idea.

"He's fine. He'll find a mate, don't worry."

She looked at me with her strange eyes. "Are you sure? There is only Gwen, and there's no indication that she will mate with him. The other crews frequently have too many males. A male without any females... it's a sad thing."

Releasing a sigh, I knew what I had to do, and I had to be direct. You couldn't hint around much with Mia. It was a waste of time.

"If you want him, go to him. Right now!"

"Really?"

"Sure. But you won't be my first anymore. You won't be my anything."

She pouted. "No... That's not what I want. I apologize."

"Yeah?"

"Yes."

And that was it. She dropped whatever had been twisting in her mind, and she didn't bring it up again. Perhaps the whole thing had been some kind of test.

We worked hard for a week, keeping *Hammerhead* flying and training constantly. Space was unforgiving, and every time we took our fighter out it required plenty of service afterward. We were finally becoming proficient at the process. Like everything aboard *Killer*, maintenance had been simplified as much as possible, but you still had to do it right or your fighter might just kill you with sudden decompression or an engine overload.

To keep my mind off the looming threat of war, I studied the technical data down-streamed from the command deck. *Killer* was a big carrier ship, but she wasn't designed that way for aesthetics. There were particular reasons why her swollen, lumpy design worked so well.

It all came down to the FTL drive. In order to jump over intervening light years, the ship had to use a stellar drive that physically required a lot of bulk and power. It was expensive, too. That meant Fleet didn't like to lose carriers. They'd designed smaller ships like *Hammerhead* to do the dying, giving the big ships a greater chance of escaping a battle that went badly.

Effectively, my ship was a screen to defend the critical carriers. We were highly expendable.

The day finally came when we were to leave the Solar System and head toward the front, my palms were sweaty. We were ordered out of our pods and into our fighters when it was time to depart. That way, we could turn on our anti-grav units and be safe. There were stories about accidents where crewmen had been found later, crushed flat by the gravity waves dumped by the big ship upon reaching its destination.

Using my sym-link, I listened into the bridge chatter. I piped it down to the rest of the crew, along with the visuals I was getting, just so they could know what was happening to them.

They all wanted to hear what was happening, naturally enough. We'd never traveled to another star before.

"Beacon star is Rigel," said a voice.

"We have a lock on Rigel."

I didn't know the pilots who flew this monster, but I'd often heard their voices when the big ship maneuvered.

"*Killer* is cleared for departure," said Captain Ursahn as she appeared on our virtual screens.

Ursahn was a large woman with a hulking physique. Tufts of honest-to-God *fur* stuck out of her suit here and there. I would have pegged her as some kind of omnivorous forest creature if there hadn't been an intelligence in her eyes.

"Initiate final singularity check," she ordered.

A series of voices reported back to her in response.

"The containment shield is as smooth as glass."

"Plasma core is cycling at seventy percent."

"Reactor is good. We've got nine hundred terajoules in the capacitors and climbing."

"Keep revving the core," Ursahn said. "Are all sectors secure?"

"All sectors reporting secure. All decks reporting secure."

The chatter went on like that as the big ship geared up to launch with the others. The Kher engineering was marvelous, but it wasn't perfect. Like first time fliers on Earth, we were concerned because we knew something might go wrong.

"Has this captain ever scattered a ship?" Gwen asked Mia nervously.

Mia looked at her in surprise. Gwen had never treated her as anything but a rival, let alone asked her a question before. I suspected Gwen's paranoia had outweighed her dislike of the girl.

"No," she said, "I don't think so. This is a big jump, but we'll make it."

Gwen looked worried anyway. Everyone watched the screens as the big ship began to make a thrumming sound.

"What's that?" Gwen demanded.

"Don't worry, it's normal," I told her.

She fell silent, but I could tell she was freaking out. We were, after all, about to jump something like twelve hundred lightyears toward the Orion Spur. None of us had ever done anything like this before.

Dr. Chang wasn't nervous at all. He seemed excited.

"This is amazing," he kept saying. "Do you realize we'll be the first humans to leave our star system?"

"You want a prize, doc?" Samson asked.

Samson was nervous too, I could tell, but he wore a tough-guy look to hide it.

"Strap in everyone," I ordered, "they're down to the final sequence."

"Strap in?" Samson asked. "We're floating."

It was true. We were drifting with our butts an inch away from our seats.

"If something goes wrong, you're going to wish you were strapped in." I told him.

"Oh..."

We all strapped in, and the computers counted down the time left in this part of the galaxy.

"Six..."

"Five... We have a portal... Stabilizers on! We've got a radiation spike!"

We stared at our screens, and I used my perception system. The rip in space appearing in front of our carrier was swirling. My sym made the invisible visible, and it showed me rays of white, deep violet and blue shooting out from the vortex. I knew that the radiation would be lethal if we weren't shielded.

"Four..."

"Three..."

"Two... Engaging pulse drive. We're moving to the portal."

The spinning region of space in front of us grew larger. I wasn't sure if this was really happening, or an illusionary effect caused by our approach. In a way, it didn't matter. The carrier was dwarfed by the maelstrom of colored light and blasting radiation in front of us.

Other ships, all a great distance away, vanished into their breaches one at a time. They'd each opened a path and followed it to its terminus. We were about to do the same.

Unable to help myself, I leaned away from the images bombarding my mind. My hands gripped the armrests of my seat like claws.

"One... Entry!"

We were moving. Plunging through a rip between two places in the galaxy, using Rigel as our beacon star.

From what I understood of astronavigation, big hot stars like Rigel helped the starship's computers target our desired destination. The gravitational influence and high radiation output served like a lighthouse in space, providing a reference point to navigate by.

Rigel was a stellar monster, two hundred thousand times as bright as our tiny yellow Sun. It was a blue-white super-giant, spectral class B.

At last, we plunged into the vortex, and we left behind our old lives, our old existence.

When our vision cleared, we were somewhere new. Somewhere humanity had never visited before.

$=22=$

When we arrived in normal space, I immediately reached out with my sym's far-seeing awareness again. With relief, I saw a dim red star. We were in some kind of star system, at least. That was good, because if you scattered, you could end up way out in the dark.

The red star wasn't too far away, indicating the navigators had done their job well. We'd ended up where we were supposed to be as far as I could tell.

All around us, more carrier ships appeared, winking into existence in blue-white flashes of light. That proved my theory. We were on-target.

"We haven't scattered," I told my crew. "This must be the right destination. There are ships popping up all around us."

Killer sailed serenely toward the small red sun with us inside her belly. We all relaxed, and soon we were given the all-clear to exit our fighter again.

Stretching on the deck, I pretended I'd never felt a moment of concern.

"These guys know what they're doing," I said. "I was a Navy pilot back on Earth. I know a professional when I see one at work."

Everyone was happy—including me. To demonstrate her approval, Mia walked past me and ran her tail up the back of my leg. I knew what that meant. She wanted a good tail-pulling tonight.

Truthfully, the girl was hard to satisfy. Unlike women from Earth, she wasn't at all shy about demanding regular attention, and she became quite irritable without it.

And now that we'd just felt the terror of the unknown and survived, a good tension release was in order. A little passion was always a good way to throw off the unsettled feelings that resulted from such risks.

We couldn't indulge ourselves right away, unfortunately. I had a ship to care for. Technically, we'd taken a small flight. Every system had to be checked. Every sensor, module and subsystem must be given a diagnostic, and the results logged.

We worked on *Hammerhead* for nearly an hour before the "day" ended. We retired into our group pod. There, to Gwen's disgust, Mia and I vigorously indulged ourselves in our private cell.

Because the cells weren't very soundproof, everyone else in the group was forced to listen to the distinctive noises emanating from our lovemaking session.

When I left my private cell, I was in a much better mood. Gwen had her arms crossed and wouldn't look at me, but I didn't care. It was time to get back to work.

"They're sucking up new recruits from a nearby planet," Dr. Chang said. "You want to watch them bash each other?"

"I'll pass," I said.

Samson and Dr. Chang huddled up to watch the vids, which were broadcast to everyone aboard on our cloth-thin computers. Mia joined them and laughed.

"This reminds me of your group," she said. "It was a great battle—very dramatic. Some races are so dull."

"These guys look like turtles that someone has yanked out of their shells," Samson commented.

"The print says they're called Terrapinians," Gwen told him.

"Turtles to me."

Gwen rolled her eyes at him.

Intrigued, I glanced over Mia's shoulder. I couldn't help myself. The species was lumpy, and their skins were mottled and greenish. They had a wrinkled reptilian look all right. Their big skulls were wedge-shaped too, which *did* make me think of turtles.

By the time we were back on duty again, the gathering up of turtles and their first bloody contests were over. The fighting had been brutal, and the surviving turtles were all banged up.

"I think it's their thick skulls," Mia said. "The losers had to be beaten with those clubs for quite a while to stay down."

We all watched them play king-of-the-hill for the final contest with knowing smiles. We couldn't help ourselves. This was *Killer*'s boot-camp, and we'd all been there. We gasped, winced and gritted our teeth—but in the end, it was over. One group won with only two members standing. Soon, they were in the group pod again, recovering.

"Let's go meet them," Mia said.

"Why?" I asked.

"Please?"

"All right... why not?"

My crew followed me out. We were armed with disruptors just in case. They wouldn't work unless the ship was attacked, but we were in the war zone now. It felt good to be armed.

The turtle-team gazed at us with unblinking eyes that looked like black drops of oil.

"We're humans from Earth," I said to them.

They said nothing. They didn't even move.

"We went through the same recruitment process you did," I continued. "We—"

"I want that one to hold my tail," Mia said suddenly, pointing at the largest turtle. "That one, Leo. Make him do it! He's looking at me with those evil lizard-eyes."

"No, Mia," I said. "We're not here to play games."

"Why are you here, then?" asked the largest turtle at last. He took a sweeping step toward us.

Their wide, bowed-out legs caused them to take large steps. They looked slow, but I knew that every step covered a lot of ground.

"We wanted to meet new people," I said. "Underneath, we're all genetically related. Officers will come soon and explain this to you.'"

"You're not an officer?" he demanded. "And yet you dare to waste my time?"

"I thought maybe we could be friends."

"Why would you think such a thing?"

"Make him hold my tail!" Mia insisted.

The turtle turned his black eyes to her.

"Disgusting creature of fur and weak bones," he said. "I will not hold your tail, except to prevent your escape while I beat you with this club."

Rebuffed, Mia backed away, showing her teeth.

Things were getting out of control, so I threw up my hands.

"I'm sorry," I said. "I know you've had a difficult time getting here. We'll leave you in peace."

"No," said the furious Terrapinian, striding forward and reaching for Mia, who danced away.

That's when Samson shot him. His disrupter hummed and the turtle went down, clutching his chest.

I was shocked to see that the weapon worked, but then I remembered we were on the front lines now. Captain Ursahn must have activated our sidearms.

"It burns!" the turtle hissed.

"Dammit, Samson," I said. "Let's get out of here before this turns into a bigger shit-storm."

The other Terrapinians gathered around their injured leader. They stared at us with hate in their obsidian eyes.

As we left them, Shaw appeared. He pointed to Samson.

"Was he authorized to damage my new recruits?" he demanded.

"No," I said, "but he acted to defend Mia."

Shaw looked from one of us to the other. "Next time, use your hands."

"But what if they're stronger than we are?" Gwen asked.

"Then you get beaten down, naturally." Shaw said firmly. "These recruits are of such low status, I'm shocked you even came out to meet them. They're worth very few points, and you gained nothing by shooting them. In fact, you probably lost a few for the violation."

I didn't bother to try to explain to him what my plan was, or how I'd hoped these Terrapinians would be different.

There was little logic to that hope, I knew. We were all Kher, and deep down that apparently made us mean, competitive and violent.

All my life I'd ascribed to the view that aliens, should we ever meet them, would be more civilized than the rowdy people of Earth. What a culture shock the truth was. It appeared that humans were more civilized than most other strains in the cosmos, from what I could see.

Among the Kher, kindness and consideration were greeted with a suspicious snarl. Friendliness was assumed to be a trick, a pretense to put an enemy off-guard, nothing else.

The more I thought about it, the less surprising it seemed from an evolutionary standpoint. The strong survived, the weak perished. That was the rule of life. There was no creature more ruthless than a predator who ran down other creatures to eat them. And who might come to dominate a planet and gain technological knowledge, other than a predator?

Even these Terrapinians appeared to be meat-eaters. They might look like shell-less turtles, but they had rows of sharp teeth in their mouths that had to be overkill when it came to eating lettuce.

"Befriending them was worth the attempt," Dr. Chang said to me, as if he could read my mind. "But it was likely to fail."

"I just wanted to make a connection."

"Think about what they've just been through," he said. "Only a few hours ago, the syms were infecting them with violent passion. Even if they're normally peaceful, they've been at one another's throats for days building to a climax that ended recently. You didn't see them at their best."

I nodded, thinking that made sense. "But I can't get the idea out of my head that we could do better, as a group, if we cooperated more."

"A noble goal," he agreed, "but one that goes against our instincts. These turtles are like any Kher-variant from any planet. They're vicious killers at heart. It was predictable that they wouldn't be interested in making friends with humans."

"I still believe a commitment to teamwork is the best way to accomplish any goal, especially military ones."

"Really? That isn't a historically based perspective. Every military on Earth is a linear dictatorship from the top to the bottom. Ranks are clear. Pecking orders are rigid. The same holds true in other organizations that function well, such as companies."

"But this is different," I said, "we're not exactly the same. We're so different in appearance, behavior, and culture."

"Like the Golden Horde…" he muttered

"What?"

"Over a thousand years ago, Mongolia conquered the majority of Asia, and a good portion of Europe as well. They didn't start with many soldiers, but they pressed others into service. Each time the Mongols conquered a city or a nation, they added them to the horde. There was no love lost between any of them, believe me, but they were very effective in battle anyway."

"Yeah…" I said with a grunt. The good doctor was kicking my ass in this argument, and I wanted out. "Well, we'll see how this organization behaves when we meet the enemy."

"I suspect it will do quite well," Dr. Chang said, "but it all depends on the strength of the enemy. If they outnumber or outgun us, we'll lose."

I had nothing further to offer.

He shrugged and headed for bed. I lay down and Mia lay next to me, curling herself up. She was hot to the touch, and her breath was warm and moist.

I stayed awake for a long time, pondering this Fleet of strangers I'd signed on with. Was I going to live or die at their side? Would I ever get to meet or talk to the real enemy in the ships on the other side? Or would we die in the cold of space, never even knowing what hit us?

There was no way of telling, and that fact made it difficult to sleep.

=23=

We flew onward for two months. Every week or so, we hopped to another star system and picked up a fresh crew for another fighter.

In all that time, we'd never seen an enemy vessel. But they were out there. I could almost feel them as we got closer and closer to the Orion Spur.

The Rebel Fleet had come from far away, close to the hub of the galaxy. There, vast glowing nebulae obscured everything. The nearness of the stars in clusters, along with the hanging dust and gases, made that corner of the universe a bright one.

When they'd launched probes from these innermost star systems toward places like Earth, we'd seen bright rips in the sky because they'd come from more luminous areas of the galaxy. Now, however, as we drove onward, ever farther away from the central hub, it seemed to be growing ever darker.

Then came another *big* jump, two thousand lightyears across an abyss that was thinly populated by either stars or life. That's when things went badly.

At first, the stellar flux seemed like any other. We were veterans of the process by now.

"Checklist complete, Chief," Gwen said, reporting to me.

I'd earned the title of "chief" very recently. Essentially, it allowed me to fly my fighter without onboard supervision from a higher-ranking individual.

Everyone in the chain of command labored hard to turn one member of each fighter crew into a chief, that way they could send us out on our own. Each successful chief, in turn, raised his officer's status in the Fleet.

"Anti-grav on," Samson said, activating the sub-system without being told to.

We were working more like a team now. We were infinitely more competent and confident. Instead of relying entirely on my earthly military training and what I'd learned from Tand, I felt my own people had become dependable. I'd steadily reassigned my tasks to them after I'd mastered new techniques during training flights.

Tand and Shaw hadn't seen fit to give me any orders in that regard. I was free to run my ship the way I wanted, as long as I accomplished the goals of my mission. That was refreshing, and unusual in any military organization I knew of.

I suspected they operated that way because each crew was so different. What might work well for a family of cats might turn into a disastrous mess for a group of hard-headed turtles. Whatever the case, I was free to operate *Hammerhead* as I liked.

So as not to be overwhelmed, I'd delegated responsibilities. I now did little other than pilot the vehicle and give coordinating commands. The others handled everything else. Dr. Chang was my navigator and support-system specialist. He'd taken plenty of mathematics in his time, and he could operate machinery like a pro.

Gwen was my computer wizard. She monitored the AI, managing the continuous incoming data-streams. Her main job was to relay a stream-lined version of key information to me.

Mia had turned out to be a good weapons operator. Our armament was sophisticated, but not terribly technical. You pretty much chose a target and ordered the ship to destroy it. Mia's reaction time was the best on the crew, and she seemed to have a natural flair for the destruction of targets during training.

Samson had been the hardest to place. Brawn had its usefulness, but it generally didn't apply when flying a spaceship. I'd decided to make him my co-pilot, and I'd given him direct responsibility over secondary elements such as the ship's hatches, defenses and safety systems. If there was ever going to be a fire aboard, he was going to be critical—but until then, frankly I hoped he could stay out of the way.

"I'm seeing power-spikes from the reactors," Gwen warned.

"Right," I said. "I see the rip forming now. We're going to fly into it about ninety seconds from now."

"Chief?" Gwen called. "I'm picking up a strange radiation reading."

I scanned my instruments, and used my distance perception to reach beyond the ship. I didn't see anything dangerous.

"I'm not getting it."

"It's internal aboard *Killer*," she said, "relaying it to your input."

I could see the problem now. One of the reactor cores had gone cold. There were eight, normally, but now there were only seven operating.

"We've had a failure," I said. "Everyone strap in."

"Report it to the bridge, Leo!" Mia said in concern.

"I already did," Gwen said, "they're well aware of the difficulty."

In my earpiece, I listened to the high command channel. They were trying to get the reactor online and failing.

"They have to abort—don't they?" Gwen asked.

"I don't know," Dr. Chang said. As our navigator, he knew the most about jumping through space. "We'll be behind the rest if we delay. They don't think they can repair the reactor for hours. Worse, if we fly late, we'll scatter for sure."

They all looked worried, and I couldn't blame them. It was moments like this that reminded us we were stuck in space with little control over our own fates.

What if we were separated from our adopted pack of predators?

Listening in, I soon got the directive from on-high.

"We're going to fly," I said. "Half the Fleet has already shipped out. If we don't go now, we'll scatter anyway. Hang on, everyone."

We winked out, plunging into the iris of the rip that had been spiraling in front of us. We tumbled through hyperspace into the unknown.

When we came into being again, we were in a spin.

No one else could feel this as the internals of *Hammerhead* were shielded from external physics such as centrifugal force.

But I could *see* it. I could reach out with my sym's eyes, beyond *Killer's* hull, to see the universe swirling around. I had to pull my focus back aboard my own ship quickly in order to keep from becoming nauseous.

"Hang on, everyone," I said. "We're in a spin."

"What do we do?" Gwen asked.

"We wait for orders."

"Shouldn't we try to get out?" Mia asked.

I glanced at her, then pointed out the see-through walls of *Hammerhead*. "Where do we go? The hangar deck is sealed."

"We're trapped in here!" she said in a frightened voice that cracked high.

"Relax, crew," I said. "I doubt things are that bad—"

"Abandon ship!" came a booming voice penetrating everyone's skull via our syms. "All crews, we're opening the aft doors. Abandon ship!"

I looked at Samson. "Release the clamps," I said.

"Releasing, Chief!" he boomed. "It's done!"

We drifted off the deck, and the hangar deck began to spin around us.

"Matching spin."

Some of the crews around us had attempted to climb out of the ship, possibly to head for the lifeboats. I could have told them that it was suicide, but I didn't have the clearance to make announcements or even the time to do it.

By lifting off from the deck, I was able to get our ship above the rest. The other fighters were beginning to slide and smash into one another. We were above them, looking down at the chaos.

A few other ships followed my lead. I couldn't identify them—there wasn't time, and it was all I could do to keep my craft from crashing into others.

The big doors at the far end of the hangar began to yawn open. People, fighters and equipment were sucked out into the void. They smashed into one another and died with gushes of flame and blood as they were jettisoned out the opening.

"Look," Mia said, "that fighter is tangled up."

I barely had time to glance in that direction. It took all my focus to keep *Hammerhead* heading in a more or less straight direction toward the exit. As the entire hangar depressurized, this grew easier. Then I only had to match the external ship's spin to get her under a steady keel.

"Leo," Mia said to me. "Let me help them. I can shoot a tow cable out there and pull them after us."

"I can't risk that," I said. "We'll be fouled up."

"It won't help. They're hung up on cables anyway," Samson said.

We glided out after a half-dozen others. The black velvet of space had never looked so good to me.

"We're clear!" Mia shouted. "Let me give it a try!"

I glanced at her. "Okay. But we have to get farther away from *Killer* in case she blows up. Gwen, are the reactors critical yet?"

"No, but they're shutting down. If I didn't know better, I'd say the carrier had been hit."

Those words ran a thrill of worry through me. I'd yet to consider the possibility we were in battle. I'd assumed some kind of technical glitch was at the root of this disaster.

"Mia, take your shot. Samson, be ready to reel them in."

The two worked together for once. I felt a tremble and heard a whoosh. The tow cable fired out, lanced the fighter with a magnetic harpoon-head, and the line went taut.

"Lighting up the engines," I said, goosing the throttle gently.

The tiny ship roared, then shook. At last, we broke free. I wasn't sure if the cable had snapped, or if we'd been successful. I was too busy dodging debris to check.

Two furry arms came up and wrapped themselves around me.

"We got them," she said. "We saved them. You're the best!"

I frowned, wondering why she cared so damned much. It wasn't like her to be the rescuing type. Then I noticed the insignia on the fighter that was drifting and bucking behind us.

"That's Ra-tikh's ship?" I asked, incredulous.

"That's right, Chief," Samson said with a laugh. "You just saved Ra-tikh, Dalton and their three cat-ladies. I wonder if you'll live to regret it."

I had to wonder the same, but with Mia nuzzling me, I didn't worry about it.

"Back to your station, Mia," I said. "Pouring on more power. We have to get clear. Gwen, tell me what's going on out there."

"Running sensor scans, but they don't make any sense."

"Why not?"

"Well, I'm picking up a lot of large ships—too many, in fact. Do you think we've merged up our group with another group from the main fleet?"

Deciding we were safe enough to take a look at the big picture, I used my perception of space around us to look deeply in random directions. I saw a cluster of large vessels, and I zoomed in on it.

They weren't carrier ships. Or if they were, they weren't our own Rebel ships.

"I think we've found the Imperial Kher," I said. "If I don't miss my guess, I'm looking at enemy cruisers."

"But we still haven't reached enemy territory," Gwen objected.

"Maybe not, but this is technically the Orion Front zone. Maybe they've invaded farther into our space. You can take a look for yourselves."

There were gasps as I relayed my visuals to the rest of the crew. They watched in astonishment.

"What do we do?" Mia asked, voicing the question on everyone's mind.

I took a moment to assess *Killer* before I answered her. The big carrier was slowing down, but she was still spinning. She clearly wasn't in any state for battle. The CAG wasn't online, and even the automated traffic control systems were dead.

It left me with an odd, hollow feeling. These people had stolen me from Earth. They'd pressed me into service and forced me to fight like a dog in a pit. But, they'd also trained me and shown me they had their own code of honor. Seeing *Killer* in her death-throes behind me didn't make me happy, and that wasn't just because without her I'd be stranded in an unknown hostile star system.

"We can't run to Earth," I said at last. "We can't run anywhere. I say it's time to find out if *Hammerhead* can fight or not."

No one answered me for a stunned moment, but then Samson grinned.

"Good thinking," he said. "I wanted to kill something anyway. It's been months!"

"That's the spirit!" I told him, and I meant it.

What the hell else could we do?

=24=

We cut Ra-tikh's fighter loose and accelerated. There was a battle ahead, well within our flight range.

Using my perception to its limits, I reached out to see what we were up against. It didn't look good. A dozen of our ships were embroiled with a row of enemy vessels.

The enemy cruisers were ugly. They were angular things with a wide flange dipping low—or high, depending on your perspective. The ships reminded me of hump-backed fish. They were misshapen, so lacking in aerodynamic lines you could tell they were never meant to enter an atmosphere.

"Kher cruisers," I said. "Heavies, if I don't miss my guess."

"No enemy fighter-cover then?" Samson asked me.

"None that I can see. Doc, give me a fuel charge calculation given this distance."

I passed my equipment's range guesstimate back to him, and he began crunching numbers.

"I'd hoped there would be fighters," Samson said.

"Why?"

He shrugged. "You can't become an ace crew without kills."

"We'll just have to kill cruisers instead of fighters," Mia said.

This set off a round of excited exclamations. My crew had no idea what they were whooping about. Samson had seen action before in war, but air battles were different. Speaking historically, a fighter in the middle of this mess was like a rowboat caught up in a pitched battle between two fleets of large ships.

This fight might be different, but I had no reason to assume it would be even after all my training. Losses would be high for everyone when fighting the Imperial Kher.

"Chief," Gwen said in sudden concern. "There's a ship pulling up on our tail. A heavy fighter—looks like one of ours."

"Identify and contact him."

"It's—it's Ra-tikh's ship. He must have gotten it under control and chased us down."

"Ra-tikh?" I called on a close-range beam. "What are you doing?"

"I'm not going to allow it, Blake," Ra-tikh's words rang in my aural nerves via my sym.

"Allow what?"

"You will not humiliate me again. You should have left me to die aboard *Killer*."

"I don't know what you're talking about," I said, "but I don't see the rest of the squadron. You wanna be my wingman?"

"Blake?" asked a new voice, overriding Ra-tikh's. "This is Shaw. Switch on your friend-or-foe transponder."

Cursing, I ordered Samson to get his ass in gear. We were supposed to turn on our transponder as soon as we left *Killer's* hold. That had been Samson's job.

"Sorry Chief," he said, activating the unit.

"There you are," Shaw said. "I'm now acting squadron commander. Tand is dead. *Killer* has been disabled. I'm taking tactical command until someone higher up the chain takes over from me."

"Got it, sir. What are my orders?"

"Circle back toward *Killer*. What are you doing so far out, anyway?"

"We saw those cruisers out there and we thought we'd go for them, sir."

He was quiet for a second.

"Brave to a fault," he said. "For a primate, you show unusually intense predatory instincts."

"Uh... thank you, sir."

"Ra-tikh will be your wingman for the duration of this action. Your orders are to locate the enemy ship that ambushed *Killer*."

In confusion, I scanned local space. "I don't see anything out here, sir."

"No, you wouldn't. They hit us the moment we jumped into this star system and disappeared. It's a phase-ship, it's got to be. They're small and slow, but they can hide in a pocket of hyperspace. The enemy will look like a sensor-ripple unless you're very close."

"Can they see us, sir?" I asked, scanning the surrounding space

"Not as well as a cruiser could, but they can passively detect local objects in normal space. Your mission is to do a sensor-sweep starting with sector 8-2-6. Check the transmitted regional mapping. Make sure the enemy phase-ship isn't in that sector."

Hammerhead was already banking, fighting against inertia. Dumping grav waves and spinning around, we were heading back toward the damaged mess that was *Killer*. The maneuver caused the little ship to shake violently, but otherwise we didn't feel the physics as we were inside our anti-grav bubble.

Ra-tikh shadowed our movements without comment. He'd heard Shaw's commands, and although he probably wasn't happy about them, he followed orders.

When we were close to the sector he'd assigned me to, I plunged *Hammerhead* into it.

"Turn on every active pinging sensor we have," I told Gwen.

"We'll be lit up like a Christmas tree, Chief," she complained.

"I know that, but we've got to find something called a 'phase-ship'. It's hidden out here, and we've got to find it."

"A *what*, Chief?"

I explained to the crew what we were looking for, as best I understood it. In our training missions, we'd learned about a broad number of topics, but we hadn't studied enemy ship classes much yet. The cruisers had been easy to spot and identify, but a phase-ship? I'd never even heard of one.

"Ra-tikh wants to talk," Gwen told me.

"Mia, free up your weapons. We might not get a lock on this thing. Look for anything strange on the sensor feed. If you see something, blast it."

"Excellent..." she purred with excitement. Her eyes were wide open, wider than a human girl's eyes could go. Her hands flexed and stretched on the controls. I could tell the hunt was thrilling her. In comparison, the rest of my crew looked stressed and nervous.

"What is it, Wingman?" I asked as I opened up a channel to Ra-tikh's ship.

He made a coughing sound. I'd heard that noise before. The cat-people made that sound when they were building up a rage.

"What is Shaw doing?" Ra-tikh demanded. "This is insane. Two ships against an enemy vessel of size? Every sector patrolled separately? Why not hunt in strength with the whole squadron?"

"I don't know exactly what Shaw's thinking," I admitted, "but we've never fought a phase-ship. I would guess he wants to find this thing before it can come out of hiding and hit *Killer* again."

"Why did it stop attacking? What is this game?"

"I told you, Ra-tikh, I don't know. Contact Shaw with your questions. Until then, follow orders."

"I am sticking to your side. Dalton is my pilot. He smells like a rodent and insults my females, but he can fly a fighter."

I smiled at that. I'd seen Dalton in flight training, which everyone had gone through in case the pilot was disabled. Dalton had been wild and unprofessional, but he'd definitely shown promise.

Ra-tikh disconnected, and I went back to scanning the feeds with the rest of my crew. We spent several minutes moving around sector 8-2-6 before giving up. We were given another sector to scan that was adjacent, and we moved onward.

In the meantime, I occasionally turned my long-range perception in the direction of the primary battle. The carriers had gotten the upper hand. We'd lost seven of the big ships, by my count, along with another half-dozen that had been disabled and sent to the back of the line.

The enemy cruisers were taking a beating, however. Without fighter-cover, they were getting melted to slag by thousands of small stinging hits. When half of them were destroyed, they pulled out, abandoning the ambush.

"They broke off," Gwen said.

"I know that. Look for the phase-ship."

"I doubt anything else is out here," Gwen said. "Wouldn't it have phased out, or whatever, and retreated to safety?"

"Maybe," I said, "but that's speculation, Gwen. We're here to destroy the ship that nailed *Killer*. We have to protect our carrier."

She shut up, and we kept scanning. There were other fighters out here doing the same. About a hundred of them. They were all patrolling sectors around the carrier one at a time, working their way farther out when each sector was cleared.

"I've got something!" Mia said suddenly.

"Blast it!" I ordered.

You didn't have to give that order to Mia twice. Her hand twitched, and twin wasps flew out of the undercarriage of our tiny ship.

Wasps were small ship-to-ship seeker missiles. They were only good for short-range battles, but they were fast and had excellent onboard AI. During training, I'd found them very effective.

The wasps darted from my ship at an angle, and I spun us around to follow them. What happened next was something of a shock. The hull of a vessel appeared, almost like a wall, and it completely blotted out my view of *Killer* in the distance.

My crew cried out or growled, depending on their vocal chords. Slamming the controls into a dive, I reversed our thrust and tried to go under the ship, rather than smashing into it.

I wanted to warn Dalton, but there wasn't time. If he hadn't seen what was right in front of us, he was doomed.

It turned out that a phase-ship wasn't as small of an affair as I'd been visualizing. It was about three hundred yards long, if I didn't miss my guess, and a quarter of that in girth. Looking like a pipe with various appendages, it was cylindrical in shape.

My wasps splashed against the hull harmlessly. They'd served to flush the ship out of hiding, but they hadn't done any serious damage. I had a moment to wish Shaw had clued me in concerning what we were going up against.

We made the plunge, and I was gratified to see Ra-tikh was still on my tail. Dalton was a good pilot, Ra-tikh hadn't been bragging emptily about that.

"Use our main cannon, Mia," I ordered. "Tear this ship up before she kills us!"

She was already on it. Her sym had her in a VR environment with the enemy phase-ship.

Streaks of radiation were visible outside our ship, connecting the fighter with the larger target. I knew these were the equivalent of virtual tracers, as the radiation wasn't actually visible to the naked eye. For purposes of aiding in our aiming efforts and to better illustrate the tactical situation, computers displayed the radiation in this manner.

It looked like we were having a paint-fight with glowing pigment. Gushes of bright blue tore into the enemy hull as we circled her at extremely close range.

Rather than breaking away and making a new pass, I hugged the enemy vessel. *Hammerhead* spiraled around that long armored tube from prow to stern.

The situation was potentially deadly in a dozen ways. Our vessel could strike the enemy hull, or some protuberance I couldn't avoid. We might be nailed by any of the defensive fire turrets that now swung and attempted to lock onto our tiny ship. Even if we were successful, a killing strike on the enemy might blow all of us up in the final release of gas, shrapnel and energy.

I could feel a presence probing for communication through my sym-link, but I couldn't compromise my focus to respond.

"Gwen!" I called out between clenched teeth, "alert Shaw, tell him we found the phase-ship."

"He knows, Chief. He wants to know what the hell we're doing spinning around it!"

"Tell him we're killing the damned thing!"

"Hull breach on enemy ship detected," Dr. Chang said calmly.

I glanced over at him. He had his eyes shut down to slits, only taking occasional glances at his screens. Maybe the wild show outside our walls was making him sick.

"Breaking off!" I shouted.

Without further warning, I threw us into a loop and swung *Hammerhead* away toward open space. We moved to the aft of the phase-ship, then she was gone to our stern.

"They've got a lock on us!" Gwen shouted.

"Cover our stern, Samson. Mia, kill your guns. We need the power."

She hissed in disappointment, but she didn't argue.

Radiation bolts flew past us. They seemed shockingly close. I ducked reflexively, even though I knew it couldn't possibly help. A direct hit on our stern would knock us out. We wouldn't even know what hit us.

"Chief..." Samson said. "The phase-ship isn't coming after us. It's going for *Killer*."

He was right. The long, tube-shaped vessel wasn't bothering to hide any longer. She'd been spotted and damaged. A long trail of plasma and gasses, made visible by software on *Hammerhead*'s walls, showed she was hurt—perhaps too hurt to run.

"They're going to try to finish off *Killer*," I said with certainty. "Where's the rest of the squadron?"

"They'll be here in one minute, tops," Dr. Chang answered.

"Chief," Gwen said, "I'm getting a reading from the prow of that ship. There's an energy surge. We have to assume it's some kind of heavy gun."

I nodded. "Yeah... I agree. Maybe we knocked out her phasing system. Or maybe she's dying. In any case, they're going to try to finish the carrier before they're destroyed by the rest of the squadron."

"Ra-tikh wants to know why we're sitting on our butts, Chief," Gwen said.

I glanced at her. She was afraid, I could tell that. We'd fought an enemy ship at insanely close range, and we'd lived somehow. But that was no reason to think we could pull off that kind of stunt again.

"Launch every wasp we have," I told Mia. "Aim at that breach in their hull. Blow it open."

"Missiles away!"

"Now, we're going to have to swing under her, to get to that belly she's hiding. We're going to have to put our gun to that hole in her gut, and you're not going to miss, Mia."

"Get me closer!" she shouted, all excitement and killer-instinct again.

I had to wonder if this was why most Rebel fighters were flown by carnivores. Maybe only they had the right reactions—even before formal training.

Ra-tikh's fighter, piloted by Dalton with smoothness that belied how green he was to this sort of thing, followed me precisely.

Hammerhead was much easier to fly than any Earth-based fighter I'd ever flown, of course. That was part of the story. In this ship, we had many technological advantages over the comparatively primitive aircraft of my home world.

But skill couldn't be ignored. Dalton had that skill, and he'd displayed it effortlessly. Sure, the control systems were so simple a child could spin one of these fighters around a goalpost, but you still had to have the guts and the steady nerve required to do it.

We swooped over the bigger ship, then dived low.

The crew aboard the phase-ship knew what we were up to. There was never any doubt. The ship spun, trying to keep her wounded side away from us.

But we spun faster. The wasps bobbed and weaved until they found their target and bloodied her further.

But the kill-shot didn't come until Ra-tikh's gunner and Mia unloaded their cannons simultaneously into the exposed guts of the enemy.

The fan-tail seemed to fall off the bigger ship. That was the first clue that we'd done catastrophic damage to her.

I was already retreating, catching splashes of defensive fire on the shielding Samson had diverted to face the enemy. Fortunately, phase-ships didn't seem to have much in the way of supporting weaponry. They had a big gun that could nail a carrier, and a phasing system that could hide them from their enemies. That was about it.

She blew up shortly thereafter, sending plumes of gas and colorful fire into space. These existed only briefly before fading into a haze of dust and background radiation.

My crew yelled out in victorious cheers that rang inside *Hammerhead*, and I joined them. They clapped my back, and they grinned, and they shouted things I couldn't even hear.

That's when I knew we'd gelled all the way through. We'd become a functional unit. Come what may, this tiny crew was going to fight together as a single, coherent force from now on.

=25=

We returned to the limping carrier in a good mood. Our laughter and boasting soon died as we got close enough to *Killer* to take a good look at her.

The carrier was damaged internally. Cracks in the external hull leaked a constant frosty breath of valuable gases.

"Are the bulkheads all blown?" Mia asked in concern. "They should have had the venting under control by now."

"Maybe they're all dead—the crew, I mean," Dr. Chang suggested.

No one spoke as we closed in and swung around to see the open hangar bay. Inside, the lights were still on. A mix of debris and stiff bodies floated everywhere.

Some of the spacers wriggled toward us in their suit jets. We were glad to see that a few had survived.

"Blake," Shaw's voice spoke in my headset, startling me. "You're approaching *Killer* without orders or authorization."

"We knocked out the phase-ship, Lieutenant. We tried to report, but couldn't get through. We thought we'd come back here and help out with the clean-up."

"You knocked out the phase-ship?" he demanded. "You were supposed to wait for the rest of the squadron."

"I know, sir, but we thought she might phase out again after we stumbled upon her."

"Send me your automated logs," he ordered.

157

"Just a second."

I nodded to Samson, who uploaded the requested electronic documents—vid files, readings and computer assessment reports. Fortunately, most after-action reports were done by machine in this service.

Shaw didn't trust me, naturally enough. Only a month or two ago my crew had hit an officer over the head and attempted to flee back to Earth. Now, we were essentially claiming to be heroes that had just saved everyone's hide. That sort of thing had to be checked out in order to be believed.

There was a delay as Shaw was no doubt perusing our documentation. At last, he came back onto the channel.

"Unbelievable. You went above and beyond, Blake. I knew you had potential, but I didn't think it would show up like this."

"Thank you, sir."

"Come aboard. *Killer* is stable enough for now, but she's badly damaged. You'll have to use your own suits for life-support."

"That seems clear, sir."

He disconnected, and I went back to the task of piloting my tiny ship into a maelstrom of wreckage. The floating debris we had to dodge and brush aside wasn't dangerous as long as we kept our pace to a crawl. Eventually, I found my way to our berth.

Guiding my ship the last few dozen yards with spurts from her maneuvering jets, I managed to ease *Hammerhead* into her cradle again.

We climbed out of our fighter with our personal life-support gear sealed. There was no one to greet us, other than junk and corpses. The surviving yard people and crews were all busy cleaning up their own messes.

The hangar was dark for the most part. Shuffling and using my boot magnetics, we had to work to keep from kicking up a cloud of obscuring dust and filings. My crew followed me at a safe distance.

"Looks like this battle is over, Chief," Samson said. "I'm not sure if we won or not, though."

"Me neither," I said, looking at the devastation.

We'd driven off the Imperials, but the cost had been high. According to the data Gwen had gathered, we'd lost half of *Killer's* fighters and plenty of regular crew as well.

Worse, the ship itself was in shambles. She could be repaired, I supposed, but it would take time.

Shaw summoned me to the command deck about an hour later. I welcomed the opportunity to take a break. We'd all been working to sort out the mess on the hangar deck, which still didn't have artificial gravity or life support. The big bay doors were hanging open to space, and fighters straggled in now and then to land.

Those doors made me nervous. I wasn't used to working out in the open with the yawning expanse of space looking over my shoulder. It was dark out there, and I felt like another phase-ship could pop up and nail us at any moment.

Crossing the hangar deck in clanking magnetic boots, I reached the elevators and rode them up to the command level. I'd only been up here once or twice, and each time it had been to receive a reprimand.

This time was different. Shaw beckoned me to enter his office and sit down.

"Wasn't this Commander Tand's office a few hours ago?" I asked him.

"That's right. As his second, I moved up a notch. Your action today helped cinch that gain."

I looked at him thoughtfully. I wasn't sure if he was grateful or viewing me as a possible threat. With these Kher officers it could go either way.

After eyeing me coldly for a time, he smiled. "You helped me out, so I'm going to offer you a temporary alliance."

Blinking, I didn't respond. I didn't know where this was going.

"No answer, eh?" he asked, leaning back. He nodded. "I knew you were a cagey man. A primate, through and through. You worry me, Blake. Your kind tends to make it to the top all too often. But I'm warning you, if you think you can plant a blade—"

"Stop worrying," I told him. "I'm new here. All I did was fight to keep *Killer* in one piece. How else were any of us going to survive?"

He nodded slowly. "That's true. But you have to understand that in the Rebel Fleet most Kher would rather not be the first ones to take a huge risk. They tend to hang back in battle."

"Not Ra-tikh," I said.

"No, his kind are different. Cats have their own sense of honor. It's more important to them than survival, I think. They'd rather die than be shown up by a rival. It's unfortunate, but they tend to get themselves killed frequently by dueling for petty glory."

"You mentioned an alliance?" I asked.

"Yes. Here's the deal: I'll put you on the fast-track to becoming an ensign. All I need is for you to keep delivering me victories in space."

I almost laughed, but I managed to control myself. This guy really thought I was a chump. But then again, maybe such a ham-handed offer would work on most Kher. Maybe he really expected it to work on me.

"I don't know," I said, as if I was seriously considering his offer. "You're telling me to take action now for a promise of action on your part later. But I've already helped you. What are you going to do for me right now?"

A low growl rumbled out of his throat. "Are you refusing to accept my generous offer?"

"I'm asking for details, that's all."

He looked annoyed, and I pretended I couldn't care less what he said next. That was easy to do, since I wasn't really seeking a promotion.

"All right," he growled. "I'm making you an ensign, right now. You're getting a silver line. But you owe me. You haven't accumulated enough status points to earn this on your own. I'll have to put all my weight behind it because you're so junior."

"Did any other fighter pilots knock out an enemy vessel?"

"No," he admitted.

I shrugged. "Well then, you've got no one else to reward, and plenty of dead crews to replace. I accept your offer, Lieutenant."

"Excellent. Now, let me show you something of the bigger picture, Ensign."

He caused the walls of his office to light up. They all could function as one big screen if you wanted them to. A blackness closed over us, broken up by pinpoints of bright light. Near at hand were the local planets.

"Red dwarfs like this local star are the most common type in this region," he said. "We were coming here to pick up another fighter crew made up of fresh recruits, like yours."

He zoomed in as he spoke, choosing a small patch of the back wall. His fingers spread, and the image magnified sickeningly. I could tell this was a perception system, working like the way my sym-link operated aboard *Hammerhead*, only better. The image was more precise, and the range seemed to be greater.

He zoomed in toward the second planet from the central sun, a cool lump of gray rock that circled the glowing ember. I watched as he penetrated the clouds, then sailed over the landscape beneath.

All around us, the walls of the office lit up with a rusty orange light. The terrain of the planet wrapped completely around the room. It was like standing inside of a globe with squared-off corners.

We saw the world from the perspective of the clouds. There were pockmarks in the terrain below us. I stared at them, knowing instantly what I was seeing.

"Cities?" I said. "The Imperials wiped out this world?"

"They did. There were few survivors, mostly from the rural regions. The enemy must have done this recently, because we didn't get a warning from our probes. Instead, when we arrived to gather recruits, we were ambushed."

I stared at the land. It looked cratered. I could see lines connecting the craters.

"Are those roads?"

"Yes. Broad highways and waterways."

"Why are the cities sunken in, rather than burnt?"

"That's a signature effect of gravity-bombs," he said soberly. "They momentarily increase the localized gravitational pull of a region. That crushes a city into itself, destroying everything. All of a sudden, you find yourself weighing ten times more than you weighed a moment before. Then the buildings collapse and crush what's left of you."

It sounded like a grim way to die, but then, I couldn't think of a pleasant path to death right then.

"How many people?" I asked.

"We don't take a regular census," he said, "but estimates put the total at three billion Kher lost. We're picking up a few crews now, hopefully they'll be eager to fight when they finish their training."

He looked up and caught my horrified expression as I studied the walls of his office.

"They weren't primates," he said, "if that's any consolation."

It wasn't. All I could think of was potentially seeing Earth's cities pulverized in this fashion. Rome, Tokyo, New York—all turned into instant graveyards sprinkled over the planet.

We talked quietly for a time about the battle and the aftermath. He gave me a short lecture on phase-ships that was mostly full of information I already knew.

Then, at last, Shaw grunted and tapped in my new rank. The insignia on my shoulder transformed in shape and color. I now wore silver lines, rather than gold points, on my epaulets.

Just like that, I was an ensign, second class.

When I got back to my crew, they were astonished to see my new rank insignia.

"I thought for sure they were going to lock you up for risking valuable hardware," Samson said. "That's how things tend to go around here."

I shook my head. "Not today. They lost a lot of people. Nearly half the carrier's complement died."

"One phase-ship did so much damage?" Dr. Chang asked. "It's a wonder the enemy builds anything else."

"I don't know how difficult those ships are to produce," I said, "but this one had a hard time escaping. I suspect they are weak and slow. Only their stealth makes them effective."

"It's enough," Gwen said. "One punch almost took out *Killer*."

"Shaw told me that this was an unusual battle," I continued. "Our carriers weren't protected by screening ships because our brass didn't think we'd run into the enemy yet. Normally, the phase-ships wouldn't be able to ambush us like that."

"They must have had inside information," Gwen said suspiciously. "How else would they know exactly where and when we would jump into this system and be lying in wait for us?"

Her idea wasn't too far-fetched, but I simply didn't know enough about this war and the technology on both sides to guess if she was right or not.

"Let the commanders figure it out," I said. "Shaw said we were to shove all the fragments that could be recycled into the refabrication vents. The rest of it goes out the bay doors. Then they'll shut the hangar up again."

"Next time it opens," Samson said, looking at deep space warily, "I hope we'll be receiving a complete squadron."

I reflected how quickly we were taking on the Rebel cause for our own. It only made sense now that we had a more complete picture of the situation around our home star.

Earth was only one tiny planet among millions. We'd built a relatively advanced civilization, but there were plenty more in the cosmos where that came from. What mattered was the level of threat Earth faced.

All my life, I'd wondered about the stars and who might live out there among them. But I'd never thought it likely I'd learn the truth.

I'd always envisioned a visitation to Earth as hopeful and positive. I'd imagined aliens that were benevolent and friendly, perhaps arriving with solutions for humanity's ills. I'd never thought they'd come as the engine of our destruction.

But the truth was a harsh surprise. We'd met up with a vast empire facing another even bigger empire, both locked in mortal combat. They'd pressed a few of us into service, but no one actually expected us to do much.

The important detail was that if the Rebel Fleet failed to stop the Imperials, that could spell the end for Earth. All those beings known as "humans" could cease to exist. Once all these facts had become clear to me and my crew, we'd turned our attention to winning this war—or at least fighting it as best we could.

At long last, the hangar doors shut, and we were allowed to rest. We slept like the dead, circled around our fighter.

Our pod had been destroyed. Most of the bedding and other personal articles—such as there were on this warship—had also been lost or gone into the recycling chutes to produce more necessary items.

Down under the decking, I could feel the thrum of the recyclers running all night. At least they hadn't been knocked out. They operated somewhat like three-dimensional printers back on Earth. Taking in a variety of finely ground pellets, they were able to spit out finished parts to re-outfit much of the ship and her fighters. Only our fellow pilots who'd perished could not be replaced so directly—even though their bodies had been fed into the recyclers as well.

It was the middle of the night shift when we were attacked again, and again taken completely by surprise during our exhausted sleep.

The attack didn't come from space this time, however. It came from an unexpected quarter—our fellow shipmates.

Mia was the only one to call out a warning. Her keener senses must have caught a stealthy sound. Whatever the case, I heard her cry out and opened my bleary eyes.

Hunched figures with bony triangular heads and powerful arms loomed over us. On a collective signal, they lifted their clubs and slammed them down.

My crewmen grunted in pain. Ribs snapped, skulls thudded, as my people were knocked senseless.

The Terrapinians, those heartless, gray-green bastards, had decided to ambush us in our sleep.

=26=

Brawling on the decks was allowed—even commonplace—but both sides were usually aware of what was coming. Such combats normally started in the form of an honest duel between chiefs, or a spat over a shared female.

This time was different. The turtles had seen an opportunity to get some status points by ambushing us, the heroes of the ship. If they could take us out in personal combat, they could demonstrate their superiority without having to risk death by fighting Imperials. But while we were asleep? Leave it to a primitive reptilian to exploit a sleazy short-cut to improve their stature.

There was no time to think, only to react. Dr. Chang barely got his arms up before he was brained and put out of the fight. Samson fared better, sweeping the legs out from under the turtle that attacked him and grappling with him on the deck.

Mia fought like the little demon she was. She was always alert, and she never seemed to awaken groggy—even after a deep sleep. She sprang up, dodging a slow-moving club, and sprang upon her attacker's head.

Gwen lay on her back, screeching and dodging the club that descended to smash her. It sparked on the deck plates, then was hoisted up high again for another swing.

I couldn't help her. I couldn't help any of them as I had my own problems.

The boss turtle had chosen to take me on. He stood a head taller than the rest, and he'd clearly decided to make it personal in my case.

Without saying anything, he stooped and smashed the deck near my right shoulder. I'd barely slid out of the way in time.

Trying to jump up, I found a massive round foot sweeping down and pressing me onto my back. A tremendous weight crushed my ribs. I could hardly gasp for breath.

He lifted his club with both of his powerful arms. His nightmarish face regarded me, his expression was singularly determined and never-changing. The oil-drop eyes stared down, and they were merciless.

Just then a large ball of flying fur slammed into the Terrapinian's back. The monster staggered, but he didn't fall. A growling sound rose up behind him, and he dropped his club, which came clanging down next to me.

The turtle reached back over his shoulders to grasp the hairy thing that was now riding him. Knowing this distraction was the only break I was going to get, I levered his huge flat foot off my ribs with both hands.

The unsuspecting monster stumbled and fell. The furry thing continued to savage him with fangs and ripping claws. Wheezing, I stood and snatched up the turtle leader's fallen club. Then I set to work on that big head of his.

The oil-drop eyes stared up at me in hate as I struck that skull again and again. It took a long time, but the light finally went out of them, and his body went slack.

"Thanks Ra-tikh," I said to the fur-bag that perched on the turtle's chest.

"No need," he said, getting up and beginning to smooth his disheveled coat. "Their attack was dishonorable. It was like the work of a primate or a lemur. I hate these turtles. They're even worse than you monkeys."

His rude comments couldn't derail my good mood. I laughed, causing sharp pains to jolt through my chest.

All around us, the fight had ended. Ra-tikh's crew had come to help, and together our crews had driven off or beaten down the turtles. Once they'd seen their leader fall, the fight had gone out of the rest.

There were no hugs or congratulations with the cat-crew that had saved us, however. They seemed almost embarrassed to have interfered.

Except for Dalton—he came to me and shook my hand.

"You owe me one, Blake," he said, flashing me his crooked teeth.

I smiled back. "For once, I agree."

The groups separated, dragging away the injured. No one had died, but Dr. Chang didn't regain consciousness for several hours. Fortunately, the officers sent a medical drone to tend to him.

Shaw appeared later and looked over the scene.

"A shame," he said.

"What?" I responded. "That the turtles chose such an evil moment to turn traitor?"

He looked at me in bafflement. "No. Not at all. Their attack was well-executed and within the bounds of ship's regulations. No disruptors were used. We weren't in combat with any Imperials, and a full shift has passed since the last battle ended. In addition, none of you were injured prior to the encounter, so—"

I put up my hand. "I know the rulebook," I said. "It just seems crazy to me. Why do you allow us to fight each other instead of the enemy?"

He stared at me coldly. "That's what an Imperial would say—that no one should be allowed to prove they're better than their superiors. We've rejected the Imperial way of thinking! They're absolute and strict in their hierarchies. A pawn born to a low-caste Kher will never ascend to—"

"Okay," I said, throwing up my hands, "I give up on the politics. You guys have your customs, and we'll follow them as best we can. What I want to know is what you meant by saying this incident was a shame?"

"Oh... well, I meant it's unfortunate that there was no clear winner. Each side took out one enemy. You ended up doing better, but since Ra-tikh interfered, any points gained after his interference were negated."

I stared at him in disbelief. "I can't believe you're still keeping track of points! I thought we'd already proven ourselves—that the fights between the different crews were over and settled. But here you are, talking about gaining status through our pain!"

"Of course. As all the combatants involved in this particular skirmish were under my command, a decisive win would have given me half the points gained by the winning crew."

Shaking my head, I limped away from him. Sometimes, the Kher were too much for me, and that went for both the Rebels as well as the Imperials. The Rebels loved freedom and individuality. They'd taken these traits to an extreme in my opinion—but no one was interested in my opinions. At best, my ideas concerning mutual cooperation for the greater good were seen as subversive and weak aboard this ship.

When our next shift started, we were all wary, sore and tired. On top of that, my crew was angry.

"We ought to *do* something," Samson told me as we worked to get our fighter back into shape. "This attack can't go unanswered."

"You mean against the turtles, right?" I asked him, working an auto-welder on *Hammerhead's* stubby wings.

"Yeah, of course. If they think they can come at us any time without warning, we'll never have any peace."

"Normally, we'd be in our pods, sleeping safely. We went to sleep without posting a guard on the hangar deck. It was a mistake, made under special circumstances."

"Nevertheless, I agree with Samson," Dr. Chang said in a scratchy voice.

I switched off the auto-welder and turned to look him over. The medical drone hummed, lifted off and left him behind. As he'd been laid out flat on the deck, he struggled to rise into a sitting position.

He managed to sit up on his own, but he was still a mess. His head was missing a lot of hair on the left side of his skull above the ear. There was a lump of false-flesh there, which looked like a giant tumor. I knew it would regrow his skin and fall off in time, but it was still hard to look at.

"You feeling okay, Doc?" I asked him.

"I'm fine," he lied.

"Why should we hit the turtles?" I asked.

"Because they won't quit until they either take us down, or they become certain they can't. They're not driven by honor or anger—at least, not much. I think they're just opportunists. The worst kind of opponent to have. They coldly judged we were a ripe target, and they took a shot while we were vulnerable. We have to teach them we're *never* going to be a good target."

Gwen was listening in now, I could tell. So was Mia. My little tigress wanted blood—but then she always did. She was quivering with excitement at the prospect of another fight. She was also smart enough to let the others make her arguments for her.

"All right," I said. "We'll take care of the turtles."

"How?" asked Samson. "When?"

"Leave that up to me," I assured him. "You'll know when it's time."

In truth, I had no plan at all. But I was just as much of an opportunist as the turtles, and I needed my crew to *feel* like I had things under control.

After stating my vengeful intentions clearly, the whole group shifted gears. They became instantly happier. They'd been simmering with resentment against the turtles. They wanted revenge, but they trusted me enough to wait.

A counterattack wasn't the best road to peace, but we all knew that peace would be difficult to find on this ship. I was in charge, and the members of my crew were my problem. I had to keep their morale up. It wouldn't do to let them—or anyone else—think we were easy to pick on.

Time passed in a blur of hard-working days and watchful nights. It was a testimony to how much my crew trusted me that they never demanded to know *when* we were going to move on the turtles. It was enough for them to know that we eventually would.

New crews came aboard *Killer*. They were all from the local planet, survivors of the vicious extermination efforts of the Imperials.

I wanted to feel sympathy for these new guys, but they were the strangest-looking bunch I'd run into yet.

They were bug-like—but they were still mammals, I was sure of that. All Kher were mammals no matter what they looked like. Even the Terrapinians produced live-born young rather than laying eggs.

But these flesh-beetles sure didn't look like cousins. They had hard brown carapaces that grew over their hunched backs. They were short of limb and powerfully built.

If anything, they looked like fleshy beetles. It was going to be hard to get used to them, in part because they were so ugly.

"Yo," Dalton said, coming to our pit and standing at a respectful distance.

"Hey Dalton," I said. "What's on your mind?"

Samson and Dalton still socialized now and then, and they both chased the cat-girls whenever they could, with occasional success. But usually, members of rival crews didn't step into the territory of another group. It was considered a threat, and there was always the chance that such a move might end in violence.

We all stared at Dalton, even though we knew him well. Maybe *because* we knew him well.

"Ra-tikh wanted me to ask you something, Chief."

Some might have complained that he wasn't using my new rank of ensign, but I didn't mind. The commander of every small boat in the Fleet was called a "chief," regardless of their actual naval rank.

I watched him for a moment, then nodded and waved him closer.

He walked right past me and entered *Hammerhead* without asking permission. I climbed in after him quickly, as did Samson. We both suspected some kind of sabotage.

Inside the cramped ship, Dalton had stretched himself out on my command chair.

"Damn, this is pretty nice," he said. "The kitties next door like it hotter than this, and I have to put up with little tufts of fur everywhere."

"Start talking," I told him, "about something that matters, I mean."

"Yeah," Samson said, "or we'll kick your ass out of here—and don't go asking to come back to our crew. We like this crew the way it is."

I glanced at Samson. The composition of my crew wasn't his call to make, but I let it slide this time.

"It's like this," Dalton said, putting his hands behind his head, lacing his fingers and leaning back. "Ra-tikh thinks you make a good sidekick. He'd like to offer you an informal alliance."

I frowned. "An alliance? What for?"

"Against the turtles, or these new skin-beetles. It's those freaks that gave us the idea. It seems unfair, doesn't it? They have like six crews of beetles, and we've only got one team each of our species."

"That's just because we lost so many crews in the attack," I said, "but I get your point. An alliance… Unofficial, of course?"

"That's right. If you need help, we'll come to help. If we need your help, we'll call for you."

"Does this go for arena fights as well as random ambushes on the hangar deck?"

"Yes—but we have to keep that quiet. The other crews will gang-up against us otherwise."

After mulling it over, I nodded at last. "I'll agree. But there's one detail that must change."

"What?"

"I'm in charge. Ra-tikh is the sidekick."

Dalton produced a dirty laugh. "The boss-kitty isn't going to like that. Why do you think you should be the—?"

"Because I'm an ensign," I said firmly. "I'm on the officer training track. Technically, I outrank him."

Dalton nodded. "I'll tell him."

He left, and Samson looked after him worriedly.

"What is it?" I asked him.

"I know Dalton. You can't really trust him. He's probably lying about something. He's got a scheme. He's always got an angle."

"We'll be careful. So far, our two teams have been helping one another. I see no reason why we shouldn't keep doing it."

Shaking his head, Samson left the interior of the fighter. I went to work on the ventilation. Despite Dalton's compliments, I thought it was rather stale inside the ship. It must really be rank in his vessel.

About ten minutes later, I heard some angry noises outside. I ducked my head out of the hatch, and I wasn't surprised to see Ra-tikh approaching. He looked like someone had stomped on his tail.

He got close enough to steam up my shirt with his breath before he stopped. Samson stood to my side, but he didn't make a move. He was like a guard dog these days.

"What trick are you up to now, monkey?" Ra-tikh asked me. "I don't like tricks."

"Was Dalton lying?" I asked him.

"About a quiet alliance?" Ra-tikh asked. "No. But you have pressed for advantage already. You make demands as if I were your servant!"

I shrugged. "No one said you were. We're just going to back each other up. But I'm not going to be your second. You're *my* second."

I understood by this time that there was no room in Ra-tikh's furry mind for a co-equal relationship. His species dealt strictly in rigid hierarchies, like a military organization or a pack of wolves.

"You insult me," he said. "I've been onboard this carrier longer than you have. I've defeated many crew chiefs."

"This is true, but you've never beaten me. I'm beginning to think that what you really wanted was a way to say you *had* defeated me—without having to actually fight."

His eyes flashed dangerously. "You accuse me of dishonor? You accuse *me* of cowardice?"

I thought about that and frowned.

"No," I said. "I take that back. You wouldn't play it that way, Ra-tikh. My apologies. Recent events have made me distrustful of others."

He relaxed somewhat. "I understand that. The turtles are dishonorable. I don't know about these flesh-beetles yet, but I think their blood will leave a bad taste when we learn the truth."

Calculating he was using an idiom, I nodded in agreement.

"So," he continued. "You have apologized. I accept your apology. You are now my second! Be welcome!"

"Hold on! That's not going to fly. I'm still the ensign here."

He looked me over with narrowed, angry eyes. "Our two crews are more powerful as a team, do you agree?"

"I agree."

"We have proved this twice over, yes?"

"You are correct."

"Then why do you refuse to bow to reason?"

"It is you who isn't being reasonable. You asked for this alliance, not me. If you still want it, you can have it. But it will have to be on *my* terms."

He glared at the deck for a time, thinking hard. "What if…" he said thoughtfully, "what if in the future I come to outrank you? Will you become my second then?"

I thought it over, then nodded. "I would agree to that."

His furry paw shot out. I took it, and he pumped it up and down powerfully. Dalton must have taught him this Earth custom.

"We have a deal," he said.

Then he turned around and left me and my crew standing in our pit. I watched him walk away, wondering where all this might lead.

=27=

We jumped through the stars again a few days later—and this time, the jump was a long one.

"All hands, prepare for vortex entry. Nine, eight, seven…"

We were nervous. We were aboard *Hammerhead*, strapped in, floating in anti-grav—but we were worried anyway.

Killer had taken quite a beating in the last battle. Three of her big engines were still off-line, and some of the reactors were pulsing at random intervals.

Like an old man with the hiccups, we could see and feel the deck as it shivered under our skids. The throbbing power, building up for the jump, was making everything unstable.

"Do you think she'll stay together?" Gwen asked.

"If she doesn't," Dr. Chang said, "we'll be dead so fast we'll never know what happened."

"As usual, that's very comforting, Doc. Thanks."

The throbbing continued building up. We could see—well, I could see using far-flung perception, that the rip in space had appeared before us. This time it spun around slowly, like a vortex in a lazy mood.

"Hold on," I said, "we're going through."

Killer vibrated and advanced toward our artificial anomaly. All around us, twenty-odd other carriers did the same.

"Where are we headed?" Mia asked me.

I glanced at her. I'd been briefed, but I'd been told not to reveal anything until we got to our destination.

"To somewhere safe," I said, giving her a reassuring smile.

"Liar," she said.

She'd come to know me too well. If I thought the truth wouldn't help and might possibly hurt one of my crewmen, I dispensed with it immediately.

Fortunately, before she could demand more accurate information, we jumped away from the dull red sun and its planet-full of dead flesh-beetles.

Soon thereafter, we were someplace new. My perception dawned slowly, expanding my mind and my consciousness.

The other end of the jump was very different. Two white stars circled one another in a close orbit. They were twins in size, or nearly so. Together, they made the skies brilliant, but not friendly. It was more like looking at an arc-welder's torch than a warm winter's fire.

Still, our mood shifted to one of relief. We'd all feared we would scatter, given *Killer*'s poor state of health. But we'd made it through once again.

There were a large number of planets circling these two suns. They ranged from burnt rocks near the center, to titanic gas giants in the waist and finished up with a crowd of ice-balls in distant orbit.

"Seventy-one planets!" Gwen said, whistling. "Never seen this many before, especially not in a binary system."

"Any ships?" I asked, scanning the feed from our long range sensors.

My perception system was superior when it came to visualizing local objects, but my crew had access to *Killer's* arrays. The powerful instrumentation could provide data I wouldn't hope to gather by my sym-link's ability alone.

"Yes," Gwen said a few minutes later. "We've got ships. I'm glad we didn't scatter. But I think there are two missing ships in the Fleet."

"Two lost? That's a high rate of attrition."

"At least *we* didn't get lost," Samson said, smiling and putting his head back to rest on his chair. "Not this time."

I didn't feel as relieved as he obviously did. We'd lost about ten percent of our force with a simple jump. They might catch back up to us, or they might not. Either way, the loss had weakened our force.

"More ships are in the system…" Gwen said. "Distant contacts."

Craning my neck around to look at her, I frowned. "Enemy?"

"More are appearing. Thirty—fifty. Different configurations."

"Give me coordinates," I said urgently.

She tossed them to me virtually, and I used them to lock in, seeking in the right direction with my sym.

A few seconds later, I saw the gathering force. There had to be over a hundred now.

"They're popping in close to the farther of the two white suns," I said. "They look like our ships—but I can't tell from here."

"Ask Shaw," Mia said.

I looked at her.

"Please?" she asked.

Her face had to contort to pronounce the word. I'd learned that her people didn't have an equivalent term in their language. Without the translator, she'd had to force her lips to form the unfamiliar sound.

"All right," I said, opening a channel to Shaw.

It was a breach of protocol, but a small one. At least I was an ensign now, no longer a snot-nosed rookie pilot.

"Blake?" he responded. "What is it? I'm busy."

"We've detected a large force near the farther of the suns, Lieutenant. Can you confirm they're friendly?"

He chuckled. "Spoiling for another fight, eh?" he said, completely missing my mood and intent. "Well, I'm sorry to disappoint. They're ours. Stand down your engines and your wasps. You'll have to wait until some Imperials show up."

He closed the channel, and I closed my eyes in a moment of silent prayer.

"We're in the clear. Those are Rebel ships out there."

"So many?" Mia said. "I didn't know we had such strength. I'm pleased with you."

She rubbed her tail over my legs, and I knew what that meant. If I could get a moment alone with her, she'd make it worth my while.

Gwen glanced at us in disgust. She'd never quite gotten over the idea that I'd struck up a sexual relationship with a non-human. Fortunately, her distress had no effect on Mia or myself.

"How long do we have to sit in this tin can, then?" she asked.

"Less than an hour, I'm sure."

"Good."

As it turned out, all the alarms and alerts were cancelled within minutes. We switched off the anti-grav, exited the fighter and stretched on the hangar deck.

"Kind of a letdown," Mia complained. "I'm bored now."

She walked away, running her tail over my suit as she passed by, as if by accident.

I followed her a few moments later, telling the others to take a break. Samson grinned at me, Dr. Chang studied his instruments, and Gwen coldly minded some unnecessary task to occupy herself.

I ignored them all and found a quiet spot to commune with Mia. She was hot and quick to get down to the action. She kissed me because she knew I liked it, and I stroked her fur because I knew *she* liked it. She knew what she wanted, and she wasn't going to stop until she got it. I was happy to help.

Well into our distracted interlude, a figure loomed nearby. Startled, I turned to face this new threat.

My immediate impression was that I was looking at a turtle. The biggest of them, their leader. But that wasn't the case. My mind had filled in the blanks in the shadows of pipes and dripping conduits.

"Lieutenant Shaw," I said. "How nice of you to come find me in person. Is your communication unit switched off?"

He took a step closer, looking around in a conspiratorial fashion.

"I can't believe this is how you spend your precious few moments."

"Phht!" Mia said, making a sound in her own language that defied interpretation. "You came here to spy on us."

"Hardly," he said. "I hope you're finished copulating because I need to speak privately to Ensign Blake."

Mia wormed up against me defiantly. "What if we aren't?"

Feeling somewhat embarrassed, I gently guided her away from me as my uniform restored itself fully to dressed condition.

"We're finished discussing that private matter until later, Mia," I said to her.

Mia got the hint and sprang away. She was ruffled, but I knew she'd get over it quickly. She was like that, quick to anger and just as fast to forget.

"Blake," Shaw said, "we have a problem."

"What's that, sir?"

"The new arrivals are teaming up. They won't fight. They won't challenge one another properly."

"You mean the beetles?" I asked, knowing it couldn't be the turtles. The Terrapinians seemed to relish a good battle. "How is that a problem?"

"They failed the tests. All of them. They stood there and burned on the decks, rather than lift a limb to strike their companions."

Frowning, I wasn't sure how to take that. "They sound like good soldiers—if they'll fight the enemy."

"It's possible they will," he said. "But we can't take a chance on them without seeing how well they can hold their own."

"Why'd you take them aboard then, sir? Why not leave them on their world?"

"We've lost too many crews. We're in a fight for our lives now. The Imperials are done playing, they'll make their big push soon. Their recon efforts are nearly finished."

"Recon? You mean, back on that last planet...?"

"Yes. That was a scouting force, not a serious fleet."

His words alarmed me. "How many ships are we gathering together here?" I asked him.

"Several hundred. We hope to trick them into attacking us where we are strong. They outnumber us greatly, but if we can find another hunter-group and destroy it with few losses, we can even the odds."

I didn't feel confident about his plan, but I didn't have a better one.

"About the beetles," he said. "I need you to... agitate them."

"What?"

"Make them fight. You're very good at that."

I hadn't thought of myself as a troublemaker, but perhaps in his eyes, I seemed like someone who fought with everyone.

"How do you propose I do that?" I asked.

"You could steal one of their females. The way you did with Mia."

I winced in horror. The idea of having sex with one of those creatures was far beyond the pale. I couldn't believe he would even suggest it.

Shaw caught none of my facial clues. "Well?" he asked.

"It wouldn't work, Lieutenant," I said with certainty. "Even if I were to succeed, they would only be angry with *me*, not each other. The point is to get them to compete among themselves, isn't it?"

"Yes... You're right... I have no choice. It's bad timing, but we must use the arena."

My heart sank. "The pit, sir?"

"Yes. Report there upon the next dawn. Bring your crewmen, and your most effective primate trickery."

He left me then, and I sighed aloud. What had been a lovely start to the day had turned into a vast disappointment.

=28=

My crew didn't take the news well.

"That is total *bullshit*, Chief!" Samson complained.

"There's no way we should have to enter the arena again," Mia said. "We've already earned our disruptors. Let the weak fight in the pit. We'll stand on the edge and hiss at them in amusement. That is how it should be!"

"They can't make us go in again, can they Leo?" Gwen asked plaintively.

I glanced at her. "They can do whatever the hell they want to. They make up the rules as they go along, I guess. They need the beetles to fight one another, and for some reason they think we can get them to do it."

"It's because of the turtles," Samson said. "It has to be."

"How so?"

"Remember when Ra-tikh came and jumped them? Right there, you had two crews fighting on your behalf."

"That's thin evidence," I protested.

"Not in Shaw's mind," Dr. Chang said suddenly. "To his way of thinking, we are weaklings, but we possess a low, cunning intelligence. We're beings that survive by our wits, rather than our brawn. Therefore, he has calculated that we can succeed at socializing the beetles where he has failed."

"Socializing?" Gwen asked. "Is that what we're calling this? We're going down there to be burned and bruised."

"We can win," I said firmly. "We've done it before, and we'll do it again."

"What if the beetles won't fight each other?" Samson demanded. "What if they all gang up on us instead?"

I didn't have an answer for his questions, so I didn't bother. I led my crew toward the pit instead.

Our disruptors were reset for low power, to be used as training units. Minutes later, we found ourselves in a colored circle, sinking into the deck again.

The other teams were eyeing us warily. Three of them were flesh-beetles. They were hunched and yellow-brown. Their flesh was warty and built with lumps of meat, bone and shiny chitin. There was no easy way to tell the individuals apart. They all appeared to be about the same size and shape.

The only surprise was the fifth team. We had come to know them well. They were led by a particularly large member of their breed, the very Terrapinian who had attempted to beat me down a few weeks ago while I slept on the hangar deck.

"Turtles?!" Samson roared. "Let's make soup out of them!"

He pointed his disruptor toward the turtles, who returned the favor. We were descending now into the pit, but the battle hadn't officially begun, so our weapons weren't activated yet.

My mind was in overdrive, trying to figure out what to do. It made sense that the turtles would be in this fight as they had yet to earn their official sidearms, but I still smelled a rat. I was certain that Shaw was the source of the unpleasant odor.

My concerns were confirmed when the Terrapinian team was placed next to us in the line-up.

"The officers know we hate the turtles…" I said. "Do they want us to fight?"

"I don't get it…" Gwen said in alarm. "If we go for the turtles right off, that will leave only the bugs to clean up the mess."

"Right," I said. "But maybe Shaw's hoping that a display of violence on our part will motivate the beetles."

"I don't think he has any coherent plan," Dr. Chang said. "He's probably hoping you've got a trick to play."

"Great…"

The pit continued to lower until we reached the bottom. Far above, a circle of smiling faces watched us. They cheered, hoping for blood. The contestants checked their weapons and were informed as to the rules.

"Hey!" I shouted at the turtles.

Two of them looked at me with their liquid black eyes, but they soon lost interest.

Desperate, I took several steps in their direction. I stood at the very edge of our circle of territory, which was delineated by a ring of colored light on the deck.

This move got their attention. The leader turned his big wedge-shaped head in my direction.

"You seek to befoul us?" he demanded. "To spread the stench of your lungs in our odor-space?"

I could tell that the translators were struggling to give us the meaning of his words, but I got the idea. He thought I stank and should shut up.

"I have a suggestion," I said, shouting over the announcer who was just about finished. "Let's not fight. The bugs will all team against us, anyway. We should unite and fight all three of their crews."

The huge turtle seemed to consider the offer. Then time ran out, and the floor went green.

"Agreed," he said to me at the last instant.

"Damn, I was going to cold-cock him right off," Samson said, lowering his weapon.

"Samson," I said with real regret, "we have to make a sacrifice. You're it."

"Ah, shit."

We'd talked about this before, and now it was time to put the plan into action. As he was our biggest teammate, he moved toward the three bug groups and threw himself down on the deck.

The rest of us fell onto our bellies and aimed over Samson, who had his broad back directed toward the bugs.

"Arrr!" Samson howled as a lucky strike caught him in the spine. "They're going to spine-meld me and put me out quick!"

"All right, time to choose targets—" I said, but I broke off. "What the—they're cheating!"

Already, things were going badly. The enemy beetles had all turned around, aiming their shiny brown carapaces in our direction. They looked like shields with legs when they ducked their heads and tucked in their arms. Now and then, they took a blind shot in our direction as they advanced slowly.

Backing up, they began a slow, plodding march in our direction. We shot their backs, but it was like striking at a shield-wall. Their carapaces seemed to be immune to our low-powered disruptors. They had a natural advantage we couldn't easily overcome.

"Shoot for their legs!" I ordered.

We fired a barrage, and one of the bugs stumbled, flopping on the deck. It had taken us fifteen shots to do it, and that single bug wasn't even finished. I couldn't help but notice that none of the bugs were shooting at each other. They were operating as a single fifteen-man crew.

That's when the first bolt landed in our midst. A second later, a dozen more struck.

It wasn't coming from the beetles, however, who couldn't even see us with their backs turned.

The turtles were doing it. They'd decided to break their alliance and shoot us in the ass. Our agreement had lasted for maybe ninety seconds.

"Those cock-smokers," Samson slurred. His mouth was bleeding from the strikes he'd sustained, and a pink foam was glistening on the deck around his head.

"Team!" I shouted, turning to face this new threat. "Everyone shoot at the big guy. Fry that turtle—no mercy!"

One weakness of the turtles was their tendency not to wear covering gear. They didn't seem to like wearing uniforms at all. This was probably due to a hot climate on their home planet—or maybe our atmosphere was too hot for them, and they wanted to cool down. It was hard to tell.

Whatever the case, they tended to wear only a battle-harness with weapons or tools on their crisscrossing belts. This left critical parts of their bodies exposed…

None of my team had any compunction. They targeted the lead turtle's balls and fired in unison.

Shocked by multiple hits and near-hits, the turtle staggered, but he didn't go down.

"The eyes!" I shouted. "Aim for those black marbles!"

We lanced at him with a dozen more shots, and that was it. Gargling oddly, he spun around and fell. We shot him a few more times, but the battle was over.

As had happened before, and I'd hoped would happen this time, the rest of his team crumpled. They stopped firing, staggered backward and some even dropped their weapons. Without their leader, they were confused and cowardly.

"Forget them," I said, "the bugs are almost here."

Samson was unconscious by this time. He'd been knocked out by so many hits to the back and head. Mia was down too, having been fried by hits mostly from the treacherous turtles.

That left me and my two weakest combatants. The closest enemy beetles, still walking backward, were only a dozen paces away.

"Forget shooting them. Grab up fallen disruptors. Let's move to the turtles and use them for shields."

We scrambled up and ran. Gwen cursed and Dr. Chang made a long growling sound in his throat. We were all taking a hit now and then, creating red swollen patches on our backs and legs.

When we reached the turtles, they looked confused. I decided to go for broke.

"You heard your leader!" I shouted at them. "He made a deal to fight with me. Now that he's gone, you're under *my* command!"

This took a few seconds to register, but when it did, the group became reenergized. Three of them were still standing. They lifted their weapons and aimed them at the approaching shield-wall of beetles.

The final moments of the fight were brutal and strange. We adopted a new tactic, rushing forward, spinning a bug around, and shooting him point-blank until he toppled, shivering and leaking fluids.

Then, all at once, the remaining beetles turned around to face us. If there had been a signal between them, I'd missed it.

There were ten of them left against our six, but we were more experienced, often larger and stronger—and we were mean.

Closing with the enemy, we placed our disruptors where we knew they would do the most damage: up against eyeballs, genitals, or fingers that held weapons.

Both Gwen and Dr. Chang, despite heroic efforts, fell. Of my three turtles, two survived to the end. They weren't fast or cunning, but they could take an impressive amount of punishment.

The last of the beetles fell with me gunning him in the guts over and over with a disruptor in each hand. I'd picked them up from fallen bugs when mine had run out of juice.

Triumphant, I lifted my hands over my head and clasped them together. I shook them at the watchers, hating them almost as much as the fallen beetles that lay everywhere around me, kicking and twitching.

I expected the announcement of the ending to come, but it didn't. Instead, the floor began to pulse yellow. It was a warning, a threat: the pain was coming soon.

After a moment, I looked around at my two-turtle army and realized what the problem was. The officers didn't recognize us as a crew. We were two crews, myself alone against two turtles.

For their part, the turtles stared at me. They didn't know what to do as no one had told them yet.

I heaved a sigh.

"Honor must be satisfied," I said. "You must shoot one another until you're both out of the game."

They turned, hesitantly, and began shooting one another from two paces apart. Their hisses of pain were enough to make me feel sorry for the gray-green losers.

Finally, they fell. I was the last man standing in the arena.

"The contest is over," Shaw declared in an amplified voice. "The humans have won—again."

Ragged cheers rang out from above. The floor stopped displaying colors and began to rise.

The battle was over.

=29=

Shaw came to visit us in our pod, which had been repaired after the initial battle with the Imperials.

My own team was still in a sorry state, however. Two medical drones were applying salves and patches to our damaged flesh. I had a dozen swollen injuries myself, and I found I wasn't in the mood to apologize to Shaw.

"What kind of plan was that?" he demanded.

I shrugged.

"A perfect one," I said. "The battle went exactly as I'd hoped. Everything fell into place beautifully. The one part I wasn't sure would go right was tempting the turtles into a backstab—but they went for it. Sometimes, I do impress even myself."

He stared at me in confusion. "You *planned* for the turtles to attack you?"

"That's what I said."

"But you utterly failed to get the beetles to fight one another! All you accomplished was another selfish victory!"

"Ah," I said, lifting a finger with a red weal on it that stung in the open air. "You don't see it, do you? I thought you were more perceptive. Oh well, not all species are the same when it comes to scheming. You've said it yourself a dozen times."

He strode closer, glowering at me. "You're telling me this is all part of some grand strategy of yours?"

"Of course. The beetles learned today not to screw with the humans. You have to understand, Lieutenant, I can't break their lifelong conditioning toward species-unity in a single step. It will take time for my lessons to sink in."

"Why should I believe any of this?" he asked suspiciously.

I gave him a sweeping gesture indicating the entire situation. "Did you somehow miss the sight of a battlefield strewn with fallen enemies? I thought it was a Rebel belief that success such as mine today should bring status to the victor. Increased status, in turn, is the *only* evidence that will prove I know what I'm doing. Isn't that how Rebels are supposed to act?"

Shaw mumbled bitterly, but he had to concede my point. Then the conversation took an unexpected turn.

"I have your reward here," he grumbled. "It is inappropriate you should receive this honor, but I can't deny that you've come out on top in the arena twice in a row."

A cargo-drone buzzed into our pod. It was carrying a large cube. The drone set down the cube at our feet.

The cube turned out to be an automated carton. It opened quietly, like a box yawning wide. Inside were some ugly-looking metal devices. I picked one up, impressed by the weight of it.

"Graviton thumpers," Shaw said, his tone indicating he believed his statement should have explained everything.

"Um… thanks," I said, looking them over.

"They're close-combat weapons," Shaw said, realizing I had no idea what the purpose of these devices was. "The barrel on top is a disruptor, like your hand weapons, but with more range and hitting power. The tube underneath the device fires the gravity-grenades."

"I see," I said, impressed. "Why are we being issued these weapons?"

He squirmed in irritation.

"Champions are often called upon in battle for special operations."

"Like what?"

"Thumpers are advanced personal armament," he said, "they're for leading boarding assaults, or repelling them. Under rare circumstances, they can be used when invading worlds and pacifying them."

"Great," I said, "can we keep our regular disruptors as well?"

"Of course. The thumpers aren't allowed to be used aboard ship unless we're engaged in actual battle."

I sighed in disappointment and put the weapon back into the crate.

"Too bad," I said.

Shaw laughed. "What? Have you already hatched a plan to ambush the Terrapinians with these unfair weapons?"

Shrugging, I admitted nothing.

Shaw left us. As the door closed behind him, he shook his head and muttered about the natural duplicity and vile habits of primates.

Mia came to me, and her fuzzy hands ran over my arms.

"You performed so well on the battlefield," she said. "I doubted you—I admit it—but I was wrong. You said you would get revenge on the turtles for their treachery, and you did it in the most artful way. They'll never consider turning against us again!"

I wasn't sure about the last part, but I smiled and nuzzled with Mia anyway.

"Never forget what you saw today," I said, grabbing her waist to pull her close.

She pressed her palms against my chest and looked up at me with a quiet growl and a smile of her own. Pushing away from me, her tail wrapped around the inside of my thigh and clung as if reluctant to break away. I watched her turn to go.

After she'd moved off, Samson came and shook my hand. "I hated those turtles, but I was still conscious when you fried the 'nads off their leader. What a beautiful sight that was."

I chuckled and looked expectantly at the other two. Dr. Chang gave me a respectful nod, but Gwen didn't look at me at all.

We went on with our day, which mostly consisted of healing from dozens of painful welts and more serious injuries. If it hadn't been for the amazing medical capacities of the Kher, we'd have been out of commission for weeks. Some of the injuries might have been permanent and disfiguring. But as it was, we were back to our duties after taking only two full shifts off.

When we returned to *Hammerhead*, I had the chance to talk to Gwen.

"What did you think of the battle?" I asked her.

"Very clever," she said, "but you didn't have to pretend with Shaw."

"What do you mean?"

"It was eighty percent luck, and you know it."

I looked at her sharply. "Eighty percent?" I demanded. "I won't accept that. Fifty percent, maybe—but even that's arguable."

She rolled her eyes at me. This bothered me more than I thought it should. Gwen was smart, a lot smarter than Samson or Mia. If she had a problem with the situation, it was worth listening to.

"Come on," I said. "I got us out of there alive. I won the battle. The turtles and the beetles all got creamed. What do you want from me?"

"A little less grandstanding would be nice. A little more humility. Why do you have to take credit when none is due?"

Growing annoyed with her, I shrugged my shoulders.

"All right," I said. "Next time, I'll make sure we lose. You can get your brains knocked in or get your butt scorched. I don't care which."

"I *did* get my butt scorched."

"Yes, but you're alive now and our status has increased. Isn't that a good thing?"

She came closer to me and lowered her voice.

"I'm not sure that it is," she said. "Have you realized that our rising status is causing us to become the focus of *more* trials? That if you keep winning, we'll keep getting our asses into more trouble?"

I nodded, but her idea hadn't occurred to me. The more I thought about it, the more she seemed to be right. Instead of making life aboard this vessel easier for us, I might be making it infinitely worse.

"Hmmm..." I said. "Do you think I should throw a fight or two?"

"You're serious?"

"Yes. Or should I keep winning—if I can?"

She shook her head. "It's up to you, Leo. It does seem crazy to lose on purpose. But consider this: the Kher Fleet is a giant pyramid scheme. They've hooked us into their game, and they're making us compete. We've been trying ever harder to win, just the way they want us to. That's great, but is it really to our benefit—or only to theirs? Who is *really* winning this game?"

"Well... I'm certain we're all on the same side against the Imperials."

"Yeah? These guys are Rebel Kher. They tell us we're fighting a holy war against a great evil—but what's *really* going on? Are we actually fighting for or against the good guys? We have no idea."

Her words troubled me. The more I thought about them, the more I wasn't sure about the answer.

It was impossible to argue with the facts. The Kher tactic of getting us all to compete had yielded dramatic results. The human team had started off as a nobody crew from a no-name planet, but we'd stood up and fought a half-dozen champions from other worlds to a standstill.

I wasn't sure if standing out and winning battles was the wisest thing in this situation—but I had to admit, I was enjoying it.

=30=

The following two weeks were exciting. The Rebel Fleet continued to grow. I now respected the Kher's use of Mongol Horde tactics. There had to be representative crews from a thousand unique planets. Most of those planets had sent a small group, perhaps five or fifteen individuals. The low-status crews like ours were only allowed to fly fighters.

But there were bigger outfits as well. Some planets had sent a full squadron of cruisers. These forces came from advanced worlds capable of building ships on their own.

The most advanced worlds had built and manned the carriers. Shaw came from one of these planets, as had Commander Tand.

Earth, being sort of a wilderness preserve, had no ships of her own. We had to be content with the single fighter we'd been provided. It soon became clear *Hammerhead* was the equivalent of army surplus. It was cast-off equipment. I confronted Shaw about this as we gathered on the hangar deck for an inspection.

"This fighter of mine," I said, "you're saying it's been in service since the last time this fleet gathered? So it's a thousand years old?"

"Yes," he said, "but it's been stored for the vast majority of that time. Kept in stasis, it's as fresh as when it was built."

I shook my head. "But surely there are newer, better designs?"

"Of course, but no one would give their best spacecraft to an unproven militia."

On my own world, I knew, it was common practice among superpowers to sell off old equipment to poor nations to fight bush wars. I guess that thinking wasn't unique to Earth.

"How can we win a war against the Imperials with old junk?" I asked.

He looked startled. "Your words are so disjointed as to be rendered almost meaningless. We don't *war* with the Imperials—not really. We wouldn't want to. We're here to resist them. To wear them down until they decide they've had enough, at which point they'll withdraw."

I stared at him. "So... we're not expected to win?"

He laughed. "We can't *win*. We can only survive. That is our goal—to keep as many of our planets intact as possible."

I thought about the flesh-beetles. They'd had it pretty rough. I'd seen their cities destroyed. Even if they were cheaters and grimly hideous, I had no wish to see such devastation on any planet.

"If this isn't actually a war," I said, "then it's abuse by a superior power. Is that more accurate?"

"Yes. We're like animals to the Imperial Kher. We share common genetics, but they don't care about that."

"So... they don't plan to conquer us?" I asked. "What's the point of all this then, from their view?"

"They do more than just kill us when it suits them," he explained. "Sometimes, they may decide to keep a planet they've cleansed of wild Kher and colonize it permanently with so-called civilized Imperials. But that sort of thing is rare. They come into our space to cull our numbers, and to prove themselves to one another. We also believe they wish to sharpen their skills against other enemies from beyond the rim."

"Beyond the rim? You mean the rim of the galaxy?"

Shaw looked at me with bleariness.

"Of course the rim of the galaxy," he said. "Now, if you'll excuse me Blake, there's an admiral coming aboard. Try not to embarrass my ship."

I stepped back into line. My team was arrayed in front of our ship, looking proud and attentive. In every pit, a similar crew stood with their fighter.

Shaw's words rang in my head. I'd gotten this same impression before, but never so clearly. The Imperial Kher were just toying with us. We were animals to them—or worse—fish in the sea. We were only worthy of being hunted for sport.

The more I thought about it, the more this situation pissed me off. These Rebels were no sweethearts, but they'd come to Earth and given us a shot at participating in this war. When Earth had beaten rival crews, they'd given us respect.

In contrast, the Imperials were heartless monsters. They'd been coming into our space periodically for target-practice for countless years. If anyone was asking me, we were definitely fighting on the more reasonable team—even if we weren't expected to win.

After having observed the Rebels in action, I wasn't surprised they'd always been on the losing side. They flew ramshackle ships that were centuries old. They fought each other at least as often as they did the enemy, and from what I'd seen of their behavior in battle, they were far from organized.

Military history had been an interest of mine, back in my days in the U. S. Navy. I recalled there'd been many battles of the past between uneven opponents. Actually, most wars in history had been very unfair contests. Logically, few countries would attack their neighbors if they thought they might lose.

The Kher situation reminded me most of the era of the Roman Empire. Rome had conquered numerous neighboring villages, tribes and nations. Most of those battles had been easily won. The victims had fielded ill-equipped and badly trained forces. They'd possessed inferior technology, poor discipline and barely understood tactics more complex than massing up and charging. The professional legions of Rome had smashed them by the thousands.

That was the situation here, in my estimation. The Imperials had much better ships and organization. They were a single coherent force. In comparison, the Rebels were a loose confederation of competing states. They were cooperating right now—but only because they had to.

Interrupting my thoughts, two high-level officers appeared on the main deck.

The first of them was Captain Ursahn. She was a creature I'd seen in ship-wide briefings but never met up close. She had a tanned body with tufts of hair at her shoulders that poked out of her uniform. Her face was alien-looking, but only to a human.

She was physically imposing like most officers. Strength accounted for a lot when it came to defeating challengers in personal combat. Her shoulders were well-rounded, and her neck was more of a sloping affair that connected her thick shoulders to a heavy skull.

The second creature walking alongside the captain had to be an admiral. He appeared to be from an entirely different branch of our shared genetic tree.

He was thinly built, but capable-looking. He eyed everything with quick, darting glances. His arms were overly long—far longer than any human's—but otherwise he looked almost like a gangly Earthman.

The admiral stopped suddenly when he came to our fighter. The captain stopped her continuous talk when she noticed his distraction, and they both looked at my crew.

"Ah yes," she said, "these are humans, Admiral Fex. A minor group from the Cygnus Carina region. They've done well for themselves."

Admiral Fex gave us a flickering a smile.

"I like the look," he said, clearly indicating we were close to him in appearance, which was true. His voice was nasally and slightly high-pitched. He addressed me specifically. "Primates, I assume?"

"Yes sir," I said, standing at attention.

Fex frowned and turned to Captain Ursahn. "Why does it present itself with an odd stance?" he asked. "Is this a display of petulance or false-superiority?"

I was taken by surprise. My stance was typical for a lower-level officer under inspection by a high-ranking one. Of course, I had to remind myself, this wasn't Earth and this was no Earthman. My training didn't match up with their culture. For the most part, the rebels were quite informal. They were the barbarians, I reminded myself, not the Romans.

With an effort, I tried to loosen up. I forced a slight smile to appear on my lips.

"Sorry sir," I said. "It's Earth custom to avoid eye-contact and familiarity with our superiors during an inspection."

"Interesting," the admiral said. "For a primate, you're very stiff and disciplined."

"Thank you, sir," I said.

Fex snorted and shook his head. He'd clearly not meant his comments as complimentary—but I didn't care. I was getting a little tired of living by everyone else's rules.

"What do you plan to do in the upcoming battle?" the admiral asked me.

"Kill the enemy, sir," I said. "All of them, if possible."

This finally made him happy.

"I understand!" he shouted. "Honor sits atop a *vicious* anger in your species. Has your home world been burned yet?"

Startled, I shook my head.

"Still, I can see it in your eyes. You simmer with rage and battle lust. All that motivation combined with ape cunning... Yes, these humans will go far. Keep raging!"

Before I could object, he turned his back and looked back at Captain Ursahn, who was eyeing me dubiously.

"Show me more misfits!" Admiral Fex ordered. "I find them amusing."

Ursahn led him away, and my crew looked after the odd pair in confusion. Samson stepped up and spoke over my shoulder.

"I think we've just been insulted," he said.

"I'm sure of it."

Gwen spoke next. "You see? We're pawns to them. Jokes."

She walked away and went back to working on *Hammerhead's* landing sensors.

I was left to ponder our status and my actions thus far. Was I proudly representing Earth—or playing the fool?

=31=

The Rebel Fleet had been occupying the binary system with seventy-one planets for days. They'd set up shop between the twin white suns, waiting.

More and more Rebel starships arrived every day, and our numbers swelled into the hundreds. Only the largest ships were capable of ripping a hole in space and wriggling through, otherwise known as performing an interstellar jump. At least ninety of the starships were carriers, with around twenty battle ships and three hundred cruiser-class vessels forming the balance.

Smaller, screening ships consisted of destroyers, gunboats and fighters. There were literally thousands of them in our massive, haphazard formation.

Altogether, we covered a region of space that was about ten million miles in diameter. Unlike surface fleets on planetary oceans, starship captains liked to have plenty of elbow room. At this distance, a fusion blast on one vessel wouldn't affect any neighboring ships—at least, that was what our commanders had told us.

My theory was different. I didn't think the rebel ships from various planets were all that fond of one another.

"See that group over there, closer to the Alpha star?" I asked my team, displaying my perception data on the walls of our fighter with the help of my sym-link.

"What about it?" Samson asked.

"You see that squadron? They have six cruisers, all tightly grouped, all from the same planet. If those ships are content to be within five miles of one another, why is the next group ten thousand miles behind them?"

"Well..." Samson said. "Maybe they have different missions."

"What missions?" I snorted. "We're all just floating around, hoping a small Imperial patrol shows up so we can jump them."

Our entire fleet was, in effect, a baited trap. Twice Imperial freighters had drifted by, only to be set upon by the massed ships and quickly destroyed.

"Everyone in this fleet hates everyone else," Gwen said. "Or at least, they don't trust one another. That's why they watch each other with their instruments at least as much as they search for Imperials."

"Exactly," I said, staring around the Fleet by turning my head. I felt disgusted by the lax discipline. "That smart-ass admiral who inspected us was no tactical genius, let me tell you. He was the worst kind of military officer."

"Maybe he gained his rank through some kind of underhanded deal," Mia said. "Let me assure you, primates everywhere are famous for that."

"Whatever the case," Dr. Chang said. "These Rebels are clearly more worried about their personal status than they are the safety of the Fleet."

"Yeah," I said, "that's how I see it, too."

No one said anything else for a time. There was little we could do about the situation, so we checked our instruments and waited. We'd been placed on scramble-alert, ready to fire out of *Killer's* launch bays the second we got the word.

It came at last, during the final hour of our shift. I'd almost nodded off when Mia sank a single, curved claw into my shoulder to wake me up.

I saw right away that the Rebel bait had worked—better than we'd expected. We'd been picking off local Imperial shipping in hopes of luring a full patrol here to defend them. We'd gotten our wish and then some.

"Chief!" Gwen shouted from her station at the main scanner interface. "Ships are pouring into the system—and they aren't ours!"

She gave me the coordinates while Samson geared up *Hammerhead* for launch.

"All fighters," Captain Ursahn's voice rang in our skulls, "prepare for launch. Signal your readiness to the CAG."

I glanced at Samson, who'd finished a final check. I signaled the CAG and leaned back.

Automatically, our pit folded open underneath us. We weren't using the big doors at the end of the hangar bay, but the launch tubes instead. We were lowered into the tube, lights flashing all around us.

Shaw contacted me as we sank into the floor. "Blake, I see you're eager as always. Please wait at your designated checkpoint until the full squadron can join you."

He didn't have to tell me that, but I acknowledged his order anyway. I'd begun to realize my crew's effectiveness in battle had gained us a reputation for being hard-charging and eager. I could have told them we were actually better disciplined than most—but that wouldn't have impressed this bunch, so I didn't waste my breath.

My heart pounded in my chest as we were shunted into the breach of what amounted to a giant cannon. The anti-grav systems were active, or we would have been crushed by the G-forces the cannon was about to apply to our tiny fighter.

The lights stopped whisking by for a second, and soon we were inside the barrel. Effectively, the launch system was a giant rail gun. Using powerful magnetics on *Hammerhead*'s tiny hull, it was designed to accelerate us to around twenty thousand miles per hour in about a second.

I knew we shouldn't feel anything when the launch system went off, but I braced myself anyway. My crewmen around me did the same, baring their teeth and squinching their eyes down to slits.

There was shaking, then a rumbling sound filled the fighter. For a split-second, everything went black. We were used to being able to see through the walls of the fighter, and the change was alarming.

We knew from experience it was because the barrel of the rail gun launcher didn't have any lights inside of it.

The barrel was rifled slightly for accurate fire, so we came out spinning hard. We were spinning so fast the stars resembled streaks of fire. I tried not to look at the twin white blazing suns which flashed around us in a corkscrew pattern.

"Counter that spin!" I shouted at Samson unnecessarily. He'd already activated the appropriate automated stabilizers.

He made no comment, other than to work his virtual touchscreens. We all had touchscreens—or what we sometimes called air-screens, because they appeared to hang in space around us.

Laying in a course toward our designated rendezvous point, I watched as our fighter slowed its corkscrew motion and arced gently toward our designated position. Behind me, I saw more fighters come out of an array of four stubby barrels. They fired in a rapid succession, like a Gatling gun.

Glowing blue streaks trailed each fighter as it poured out. Each tiny craft swung onto a new course as soon as it was able, banking to join its squadron at our checkpoint.

I made sure I applied no additional thrust, other than what the rail-gun had given me. We were one of the first fighters out of the gate, and I was going to have to linger and give the rest a chance to catch up.

This brief period gave me the opportunity to take stock of the situation directly. Reaching out with my perception system, I saw the bulk of the Fleet off to my starboard side and below us in angle.

The big ships were on the move, just as we were. They looked like a bunch of scrambling soldiers, puffing out fighters, dumping acceleration waves and maneuvering drastically.

Why should such a thing be necessary now? I asked myself in frustration. These captains had been waiting for this outcome, supposedly. Now that they were finally faced with the forceful response they'd hoped for, they seemed surprised and out of position. No Earth Navy would've been caught slouching like this.

Ahead of us—that was where it became interesting. Our fighter squadron was being deployed ahead of the main body of the fleet, that much was clear, because the enemy force had begun to appear there.

The stellar rips in space-time were numerous, and they all glowed with red fire. Wherever this opposing fleet was coming from, it had to be a single location.

"Dr. Chang, what are we facing?" I asked.

"I'm seeing two hundred fifty-six breaches. Not a single ship has come through yet in this region."

I nodded to myself. "They have to be Imperials," I said. "They know how to read a clock. Samson, all defenses forward."

"Active."

"Mia, gun-check."

"All green," she said. "Can I fire to be sure?"

I glanced at her. "Sure. Go ahead—but keep it to a short burst."

A pulsing streak of projectiles ripped ahead of us.

"Main gun ready. Wasps ready—can I fire off a few of them, too?"

"Negative. Let's save our ordnance for the enemy, huh?"

She pouted a bit, and I laughed.

"Don't worry," I said, "if we make it to their line at all, you'll get to fire every missile we have."

That brightened her expression.

"The enemy is coming through now, Chief!" Gwen said from the back.

I threw my attention forward again. Looking outside the ship, zooming toward a target with my mind, had become almost second-nature for me. That part of the Rebel training had been effective.

Two hundred and fifty-six rips in space all gave birth at once. Each of them emitted a single cruiser. I doubted a single Imperial ship had scattered. The Imperials didn't screw up like that.

"What have we got?" I asked Gwen.

"Cruisers, mostly. I'm seeing some bigger ships—battlecruisers. A few carriers are setting up in the back line...

Wait a minute… some of the rips are flickering like they're active, but I don't see anything coming through."

"Throw me the coordinates of one of them," I snapped quickly, already having a suspicion.

She did, and I saw the situation for myself. A rip in space tended to shimmer when a ship passed through it, and every one of the rips were reacting now. But the one she'd sent me wasn't showing any kind of silhouette slipping through.

"That's got to be a phase-ship," I said. "They're sliding through already phased. I didn't even know they could do that. Connect me up to Shaw, Gwen."

She worked the air with her fingertips, and Shaw answered.

"Don't get impatient, Blake," Shaw said. "The bulk of my fighters are right behind you."

"Sir," I said, "we've spotted breach points that show wavering radiation, but no visible ship coming through."

"What are you talking about?"

"I'll throw you a clip," I said, nodding to Samson.

He looked alarmed. He worked his fingers, but he shrugged helplessly.

"Dr. Chang?" I called to the back. "Could you pull that out of the stream?"

Dr. Chang did as I asked quickly. I tossed it to Shaw and waited for him to analyze it.

Soon, fighters were streaking by us. I put on a little gas, chasing after them. The latecomers were suddenly eager to get to our checkpoint before we did. Everything was a race with these people.

One fighter, however, didn't plunge ahead of us. It came up on my wing and stuck there. I didn't even have to look, knowing it was Ra-tikh.

"Blake?" Shaw asked. "I kicked that file up to the CAG. He said he's gotten two other reports, fleet-wide, of the phenomenon."

"It's a phase-ship, isn't it, sir?" I asked.

"I think it must be. But our knowledge of phase-ships indicates they can't do that. They can't come through a breach already in subspace. That's very strange—and worrisome."

"It's been a while since we've fought the Imperials, right Lieutenant?" I asked. "Maybe they've improved on their tech."

"Let's hope not, by the stars. We're outclassed as it is."

"But sir," I persisted. "We outnumber them by almost two to one. This is what the admirals wanted, isn't it?"

Shaw didn't say anything for a second. "We'd hoped for less opposition," he said at last, then cut the connection.

That last part worried me. Shaw hadn't sounded confident. He had sounded very concerned.

=32=

We massed up our fighter squadron in the assigned sector and once we were all there, we were given the go-ahead to attack.

The other two squadrons were given the same target, thank God. I hadn't wanted to fly into the teeth of an Imperial fleet with only my staunchest brothers on my flanks.

"Our mission is to swing out of the plane of battle and dive low," I told my people, showing them our orders as soon they were received by my command unit. "Then we'll reverse and come back up under their carriers. Those are our primary targets."

The Rebel Fleet commonly used concepts such as "low" and "high" despite the fact there was no such thing in space combat. As a matter of expediency, Command used a flat plane as a baseline for explaining battle positioning. It was artificial, but it helped many of the more primitive crews to cope with three-dimensional battles outside of their experience. They simply weren't used to fighting outside of their home planet's gravity-well.

My crew sighed with relief at the orders. Most of our fighter wings had been ordered to plunge directly into the teeth of the approaching fleet. We had a lot of fighters, about ten times as many as the enemy had, and our admirals had apparently decided to send them out as screens to give our bigger ships time to position themselves perfectly.

This made me grind my teeth. The waste was going to be tremendous. Sure, no one could have known *exactly* where the enemy would appear and have built a perfect formation to face them. But did that mean we had to throw away our fighters in an early, unsupported attack?

Reminding myself I wasn't brass, I banished such thoughts from my mind and kept pace with my swarming brothers. The squadron was plunging downward now, out of the line of fire in-between the two fleets.

We came to the low point all too quickly and had to turn upward again. The bulk of the enemy cruisers were now arrayed above us, forming an oval-shaped plane of ships. They were so tightly organized they looked like they were having a parade up there. My own squadron, in comparison, looked like a swarm of bees who didn't know where the flowers were. Similarly, our main fleet looked like a ragged line of charging warriors.

"Here we go," I told my people, "I'm ramping up for a high-speed pass. Since Shaw hasn't seen fit to give me a specific target, I'm going for the last carrier in the line."

"Chief!" Gwen shouted. "I'm tracking incoming fighter cover."

"Display them."

The air around me lit up. A squadron of interceptors had been deployed to guard the carriers' flank. We had to get through them first.

The Imperial fighters were quite different in design. They were much smaller craft, for one thing. I doubted they had a crew of more than two men each.

Dark and sleek, they looked more agile than our heavy fighters, if not as tough. If I had to guess, I would say they were designed to operate as short-range interceptors, meaning they were fighter-killers. That made good sense given the fact our Rebel forces had so many more fighters than the Imperials did.

"Shaw," I said, "do we fight them or punch straight through?" I asked.

"Fight them," he said. "If they get behind us, they'll melt us before we get close enough to fire on the carriers anyway."

I'd come to the same conclusion, but I'd wanted to hear it from him. A few moments later the squadron spread out and slowed down. We wanted to finish this in deep space. If we got closer to the main line of big ships, they could help the interceptors burn us down with their secondary weapons.

We met the interceptors at speed. Our main gun sprayed bright gushes of radiation, and Mia released her wasps in trios without asking. I didn't mind. She knew her job by now, and I had plenty to do just piloting.

Large shapes came out of nowhere a few seconds later. Two of our nearby fighters were instantly transformed into their component molecules.

"What the hell was that?" Samson demanded.

The answer came from Shaw to the entire squadron, even though he couldn't have heard Samson's question.

"They're firing magnetized kinetics. Start randomizing your positions and deploy countermeasures."

Kinetics were dumb-fire weapons that struck fighters without using AI and rocketry to guide them. They contained very powerful magnets and simply got in the way. When a small ship was moving at speed, hitting a flat rock was like hitting a brick wall.

Kinetics were hard to detect, but deadly when the targets made their intended course obvious—as we'd done.

"Turn on our magnetic sensors, full amplification!" I demanded.

Gwen did as I asked, and a wave of incoming projectiles appeared. I danced our fighter with violent movements. We were going so fast, escape was largely going to be luck, but I worked the controls anyway. If nothing else, it made me feel better about facing death.

Three more of our fighters vanished before we closed with the enemy. We were now outnumbered and shaken up.

Some of our pilots panicked at this point and broke off from the core of our squadron. Pairs of Imperials, moving like smooth predators, swung after these stragglers and began to destroy them.

"Ra-tikh, stay on my wing!" I said.

Technically, I had little grounds to give him orders, but he followed them anyway. Maybe he was beginning to believe in me.

We plunged after a pair of Imperials who had run down one of our fighters. Even as they riddled the hapless ship with close-range fire, we came in blazing. Ra-tikh and I both concentrated on one fighter, then the other. They both blew up with a satisfying puff of decompressing gas and plasma.

Our move hadn't gone unnoticed, unfortunately. More enemy fighters peeled away from the main force and chased us. We did a stunning turn-around, a maneuver that would have killed a pilot without an anti-grav field, but it only served to leave us facing nine incoming enemy interceptors.

"Mia, stop firing that cannon!" I ordered. "Release a cloud of wasps instead. Samson, full forward defenses."

Ra-tikh mimicked my moves. We survived the pass, but we took hits and I heard a hiss in the back.

"We've got a breach," Gwen said.

"I'm on it," Samson said, climbing out of his harness and drifting back to the aft region with a patch in his hand.

Taking a chance, I swung toward the core of the squad which was fighting in a tangled mess with the Imperials. Getting caught isolated from our comrades again would be deadly. We'd used up most of our limited supply of countermeasures.

I was hoping the nine fighters we'd slipped past would seek an easier target, but it wasn't to be. Either they were raging because we'd nailed their buddies, or they'd decided we were still their easiest prey.

They did a one-eighty and plunged after us. They accelerated so smoothly, so powerfully, that I felt outclassed by them for the first time. They were going to catch us before I could rejoin the mass of Shaw's squadron.

Looking around desperately, I saw a group of six of our allied fighters standing off from the battle. They were hanging there, at range, barely firing at the enemy interceptors and refusing to engage with the maelstrom in front of them.

Narrowing my eyes, I veered toward them.

"Dalton," I called, contacting my wingman's pilot. "You see that bunch—the ones farting around at the rear of the battle?"

"...yes... What's the call, Chief?"

Dalton sounded like he was nervous, and he had good reason to be.

"Let's head straight into that group of laggers. They can either help us, or they can eat these nine interceptors for breakfast."

"Roger that."

We swung around and flew right toward the chicken group. They didn't do anything for a few seconds. The enemy interceptors meanwhile were poking at our tails with laser-fire. Two more holes were punched through *Hammerhead*'s ass despite the fact Samson was dumping aerogels in our wake. Once they caught up to us, they'd take us out fast.

Finally, the laggers woke up to the fact we were bringing the fight to them. They had two choices: they could run, in which case Ra-tikh and I were toast. The problem with that plan was the fact nine interceptors were almost certainly going to chase down the laggers next, as they would be nearby and separated from the core battle.

Their second option was to join the fight. That's what they chose to do, fortunately. As a single coherent team, they approached us, firing at the interceptors on my tail.

The battle was fierce, but it was decisive. We whirled and joined in before the end. Our heavy fighters pounded the interceptors, who were faced with head-on fire.

Maybe the Imperial pilots had made a mistake, I reflected when it was over. They'd been so angry, so determined to kill Ra-tikh and I, that they'd plowed into a head-on stream of projectiles and radiation.

Whatever the case, we killed all nine with only one lost ship. Our chicken-shit friends were down to five ships, rather than six. It was hard to feel too sorry for them.

"Incoming communication request," Gwen said.

"From the laggers?"

"Right."

I displayed the face that appeared in front of me for everyone aboard to see.

It was ugly, it was bug-like, and I was pretty sure it was angry. It was hard to tell for sure, though.

How were you supposed to know if a flesh-beetle was glaring at you or not?

=33=

Although I'd had a couple of run-ins with the beetles, I'd never actually talked to one of them. I found myself looking forward to the experience as I banked my fighter and headed back toward the rest of the Squadron.

"Chief," I said, greeting the hideous face that hung in the air before me. "Thanks for helping me defeat those Imperials."

"Your gratitude is not helpful," the being said. "We've lost a ship. A full crew of five died due to your actions."

"Yes, but we destroyed nine of the enemy, and both of my ships are intact. That sounds like a bargain to me."

The bug looked at me for a second. I wasn't sure if he was thinking over my statement, or what.

"Again, you fail to grasp the obvious," he said at last. "Your actions have caused five of the Chosen to die. This is unacceptable."

I was beginning to lose interest, so I cut the channel. Ahead of us, Shaw's group seemed to be winning the battle. We'd lost about half of our total fighters—a grim price—but we'd won through. Our heavier ships were better able to face the interceptors when they stayed together and fought in formation.

"Chief..." Samson said, "the bugs are swinging around and pulling up behind us. They're right on our tails."

"Good," I said. "Maybe they've learned they can't sit this battle out."

He shook his head. "I don't think that's what's going on in their bug-brains."

I glanced over the incoming data, and my victorious smirk transformed into a frown. "What the hell... they're lighting us up?"

"They've got a target lock, Chief," Gwen said.

"Permission to deploy defenses aft, sir," Samson said.

I shook my head in disbelief. "They won't shoot at the enemy, but they're willing to blast our tails off for bringing the fight to them? What selfish pricks."

Samson shrugged. "They do look more like cockroaches than anyone else in the Fleet."

"Reconnect me with that bug," I ordered.

A moment later the air in front of my eyes glowed. Chief Super-ugly worked his mouth-parts at me.

"Chief, we're not the enemy," I told him. "Firing on my ship would be a violation of Rebel Law."

"We're examining that right now," he replied. "That's the only reason we haven't dismantled you yet."

"What's your problem, bug?" I demanded. "You sat back and let the others do your fighting for you. That's cowardice, plain and simple. Now, because we needed help and brought the fight to you, you're contemplating treachery. Just what kind of a race of cowards are you people?"

"We are the Chosen. We are the last. By logic and law, we are more valuable beings than you are."

My eyes squinched together in confusion, but I thought I understood what this roach was talking about.

"You mean you think that because your population took a hit, you're more important than the rest of us?"

"You state the obvious. Our estimations of your intellectual capacity are improving."

"Great. Okay bug, here's what I think: you're arrogant and selfish. Those traits aren't all that unusual for anyone of Kher descent, but you've taken it to an extreme. Plenty of the combatants here have lost their home world."

"That is undoubtedly true," the bug said, "but we aren't concerned with the reproductive lines of the non-Chosen."

"Well, I'm becoming less and less concerned with your continued existence as well. Go back to your dim red sun and the rock circling it, if you want to."

The bug began to explain to me how that was technically impossible, and to suggest I was some variety of idiot for mentioning such a line of action. Clearly, bugs didn't have a good grasp of sarcasm.

I disconnected. "Watch them," I told Samson and Mia. "If they fire on us, shoot back without hesitation."

Our return to Shaw's squadron was tense, but we made it without taking a beam in the backside.

Shaw didn't talk to us right away, he was too busy giving the entire squadron orders.

"Pilots," Shaw said, addressing the entire squadron, "that was a miserable performance. We outweighed and outgunned the enemy. We should have destroyed those interceptors with few losses. If you all stay together and hold your formations, we'll do much better when we hit the carriers."

There were some grumbled complaints, but no one swung their ships around to run. Such poor discipline made me sick. These people weren't real military, we were more like a band of gangsters or Apache warriors. Individual crews were often brave enough in their own right, but the squadron hadn't yet gelled into a determined force.

Lt. Shaw lit up the target, the closest of the carriers. We applied thrust and approached in a parabolic formation, giving everyone a free range of fire.

Long before we reached effective range, defensive fire began coming at us from the enemy vessel. She was big and ugly—possibly even uglier than *Killer*. She had bulbous projections that extended from the forward part of the craft in a trio. It made the carrier look like a shark with three snouts.

"I see them firing something out of those large forward cannons," Gwen said, her eyes glued to the scope. "I… I think those must be launch bays. They're deploying more interceptors."

"Great," I said, "hold your fire, everyone. We're way too far out."

Around us other fighter pilots weren't so professional. They beamed radiation and fired wasps at the looming ship. Shaw soon shouted at them, pointing out they hadn't been given the all-clear to shoot yet.

"Blake?" he called to me. "Take point on the first run."

"Me sir?" I asked, my heart sinking.

"Yes. You can thank me for the honor later. I was very impressed with the way you took out that hunter-killer group, then rounded up the straggling beetles."

I puffed out my cheeks and shook my head. I thought about telling him the beetles were contemplating waxing my ass for my heroic efforts, but I passed on the idea.

"I'll need two more wingmen, Lieutenant," I said.

He chewed that over then ordered two ships to join me on the front lines. Together, four fighters accelerated toward the looming carrier.

The Imperial ship hadn't been slacking. They'd pumped out a new, small group of defensive fighters and begun firing radiation cannons that beamed short, accurate bursts in our direction. One of my assigned wingmen was dead before we reached effective range.

Just as we got within shooting distance, the big ship powered up her shields. They were bluish in color and looked like a nimbus around a cloud that's slipped between the sun and the eye of the beholder.

The incoming fire ceased as the carrier wasn't configured to fire at us with her deflection shields up, but we still had her deployed fighters to deal with.

The enemy captain's plan was clear. He would sit inside the safety of his shields to see how his interceptors did. Already, Imperial gunships were detaching from the main battle lines ahead and approaching to defend the carriers. They'd called for help, and we didn't have much time.

"We're only going to get one shot at this big bastard," Shaw said. "Let's do what we came for—make an attack run at her core, strike amidships. Enough damage there will buckle the shields."

Superimposed on my vision, the carrier now had a red circle low and in the central belly region. That was our target, and I dove low to come up and get a focused shot at the monster's gut.

The defending fighter group didn't go for my team. They'd decided the rest of the squadron was a bigger threat, and so they roared out to meet them.

"We've got a chance," I said. "Stay together and fire together. Everyone on that target on my mark. Three… two… one… mark!"

We blazed furiously at the weak point in the enemy defenses that Shaw had designated. Behind us, the rest of the squad tangled with the interceptors and broke through. They poured on fire as well.

The tactic worked, and the bluish-silver shielding flickered. I could see sparking strikes were getting through, melting the hull underneath and making it run like dark wax.

Suddenly, the central module of the big ship imploded. It was the strangest thing I'd ever seen. One second, she was there taking fire, and the next the belly folded in on itself like a crushed can. After compressing inwardly for a second, the reaction reversed in a larger, brighter explosion outward. The hull had been compromised, and the gasses inside the vessel were gushing out into space.

The running lights on the carrier went out. She wasn't completely destroyed, but she'd been knocked out of the fight. The shield flickered and died.

"Let's finish her," I said, swinging my group around for another run.

"Squadron," Shaw said before we were half-way turned around for the next run. "We're being recalled. All fighters return to *Killer*. CAG's orders."

"Fuck!" Samson yelled. "All this and they call us off? The Imperials will repair this monster and we'll have to fight her again."

I couldn't argue with him. "Orders are orders," I said, "Dr. Chang, plot me a safe course back to our carrier."

Samson stared at me, shaking his head. "No one else in this outfit follows orders. Why should we?"

He had a point. The bugs were already leading the pack away from the battle. A few other fighters were dog-fighting with interceptors or making runs at the crippled carrier.

I sucked in a breath and contacted Ra-tikh with my sym.

"What do you think?" I asked him. "Should we obey Shaw or destroy this carrier?"

"Shaw can mate with his own tail," Ra-tikh said. "I vote we destroy the enemy while it is weak and helpless."

"One more attack run," I said. "Let's hit that damaged belly-region again."

It took a full minute to swing under the big ship and come at her from the right angle, but the results were magnificent. The carrier was torn apart and pieces went spinning off into the void.

"We must have nailed her core," Mia said, awestruck. "That was glorious."

Her predator side was enamored. It almost made me shiver. Most humans showed at least a fraction of remorse after inflicting mass casualties. But Mia's kind was different. Killing obviously gave her great pleasure. Her big eyes glowed as she soaked in the destruction she'd helped cause.

"Wingmen, stay with me," I told my group. "Let's head home."

=34=

We were far from safe. The battle was effectively over, and it had ended in defeat, despite our best efforts.

The Rebel Fleet was pulling out, retreating. We'd done well against the Imperial carriers, and there were other bright spots, but the overall battle had gone badly.

The massed Imperials had focused firepower in coordinated strikes. They'd methodically destroyed ship after ship, and their tight formations had interlocked their shields, making our weapons less effective.

From what I could gather from the chaos, the enemy phase-ships had broken our front lines first, then the concentrated fire of the highly organized fleet had done the rest. The enemy had broken us.

As we zoomed away from the drifting wreck of the carrier we'd gutted, we had the chance to see the reality of the situation. The battle was turning into a rout, and even now it was sinking into a disaster.

Instead of retreating in an organized fashion, the Rebel captains all tried to save themselves. There was no thought of covering for the wounded to escape first. As soon as any ship was able to open a stellar rip it plunged into it and vanished, leaving their comrades behind. The ever-shrinking circle of survivors was blasted to pieces by concentrated Imperial fire.

"Chief!" Gwen called to me. "Interceptors on our six!"

I used my sym to perceive what followed. After counting nineteen of the sleek little fighters, I stopped bothering. If they caught up to us, we were doomed.

Already, they were peppering us with low-powered strikes. We were inside their maximum effective range.

Fortunately, most of my fellow wingmen had enough defensive systems left to survive these pinpricks to our tails—but not *Hammerhead*. She was a good, tough little ship, but she'd taken too much abuse today.

"We've got two more hull breaches," Samson said, moving around with the patches.

"Get them sealed up," I ordered pointlessly.

"We're out of nanite juice. We're out of everything."

Mia was the only happy member of my crew left aboard. She fired her cannon continuously. She was breathing hard and seemed oblivious to the fact we were doomed.

Looking ahead, I gave it everything our engine had. If we could make it back to our carriers—any carrier—I'd jump into the first hangar I found and take my chances.

But it wasn't to be. The engine shivered, setting up a grim vibration that made my butt hurt right through my seat, the padding and my spacer's suit.

"What's the situation?" I demanded.

"I think we're losing the engine," Dr. Chang said. "Performance is down by thirty-nine percent."

Sure enough, our acceleration arc was falling. We weren't slowing down as there was no air-pressure to put drag on our ship, but we couldn't push any faster. The enemy interceptors were still gaining.

Then the ship to my side blew up. Most of the incoming fire had been targeting her. They'd all died in an instant.

Now, the enemy turned their guns on us, the next easiest target.

I was gritting my teeth, an instant from flipping around and charging into their faces. My only hope was to ram one and take him down with me—but then, I got an idea.

"Team, keep running," I told Ra-tikh and the rest. "We're breaking off. They'll probably follow us, as we're wounded."

Ra-tikh took a moment to manifest into my mind by way of his sym-link. He nodded to me.

"You spread your scent so the predators follow," he said. "An honorable effort. You will be remembered in our dreams."

Before I could answer, he cut off the channel. We were alone.

Well, not quite alone. We still had a pack of angry interceptors on our tails.

My idea was a simple one, but it was very risky. Our carriers had been in the rear of our formation, so they were too far away to shield us. I had to find a closer refuge. Instead of trying to reach a carrier, I headed toward one of our damaged ships that was trying to escape.

Banking sharply and working the shivering engine to its breaking point, I streaked toward a nearby destroyer. She was running, just like the rest of them. Locked in a struggle with a larger heavy cruiser, she had no chance, and her captain had decided to open a rip in space to exit the battle.

Under my guiding hands, *Hammerhead* plunged directly toward this flux zone. It was a crazy thing to do, I knew that. Fighters weren't built to go through hyperspace alone. The hulls hadn't been designed for it, and we had none of the physics-stabilization systems aboard that would help us keep our form.

But there wasn't anything else I could do. We had no better chance to live.

When we got close to the big ships, it seemed like we shrank. Our fighter was tiny in comparison. We were like a gnat zipping between battling titans.

Any of them could have fired upon us, destroying us, but they were all too busy hacking away on a bigger prize.

Mia had stopped firing her cannon. She was out of missiles, and her main gun was either damaged or overheated. She climbed to my seat and wrapped an arm around my neck. I let her do it, as we were probably all dead anyway.

In the last moments before we plunged into the plasma-edged rift, I had the opportunity to look down at the inhabited planet we'd been protecting.

The world had joined the Rebel cause and provided us with fresh crews. Now, they were paying a gruesome price. As I watched, gravity-bombs fell and their bright, flat cities were sucked up, drawing all the local mass into a conical shape. New dark mountains appeared at every population center.

When we hit the rift, I let out a roar of defiance—but I didn't hear any sound. I couldn't see much, either. Then there was a dim glow around me, coming from beyond our thin hull. I could hear and see again, but it seemed like every subsystem on our ship had been switched off.

"Dr. Chang…" I said, my voice sounding loud in the sudden, eerie silence. "Are we dead?"

"Probably," he replied calmly. "We can't hear our ship, that much I know. Does that mean it doesn't exist, or that it has ceased to operate? I have no idea."

"I'm getting some instrument readings," Gwen said. "The central computer appears to be rebooting. There's no output from the engine. No emissions at all. Nothing is exiting our central mass."

I looked around at our instruments. We appeared to be drifting. Outside the transparent parts of *Hammerhead*'s hull, there were no more stars. There weren't any bright lights either though.

There was nothing but a faint, variegated grayness. It was as if we'd been becalmed in an endless underground river, encapsulated by fog.

Before I could open my mouth to ask another question, the journey was over. We'd leapt a great distance. One lightyear or a thousand—I had no idea which, and I wasn't sure that it mattered.

When we came out of the rift on the far side, the sudden reappearance of stars took me by surprise. It shouldn't have, but it did. I chalked it up to a lack of experience on my part.

When we reappeared in normal space, we were thrown into a spin. Possibly, part of our propulsion system had been operating while we were transiting the rift. Or maybe we'd come out with our engines thrusting unevenly. Whatever the case, I fought the controls.

"Chief!" Gwen called out. "We're going to ram the destroyer!"

I envisioned it the second she spoke. My sym cast to my mind the location of the starship, and it was a good thing my sym was on the ball. We were still spinning, and evasive action on my part was desperate.

Accelerating out of the spin, *Hammerhead* did a sickening double-backflip before I could level her off. We slid by the destroyer's belly. It was so close the big ship's shields flickered and sparked.

With a sick sigh of relief, I leaned back from the controls.

"We're clear," I said. "Hail the captain of that ship."

A moment later, an amused alien-looking face regarded me. I had him pegged as some kind of desert-dwelling reptile the moment I saw him.

"Captain Behir of *Talon* here," he said. "You're a crazy pilot, even for a primate."

"Thanks. Have you got a fix on the location of *Killer*?" I asked him. "We're part of her 2nd squadron."

Behir made an odd, huffing sound. Laughter, maybe?

"We don't have a fix on anything, Chief," he said. "Take a look around—we've scattered."

For the first time, I cast my perception far and wide in this new system.

I saw an F-class star, hot and white—but it was a long way off. There were no planets nearby and no other starships. Nothing, not even dust.

His words sank in, and I began to worry.

Scattered, I thought to myself. It was the whispered doom-word of everyone in the Fleet. Always, there was the possibility a given ship might miss a jump, lose its fellows and end up somewhere in deep space, alone.

Under the best of conditions, scattering could happen to any starship on any jump. In this case, it was far more likely. We'd horned into a rift built by *Talon*, a risky move at best. But because the starship had opened the rift in a panic, without communicating with her sister ships, she'd been almost bound to scatter. Hell, Captain Behir might not have known where to jump to in the first place. I wouldn't put it past the Rebel admirals to have no contingency plan in case disaster struck.

Turning back to the thing on the screen, I forced a smile.

"Well then," I said brightly. "Looks like we're going to have to become best friends."

Captain Behir looked at me dubiously, but he didn't argue. I took that as a plus.

=35=

Captain Behir signed off after telling us to come aboard at our leisure. Unfortunately, we never got the chance to accept his invitation.

"Chief," Dr. Chang said. "You'd better take a look behind us."

I would have done as he suggested, but there was something going on directly ahead that I was more concerned about.

What I saw was the receding fantail of the destroyer, *Talon*.

"How can we dock with them when they're running off like that?" Mia demanded.

"It doesn't make sense…" I said.

"Chief, check your six—" Dr. Chang said, but he broke off.

Just then a huge shadow flew by us. It was a ship, a starship, and it was much larger than our ship or *Talon*. It bore the distinctive emblem of the Imperials.

I'd seen the symbol before. To me, it looked like a golden ribcage on a circular field of red. But I'd never seen one this close.

As I dove *Hammerhead* away from the hulking enemy, Samson didn't have to be told to engage every defensive measure we had left.

"It's the enemy heavy cruiser," Gwen said, "it must have come after *Talon* through the rift."

"The commander must be crazy," I said, staring. "The rift is almost gone."

"No crazier than we were trying to navigate it in a fighter," Dr. Chang pointed out.

"It's got to be the same ship that was fighting *Talon* in the battle," I said. "At least it's ignoring us for now."

The ship shifted course in an arc to follow *Talon*, increasing speed. Fire leapt out, digitally enhanced by my sym for my senses, which weren't sensitive enough to detect radiation outside the normal visible range.

The two ships were already pounding one another. They were locked in combat. Missiles flared, shields flashed and beams of deadly radiation criss-crossed the void between them.

"I'll try to give us some room between *Hammerhead* and this new fight," I said, turning away.

We whirled around sickeningly and inverted. The heavy cruiser was now on the other side of our last few operating deflector shields.

Even as I did so, it occurred to me that escaping the cruiser would be pointless. We were trapped in deep space. Without the destroyer to hitch a ride home with, we would soon die out here. No fuel, no food, no water other than emergency rations that would run out in about a week. The air might run out even before that. The carbon-scrubbers were running constantly, but they weren't the best.

The heavy cruiser plunged past us intent on its prey. We weren't even worthy of notice.

"Drop our shields," I ordered Samson.

He looked at me as if I was crazy, and he had a good point.

"Now," I ordered, "we're only wasting power. If they fire one of those cannons at us, we'll be blown right out of the sky anyway."

Reluctantly, he powered down his defenses and slumped back in his seat. "What are we going to do, Chief?"

Instead of answering, I banked and pulled a hard U-turn. We managed it because we weren't going very fast yet. The faster you went in space—or anywhere else—the longer it took to turn around and go the other way.

Fortunately, *Hammerhead* was quick on her feet. We were zooming after the cruiser seconds later.

"You're going to attack?" Gwen cried out. "You're crazy!"

"*This* is the way to die!" Mia said with a display of long, white teeth. "You should have been born on Ral, Leo."

"He's not crazy," Dr. Chang informed Gwen. "Our situation is grim. If the cruiser wins this fight, we'll die out here anyway."

"Mia, hold your fire until we're inside her exhaust plume. Then, burn her engines to slow her down."

"Not a winning tactic," Dr. Chang said, changing his mind. "If you do slow them down, they'll certainly destroy us."

I shook my head. "I never said we were going to survive this. The least we can do is give the destroyer a chance to run. She can't beat this behemoth—she's outclassed."

It was all true, and I saw the brief flare of hope that had blossomed in their eyes fade. I wasn't trying to save them—I was trying to die well.

Only Mia was happy. She grinned and sighted her weapon, intent on giving the big ship a sharp jab in the butt. Live or die, all she wanted to do was fight.

We got close, I'll give us that much. We reached the exhaust plume and plunged into it. When the streaming radiation bathed our ship, the number of rads entering the cabin shot up, causing the dosage counters to beep in panic.

Mia started firing. She'd already locked onto her target—but unfortunately, so had the crew of the cruiser.

A big ship like the enemy vessel wasn't without smaller weapons. Many of them were pointed forward as heavy cruisers were attack ships. But she had defensive armament on her stern as well.

Red flashes impinged on my senses for a fraction of a second, and just like that, we were hit hard.

Hammerhead went into a tumble. I lost the main engine, and since it powered everything else, the fighter went dark.

"Emergency power!" I ordered.

Samson battled his sudden weight. We were being spun around, thrown hard against the hull. Reaching up with trembling fingers, he strained with all his strength.

I was impressed as I could hardly move.

He managed to touch the proper control, and the anti-grav system came back on. We came away from the walls puking and bloody.

Dr. Chang was unconscious. Mia had suffered broken ribs. One of Gwen's eyes was bloodshot and half-closed. There was blood on her cheek.

"Good job, Samson," I gasped. "Turn off everything except for basic life-support and the anti-grav. We have to play dead now and hope for the best."

Spinning still, we drifted away from the ship we'd dared to attack. The cruiser roared after the destroyer, not bothering to waste any further time on our wrecked fighter.

I used my sym to reach out and watch the uneven battle that ensued. There was nothing else to do other than nurse one another and patch holes in our leaking hull.

When the big ships were far away, nearly an AU distant, the struggle ended. Captain Behir had run the entire time, firing what he had and using his stern defenses doggedly—but it was no good.

Without mercy, the Imperial cruiser blasted *Talon* apart.

By that time, we had everyone aboard breathing again and patched with flesh-growing bandages. We'd also managed to get the ship to stop spinning with careful squirts from our steering jets.

"Okay," I said, watching the destroyer break apart in the distance. "Time to play dead again."

"Why bother?" Gwen asked. "You said it yourself, we'll suffocate out here."

"We can't fight," I said. "So this is about grim choices. Do you want to die now or a week from now?"

She stared at me as if thinking it over, then she punched off her systems angrily.

Samson killed the emergency power—everything. The tiny ship went dark, and we floated.

Easing myself back into my chair, I looked out through *Hammerhead*'s walls at the patchwork of stars. Back home on Earth, they'd always fascinated me, these distant pinpoints of light. High in the Rocky Mountains of Colorado, where I'd grown up, the stars were often spectacular. The heavens back then had looked the way they were supposed to look, like the playground of gods.

But from space—open, deep space—the view was even better. A velvety black expanse with a thousand glowing lights moving slowly across it. The cold, glittering stars were perfect tiny fires, and there were literally millions of them that my eye could pick out with the help of my sym.

"Chief?" whispered Samson several minutes later. "Where's the cruiser?"

I looked at him and smiled. I'd forgotten about our nemesis. Casting in the right direction, I spotted her.

She was growing larger. The exhaust behind her flared. She was thrusting in our direction. She'd taken the time—and probably a lot of fuel too—just to turn around.

Why was the captain of that ship working so hard to come back here and check on our dead little scrap of metal and flesh? Were they angry? Curious? Or only obsessively thorough?

It hardly mattered. I chuckled aloud.

Samson looked at me with hungry eyes. He wanted to know his fate—or at least, he thought he did.

"They're gone, big guy," I said. "Take a nap."

He smiled at me, and I knew I'd told him the right lie. The one he wanted to hear. The one that gave him hope that this nightmare had passed.

At least he could die now with this one last moment of peace in his memory.

=36=

When the heavy cruiser loomed near, I wondered what they were waiting for. We were running on nothing but suit power. Surely, we had to be in easy range now. We were sitting ducks.

Like a lion prodding prey that plays dead, the big ship circled around. They were scanning us. My sym showed me lavender waves crisscrossing our hull.

I thought of various plans. Perhaps we could get close enough and magnetically adhere to her hull. Then, her crew would have a choice. If they came out to pry us out of the fighter, we could blow up the ship in a final act of defiance.

On the other hand, there was a remote chance that they'd ignore us and simply create a new rift. We'd tag along, and take our chances wherever we ended up.

Impatiently, I waited for an opportunity to make such a maneuver. But the enemy pilot was cagey, and he never got close enough for me to try it.

Finally, I grew irritated. "Samson, turn on our com system," I ordered.

"You're going to talk shit to them, aren't you?" Mia purred.

She loved it when I spat at defeat. No wonder we'd gotten along so well. She'd never heard of the concept of diplomacy. It wasn't in her genes.

"Yeah," I said. "Something like that."

Samson lit up the com system, and a funny thing happened. A repeating message came booming over the speakers.

"...trying our patience, pilot," said a voice. It was a commanding feminine voice. "This is your last opportunity to—"

"Hello?" I said. "This is Ensign Leo Blake, Earth crew."

"Blake..." she said. "I don't know you. A pity. I thought I knew all the brave ones that remained. You disappoint me greatly. This kill will bring no honor."

My mind raced. This had to be an Imperial. What would they be like? I'd talked to the officers aboard *Killer*, and my impression was that they were quite similar in mindset to Wild Kher. Except that they were infinitely more arrogant.

But I'd learned how the status-based civilization of the Rebels worked. If the Imperials worked the same way, I had at least an inkling as to how to proceed.

"Not so," I said. "Your kill has brought you great honor. My ship personally destroyed one of your carriers."

There was a moment of silence.

"Your claims are incredible," she said. "But I've checked, and according to reports that came in during the... 'battle', if you wish to call it that, a few carriers were destroyed."

"Exactly. By heavy fighters. *My* heavy fighter in fact, supported by *my* squadron, did the deed."

"Hmmm..." she said. "This does change matters. If you are truly—"

"I am," I snapped. "I would have destroyed your vessel, if I'd had a dozen wingmen to help."

She laughed then. "Such boasting! I like it. You will be fun to destroy and not as worthless to my records as I'd thought. Thank you for this—"

"Thanks are not good enough," I interrupted. "Neither is your limited understanding of your own interests."

"What? Insults now? On top of—?"

"Hardly. I'm trying to help. I'll speak slowly, so as to make sure you understand. I've been told Imperials are slow to grasp unfamiliar concepts."

I was getting urgent cautioning gestures from my crew by now, except for Dr. Chang, who watched with thoughtfulness, and Mia, who watched with glee.

Turning away from them so I couldn't see their frantic waving, I stared at the big ship that stood off at a safe distance, watching us.

"You will pay for your insults," the voice warned dangerously. "Enjoy your final moments—"

"How can I pay further?" I laughed. "You're going to blast me out of space, right? How unimaginative. How wasteful. I hadn't believed my officers, but now you're proving their points one after another."

"What points?" the voice demanded loudly. "What might be gained by doing anything other than destroying you instantly, you insect?"

"First off," I said calmly, a grin spreading over my face. I knew when a mark was taking the bait. This captain was mean, but she reminded me of petty bureaucrats everywhere. "You're missing a grand opportunity. I'm not just a fighter pilot, I'm a Rebel hero. You could capture me and parade me at your base. You could—"

"Ah!" the voice said suddenly. "I get it. Public dismemberment! The acid baths! The genital mutilation! You crave treatment beyond your station, insect."

For just a second, I was at a loss as to what to say. I'd been envisioning the life of a beaten hero. A prize to be shown off in a sumptuously appointed prison cell, perhaps.

"Uh… right," I said. "Perhaps not that, although—"

"You've convinced me," she said. "Stand-to as we lock onto your vessel. If you attempt to escape the gravity beams, or even power up your ship, you'll be instantly destroyed."

The channel fell silent, and a liquid-looking beam of sickly green reached out, enveloping our tiny ship. Only I could see it with the aid of my improved perception.

"*This* was your plan?" Gwen demanded. "Genital mutilation?"

"She's just trying to scare us," I assured her.

"Well, it's working."

I looked around the group. "Who votes we blow ourselves up when we're sucked into their hull?" I asked.

They looked trapped and indecisive.

"I do," Mia said, going first.

Gwen shook her head, breathing hard.

"No," she said. "Let's take our chances. Perhaps imprisonment won't be as awful as she said. Maybe we'll get lucky. We've come so far…"

"Yeah," Samson said. "Maybe they'll only mutilate Leo."

"You really want to surrender?" I asked him.

He looked at me for a second and shook his head. "Nah, I'm with Mia. Blow us up. Blow this ship's guts out."

Already, beyond our thin hull, I could see the yawning portal we were being drawn into. It looked small from where we were, but it was rapidly growing in size.

"Dr. Chang?" I asked.

He squinted at me thoughtfully. "I'll go with your instincts, Leo," he said. "So far, they've been exceptional. Besides, you'll do whatever you want in the final instant, anyway.'"

I smiled at him. Perhaps, in the end, he knew me better than the rest of them.

"We'll die then," I said, "the moment they suck us up inside their ship."

Samson and I worked on rigging it up. The plan was to power up the core briefly, overload it, and set it off. The process would take no more than a millisecond. We wouldn't feel a thing.

With one finger on a pressure-switch, I watched as we drifted closer and closer. The moment was almost upon us.

I discovered then that blowing yourself up is much harder to do than it sounds. Your mind fights against it. You come up with a thousand excuses to avoid going through with it.

I'd always wondered, when watching vids of people wait for their executions, why they weren't struggling, howling, fighting to the last.

Now, I knew. It was a sense of unreality. A moment of futile hope that wouldn't recede. I was mesmerized, trading obedience for one last second of life, one final lungful of air…

=37=

When we passed through the shimmering shields and into the armored hull, I pressed the self-destruct button—then I did it again.

Nothing happened. I sat back, defeated.

"They drained our power somehow," Samson said. "The core is empty. There isn't enough left to light a candle."

Nodding, I knew the truth of his words. It made perfect sense. The Imperials weren't stupid, no matter what I'd implied. They would never snuggle with a viper without being certain its fangs had been pulled first.

"Assault weapons," I said, "get your thumpers out!"

My crew looked startled for a moment. Then they scrambled to obey. We pulled out the graviton thumpers we'd won back aboard our carrier and checked them. They were loaded and ready to go.

The sickly green beam pulled us into the guts of the cruiser and set us on the deck. We had gravity again—it was artificial, but it felt good to be on steady feet.

Everyone was locked and loaded. We aimed at the hatch.

Outside *Hammerhead*, we saw a delegation approach. Six hulking brutes in body armor clanked in the lead. Behind them walked a very different figure.

She was tall, fine-boned, and lovely. Her clothing was spare, but what she wore was regal and flowing. There was a hard cast to her features, however. A stern, unsmiling look that I knew instantly was capable of evil deeds. To me, she looked like a devilish queen.

Could this be the captain?

"Do we fight?" Samson said, gripping and regripping his thumper.

"Yeah," I said. "Might as well. Take out the tin cans in front. If we can capture the captain, maybe we can—"

The hatch blew off and clanged down onto the deck at that moment. One of the metal-encased guards had done it.

Startled, my crew didn't need any more urging after that. They fired their weapons. Five gravity grenades flew out, thumping and clanging on the deck like ball bearings. They went off a second later, surprising the enemy.

All six of the armored hulks crumpled, crushed inward by the sudden intense weight of the very armor they wore.

We leapt out of the ship, spraying disruptor fire at those of the enemy who were still struggling to rise or lift a weapon. They shuddered in agony.

The captain's fine hand twitched then, and we all fell onto our faces.

I couldn't move. My body felt as if it had gone to sleep. Every limb tingled with numbness, even my cheeks were numb. My eyes were locked open and unable to blink.

The captain walked near to stand over me. My eyes couldn't even close to shut out her image. They were beginning to sting, but I was helpless.

She examined me closely.

"Allow me to introduce myself," she said calmly. "I'm Captain Lael, Rebel. Welcome aboard my ship *Splendor*."

She looked at me expectantly, but of course I couldn't move or speak.

"Ah, not in talkative mood? We'll fix that soon enough."

My eyes shifted to a wand-like device she was holding. I could swivel my eyeballs now, but not blink. Tears ran down my face.

She held her wand close to my face. I wanted to shy away, or even just to close my eyes, but I couldn't.

"This is a neural paralyzer," she said, holding the thin metal rod an inch from my left eye. "I considered using it the moment you came aboard, but I wanted to gauge your responses first. I'm impressed. You attacked without hesitation. It's the same vicious behavior pattern you exhibited when you shot-up my ship's stern."

I looked up at her, and she stared back curiously. I felt some of the numbness wear off, allowing me to blink. That was a relief.

Captain Lael was lovely, in an ethereal way. She didn't look quite human. She looked... *beyond* human. Her limbs were all shapely, though slightly elongated. Her cheekbones were high, her chin narrow, her ears small and perfectly shaped.

Her eyes were the most enchanting part. I'd met a thousand women who spent time in front of a mirror every day to make their eyes look like that—but she wasn't wearing any makeup at all.

"You're an interesting specimen," she said. "I don't think I've encountered your type before. Very much like an Imperial, but squatty and built with dense bones... there's so much body hair..."

Captain Lael spread her long fingers over my scalp. They were cool to the touch.

"The cranium appears to be small," she said, "but not so small as to suggest impairment."

More armored soldiers had appeared by this time. I could see them as I could now move my eyes freely. The paralysis effect was slowly wearing off.

"I'm intrigued," the captain said, standing again on her long legs. "Bring this one to my private chambers. Put the rest into the algae tanks."

They lifted me and my crewmates up, taking us away as if we were children riding upon the backs of athletic fathers. This level of strength surprised me because the Imperials appeared to be slight—even frail. It occurred to me that their strength had to come from their armored suits. Inside them marched long-armed Imperials like the captain, aided by the powered constructs they wore.

I was placed inside a cube of force. There was no escape—I couldn't even touch the walls without a stinging sensation burning my fingers.

The Imperials seemed to be physically weak as individuals, but their technology made them powerful. I thought that over while I waited inside my shimmering cage for the captain. Perhaps I could use my superior strength to my advantage.

It seemed like a long time before she showed up.

"You will now answer my questions," she told me when she finally did.

"Where's my crew?" I demanded immediately, glaring at her.

I stood as tall as I could inside the force cube, but I couldn't straighten my back fully without zapping the top of my head. Perhaps that was by design.

"You demand punishment already?" she asked. "I thought you were capable of understanding your situation. Perhaps I was wrong."

Her steel wand-like device came out again. She'd used it as a neural-paralyzer before. She made a motion with it, and I found myself falling into a crumpled heap on the deck.

This time, I hadn't gone limp. She'd done something with my muscles, however, making them spastically contract. Struggling against the effect, I lifted my head and my body, pushing up off the deck. My throat made an angry gargling sound of effort.

She threw me back down again and laughed.

"You don't learn quickly," she said. "We usually eliminate slaves of such poor quality immediately. But I've held back so far because you amuse me."

I began to rise again, slowly. This time I was ready to catch myself in case I was thrown down again.

"I'm not a slave," I said, "I'm a prisoner of war."

She laughed. "Such wild claims! You're no such thing. You're a beast of the field. An insect that apes its betters. A mongrel in the shadow of an Imperial."

"We're at war. I'm your prisoner. Therefore, I'm a prisoner of war."

Captain Lael shook her head. "I see you don't understand. In order for two creatures to be at war, there must be an opportunity for both creatures to harm the other. If you catch a fish, are you at war with all fish? If you shoot down an air-swimmer, are you at war with the entire species?"

Before I could respond, she went on to answer the question herself.

"No," she said firmly, "no one says the huntress makes war upon the rodent in her sights. War requires equal participants."

"Agreed," I said. "But by your own definition, we're at war."

"How so?"

"I destroyed one of your carriers personally. If my full squadron of fighters had been here, I could have taken out your ship. You're talented and well-equipped, but your ship is nothing I couldn't handle under the right circumstances."

She tilted her head in a manner I found enchanting, despite my discomfort. I warned myself not to go easy on her if I was to get the upper hand somehow. Just because she was pretty didn't mean she wasn't a deadly enemy.

"You've made that claim before," she said. "There *was* a carrier knocked out at the rear of our formation…"

"Now that we've settled our definitions," I said, "I require that you treat me—"

"And what about physical combat?" she asked, as if she hadn't heard me. "Do you think you could defeat my warriors?"

I shrugged. "Of course," I said with certainty. "I'd love to have the chance to prove it."

"I'd enjoy watching that. Whip-blades would flay that attitude off your face."

"No weapons," I said quickly. "No false skins of exoskeletal armor, either. Just two people in a fight to the finish."

"No weapons?" she asked, scandalized. "Why should I honor any of your requests?"

"Because, your way would prove nothing. Your weapons are as unknown to me as mine are to you. Send out your champion—or would you dare to take up my challenge yourself?"

My speech had made her increasingly unhappy with every word. It seemed that suggesting I could beat her in a fight had thrown her into a rage.

She stood with her hands on her hips, staring at me through the force-walls of my cube prison. She was tall, almost as tall as I was—even taller when I was left hunching inside her glowing cage.

"This talk of duels is a fantasy," she said. "Let's get to business. I'm not interested in your bravado. I'm here to gain answers from a captive. You'll be coerced with pain until I hear what I want to know."

"So this is an interrogation?" I asked. "Why me? Why not some admiral or other?"

"I don't have an admiral on hand, but I do have a wild-thing that attacks without warning or hesitation. I want to know what you know. Will you answer my questions, or shall we begin with a session of unpleasantness?"

She tapped on the force-walls with her wand. Each time the handheld device made contact, a buzzing sound came to my ears, and my body tingled. Her slightest movement created nausea and pain.

"I'll answer every question I can," I said, "if you'll accept my formal challenge to—"

She lost patience and zapped me. My balls shriveled into my body, and my knees came together. A feeling of intense electrical shock ran through me.

There were no visible wires, but I was being electrocuted, nonetheless.

Summoning what little self-control I had left, as soon as the pulse let up I showed my teeth in a savage grin. "Sitting safely outside a cage, tormenting people? Does this sort of thing get you off?"

She made an exasperated sound and cranked up the power. I fell to the floor of my cage and lost consciousness.

I felt heat spreading throughout my body as I lost consciousness. I hoped my bladder hadn't let go, but I thought that it might have.

=38=

When I awakened, I knew why everyone aboard *Killer* had hated my kind so much. We were too similar in appearance to Imperials.

Apparently the original Kher, the base stock of all our races, were primates. Smart, technologically capable—and ruthless.

No one had ever shown me a picture of an Imperial, but the officers had to know what they looked like. They'd leaned on me because of the resemblance, even if they weren't doing it consciously.

None of that mattered now. I found myself on a cold metal deck. The surface was rippled with hard ridges, and they'd caused red painful lines to appear on my slack cheek.

I staggered up and looked around. I was still inside a force-cube in the Imperial captain's bedroom. The captain herself was gone.

Taking stock of myself, I found no weapons, but I had something else I could use: my sym.

Closing my eyes, I willed the synthetic lifeform that resided in my body to contact its brothers wherever they were. I had to know what was happening to my crew.

There was a pause. The sym never talked to me directly, but it could be encouraged to do complicated things. It was especially good at communications tasks. As I understood it, the nanites that formed part of its structure were powered chemically by my body. They allowed it to send radio transmissions.

After a long time, I thought I saw and heard something. A snatch of a scream. An echoing conversation. Was that Samson's face?

Then, the vision came to me in full-force. My sym had hacked into the ship's network and found a pathway to my crew through the ship's surveillance system. Unfortunately, the vision it presented wasn't a happy one.

At first, I thought they were drowning. They were in cold-looking water up to their necks. They were all splashing and pushing away growths of some kind—could that be the algae the captain had mentioned earlier?

"Dr. Chang," I said, pressing to make contact. "Can you hear me?"

He twitched and frowned, but he seemed too distracted to talk. He dragged a patch of green-black seaweed-looking stuff from his arm. It left a red weal behind. Could the algae be consuming them?

"Doc!" I shouted, forcing the sym to carry my urgency.

He reacted as if startled, and he looked around. His sym tipped him off to look for a camera eye somewhere, and he spotted it.

"Is that you, Chief?" He asked. "Get us out of this tank! This organism is carnivorous!"

I felt a surge of worry in my gut. My crew was my responsibility. I had to get them out—but how?

The following few minutes I tried to hold a conversation with the group and to explain my situation. It didn't help much. They were too distracted to talk or think. My tortured crew didn't know the layout of the ship, but they thought they were in the lower decks, in what we might have referred to as "the bilge" back on Earth.

After reassuring them I'd do something to save them, I cut the connection and pressed my sym further. I urged it to "see" beyond *Splendor's* hull.

My perception tricks were really generated by mass data input through a ship's sensors which were filtered into a form my mind could take in directly as visuals. Accomplishing the same thing aboard an Imperial ship might have been impossible—but it wasn't.

After a few minutes of trying, perhaps driven to greater concentration by the fact my crew was dying below, I broke through. It felt strange, as if a plug had been pulled out of my skull, and the contents of the ship's sensors were being poured inside.

The heavy cruiser was in flight. *Splendor* was no longer in the same empty patch of space where we'd been captured. We'd jumped to somewhere new. A group of five vessels had gathered here.

There was a planet, the target of the hunting party. They were circling the target like sharks. Bombs were being readied, gravity-bombs that would crush the inhabitants to pulp when they fell.

My mind was brought back to my body with a sudden shocking sensation. I opened my eyes to find myself confused and writhing on the deck again. My muscles had contracted, and I'd crumpled to the floor.

The captain was back. She was breathing hard, standing tall.

"I see it," she said, "but I don't believe it. *You* hacked our networks? From inside a force-cube?"

I looked up at her, deciding how to play the situation. Slowly, I got to my feet. I lifted my chin and shrugged.

"Of course," I said. "Are you surprised? I thought since you left everything open—"

"Shut up," she said dangerously. "Drop your device on the floor of your cage, and your life will be spared."

"Device?" I asked, as if confused. "Oh, I see you don't understand. There is no device. You can scan me if you want to. It's an innate ability."

I was gambling hard, but with my crew in jeopardy, I felt I had to. My sym was mostly biological, with only trace amounts of metal. I hoped the nanites wouldn't show up on an electromagnetic scan.

She paced around the cage angrily. She obviously didn't like the idea that I possessed any kind of tech that she didn't.

"We'll have to dissect you. The lot of you."

Captain Lael lifted up her hand and spoke to her wand. "Remove the prisoners from the tanks. Feed the bloom some other kind of protein source. I need to study all of these vermin."

I felt relief, but I didn't show it. I looked at her blankly. One of the keys to getting away with any con was to look like you didn't know what was happening.

She studied me in return.

"This can't all be a coincidence," she said. "A vicious streak. A mad assault on my ship—wanting to be captured, perhaps? Now, you invade my networks from inside a force-cube? No, this has been carefully planned."

"You'd best kill me now, then," I said. "It's the only safe thing to do."

Her face tightened. She was paranoid as well as arrogant, and I was feeding her worst concerns.

"You'd like that, wouldn't you?" she asked. "The only reason you'd make such a request is because you've already finished your mission. Have you downloaded and transmitted any design information? Force intel?"

Her eyes widened as I continued to stare at her with my best innocent-rabbit expression.

"A trap!" she said. "This is a trap! You've called Rebel forces here. I'm reporting this immediately—and don't worry, all your secrets will be torn from you in time."

Turning, she left the chamber. I heard her say something about the bridge as she marched down the passages. A squad of clanking troops in heavy armor followed her at a jog.

It was time to do my worst now, I figured. I reached out with my mind and tried to get my sym to engage the ship's controls.

It was easier this time around. I'd thought they might have put up a firewall or something, but whatever work-around the sym had figured out was still functioning unabated. I continued to browse their ship's network with impunity.

It would probably be only a matter of time before they shut me out, so I knew I had to do something drastic, and do it fast.

When you've got an advantage, it's best to work it hard while you can.

Skipping weapons, communications, sensors, life-support... I went to the security systems.

Things were difficult there, but I found what I was looking for at last: the force-field generator and its all-important control unit.

I thought about switching them *all* off. That would surely mess things up—but it might be deadly, too. The warp core was contained by a force-wall on Rebel ships. I figured that might be true on this ship as well. Singlehandedly destroying a heavy cruiser would be an impressive final act, one I'd been willing to settle for a few hours ago—but now I was becoming ambitious. I wanted more.

Figuring out exactly which force-wall was surrounding me right now was too difficult, so I killed all the security walls at once. Every prisoner on the ship was instantly released, including me.

The first thing I did was stand tall and stretch out my spine. That felt good!

A moment later, I walked to stand to one side of where I knew the door had been. The ship's doors were like those on *Killer*, they simply vanished and reappeared when you touched them.

I considered exiting the chambers, but I knew that was likely to end in death. The guards would spot me. I wouldn't stand a chance against those guys. They were well-armed and armored.

Instead, I walked to the captain's bed. I gathered up all her bedding and threw it on the floor where the force-cube had been. Then, I stood against the wall again near the entrance and waited.

It was a long wait, but she showed up at last. Behind her, guards were clanking. I could hear them in their metal suits. This was going to be tight, if it could be done at all.

Holding my breath, I saw the door vanish to reveal the passageway and the captain—and then I made my move.

=39=

Captain Lael stepped into the room and saw the pile of junk I'd thrown on the floor. It was just a diversion, but she fell for it.

Any magician will tell you the real magic behind any 'trick' is to get the mark's eye to watch something that doesn't matter while you do your worst to deceive them. In this case, she was left thinking for a fraction of a second that I'd somehow turned into silky pillows and sheets—or perhaps that I'd buried myself under them.

Whatever she thought, she stepped into the chambers with her attention riveted on the distraction.

I moved, and I moved fast. My hand shot out, grabbing her wrist. I plucked the wand-like device out of her slender hand and took it from her.

The machine-looking guards behind her were not amused. They surged into the doorway after me. Their arms were upraised, and I had no doubt the black, muzzle-like tubes they were lifting in my direction were deadly.

Then suddenly, they all tumbled onto their faces and shivered there. I'd activated the neural paralyzing effect, exactly as I'd seen her do earlier.

Grabbing her wand had been a big gamble, but it had paid off. I would never have tried it if I'd had a better move—but there hadn't been time to come up with anything better.

I shuddered to think what might have happened if the paralyzer had affected me and not them. Or, if the body armor had rendered the troops immune.

None of these things had been the case, and I knew I'd lucked out.

The captain had been paralyzed along with her troops. I took a moment to grin and squat next to her, placing myself within her field of vision. Her beautiful eyes, wide-open and motionless, saw me but were unable to acknowledge it.

"See?" I told her. "Weapons are unfair in any duel."

I stood up and reached out with my sym again. I held the wand tightly in both hands, hoping it would help somehow.

It did. I could see more now, I could move through the ship more quickly. It seemed I no longer needed to rely on my sym for any kind of security hack. Apparently, I had unfettered access to everything.

As if flipping through pages, I reviewed the decks. Everywhere there was a security camera, I could see through it. There was an overload of information, and I ordered my sym to collate it all, to gather it into a single unified interface. It did this quickly, as that was what it had been designed for.

When I found the deck I was on, I saw myself standing over the fallen forms. My eyes were closed, yet it felt as if I were outside my body, looking down at myself. This was virtual reality at its finest.

But as I looked around the deck, reaching out farther down the local passages, I became alarmed.

My actions hadn't gone unnoticed. A veritable army of troops were coming now, clanking in teams of six from both directions toward the passage outside. I saw unarmored officers among them as well. The unarmored officers were women, and they guided their armored males in my direction.

They paused at the far ends of the passage outside. The officers touched their troops with wands, making their armored suits glimmer with new fields. Could it be they were making them immune to the neural paralyzer? I couldn't think of a better explanation.

My eyes snapped open. Breathing hard, I dragged the captain's limp form into the chamber, and rudely rolled and kicked the armored troops out. They were quite heavy in their metal suits. After a moment, the door snapped back into place.

Picking up the captain again, I found she was shockingly light. She couldn't have weighed more than a hundred pounds. That was extremely light given her height. Maybe her bones were thin—I tried to be careful with her.

Laying her down on the pile of pillows, I stood beside her and turned on the force cube again. It closed around us, locking us in. All over the ship, the force-walls in security systems glowed in place once more.

This time there was a difference. Instead of keeping the inhabitants within and shocking them if they touched the walls, the security barriers were set to operate in reverse. They now kept things out, rather than keeping them in.

Doing this was simplicity itself, as it turned out. All I had to do was the equivalent of changing an option in a database field. The "type" of field was changed from security, to defensive.

The door opened again a moment later, and a squad of angry, robot-looking troops marched in. I could see their long-chinned faces through their faceplates, sallow and snarling, as they rushed to my force-cube.

I couldn't suppress my grin as they reached for my protective walls and banged on them in unison.

When the captain had tapped on my cube before, it had sickened me. It was their way of tormenting prisoners. I guess the captain would have experienced the pain too, if she'd been fully in charge of her senses.

But that wasn't what happened. Instead, because the field had been reversed, the troopers shocked themselves. They recoiled with alarm and surprise.

Two of them fell on the floor outright, their own fields flickering. Maybe they'd shorted out their suits.

Three more were left reeling and fell onto the deck. They scrambled weakly, unable to completely control their limbs. These men had not touched the force-walls directly but had been stunned by the rippling effects.

The last guy in the back wisely marched back out of the chamber to where the officers waited, scolding their troops. I laughed at him quietly, and I closed my eyes again.

I didn't have much time for my next trick, but I knew I had to make it a big one. Sooner or later someone was going to figure out how to stop me from hacking their ship.

This time, I sent my consciousness down to engineering and examined the engines.

I think, in the end, someone down there knew what I was up to. They tried to shut down the core. But doing such a thing takes time. You have to do it right, or the whole vessel will explode.

Using all the tricks I had, I ordered my sym to open a rift in front of the ship. That part took time as well. Several minutes of thrumming followed as the generators built up a charge.

Without their captain, and in general disarray, the ship's crew seemed to forget about me. They were no longer mounting an attack on their captain's quarters. This was a mistake, as it gave me more time to work mischief.

The rift appeared directly in front of the ship. I froze the helm controls so that the frantic bridge crew couldn't divert our course.

The entire ship's complement watched on in horror as we sailed into the rift and vanished.

The scary thing was that I had no idea where this rift might take us. I hadn't bothered to figure that part out. I hadn't had the time.

And I'd bet a million bucks no one else aboard knew where we were going, either.

=40=

They began hacking back the control systems at about the same time Captain Lael came out of her paralysis.

It was a lot to handle at once. I had to pretty much sit on the captain—which she didn't appreciate at all.

"Get off me, you worthless ape!" she snarled, writhing around weakly.

"Just a second, your people are giving me problems."

My sym had gained control of the Imperial interface due to a heavy reliance on certain top-level security systems. They were built in to bypass everything else, to allow the top officers easy access to whatever they needed to do.

The problem for them seemed to be that they hadn't considered a hacking attempt, even a simple one. Apparently, Imperials were a pretty docile, law-abiding group. These people did what they were told and didn't go up against each other much if I had to guess.

My sym had been developed by people from a very different, chaotic culture. We weren't good at lining up, me and my wild-eyed Rebel brethren, but we knew how to break things.

As my sym worked to regain control of the ship, I took a moment to reflect upon the current situation. I couldn't help but see this as an example of the advantages afforded to those living among varied cultures and backgrounds. A ship that came from a planet full of thieves, for example, was bound to have solidly built locks on everything, while a ship from a world without crime would have few, if any.

When my sym came through again, I was disappointed that I didn't have complete control any more. I couldn't even see where we were in space. All I could do was control some basic things like life-support, force-walls and various chemical processing systems.

Deciding to give the Imperials as much trouble as I could, I turned off the air then took a look at the chemical systems. That rabbit-hole led me down to my crew, who had escaped in the confusion—most importantly, they'd gotten past the force-walls that had kept them in the algae tanks. Using the security cameras and transmitting to their syms, I finally got their attention.

"Hey..." I said with some excitement. "Gwen, can you hear me?"

"Leo?" she asked, looking around wildly at the walls. She spotted a camera stick tracking her and stepped up to it. "Are you behind all this chaos?"

"Naturally. Listen, you need to find an oxygen supply. I cut off the ship-wide distribution matrix."

"How in the hell—?"

"No time to explain, but you might be able to do the same thing with your own sym if you focus hard enough. Reach out with it to the chemical processing facilities. They're all located in your area. See if you can use them to your advantage."

"All right... I'll try."

She was a good hacker, I knew that. She'd demonstrated her powers several times in the past. But she wasn't as used to using her sym in that way as I was. It was going to be a challenge.

I had no more time for Gwen. In fact, I'd just felt a powerful pinch in my hindquarters.

Opening my eyes, I found Captain Lael was trying to take a bite out of me. I restrained her and talked to her seriously.

"Tell your crew to stand down," I said, "or I'll kill everyone aboard."

"You couldn't—"

"I killed the force-walls, didn't I? I can kill the ones containing the reactor core just as easily."

Her wide eyes widened further. "You wouldn't. The ship would be destroyed."

My face presented her with my best grin. "Exactly. I've already tried to take you out twice, you know that. And I don't care if I die as long as I achieve my goals—you know that, too."

She looked at me in growing alarm. I could tell she was paranoid to begin with, and after the events of today, I'd done nothing to reassure her.

"I'll tell them," she said, "but they may not listen. I'm your captive, therefore my orders are nullified."

"You'd better sound convincing then."

I let her sit up, and when she reached for her wand, I moved it out of her reach. I activated it myself and allowed her to speak into it.

"This is Captain Lael. The situation is under control, the barbarians have surrendered. The Empire has prevailed, as it must."

I waved my hand at her, suggesting she speed it up. She kept talking while I listened with gritted teeth.

"Security techs are ordered to return all passcodes to their original state for the convenience of the officers. Everyone else should focus on damage control. That is all."

I killed the transmitter. We looked at one another, and I smiled thoughtfully.

"You *really* do want to live, don't you?" I asked her. "I should have realized that when I sensed your paranoia. Who would be paranoid if they didn't value their own lives very highly?"

"It's a natural instinct," she said. "There's nothing in this part of the galaxy worth my life."

I nodded. To her, this wasn't a war at all. This was a hunt. An exercise designed to bring pleasure and training opportunities to her kind. Who went hunting willing to die just to bag the prey?

Not Captain Lael, anyway. She had no intention of sacrificing her life or her ship for honor, or anything else.

That simple fact gave the Rebels an advantage. This was *real* to us. We were losing planets, whole civilizations. If we could only get our act together, we might win this war simply because we cared more about the final outcome than the Imperials did.

Morale. I'd learned back in my officer training days in the Navy that battles and even wars were often won before they started. If one side didn't really want to fight, they often lost by default. That was how so many nations had lost their colonies to rebellions in the past—they just didn't have the stomach to lose all that blood and treasure over some distant outpost.

"Okay," I said as I felt my sym regain control over the ship's systems, one after another. I could hardly believe she was allowing it, but then, I was effectively holding a gun to her head and that of everyone aboard.

"Let me go now," she said.

"No... I don't think so. You'll stay here as my hostage and go-between. I want to take this ship back to Rebel territory."

"What?!" she demanded in shock. "I'll never allow that! You're a mad creature and—"

That was all she said before she took a "nap." I'd activated the neural paralyzer again. She slumped stiffly onto the pillows that surrounded us.

Knowing I had a few minutes of peace during which to concentrate, I took a look around.

We were inside some kind of big nebula. That was interesting all by itself. A gassy cloud of dust and vapor surrounded the ship, and it made our shield sparkle with thousands of tiny impacts.

Sand-sized particles flared into energy as the ship ran into them. Now and then, a sheet seemed to ripple across the vessel, lighting it up like the Fourth of July.

There were stars nearby too. Big, blue-white giants. By "near" I'm talking about half a lightyear or so, but still, at this distance they were lovely to behold.

Recalling what little I remembered from my only college class in astronomy, I figured out this was what they called a "stellar nursery." A place where young stars grew from accumulated dust and were flung to become independent burning chunks of matter in the heavens.

I tried to get my bearings, but I had difficulty. I couldn't see the way home.

"Mia?" I called, trying to reach out to her again.

"Here, Chief."

"How are things with you?"

She gave me a mean giggle. That surprised me, as she wasn't much for laughter even when someone told an excellent joke.

"Are you drunk or something?" I asked in concern. "Is the oxygen running out already?"

"No," she said. "Look here—follow my sym."

I piggybacked my sym onto hers, and I let her lead the way. We raced through cameras and conduits until I saw the algae tanks again.

Only this time, the crawling, green-black mess in the tanks wasn't contained in the tanks. It was sliding around the passages, attacking people. Several were mired in it, and even the armored guys were having trouble.

"Those monsters fed us to that slime," she said. "I hope they get their skins peeled off!"

"Uh... that's great," I said, wondering if her own sym was influencing her emotions less than optimally. "We need to do some navigating. I can jump the ship again, but I don't have any coordinates to target."

My vision retreated to her location, and she shrugged. "Try finding a beacon star—like Rigel. That's an easy one."

Of course. I was an idiot! When jumping between the stars, we'd always tried to use a beacon star. A big, massive lighthouse of a star that could guide us to the correct destination.

I didn't know if Rigel was still in our effective range or not, but I felt I had to give it a try. The ship's crew had already begun their effort to retake control using stealthy techniques. My sym revealed that they were crawling down the passages shutting down systems they didn't need and reactivating essential ones. Already, they'd turned life-support back on.

Captain Lael had given them my orders, and they were following them, but it was only a matter of time before they figured out who was really calling the shots. They had to be suspicious by now. The wand I'd lifted from the captain was vibrating almost constantly, and I was pretty sure there were something like cell phone calls coming in which I couldn't afford to answer.

On the floor, the captain was beginning to twitch. Her eyes were swiveled up, almost rolled up into her head, just so she could glare at me.

Closing my eyes again to eliminate distractions, I reached out with my perception and used the ship's navigational interface. Where was Rigel? Where was the biggest class B giant star in this part of the galaxy?

After a minute or so, I found it. With an effort of will, I directed the ship to open a new rift.

The people on the bridge reacted much faster this time. They knew something very fishy was going on. They implemented their new security protocols, and shut down all my access to the rift engines.

But it was too late as the space-time rip I'd created was right in front of us. They reversed the engines, but you don't turn on a dime in space. We were going around a thousand miles a second, and even though they managed to slow that down by half, with our rudder controls frozen, they couldn't turn away.

In those final moments, I could imagine the panicked shouts by the bridge officers as we plunged into another rift that led to God-knew-where.

The thought made me smile.

=41=

My biggest worry over the next few moments was that we'd scatter again. There was only one ship in this train, and she had a beacon star to guide her, but I was still worried. After all, it was only the second stellar-jump I'd performed in a lifetime.

The computers did their magic right this time, however. I needn't have worried. The gravitational forces caused by the immense hot mass of Rigel guided us in with ease.

All over the ship, alarms were wailing, and people were panicking. It took me a second to realize *Splendor's* crew had been called to battle stations. After all, this was enemy territory to them, and this cruiser had no backup.

Standing up, I took two seconds to look at Captain Lael. She was in control of her eyes again by now, and she looked up at me with the most malevolent stare I could recall having seen from a lovely woman.

I gave her a grin and blew her a kiss, then ran out of the place.

Sure, I should have zapped her with the wand one more time to keep her from causing trouble, but I felt bad about having done it twice already.

Needing a distraction, I killed the external force walls around the forward section of the ship. They were going down in the same order as before. They were trying to block me, but I could still manipulate their force fields.

I knew shutting down the force walls would panic the officers. The radiation levels in this star system were extremely high. I was glad to be far from the core suns. The suns were about a hundred thousand times as bright as Sol, but we were a lot farther out than Earth was. Even so, without a protective force field, orbiting Rigel was like being inside a blast furnace.

As I ran below decks, plenty of skinny guys in space suits came up toward me. They were repair crews heading toward the region I'd just sabotaged.

They were stunned to see me. I took that moment's hesitation to attack. I paralyzed the ones wearing armor. Those not wearing armor got knocked to the deck with a left hook. Either way, they all went down. It seemed to me that Imperials simply weren't good at handling surprising situations aboard their own ship.

Gwen and the rest of my tiny crew had broken free and were coming up to meet me the other way. We found each other on deck seventeen, and everyone was out of breath.

"These guys are wimps," Samson puffed. His red knuckles were the only explanation I needed.

"Yeah," I said. "I think they're used to less gravity where they're from. Maybe they're born in space, I don't know or care. What I want to know now is how we get the hell off this ship."

Gwen shook her head and put her hands on her knees to pant. "I've been scouting with my sym. There's nothing but a few life pods for the officers. They won't get very far."

I nodded. "To the hangar then," I said.

"What? Back to *Hammerhead*?" Samson asked. "We barely had any fuel, and the core was drained anyway."

"I know, but she's all we've got. Besides, we know how to fly her."

We ran to the midsection of the ship, the belly itself. We reached the cargo bay where our ship was, and I was surprised to find very few people there. Apparently, calling battle stations didn't send a large contingent to this part of the ship.

We found *Hammerhead* and jumped aboard. Our reactor coil had regained some juice, and we were soon whooping.

"The Imperials drained our core, but it was a temporary effect," Dr. Chang said. "The core has slowly recharged itself. We're about a quarter full now."

"That will have to be enough," I said, climbing into the pilot's seat.

Focusing my mind, I communicated with my sym: "This is it. We've got to open that big door."

I concentrated, but nothing happened.

"They're blocking us," I said in a panicky voice. "I can't do anything."

"Let me try," said Gwen.

She concentrated. A minute passed, then another.

I was becoming impatient. We had the cannon online again. I directed Mia to swivel it around and aim it at the big bay doors.

"The back-blast will kill us," Dr. Chang cautioned.

"To say nothing of the decompression," I added. "But we have company."

Crawling out onto the hangar deck was a small army of armored troops. They were spread out, with weapons lifted high.

"Mia," I said, "take care of those guys, will you?"

She swiveled the gun smoothly. The enemy, seeing the danger, scattered and threw themselves behind cubes of cargo.

Mia released a happy sound that could have been a growl or purr—it was hard to tell sometimes. Then she opened up with her cannon.

Troops were blasted, and the red contents of their armor splattered the walls. Scorch marks and gouges showed on every surface touched by the big gun.

The troops returned fire, throwing gravity grenades that rocked our small ship. A hundred flashes of energy splashed over the wings and hull, pitting and pockmarking my poor, heavily abused fighter.

I heard a gasp, and then I found we were in sudden, unexpected flight.

The gasp had come from Gwen. She'd thrown her eyes wide at last, and it was as if she'd come up from a deep, deep dive into the sea. Perhaps she'd been holding her breath all this time, without knowing it. Whatever the case, she'd managed to get the big bay doors open.

Bodies of armored troops flew up out of hiding and tumbled past us, limbs flailing. All around them sailed the crates they'd used for protection.

Merciless, Mia shot at them, swiveling her gun this way and that.

Then we were flying, too. The hangar door had blown open, and *Hammerhead* was sucked out into space.

It all happened so fast. I barely had time to register it all. But by the time the velvet black of open space appeared, I had the controls in my hands and spun the fighter around to face the exit.

"Rigel…" I said. "Samson, put up every radiation shield we have or we'll be cooked!"

He worked the air around his seat like a pro. I was glad to have him in that moment. There was no substitute for a good support-man in a cockpit like this one.

Driven out into open space with the rest of the debris, the blinding light touched each armored troop and cargo crate like an intense torch. They went white, so white that no unshielded human eye could bear to watch without being damaged.

"Dampen the hull ninety-nine percent!" I ordered.

The chamber dimmed, but it wasn't enough. The light was still blinding us.

"Full opacity!" I ordered, keeping my eyes shut. Even through my helmet, the darkened hull, and lots of other filters, the light was intense and painfully leaking into my eyeballs.

Samson's fumbling fingers found the right part of his interface at last, and the light suddenly cut out. We were enveloped by darkness. I opened my eyes and looked around in a wary squint.

The hull was solid steel again, emitting no light at all. Outside, the glare had to be extreme. We'd come out too close to the beacon star when we'd jumped, I realized now. It was a rookie mistake, but after all, I wasn't really an astronavigator—not an experienced one, anyway.

Soon, we regained control of our battered craft and flew purely on instruments.

"Radiation levels are high," Dr. Chang said in a remarkably calm voice. "We'll be eating potassium iodide tonight—assuming we live."

"Break out the pills now," I said, and we all took a handful.

I chewed the bitter compound and swallowed it, coughing. "Any report on *Splendor*?" I asked.

"She's gone, Chief," Gwen said. "She was venting, but they must have regained control long enough to jump out again."

"I thought starships couldn't jump again that fast…" I said.

"They can if they're willing to take grim risks," Dr. Chang explained. "Let's hope the ship was destroyed."

For some reason, that thought gave me a pang. As mean of a woman as Lael was, I didn't want to think I'd caused her death.

"Why didn't they destroy us?" Samson asked.

Gwen grinned. "I took the liberty of disabling their weapons systems when I had the chance."

"Damn," I said, looking at her. "Why didn't I think of that?"

She beamed, eating up the praise.

=42=

Despite the turbulent nature of our brief time in each other's company, I found I couldn't stop thinking about Captain Lael. We were lightyears apart now—and she might well be dead—but to my all-too-human mind, that didn't matter. I felt I should be able to look around and find her again because I'd been with her so recently.

Why was I still thinking of her? It wasn't *just* because she had possessed haunting beauty. I'm not that shallow—at least, not all the time.

An outside observer might reason I could be dreaming about revenge for her mistreatment of my crew, but it wasn't like that, either.

What I was feeling was a sense of pride. I'd beaten her fair and square. If her ship had survived the damaged force-containment fields I'd left her with, I was pretty sure she was thinking of me right now, too.

How could she not be? Leo Blake, a lowly savage to her way of thinking, had waltzed aboard her ship and commandeered it for a spin. Just thinking about that made me grin.

"Why are you so happy?" Mia asked me with a hint of suspicion. She was eyeing me, and I gave a guilty start. "What did that bitch-captain do to you in her quarters?" she asked.

"She put me in a cage and shocked it, mostly," I said. "But I managed to get the upper hand using my sym in the end. I'm just happy we all got away with our lives."

"We did more than that," Dr. Chang said. "Much more. We embarrassed the enemy. That could be good—or very, very bad."

"How could it possibly be bad, Doc?" Samson asked.

"Because, now they know who we are. The Imperials have noticed the creatures known as humans, and they've singled us out as dangerous. The only question is: what are they going to do about it?"

My grin faded. I realized he was right. The Imperials weren't the kind to take a setback lightly. They were hard-assed, arrogant, and intolerant of any kind of rivalry. They might even come after Earth.

"We have to get back to the Fleet," I said. "We need to report in, pronto."

"Leo…" Gwen asked, "why didn't you just take us home? You could have taken that Imperial ship anywhere."

I gave her one of those, "are you crazy?" looks.

"What you're suggesting wouldn't have been easy," I said. "Getting home on our own would have required a very long stellar-jump. Earth is deep in Rebel territory, far from the Orion Front. And old Sol isn't much of a beacon star for navigation. Remember too, I barely knew what I was doing. If I'd tried for Earth, I'd probably have scattered us to Andromeda."

"For another thing," Samson said, taking my side, "I don't think Earth needs an enemy cruiser in orbit."

"No, but…" Gwen went on thoughtfully. "Leo, I guess you should have destroyed that ship. You should have exposed their core as we escaped."

Coming from Gwen, the idea seemed uncharacteristically ruthless. I looked at her in surprise.

"You really think I should've killed them all?" I asked.

"That's what I would have done," Dr. Chang answered for her. "Our situation is infinitely worse now. You revealed we had power over them. I know you had to in order to allow us to escape, but the mistake you made was in leaving them alive to tell the story."

"You've got a point…" I said. "But they just took a blind jump away from Rigel with a damaged ship. They might be dead or lost."

"You can't *know* that," Gwen insisted, "and now, they know we came from Earth."

"True…" I admitted.

Despite our escape, they appeared to be unhappy. As I thought about it, I decided I couldn't blame them. We'd seen enough dead worlds that were dotted with cities compressed to black mounds of ash. We all knew humanity's survival was at stake.

"As it is, we're going to have to rejoin the Rebel Fleet," Gwen said, sounding depressed. "I'm not looking forward to that."

Looking around *Hammerhead*'s cramped main deck, I realized it was time for a pep-talk.

"Like it or not," I said, "we're the best fighters Earth has right now. We're her best hope for a defense in space—for your world too, Mia."

She nodded.

"We're trained," I said, "we've got new know-how when it comes to hacking enemy systems, and we're flying a warship again."

"A tiny one," complained Samson.

"Gwen," I said, "have you got a fix on the Rebel Fleet?"

"I've got a signal, but it's garbled. Rigel A and B are putting out so much radiation I can't get anything other than a directional fix."

"Give it to me."

She did, and I set our course for the distant outpost I hoped was waiting there. The course intersected with a large rock in space about the size of Earth's Moon. The region around Rigel's stars was so saturated with light and atomic and subatomic particles, we suspected the Fleet had taken refuge behind this star-blasted rock for protection.

Rationing our fuel, I figured we could make it out there in two days. The main worry was that the Fleet would pull out before we got to them. If they did that, we'd likely sail out into deep space and never be found again.

"We've got a choice to make," I said, working the numbers. "We can either blow our fuel and get up to high speed, taking us to that rock faster. That's option A."

"What's B? Self-destruction?" Samson complained.

"Either of these paths might lead to that," I admitted. "Option B is to coast, saving enough fuel to slow down when we get out there to that rock they're hiding behind."

Gwen shook her head. "Why bother doing that? The Rebels can chase us down and grapple us or refuel us with a tanker. I vote we blow the fuel to get back to them as fast as possible."

"Hold on," I said, lifting my hand. "If we do it that way, we'll be going pretty damned fast by the time we get there. If they leave that rock before we arrive we'll sail away into the dark. Even if they come back later, they'll never find us."

"Oh…" she said, thinking it over. "I get it. We'd have to use more fuel to slow down, and they might be occupied or just miss our fly-by. We don't know when they'll gather here again at this beacon star."

"You got it. Well, which option sounds best?"

They all looked glum and uncertain. My fantasies about passing the buck on this one were fading fast.

"Hmm…" I said. "I think we should split the difference. We'll fly out using most of our fuel, but save enough to slow down when we get close. That should at least give us a few days to hang around the area and get noticed."

They agreed reluctantly. What I wasn't telling them was that, according to my calculations, we only had about two weeks of good air left. We had to get rescued soon, or we were going to suffocate. Rebreathers and carbon-scrubbers only worked for so long before a small ship with five passengers became toxic.

With our plan in place, things were fairly quiet on the flight outward. After about thirty hours, Gwen came to me and whispered in my ear.

"Leo?"

"What's up?"

She looked guilty. It was an expression I wasn't accustomed to seeing on her face.

"What?" I repeated. "Did you eat the last candy bar or something?"

"No, nothing like that. But the radio signals we've been following—they're gone. I'm not getting anything from that rock we're flying toward. There's nothing else out here to get a fix on, either."

I stared at her, and she lifted her eyes and stared back.

Was this it? I thought to myself. Were we screwed, destined to float away in space forever? We'd be dried out fossils inside of a month.

"Hmm," I said, "I can't do much with our course or speed. We're locked."

"I know," she said. "I ran the oxygen numbers after we decided to do this, and I saw why you'd chosen to take this option. There really wasn't much of a choice, was there?"

"No," I said quietly. "Don't bother to mention that to the others. No point."

She shook her head. "No point."

We parted, and I caught Mia watching us. She had a funny look on her face, but I didn't know what it meant. Her facial expressions were just different enough from human ones that I had trouble tracking them. Was she worried? Jealous? Pissed? I had no idea. Hell, I wasn't even good at reading the emotions of human women.

I smiled and gave her a friendly nod then went back to my station. I felt her predatory eyes on me for several seconds afterward, and I finally couldn't stand it any longer. I turned to look at her and demand to know what she was thinking—but she was gone.

The feline types were good at vanishing quietly when they wanted to.

The next two days crawled by. Periodically, I conferred with Gwen—but there was nothing else indicating life or technology in the system.

We began the deceleration process on schedule. The ship had been coasting for a while, but now we wheeled around, put all our shielding toward Rigel, and braked hard.

The rumble of the engines was continuous. To save fuel, I had Samson turn off the anti-grav system. That made us uncomfortable, but it gave us several more hours of time to be spotted.

To keep himself busy, Dr. Chang had been working on a gizmo. He showed it to us on the third day of the journey.

"It works like this," he said, displaying what looked like a lead-lined crate with some electronics packed inside, "this transponder will beep every six minutes for about a month. We'll fire it out of the airlock toward the back of that rock as we pass by. With any luck, it will survive impact with the planetoid and sit there beeping for attention."

By this time, my crew had all figured out that there wasn't any welcoming committee out here—if there ever had been.

"That's great, Doc," Samson said. "But we aren't going to last a month. We've got less than a week, tops, before the air runs out."

No one was happy about our situation, but they seemed resigned to it. They weren't depressed or angry. All I sensed was a serious, quiet desperation.

"We'll try it," I said. "I assume you put information aboard the device about our course and speed?"

"Certainly. Anyone who finds this will be able to locate us."

I nodded, and we all worked together to make it happen. We loaded the transponder into our airlock and shoved it out into the brilliant blue-white light. Even at this distance, with every filter set to maximum, Rigel was blinding and deadly.

The following hour was a bleak one. We all kept quiet, conserving our air. We were out of happy-thoughts to spread around to cheer one another up. Morale was scraping the bottom of the barrel.

Then, at the one hour mark, a funny thing happened.

"Chief...?" Dr. Chang called to me. "Blake... I don't—take a look at this."

I pulled up his sensor data and displayed it for everyone. We all stared and gaped.

"What the hell...?" Samson asked. "How many are there?"

"I'm getting a count..." Dr. Chang said. "We're running entirely on passive sensors now, so it's bound to be inaccurate, but I'm picking up over two hundred contacts."

"It's the Imperials," Gwen said with a dreadful certainty. "It has to be. Maybe Captain Lael brought them back for us. Or maybe, the Imperials destroyed all the ships in the Rebel Fleet and waited to see if—"

I shushed her with a hand. "They aren't firing. Can you get a reading on their hull configuration?"

"No," she said. "There's too much interference from Rigel for that. What do we do?"

"We play dead," I said, "what else can we do?"

"It's not going to be much of an act," Samson said sourly.

We waited for several tense minutes. Then our tiny ship lurched sickeningly.

"Gravity beam," Gwen said. "They've locked onto us. Why not just blow us out of the sky? Why torment us further?"

She began rubbing at the healing scabs on her arms. The carnivorous algae had done a number on my crew. Memories were causing them to itch.

"We don't have our thumpers anymore," Samson said, "but you've got Captain Lael's wand."

I pulled it out thoughtfully. I had no idea if this thing was going to work on a different Imperial ship's security systems. It didn't do anything aboard *Hammerhead*, so I hadn't given it much thought.

Holding our disruptors, we waited for the hatch to be ripped open again when we were sucked up into a hulking ship's interior. I thought about igniting the engines to burn whoever was outside, but there wasn't enough fuel. I considered making the hull transparent again, but even that would take some energy. Every ounce of power in *Hammerhead's* systems had been rerouted to shielding and similar efforts. Our active sensors were all dead.

The hatch sprang open. We all twitched, lifting our disruptors in a final hopeless act of defiance.

But when the scene outside was revealed, we blinked in confusion.

The environment was one we knew well. It was the hangar deck of a carrier—a Rebel carrier.

Then, a familiar figure strode into view. His tail flicked from side-to-side violently.

"Blake?" Ra-tikh demanded. "Come out of there! You better not have lost my fourth!"

We lowered our weapons and laughed. Everyone poured out onto the deck.

We were home again aboard *Killer*—although I was at a loss to explain how, or why...

=43=

We were debriefed almost as vigorously as we'd been interrogated by the Imperials. The Rebel officers in charge of such debriefings seemed to have a great deal of difficulty believing my story.

The fact that everyone in my crew had told the same tale separately helped. Our suit recorders also verified the tale, and that seemed to convince them. After a long process, they delivered me back to Shaw who asked me many of the same questions over again.

"Unbelievable..." Shaw said for the tenth time, "simply unbelievable. You say you did all that damage using the symbiotic units in your bloodstream and some simple network transmitters?"

"Yes, pretty much," I said. "The Imperials seem to have very little in the way of hardened security systems. The sym found them easy to break. One passcode, for instance, allowed me access to every subsystem on their ship."

He was pacing around his office, shaking his head and throwing his arms wide now and then. I'd gotten used to this odd, alarming gesture. For his people, I guess it was like clearing a throat or tapping a foot. He seemed to do it more often when he was excited or thinking hard.

"I can't even imagine how many status points this might be worth," he said. "But I'm also unsure how to prove it. To claim my just reward for—"

"Come on!" I said. "Forget about your status for one second, Lieutenant. We have to use this information to help the cause. We have to spread it to the top brass."

He blinked at me like a man coming out of a dream.

"That's not our responsibility. You were debriefed by professionals, and they'll decide what to do with your testimony."

Frustrated, I thought hard for a moment. "Lieutenant, what do the interrogators get points for? What would improve *their* status?"

"Eh? Well… successfully breaking a prisoner is the usual metric. They're supposed to be working their arts on captured Imperials—but we don't get many of those. When we do get one of their clueless males, they sputter and snarl until they give up what little they know. Then, they usually expire."

"Great," I said. I knew enough about Rebel culture now to understand how they thought. Everyone was out for himself. They usually only did their jobs in-so-far as it helped them personally. Oh, when their lives were on the line in combat they cooperated well enough, but it wasn't anything like a well-oiled, disciplined effort.

"The interrogators will sit on this, won't they?" I asked him. "They'll downplay the details—hoping they can personally benefit from them at some point. Only then they will log a formal report and hope for a new Imperial captive to torture to death."

"Now that would have been a boon," Shaw said, only half listening to me. "You should have brought that captain here as a captive. We could have made serious points from that. We'd both gain a rank for sure."

Hopping off his table, I came close and gripped his shoulders. He glared at me, unhappy with this intrusion into his personal space. Rebel troops were far less formal than their Imperial counterparts, but they still had some sense of decorum.

"Lieutenant," I said earnestly. "I can get us both rank. I guarantee it."

"How?"

"Let's go talk to Captain Ursahn. She's up on the command deck, right?"

He stared at me. "We can't just go up and talk to the captain. She'll rip our throats out."

I'd seen the brutish woman in action, and he might be right, but I was desperate.

"*Thousands* of status points," I said. "Just think of it. You'll get rank for sure. Maybe wing commander, or even a trainee slot under the CAG."

"How? Tell me how this is possible?"

Letting my hands drop to my side again, I gave him a smug smile. "Let me talk to the captain. Then the admiral—that primate guy. What was his name?"

He twitched, then he told me. "Fex."

"Right. We need to see him, too. He's still alive after the last battle, isn't he?"

"He is indeed, but he lost a step due to failure. His ship was one of the first ones to jump out of that slaughter at Cygnus Minor. He's a rear admiral now."

"Of course…" I said thoughtfully. "Even better."

"You're scheming," he said with a mixture of disgust and fascination. "I know that look—that monkey-mind of yours is turning things over. It's a wonder you don't have a tail and more fur."

I let his insults slide, because I didn't care what he thought. I only wanted his cooperation, and I thought I knew how to get it.

"Come on," I said. "We need status points, and our admiral needs his rank back."

Shaw followed me. I needed his passcode to get up to the command deck, to get access to the brass aboard *Killer*. As an ensign, I wasn't a full-fledged officer, I was an officer in training.

In the Rebel Navy, junior crewmen weren't fully trusted. We were, after all, recruits from the wilder planets.

But I wasn't going to let any of that stop me. I was on a mission.

"Use your code," I told Shaw, gesturing toward the intelligent panel that prevented non-authorized persons from operating the central lift.

He eyed me for a moment. "You really think you know something that will make a difference?"

"How do you think I managed to escape an enemy heavy cruiser and get back here to tell about it?"

"You're tricky," he said, as if this explained everything. "I assume you tricked the enemy, and hacked your suit-recorders. What I'm not sure of is how much of your story is true."

"It's all true. Open that door so we can get rank."

Reluctantly, he did as I asked. He had the resigned air of a man who didn't believe in the hype, but who was willing to play along just in case there was a grain of truth to it.

The doors swished open—real doors this time, not some vanishing trick of light and soundproofing. We were about to step into the lift, but halted.

We were face to face with *Killer's* captain. She was still big and impressive, but she wore a new expression, one of distrust.

"My sym relayed your report to me, human," she said, looking at me. "You can't expect me to believe it."

"It's the God's-honest truth, Captain," I said, staring into her eyes.

"You threaten me?" she asked.

I blinked. "Uh... no. Sorry. I forgot that predators considered direct eye-contact frightening."

Stepping close to me, she let out a chilling growl. "Not *frightening*. Disrespectful."

"Of course. Sorry again, sir." I found a good spot on the edge of the door to stare at.

Ursahn flicked her eyes toward Shaw for the first time. "Dismissed," she said.

"But sir—"

"You'll get your points—if you deserve any, which I doubt."

Awkwardly, Shaw retreated, and I stepped onto the lift with the captain.

"Presumptuous," she said. "Believe me, I have no intention of becoming one of your cross-species conquests, Blake."

After taking a moment to suppress a shudder, I forced a pleasant smile onto my face instead.

"What?" I asked. "Oh—no, no, Captain. That wasn't my intention at all. I just figured you might want to discuss this in your office rather than here on the lower decks."

She stepped onto the lift at my side and glared at me. I knew she viewed me as an interloper. It didn't help at all that I was a primate. That was like being from the wrong side of town. These people suspected my kind of all sorts of deviltry.

The doors snicked shut, and we were whisked away upward. The sensation was alarming, and my knees almost buckled. She watched this and showed me her teeth.

"Amusing," she said. "Physically weak, but mentally strong... I'll enjoy breaking you to discover the nature of your deception."

"I'm not deceiving anyone, Captain... at least, not right now."

We rode upward for a few seconds more before the lift stopped as suddenly as it had started. The damned thing stopped so fast I was worried I'd be thrown up into the ceiling. As it was, my feet left the floor by an inch.

But the lift had been well-engineered. The doors snicked open, and I saw the command deck for the first time.

The place was bustling with large predators, along with the occasional primate. The primates were arrogant and small, but they were usually in charge. It was interesting to see brains winning out over brawn in repeated cases.

"Your kind isn't loved," the captain said, eyeing me sidelong. "You're tolerated. Do you understand the difference?"

"It's all the same to me, Captain," I said. "I just want to defeat the enemy."

To me, that seemed like a safe statement, but it garnered an unexpected response.

"There!" she boomed suddenly, extending a long arm with an accusatory finger at the end of it. She pointed into my face as if she'd spotted a demon.

"There what?" I demanded.

"There it is! The ultimate arrogance. You speak of *victory*. No one else talks like that."

I looked at her curiously. "Why not? Wouldn't you like to win?"

She came close, puffing down hot breath from her twin nostrils. Each of those holes were big around enough to fit my thumb inside—but I certainly wouldn't want to try it.

"Arrogance. Cocky self-assurance. That's the path to total defeat. We're not in this war to win, Blake. We're in this war to cause twinges of pain to the Imperials. If we can inflict enough tiny stings, they will retreat to their star cluster for another thousand years. It's the best we can hope for."

"Why not go for the gusto, sir?" I asked her. "Why not strike deep? We could fly right into their tight knot of stars and drop a few gravity-bombs of our own."

Ursahn laughed tiredly. "Would that we could… I'm relieved by your foolish statements. They prove to me that you're not scheming—you're an ignoramus. Here, follow me."

Reluctantly, I followed her to her office. Along the way, I found the command deck was better appointed in every conceivable manner. Countless details were upgraded when compared to the Spartan environment I was familiar with below decks.

The passages were wider and more brightly lit. There was plush padding under my feet and covering the walls, while the lower decks were adorned with nothing other than hard metal. The padding wasn't exactly a carpet, but it was certainly softer on the feet than pure titanium.

Several prying eyes and flicking ears followed us as we passed them by. We were obviously generating a lot of curiosity, but she remained stoic.

She walked me to her office, which was minimal in furnishings. There was no desk—there wasn't even a chair. Instead, I saw a set of short thick stumps. She squatted on one of these and looked at me expectantly. I imitated her pose—putting my hands on my knees, but I didn't find it comfortable. It was like perching on a metal fencepost.

"Prove to me you didn't fabricate your report," she ordered.

I laughed. "I can't—but I don't have to."

"What? You try to manipulate me so baldly? I'm not a simple feline, Blake. I don't want you to play with my tail."

"Um… yeah…" I said. "I'm sure we're both happy about that. But what I'm trying to say is that the facts are self-evident. You've got the ship's data, you've got our suit-data—"

Her hand waved for my attention. "Enough. All of these things can be faked."

"Maybe," I admitted. "But I'd have to have a lab packed with techs, and a month to pull it off. I had neither."

"Nevertheless, I can't accept what you're saying. I can't accept that an Imperial ship was so easily hacked by amateurs."

"Has anyone else been captured by these guys and reported back?" I asked.

"Captives are extremely rare. The Imperials prefer to kill those who dare to beg for mercy. That's another reason that your story doesn't make sense, and it makes me suspicious of all the rest."

"Then what's your explanation for our return? Do you think I just went through a rift with a cruiser, then sat out there in space and fabricated an elaborate scenario? If that's how it happened, how did I get back to Rigel?"

She eyed me stubbornly.

"No," she said at last. "I do believe you were captured, but that's where your lies begin. I think you sat aboard the Imperial ship and fabricated the rest of this tale—or rather, that they did it for you. The Imperials falsified this 'evidence' to support your mad story."

"So… I'm a traitor?"

"Yes," she said. "That is the inescapable conclusion. Now can you understand my hostility?"

"Sure, but why don't you just space my entire crew right now if you think that's what happened?"

"Because we're not completely certain. That's the diabolical genius of this plot. It stinks like ape-scat—but we can't be absolutely *sure* that it is."

I spent a moment thinking hard. There had to be some way to convince this battle axe I wasn't bullshitting her.

After a moment, I snapped my fingers in the air. Ursahn recoiled sharply, as if the unexpected sound heralded some kind of personal attack.

"Listen," I said, "Why the hell would I—or the Imperials—come up with a convoluted story like this? Why not something simple?"

"Because they want to trick us into a foolish attack that can't possibly succeed," she said. "You want us to expose our fleet: to face the enemy in a large battle with a great trick to play—only, the trick will be on us."

It was my turn to sigh and shake my head.

"What do you take me for?" I asked. "The worst traitor that ever lived? These Imperials might come and destroy Earth, you know."

She leaned closer.

"They might indeed have that intention," she said, "and that might be the very reason you're cooperating with them. Did they threaten your home world, Blake? Did they promise not to harm your people in return for planting this mad story?"

I leaned toward her.

"Look," I said, "aren't you tired of being pushed around out here by the Imperials? Don't you want a little slice of revenge?"

"Of course I do."

"Well then, listen-up. I'm going to tell you how it works, and how we can *prove* it works without endangering more than one warship."

I had her listening at last as I laid out my plans. Before I finished, she contacted Admiral Fex. He came to our ship via shuttle, and he listened to me as well.

Neither of the officers was thrilled with my plan. They were intrigued, but they weren't yet total believers.

It was my job to change their minds.

=44=

With Admiral Fex backing us, we were quickly granted permission to fly *Killer* off on a private mission. I think it was his personal greed for glory points that made it all possible. He was still stinging from losing a rank. He wanted his points back, and he was willing to take risks to regain them.

The next day, *Killer* performed a stellar-jump from Rigel to a location that was about six hundred lightyears closer to Orion. Sadly, our front lines had been pressed back that far. Our forces had been driven deep into friendly territory by the loss at Cygnus Minor.

"This is it, Blake," Captain Ursahn told me. "We can't go any farther without running into enemy patrols."

I turned to the admiral, who'd been watching me with sidelong suspicion the entire time.

"Admiral Fex," I said, "do you believe me?"

"To a point," he said. "I *do* believe that you had an unusual experience out here."

I rolled my eyes, but fortunately the others didn't know enough about human gestures to be insulted.

"Do you at least trust me, sir?"

"Not at all."

"Then we might as well turn back now," I said, crossing my arms. "I'm sorry the captain and I wasted your time."

The captain looked alarmed. She'd been enjoying the admiral's reluctance, but she didn't like the idea of being blamed for wasting the admiral's time.

"What?" she asked. "Blake, I order you to proceed. Perform your test!"

"Can't do it. We must have an enemy patrol—preferably a small one—to test my theories."

The captain sputtered then turned to the admiral. "Well? What should we do, sir?"

The admiral looked at me with hooded eyes. He smirked then nodded.

"All right, Blake," he said. "We'll try it your way. By the way, I admire the size of your genitals."

This last statement made me blink for a second before I figured out the translator was probably struggling with an idiom. I nodded to him, and the captain sighed as she gave the order.

We jumped again, a short hop this time, which led directly into enemy territory.

There were three ships in the system. There were planets as well, but they were dark and dead.

"They've bombed them out," the captain said. "Monsters. They deserve to die. If you can kill these Imperials, Blake, I'll hold your tail myself!"

Grimly, I accepted her statement without comment. She'd apparently forgotten I possessed no tail, but I still understood the heartfelt nature of her emotions.

"We have to get closer," I said. "Under a million miles. Then we have to knock down one of the ship's shields."

They both looked at me in surprise.

"This is a carrier Blake," Admiral Fex said. "We have only fighters to perform attacks at range."

"That's right sir. I think you should release them all and have the mothership hang back. Let me lead the squadrons… or—" I said quickly as I saw their expressions, "—or have Shaw command, with orders for him to get me in close. We must take down one shield of one ship."

"That's all?"

"Yes, that will do it. Their computers will be able to receive our transmissions with a shield down. If *Hammerhead* isn't destroyed before we can get in close—"

"*Hammerhead*?" the admiral asked.

"The name of Blake's fighter, sir," the captain filled in.

"Oh, I see... All right. Have your CAG fly out a squadron in a tight formation, Captain. Immediately."

She blinked a few times, but she didn't argue. She gave the orders. As I turned to leave, I heard Admiral Fex say to her quietly: "If he fails, at least we'll be rid of him."

With my stomach churning, I took the lift back down to the hangar deck and climbed aboard *Hammerhead*. She'd been left revving and floating above the deck in the hangar.

My crew was full of questions, but I waved them into silence. Flying down the closest chute, we were fired out of a cannon and into open space.

"Orders, Chief?" Samson asked.

"Deflectors angled forward. Accelerate to attack speed and start praying."

"I don't know how, Chief," he complained.

"Then start learning fast."

We crossed the star system with alarming speed. About two hundred similar small craft cruised nearby. We were all within a zone that was no more than a hundred miles in diameter.

At about a million miles out, the Imperials finally took notice of our approach. Up until then, they'd ignored us. Maybe they'd calculated that our suicidal launch was too weak to be anything other than a show of force.

But as we closed in deadly earnest, they left orbit from around the dead planet they circled and came directly toward us. Big bolts of energy came driving out through space, sweeping away a fighter every now and then. We were all bobbing and weaving like mad, but they were still scoring hits.

We'd lost about ten percent of our fighters before we could throw our first shot back at them. The big cruisers shrugged off our bolts with disdain.

"Blake," Shaw said in my ear via my sym, "you'd better be right about this, or we're all dead. In fact, we might all be dead anyway."

"Lieutenant," I told him, "you have to get them to stop firing. We must be in close enough to drop a shield. Otherwise, we're wasting our time."

He sighed, but passed along the order. The group's formation was becoming ragged by the time we were within a hundred thousand miles of the enemy. We'd taken losses, and some were hanging back. No one seemed interested in charging forward.

I was with one of the groups hanging back. I felt bad about doing it, but it was necessary. If we were shot down, this whole exercise would have been for nothing.

I'll say one thing about Rebel fighter pilots, they might be disorganized and feisty, but when push came to shove they were almost all individually brave. Even the beetles were pulling their weight today, zooming along with the rest. Maybe it was the dead planet that had them angry enough to fight.

"It's down, Chief!" Gwen shouted from the back. "Shield four, topside."

"Let's do this before they get smart," I said, reaching out with my sym.

By this time, I'd taught the rest of my crew how to do my tricks. I hadn't had time to show anyone else, not that they'd get it anyway without this demonstration.

We let our syms go. That was most of it. Mine had trained the others, and with a burst of what looked like simple RF on any scope, we managed to penetrate the network aboard the Imperial vessel we'd targeted.

In less than a minute, the central vessel had stopped firing. We all whooped excitedly.

"Good," I said, "we've disabled her weapons. But that's not good enough."

"Let's drop her shields, Chief," Mia said. "We could tear her up if she had no shields."

She was gripping and re-gripping her gun mount excitedly, like any predator that smelled blood. But I shook my head.

"We stick to the plan. Gain helm control. Everyone, together now."

This time, the task was harder. Our syms were into the Imperial ship's network, but shutting down a system was much easier than assuming control of it.

Worse, her shield was flickering on again.

"Dammit!" I yelled, "Shaw! They have to keep that shield down!"

"The middle ship is no longer firing, Blake. The wings have switched targets."

"No, no, no!" I growled. "You'll kill us all."

"I don't like your tone, Ensign."

I closed my eyes in intense frustration. "Keep one shield down, *please*, sir."

"All right."

They resumed pelting the middle ship, and the flickering shield died. Our syms were in control again a moment later.

Then, like magic, the big ship started to change course. She swung around ponderously at first, engines flaring blue.

"She's going to do it," Samson said in awe. "She's really going to do it."

The rest of us said nothing. We just stared until the ship we'd hacked slammed into her nearest partner.

The ramming effort was a spectacular success. I could only imagine how the Imperials aboard must have been howling, fighting their controls in disbelief.

The second victim tried to dodge out of the way initially, but she'd been too busy shooting down incoming fighters to worry much about a sister ship that was getting overly friendly. They were utterly taken by surprise, that much was clear.

Both ships went up in a conjoining sheet of flame and released gases. It was both spectacular and grim. Thousands of lives had been snuffed out. Not a soul got away as far as I could tell.

The last ship finally realized something was horribly wrong. She fired up her engines and zoomed right through our lines. At first, I thought she was rushing *Killer*—but she had other plans.

"The last ship is shaping a rift," Shaw said in my ear. My sym projected his voice into my ear as though he had been aboard *Hammerhead* with me. "She's running for her life. A job well done, Blake. I have to say, I wouldn't have believed—"

"We have to kill the last cruiser, Lieutenant," I said quickly.

Already, I'd flipped *Hammerhead* around and zoomed in pursuit. Others were following, but they were doing so at a lackadaisical pace. As far as they were concerned, the battle had been won.

"Such blood-thirst, Blake! I do admire that in a pilot, but this time—"

"Listen," I told him, "we've got to stop that ship. If she gets away and reports on what happened here, our surprise will be lost the next time. We can't let that ship escape."

"How can we stop her? She'll be gone in a few minutes."

"Knock out her aft shield. That's all you have to do. Take down her stern shielding and keep *Hammerhead* alive. We'll do the rest."

He grumbled, but he relayed the order. The fighter wing swung around and formed up into a loose mass. We began firing at the escaping ship. Already, the telltale signs of a growing rip in space-time were beginning to manifest.

It was a close thing in the end. We barely managed to knock out her shield, and then it was only for thirty seconds or so.

But that was long enough. Our syms were primed. They had done this before and were ready to go again. Their collective assault on the ship's networks was soon effective.

The ship turned then, reluctantly. It was almost like watching a sailing vessel fighting a powerful wind.

But she did turn. She missed the rift that now hung open before her. She locked onto a new target, and she plunged toward it with single-minded determination.

In the end, she outran us. We couldn't follow her safely to her final destination.

I thought I saw the Imperials regain control of their ship right at the end, but by that time, they'd already entered the smoky atmosphere of the planet they'd bombed into oblivion.

They vanished for a brief moment into the dark clouds, then a white flash lit up the surface of a dead world.

"It was a fitting end for those arrogant assholes," Samson said with feeling.

The rest of us said nothing in return, but we all felt the same.

Down on the planet, the atmosphere boiled and rippled like a disturbed pond for several minutes.

=45=

One would think that after a great victory honor and swift promotion would follow, but the Rebel Fleet operated by its own obscure rules.

When we returned to *Killer*, we landed and stepped out onto the hangar deck proudly. A dozen fellow pilots came out to eye us in alarm.

Some of them had overheard my conversations with Shaw. Word had spread quickly that we were the source of the voodoo show they'd all seen out there. They didn't know what to make of it.

The first group to approach me was the Terrapinians. I hadn't spoken to this particular crew of assholes since we'd fought to a grim finish in the arena.

Reflexively, we all put our hands on our weapons. They came toward us unarmed, but we didn't trust them at all.

"What do you want?" Samson demanded.

The leader's big head turned to regard him, but he made no response. He looked back to me, as if I was the only one worthy of note. Perhaps, in their culture, being questioned by a subordinate was an insult.

"I would speak to you, Blake," he said slowly. The voice was deep and it carried.

"Talk," I said. "I don't have much time. I'm going up to the command deck again soon."

"I know this. I see the truth of what others have told us—you are not like the weak here who toil and die in this steel box."

"Uh... okay," I said, pretty sure he was complimenting me. "You fought well out there, too."

"I'm glad you noticed. I wish to offer my fealty, as you no doubt expected."

I blinked and frowned. "What? Why?"

"Because you have repeatedly bested me. You challenged me immediately, and you have always won. There is no longer a need for rivalry between us."

I narrowed my eyes. "Last time we made a deal, you backstabbed us. Why should I trust you now?"

His black shiny eyes stared at me. "You don't understand. I'm not offering you a partnership. My people don't accept such things. We know only lords and vassals. I wish to be your vassal."

"Huh..." I said, uncertain as to how to take his offer. "Well... okay. You're my vassal. But I'm only one step above you in rank. What if we rise further? What if you outrank me someday?"

"I find that unlikely," he said. "But if it does happen, I would be dishonored, as you are my lord. This military—"

He made a sweeping gesture that seemed to encompass the entire Rebel organization. "This is strange to us. Meaningless. We do not cooperate that way. We are lords, or we are vassals. No one we've met until now has been worthy, in our opinion, to rule us."

"So..." I said, beginning to catch on, "if I gave you an order, and Captain Ursahn told you to do something else, which order would you follow?"

"Yours, of course."

I nodded, seeing possibilities. "All right," I said. "I accept your oath. I hereby order you to follow the orders coming from the Rebels for now."

"It will be as you command."

The Terrapinians retreated then, and my crew stared after them, shaking their heads.

"Real freaks," Samson said. "At least we'll no longer have to post a watch every night."

"At least we've got that going for us," Gwen agreed with a hint of sarcasm.

Captain Ursahn summoned me soon afterward, and I took the lift up to the command deck. Stepping onto those plush floors like I owned the place, I walked toward her office.

But I was waylaid long before I got there.

Fleet regulars stepped out and surrounded me. I noticed they all looked similar to Captain Ursahn. They had to be from the same planet. They were tall with corded necks and dark lips that twitched as if they were perpetually about to snarl.

These regulars grabbed my arms and held them. Only then did the captain appear herself.

"What's this bullshit?" I demanded.

"I'm sorry about this, Blake," she said. "You've scared people, that's all. What you did today was impossible."

That's when Admiral Fex finally showed his snout. I sneered at him.

"I'm a hero, haven't you heard?" I demanded. "You're supposed to give me a medal or something!"

"Maybe," he said, looking at me like I was a bug that could talk. "Or maybe you're the worst danger we've yet to encounter. The Rebel council will decide."

He made a gesture to the Fleet regulars, and they produced stunners.

Before I could object, they applied them repeatedly to my skull. The stunners hit me with sonic waves of such intensity, it was like being beaten over the head with soft mallets.

It took them three shots, to my credit, before I crumpled to the deck at their traitorous feet.

* * *

It was hours—or possibly days—before I woke up again. I found myself stripped and hung in a suspension system of gray straps.

There were needles buried in my arms, my neck and my back. Some of these were connected to wires, others to tubes. I didn't like either kind.

I struggled wearily, trying to wake up.

"What the hell...?" I mumbled.

"He's coming around," said a voice.

The owner of the voice turned out to be a guy in a fur suit. He was an ape of some kind—a real hairball. He looked like a gorilla, but his hair was silver rather than black. He was also rather small. No more than five feet tall.

Moving around me, he poked and prodded me with his instruments.

"Careful," I told him. "Or I'll make you rip your own dick off."

This statement startled the ape for a second. He galloped away a few paces, moving sideways almost like a crab. Then he straightened and cleared his throat.

"Very funny," he said. "We know you can only control Imperial computer systems."

"Why'd you run, then?" I asked.

He came closer and peered up at me. "You really *are* a primate," he said. "The worst of our kind. The ones that most resemble the Imperials themselves. That's your problem. It will *always* be your biggest problem."

I frowned, trying to grasp what he was saying. Was he trying to help? Or was this a threat? I wasn't sure, but I got the idea humans weren't favored for good reasons. We just looked too much like the hated Imperials. Worse, I'd now demonstrated tech that the Rebels didn't understand.

Still fuzzy, I was trying to wrap my brain around what I should do next. I didn't come up with anything immediately, other than to try to get more information out of my caretaker.

"Hey! Hey, ape! Come back here."

But he didn't. A delegation of primates arrived instead. Among them was Admiral Fex. The others looked like they were politicians, scientists, or what-have-you.

"It doesn't *look* dangerous," said one of the political types. He wore a suit of shimmering light. It took me a second to realize it was a projection of some kind. Underneath, he was hairy and built with lumpy muscles.

"You're the leader of this bunch?" I asked him.

"Not exactly," he said. "I'm an interstellar liaison. I coordinate the requirements of our many allied worlds."

"Hmm…" I said. "A bureaucrat? What's your title?"

"I'm Secretary Thoth," he said, as if this should explain everything.

In a way, it did. The Rebels had never seemed to me to be overly organized. They were an alliance of necessity. They reminded me of the UN back home, or maybe NATO. Worse than that, even.

"Well, why am I hanging in straps with a rubber hose up my ass?" I demanded.

A few of the delegates twisted their necks and peered, no doubt trying to catch a glimpse of this imaginary hose. I let them look.

"We must apologize," the Secretary said, "but you've put us in an awkward position."

"How so?"

"Your… *experiment*… should not have been allowed. It may even have doomed more of our planets."

Frowning, I looked from one to the next. "Cut me down from here, sirs," I said. "Let me show you how to do what I did today."

"That was four days ago, actually," said one of them.

"Whatever. We destroyed three cruisers with a single carrier. I can do more than that. Let me show you how."

"It's not that simple," the Secretary said. "We don't want an escalation."

"An escalation?" I asked incredulously. "What are you talking about? The Imperials are destroying whole worlds out there!"

"Yes. But they weren't angry then, just having a little fun. If we were to hurt them badly, however, they might take this to the next level."

"What do you mean?"

Secretary Thoth came near. He seemed to have more balls than most of them.

"You have to understand our position. I've recently researched your world. You have historical precedents. You have nuclear weapons, yes?"

"Of course we do."

"But do you use them in every conflict? Do your leaders drop one, for example, when a city riots?"

"No, that would be absurd."

"Exactly! A clear overreaction. Now, what if a hunter stalks and kills game animals—but one of the animals gets lucky and kills the hunter. Would you blow up the entire forest?"

"No..." I said, almost laughing.

But a part of me was beginning to understand what he was saying.

"You mean..." I said, "that we have to be careful, because the Imperials have more power than they were displaying against us right now?"

"Exactly. The ships they've sent to invade our space are only training vessels. We don't want to face their actual warships."

I nodded slowly.

"What's our strategy then?" I asked. "How do we go about defeating the Imperials?"

The scientist ape who'd been prodding me earlier turned toward Admiral Fex who I now noticed was at the rear of the pack. "You're right. He's a smart one. Dangerous..."

Admiral Fex nodded nervously. I had the feeling he'd also stepped in this without meaning to.

"We've determined that you're operating your technical miracle purely out of your sym," the Secretary said. "That's very impressive. Doctor Shug, here, is to be credited."

He waved forward the ape I'd met first—the short guy with the fur coat and the lousy bedside manner.

"Doctor Shug," the Secretary continued, "is the being who invented your sym. You've done more with it than we'd ever thought possible."

"That's right," Shug said, "the syms were designed to quickly build up a coherent force from an incoherent mass of recruits. They sped up the selection process, facilitated translation and training—many things."

"Right," I said, "but by giving us a universal interface that can work with networks, you created a hacking platform that we humans were able to use to our advantage."

"Exactly," Secretary Thoth said, bobbing his head happily. "I'm very glad we had this talk. Your understanding of the situation wasn't entirely necessary, but it will make the rest of this unfortunate process so much easier. Thank you."

"It will stand up in court, if challenged," announced another skinny fellow in the back. "As the state's attorney, I'd now be willing to argue the execution was done appropriately. It's a sad case, but unavoidable."

My expression went from a baffled frown to one of alarm. "Execution?" I asked.

"Yes," Secretary Thoth said, turning back to me. "Isn't it obvious that's why we're here? We're a Rebel Tribunal, Blake. A duly appointed group of representatives. Your case was tried over the preceding days, and your public defender was most eloquent—where is she, by the way?"

He looked around the group, but no one raised their hand.

"Well, no matter," he said. "She failed to convince the body at large you were innocent by reason of ignorance. Execution was the verdict, but legally we had to inform you. You've now been formally and publicly sentenced, with all the appropriate officials present. The bylaws have thus been satisfied, and we can proceed."

"The bylaws…?" I echoed, stunned. "You people are insane! I saved your hairy asses! I can save more of you if you'll let me out of these straps. I'll lead your ragtag fleet to victory, if you just—"

"The prisoner is becoming agitated," Secretary Thoth said smoothly. "Shug?"

The short ape trundled forward, giving me a reluctant shake of the head. He tapped at a bulb at the end of a needle stuck in my neck. The bulb shivered and pumped.

I felt woozy. They were drugging me. In immediate reaction, I went limp and drooled on the floor.

"You gave him too much!" Secretary Thoth admonished.

"Strange..." Doctor Shug said. "Well, I am new to his biology. Perhaps the stress cortisones in his system reacted with the—"

"Who cares? Did you kill him?"

"No..." Shug said, consulting his instruments.

"Good... We'll do it right then, in public, tomorrow. Record everything in case the Imperial Hunting Council demands an accounting. Admiral Fex, you're lucky you're not the one hanging up there by your balls."

"Yes Mr. Secretary," I heard Fex say. "I'm so sorry, sir."

"Save it, Admiral," Thoth said. He indicated me with a head gesture, which I could see through my half-closed eyes. "Don't screw this up, Dr. Shug."

"No, Mr. Secretary. That's not my habit."

Then the group shuffled out. I let myself dangle in my straps, as limp as a wet dishtowel.

After a full minute, I felt a hairy presence under me. It breathed, and it stank, forcing me to finally crack one eye.

Dr. Shug grinned up at me.

"I knew you were faking," he said. "You *are* the best of our breed, Blake. Every trait is present in your genes, outlined in glorious detail. Devious, resourceful—it's going to be a shame to toss your corpse into the furnace."

Then he followed the rest of them. He made a tsking sound as he shambled off.

=46=

My next play wasn't going to be an easy one. Rebel tech wasn't like Imperial tech. It was built to keep devious types out.

But I had experience now, as did my sym. The symbiotic was really the key to the whole thing. It was, as far as I could tell, the single biggest advance the Rebels had made that went beyond what the Imperials could do. The ironic thing was that they hadn't invented it to break into security systems. It was built to influence emotions and provide a standard interface for countless people from many different planets.

It performed with nearly flawless precision on those accounts—but it was the extra, unexpected ability I was interested in now.

"Sym, my old friend," I said, talking to the loose collective of cells that resided in my body with me. "I need some magic now. Get me out of this harness."

Fortunately, even the Rebels worked with high tech gadgetry in their labs. They didn't use mechanical locks with keys or combinations. They used electronics.

Tight bands of metal wire were inside the straps that had me bound. They were very strong. Not even the biggest primate could have broken them.

But I didn't have to use brute force. I simply gave my sym the order and waited. Now and then, it tossed back a report that printed on the inside of my retina. It was trying out combinations of signals to hack the locks on my wrists.

This went on for more time than I felt was reasonable. I tried not to look nervous or to fidget while waiting, but it was difficult.

My life might very well depend on some sentient slime that coursed through my veins. That was pretty much what a brain was, of course, but somehow this time around it felt different because I wasn't in conscious control of what the sym was doing. It was like having to depend on your subconscious to solve your problems.

After nearly an hour, I was beginning to despair. I told myself I should get some sleep, that maybe I'd get a chance to break free in a more conventional fashion in the morning.

But there was no way I could do that. My body was humming with adrenaline. I was hungry, my limbs ached, and I wanted to get the hell out of here immediately.

At some point during the second hour, I heard a familiar shuffling gait. Dr. Shug was coming back.

Shit, I thought. Could it be morning already? Could I have misjudged the time, or perhaps they were on a different schedule in this star system? I had no idea, but I knew I didn't want to be marched to my execution yet.

When I saw him, he looked me up and down, and a new worry gripped me. Did he know what I was up to? Was he monitoring net traffic and therefore been alerted to the clumsy efforts of my sym? It was perfectly possible. These guys were far more sophisticated when it came to security compared to the Imperials.

He put his hands on his hips, which I found to be a very human gesture.

"Disappointing," he said.

"Who? Me?"

"Yes. I've gambled and lost this time."

He sighed and began working on a panel off to one side of the room. I saw numbers flash up, but I had no idea what they might indicate.

"I don't understand," I said.

"Of course you don't. You got lucky out there against the Imperials, that's all. I'm a fool."

It was right about at this point in the conversation that my left wrist came free. I almost blew it by yelping aloud as it fell and dangled. *Damn* it was sore, and a little bit numb. I drew a sharp breath, trying not to hiss.

"Yes," Dr. Shug said, "I see these clumsy transmissions. Simply repeating codes until you get the right one? The stuff of amateurs. This log of access-attempts is a disgrace."

My left arm was operating now, but it was still sore and weak. I reached to unbuckle the central strap that held my chest, and it fell away in my hands. It had already been unlocked.

Dr. Shug scrolled down the data listed in front of him. I knew now that he was looking at a sequential log of attempted security hacking. The work my sym had been doing over the last hour or so.

"Hmm..." he said, pausing. "This is different. It's advanced several notches. The data from the earlier responses is being used as feedback... Could it be learning from its mistakes?"

I didn't answer. I was too busy struggling with the last major buckles. All the locks were off and dangling. If Shug had been looking at current data instead of an old log, he would have surely noticed this. But like many technical people, he was lost in the details.

The next thing that happened was very painful. I'd forgotten about the needles and tubes stuck into my body. When the harness let me go, these all ripped out in a wave of pain. It was like being stabbed by a dozen long forks at once from every angle.

I landed on my face with a meaty slap. Summoning what I had left in the way of physical prowess, I forced myself to my feet, grabbed one of these dripping, pencil-thick metal needles and approached the doctor.

He'd turned around by now. He stood there, mouth agape, transfixed by what he saw. I must have looked pretty scary. After all, he was a small primate.

My right hand jabbed forward. He caught it in both of his. He was quick and strong—stronger than he looked. If there was one trait a primate typically possessed, it was physical power.

My left hand jabbed then. My right had been a fake. It no longer held the needle. I got him in the belly.

I felt a pang of sorrow about all this. I kind of liked Shug—but I liked breathing even more.

He gasped and made a choking sound. He looked down in disbelief.

Then, he did something I wasn't expecting at all. He looked up at me and smiled.

"Well done, you tricky savage! Well done! There is hope!"

I heard clapping behind me. I whirled around, almost falling as I was still off-balance from spending hours in those dangling straps. The needle in my hand glinted with a splash of fresh, red blood dribbling from the tip.

There was the gaggle of other apes. Two of the guardians were with them, stunners leveled.

Everyone but the guardians seemed happy about the situation.

"Tell me," Dr. Shug said, hobbling around to face me again, "why did you wait so long to make your move? Did you want a hostage? I'm intrigued as to the cunning details of your plans."

I gaped at him, then at the delegation. The Secretary was among them. I addressed him first.

"What the hell is wrong with you people?" I demanded. "Was this all some kind of joke?"

"No," Secretary Thoth said. "Not at all. As you can see, we're not laughing. We had to test you. It's our way."

"Yeah," I said, seeking a chair and sinking into it. "So, you're not going to execute me at dawn?"

There were a few twitters from the group at that. Apparently, some of them had a sense of humor.

"No, of course not," Secretary Thoth said. "We owe you an apology, but you have to understand, if we follow your methods in a large battle, we're risking all of our home worlds. You can understand how serious this is, can't you?"

"I guess..." I muttered in irritation.

Dr. Shug had been working a healing patch onto his skin where I'd stabbed him, but now approached me. He had another handful of patches, so I let him do his work. He sealed up the holes the needles had left in my skin, and I soon felt better.

"You're one tricky fur-ball yourself," I told him. "Did you turn your back on me to encourage me to make my move?"

"Yes. We've all been watching for about two hours while you did virtually nothing. We were growing bored, so we came up with this charade to get you moving."

Every complaint about primates I'd heard for months echoed in my mind. I was beginning to really get why the other groups found them irritating.

The Secretary stepped closer and smiled at me. "You did perform in the end, Blake. Admirably. We locked you up with standard hardware, no cheating. To pass the test, you had to successfully escape this room."

"That's great..." I mumbled, rubbing my head. "They told me during my training that primates were tricky, but I had no idea."

"Now, now, don't sell yourself short," Shug said. "That switch of the weapon from one hand to the other—that was masterful."

"Glad you liked it," I said. "I also enjoyed sinking that icepick into you as payback."

His face faltered for a second, and that brought me a small tickle of happiness. I didn't want these clowns thinking they could relax completely around me.

Shug shuffled back a few steps, and I knew I'd earned his respect.

"This is interesting..." said the Secretary. "You're a predator *and* a primate. That's a rare combination. I can see why you've climbed our hierarchy so rapidly."

"Listen," I said, "is there any chance I can get some sleep in a real bed now? And where the hell is my crew?"

"There will be a few hours for rest before the next phase. As to your crew, they're all in cells awaiting the outcome of this test."

"What would have happened if I'd failed?"

"Well..." the Secretary said, fidgeting with his hairy, overly-long thumbs. "It's best not to think about that... The good news is that you *didn't* fail. You won through, and we've all agreed to give your plan another try on a much bigger scale."

"What's my part in this Charley-Foxtrot going to be?" I asked him.

He looked confused. "What's the meaning of that idiom? The translation system has failed."

"Never mind," I told him with a grin. "What do you want to do next?"

He told me then, and before the end of his explanation, I had a fresh headache to contend with.

=47=

We spent the next several weeks training others how to use their syms to take over an Imperial network. One of the problems we had was the requirement of getting in close enough to the enemy to subvert their security systems. The only viable ships we had that could do it were fighters.

"Here's the core of the plan," Shaw said, marching back and forth in front of the fighter crews. "Our big gunships are going to knock down the shields on every tenth enemy vessel. Then, a group of five fighters with trained crews from *Killer* will do the hacking attack."

"What will prevent the enemy from wiping us out?" Ra-tikh demanded.

"A full squadron from another carrier will lead the way," Shaw explained.

"Ah…" Ra-tikh said happily. "I like that. They will be lifting our tails for us, killing themselves to keep us safe."

Shaw didn't answer, he merely shrugged and went on outlining the plan. I hardly listened as I knew the details by heart—hell, I'd come up with a lot of them.

Before long, we were strapping in and getting ready to launch. Extending my perception, I reached out with my sym and saw the Rebel Fleet begin to create rifts and plunge through them.

A dozen cruisers vanished, then fifty more. The battleships followed—we only had six of those left. Last in line, the carriers exited the system. *Killer* was the very last ship to vanish from this part of the universe, and a moment later we reappeared somewhere else.

When the carrier exited the rift, I relaxed at first. There was no incoming fire, and I was glad we hadn't jumped into the middle of a pitched battle.

But as I scanned our surroundings with my sym, I realized we were far from anything at all…

"We've scattered!" I shouted in disbelief.

"Are you sure?" Samson asked.

Gwen and Dr. Chang worked at their screens.

"It's true," Dr. Chang said at last. "I'm getting a direct feed from *Killer's* external array. There isn't anything out here. Not even a star."

My heart pounded, and I contacted Shaw. I wasn't supposed to do that yet, but this was too big.

"Lieutenant?" I asked. "We've scattered. You know that, don't you?"

"No shit, Blake," he said, although I was sure he'd said it differently in his own language. "The pilots are panicking. *Killer* is trying to build up a charge to jump again. It will take several minutes, even if nothing goes wrong."

"Several minutes? Without our secret weapon? Can't we tell the other ships to pull out? To withdraw from battle?"

"No," he said. "We're too far away. A couple of lightyears at least. The rest of the fleet jumped in close to the enemy in order to get the fighters into hacking range—but *Killer's* fighters won't be there."

"They all know the theory," I said. "Maybe they'll be able to work it out in the heat of battle."

Shaw shook his head. "I doubt it. Even on this ship, your crew is the best at this particular bit of sabotage."

He was right, I knew. I'd been surprised how poorly the Kher Rebels did when it came to hacking with their syms. I supposed every sub-race had their specialties. Some had better reaction times than we did. Others could take more injuries and stress. The cat-people, for example, couldn't even use basic perception tricks. Their syms served mostly as communication devices.

But there was something about our human brains that was different when they combined us with symbiotic slime.

It all came down to our brain structure. The syms worked with the materials they were given, and they synched best with our brains. They didn't replace our intellect, but they worked to enhance what we could already do. In the case of individuals like the turtles or the beetles, you couldn't do much for them. It was like putting a turbo engine on a skateboard. Small wheels could only spin so fast before they melted.

Despite the fact they weren't well-suited for it, I'd done my best to train the others. Those few who were primate-related did the best, along with the wolf-packs. Those were the only sub-groups with minds capable of doing this kind of gymnastics.

We waited for long minutes while *Killer* recharged and formed a new rift. When we dove through the rip in space-time at last, we were prepared to encounter the worst, and we weren't disappointed.

Our Rebel Fleet was half the size of the enemy flotilla, and it was immediately obvious their ships were better organized.

The only piece of good news was we'd taken the Imperials by surprise. We'd rammed right into the midst of their fleet, causing confusion.

While we'd been lightyears away, the Rebels had fought hard and done fairly well all things considered. But the superior weight of the Imperial Fleet was beginning to change the tide of the battle.

At first, the Imperials had been startled by the ferocity of the Rebel attack, and they'd retreated into a defensive sphere formation. Then they'd realized there weren't another thousand ships coming in behind the first few hundred that had assailed them, and they'd begun to counterattack.

That's when *Killer* finally showed up.

"Launch!" Shaw shouted, his voice almost cracking. "Open the bay doors! Launch everything we've got right now!"

The ships had been lining up to be fired out of the launch cannon, but that approach would have taken several minutes.

Instead, the big doors yawned, and a growing rectangle of black space stretched between them.

Sucked out with the ship's venting air, we were lifted up and tossed out into space with the rest. We did our best to avoid slamming into other fighters before we were outside and able to fire up our engines.

Instead of moving directly to the predetermined rally points, I shot upward, away from the central mass of fighters. A moment later I executed a hard banking turn and poured on the power. We were flying toward the battle at maximum acceleration.

Only a few pilots had matched my move. Most of them trailed behind us.

"Chief," Samson said, "Ra-tikh is requesting that we wait for him and follow the plan."

"Imagine that," I said, "a tiger begging to follow my orders. He just wants to get in on the glory. That bunch couldn't hack a joystick—no offense, Mia."

She shot me a look and lifted her lip to show me a fang. "None taken," she said.

"They've got Dalton aboard that ship," Gwen said from the back.

I cranked my head around to look at her. "Yeah… they do. All right, but tell them to catch up fast."

Easing off on the throttle, I allowed a group of fighters to straggle closer. They'd all been assigned to me, and I knew they couldn't do much without my help. All the same, waiting for them to catch up was almost unbearable.

By the time we fired up our afterburners and accelerated on our attack approach, two more cruisers had blown up in the distance. Both of them were Rebel ships.

Unfortunately, I knew our Rebels by now. They would soon break and run if things didn't improve. That would result in a rout, and further losses.

At last my group was ready, and we were accelerating at full throttle toward the battle.

"Blake, you're out of position," Shaw called to me a few minutes later.

"Negative, sir," I said. "We're going for the nearest enemy ship that has her shields down."

"Dammit, that's not the plan!"

"None of this is going as planned, Lieutenant," I said in exasperation.

"You're going to cost me every status point I have, aren't you?" he demanded. "Before this is over, I'll be playing support-man on that fighter with you. Is that your secret plan for revenge?"

That made me laugh. "I'll assign you to cleaning out the black-water tanks, sir."

He didn't seem to think it was funny, and he closed the channel. I was glad to have gotten the last laugh.

We plunged on in silence for a full minute before enemy defensive guns began to strike along our line. One of our fighters blew up—I wasn't sure if it had run into a mine, or been caught by a lucky hit from the target ship. Either way, the whole crew had died instantly.

I kept pouring on the power, pushing *Hammerhead* to her limits. We weren't close enough, not yet.

One of the beetle ships exploded next. I actually felt bad about that. Those guys had shaped up since we'd last fought together, and they were close to becoming extinct.

"We're within range now," Gwen said. "Someone has knocked the target's shield down."

"Samson," I said, "go all-out with our defensive measures while our syms work the math."

Mia made a sound of disgust, throwing her hands in the air. She wanted to work her heavy cannon, and I was screwing that up for her. She crossed her arms over her breasts in frustration.

Samson was the busiest of us after that. He was our countermeasures specialist, and he was also the worst of my bunch when it came to hacking. He performed the critical function, however, of keeping my tiny ship in one piece.

Samson was reporting casualties into my ear as we let our syms do their work.

"We've lost twenty-two percent of our capital ships," Samson said. "No enemy interceptors yet in our quadrant—but it's just matter of time."

Dalton responded with a nasty chuckle. "Only a matter of minutes before these cowards pull out and run. We'll be in the soup then, won't we?"

"Yeah..." Samson said.

I wished they would shut up, but they were doing their jobs.

I could *feel* the target now. It was a small ship—an Imperial destroyer. I hadn't chosen it for its size, but rather for its availability. As a screening ship, it had been out in front of the Imperial battlewagons.

Our hack went smoothly. I was shocked by how easy it was to complete. Either our syms had gotten better at this through training, or we had. In either case, it was clear the Imperials had no defense against this kind of attack. I suspected they weren't even aware of the influence we were exerting over them. They must not have gotten any reports indicating what we were capable of.

With contemptuous ease, I flipped the enemy destroyer onto her back. Then I directed her toward the nearest enemy cruiser.

"Wait!" Mia called, gaining my attention.

I looked and saw she was gesturing wildly toward a battleship in the middle of the enemy forces.

"Go for that big bastard, Leo," she said. "We have to gamble to win this now."

"The destroyer we've gained control of is too small," I said. "It can't build up enough velocity in such a short distance to take out such a large—"

She shook her head. "No," she said. "We won't kill it. But we could knock down her shields. Just *one* of her shields."

I thought it over for about a second then went with her plan. The destroyer swerved drunkenly and slewed around to go roaring toward the battleship. We followed directly in the destroyer's wake, and the rest of our fighters followed me.

In the final moments before impact, the captain of the battleship recognized the danger. He fired on the destroyer that was bearing down on him. Dodging wasn't going to work—it was all happening too fast.

The destroyer went orange with incoming fire, then flared white. She was breaking up. But such was her velocity and mass that she slammed into the battleship's prow anyway. The larger ship's protective shield flickered and died.

"Now," I told my crew, "it's time to earn our pay."

"But we don't get paid, Chief," Samson said.

"Shut up and focus."

He fell silent, and we all reached out to grab hold of the biggest vessel on the battlefield. She was bigger than any of the Imperial ships, even bigger than our battleships.

It took only a half-minute or so. Somehow, I'd expected a larger vessel to be harder to hack, but it really wasn't. A computer was a computer, no matter what it was attached to.

The big ship became ours, and I didn't waste any time. It was impolite, but I first had to get rid of the Imperials that were manning her.

"Open the hatches," I told my crew. "All of them—all at once."

They did it, and the results were as predictable as they were dramatic. Bodies and debris went spraying out of the big ship in every direction. Tiny flailing forms tumbled into space, ejected explosively.

Then, with her defenders helpless, we took full ownership of the behemoth. We forced her to turn ponderously, focusing all her weapons on the nearest Imperial cruiser. She blasted her ally out of the sky inside the span of three fast heartbeats.

It was wild and glorious—and a little bit sad to watch. One at a time, our treacherous monster blasted her sisters. They were so close and stuck in their formations at point-blank range. It was a disaster they were unprepared for. All their shields were positioned to defend against Rebel ships, not an attack from one of their own. A series of massive shots in the flank took them down one after another in rapid succession.

After the eleventh kill, the Imperials figured out something had gone horribly wrong. They turned on their queen, and they tried to kill her.

This greatly disrupted their formation. Our Rebel ships, many of which had been about to flee, suddenly took heart.

They joined the fight in earnest, hitting the confused Imperials from two sides at once.

As I watched, other Imperial cruisers occasionally switched allegiances to join us. Others I'd trained had gotten into the act and managed to commandeer more ships.

The hacked ships ejected their crews, and then turncoat vessels began to pour fire into their former allies.

It was a sweeping victory. Less than one Imperial ship in five managed to escape. When it was over, we were left with more ships than we'd started with, due to our numerous captures.

Transmitted cheering went on and on after the battle had ended. It wasn't just my crew making a racket, either. It seemed that every Rebel in the fleet was hooting and screeching at once.

Letting *Hammerhead* drift, I surveyed the situation. I felt good—how could I not?

But I was worried, too. The Imperials wouldn't like this. They weren't used to losing. How would they react?

It was anyone's guess.

=48=

After the destruction of their core fleet, the Imperials stopped coming into our region of space. The Orion Front fell silent. A thousand inhabited planets were spared destruction, but many others hadn't survived. Nearly two hundred islands of life had been left smoldering and devastated in the enemy's wake.

"Looks like they've given up and gone home," I said to Shaw several months later.

We were near Epsilon Aurigae, a beacon star in the Orion Spur. It was closer to the front lines than Rigel, and the fact we were able to stand guard here demonstrated how far we'd driven the enemy back.

"Yes, they've pulled back," Shaw said. "If you read our histories, the situation is unprecedented."

I shrugged off his fears, but in truth, I felt uneasy as well. It would be easy to assume the enemy had been permanently beaten, but I knew they might not be. They were back inside their cluster licking their wounds.

"But—" I began to argue with him. An incoming call on my sym stopped me.

"Blake?" Captain Ursahn said. "Get up here."

"Got to go," I told Shaw.

He nodded thoughtfully and watched me head for the lifts. I could only imagine what he was thinking. He might be jealous, or he might be overjoyed. Either reaction was justified.

I'd garnered a lot of points for old Shaw by the end of the war. He was up for a promotion to lieutenant commander. It was even possible I'd make lieutenant myself, but I had to go through officer training first in order for it to become official.

When I arrived at Ursahn's office, I found she wasn't there. A burly member of her species directed me toward the command module.

I headed up the final set of broad steps with banging boots. All these big Kher seemed to walk with a heavy step. It was my turn to be heard at a distance.

Captain Ursahn was on her bridge, standing in the middle of a team of Fleet officers. They were going over a vid file.

I stopped dead in my tracks. I considered doing a U-turn and heading back to the hangar. Only the fact I couldn't come up with a viable excuse for dodging her kept me from doing it.

Projected in the air in front of her like a misty dream was a three-dimensional representation of Dr. Shug's laboratory. I was hanging spread-eagle in the middle of the scene.

Damn, I looked awful. I had bags under my eyes, puckered needle-tracks on my limbs and back, and not enough straps to hide anything important.

The only consoling detail was that fact that while my junk was hanging low, my head was held high.

"There you are, Blake," Ursahn said over her broad shoulder. "Get up here and explain this."

Reluctantly, I joined the throng on the bridge. This wasn't the imagery I'd hoped to see on display when I finally was summoned to *Killer's* nerve-center.

"What do you want to know, sir?" I asked her.

She stared and frowned at me for a moment.

"This is abuse," she said at last. "This is unsanctioned. Did you offer some kind of offense to the Secretary or his team?"

I shrugged. "You arrested me and took me up there yourself, Captain," I pointed out. "Don't you know what the charges were? Don't you know why they tormented me in Shug's laboratory?"

She narrowed her eyes. "No, I don't. That's why I'm concerned. This isn't a contest. This isn't a chance to advance in rank. Neither is this an interrogation of an enemy combatant."

"It's illegal, then?" I asked hopefully.

"As far as I'm concerned it is."

"Well, what are you going to do about it?" I demanded suddenly.

"Do?" she asked as if startled. "I'm going to seek the truth."

"That's all? You were duped into playing a part in a crime. All you want is an investigation? Maybe you should send them a strongly worded text."

She looked at me curiously. "How did you get out of that situation, anyway?"

"It was a test of sorts," I explained. "They wanted to know if I could hack my way out of my bonds. I did so, and they were so impressed they backed my attack plans."

"Hmm…" she said, and I could see she was thinking hard.

"You're not actually going to do anything, are you?" I demanded. "Are you afraid you'll lose status points?"

"Not at all," she said, her hackles rising visibly on her neck. "I plan to *gain* points. I'm trying to figure out a way to use this to my advantage. Perhaps you could aid me in this matter instead of hurling insults."

I smiled. "If it screws this bunch of primates, I'd be happy to help."

She led me to a shuttle, and we cast off a few minutes later. We traveled to the battle station in orbit around Epsilon Aurigae.

The star itself was quite far away as the station had been built at a safe distance. The central star was a white, F-class supergiant. It had a strange companion which I'd learned had puzzled human astronomers for years.

Every twenty-seven years the main star dimmed. This had been observed from Earth for centuries. For about two years, the star's brightness dropped a great deal, causing humans to classify it as a "variable" star.

The truth was quite interesting. The orbital companion that dimmed the central star had turned out to be a sphere of heavy dust that was forming a large planet over time. When this dustball happened to get in between Earth and the star, Epsilon Aurigae appeared to dim from our perspective.

It was at just this distance that the Rebel Fleet had decided to build their battle station. The dust cloud had solid debris in it, some chunks which were as big as asteroids. Mining this region produced all the components required to manufacture a new station in space.

Parked around the station were several hundred ships. Seeing Imperial designs among them at first made me jump—but then I recalled they'd been captured.

The guns on the battle station had been salvaged from the Imperial battleship I'd helped deliver to our side. One would think that after such a great victory, I'd be rewarded—but then, the Rebel culture was different than that of my Earth.

When Captain Ursahn landed her shuttle and we climbed out, we were immediately set upon by a gang of dockyard thugs.

This event, in and of itself, wasn't too unusual. Rebels were, by definition, a rowdy group. Even in Earth's history, rebel nations had rarely been full of the most generous and forgiving souls.

Two of the ruffians grabbed Ursahn as she was the first to exit. Two more reached for me—but they got a surprise. My disruptor was out and blazing.

Unlike the practice weapons I'd used in the hangar deck arena back on *Killer*, my sidearm was fully charged and set to deliver maximum pain.

The first of my attackers went down in a fetal ball almost immediately. He didn't even scream, but he did shiver and wet the deck.

The second man—if I could even call him that as he had scales running up and down his thick arms—ripped my disruptor from my hands and tried to use it on me.

That was an error. My human team was tricky, just like the predators aboard were always claiming. We'd added a safety feature to our disruptors, so they were able to distinguish friend from foe.

In this case, anyone who wasn't a member of my crew had been designated a foe. We rigged our disruptors to detect a significant change in the body temperature or the DNA sequence of whoever used it. The gun would short out if it a non-human grabbed it, giving him a jolt of power.

His teeth set to clacking, and his eyes popped open comically wide. I kicked him once, and he toppled onto his back.

Captain Ursahn was faring worse. She was stronger than either of her assailants, but she was outnumbered and weighed down. She had a firm grip on two clumps of fur—something that grew disgustingly from between the scales on the arms of the attackers.

Still, they held onto her and wouldn't let go. Snarling and roaring, she flailed, knocking them about until I came up behind them and bashed them on the head.

All four of the yard dogs soon lay in a heap on the deck.

"Who do you think sent them?" I asked her.

She looked at me in surprise. "No one *sent* them. They want status, that's all. The question is, who tipped them off? Who told them the hero of the Fleet was on his way over here?"

I looked at her in alarm. "You mean they attacked us because I did well in the last battle?"

"Of course. Think about it: now that the war might well be over, how is anyone going to achieve a rapid rise in rank? There are no more enemies to kill. Everyone is turning on one another with hungry eyes."

This was a stunning concept for me. These people understood nothing of peace, let alone fair play. They had their rules, but it seemed to me they were the rules of the Dark Ages. Crazy, vicious tribesmen, loyal only to themselves and their immediate circle of companions.

"How can the Rebel Fleet stay intact if we're all going to start attacking each other?" I asked her.

"It can't," she admitted. "It never does. Once it serves its purpose, which is to get the Imperials to grow tired of their sport, we always disband. Once every millennium, the process is repeated."

"But what if we're wrong this time?" I demanded. "What if the Imperials are only taking a break, or refitting their ships?"

"Ah-ha!" she said, throwing one long finger upward. "Now, you have divined why we're still cooperating. We aren't yet *certain* that the Imperials have left our region of space."

Feeling another headache coming on as I followed her into the battle station's labyrinth of passages, I wondered what was coming next.

=49=

We didn't alert the Secretary about our visit, but somehow he already knew we were coming.

Instead of greeting us personally, he sent Admiral Fex to do the job in his stead.

"I'm sure you'll understand that Secretary Thoth is a busy man," Fex said smoothly. "He's wrapped up in declaring this war to be a success as soon as today."

"We want to talk about our status," Captain Ursahn said. "We've received no points for winning this war."

Admiral Fex blinked in astonishment. "Winning…? You?" He laughed then, long, loud, and from the depths of his belly. "Come now, Ursahn, no one enjoys a good joke as much as I do, but—"

Captain Ursahn moved quickly. She gripped him around the throat with steel-like fingers.

Admiral Fex hadn't gotten to his vaulted rank by being slow, however. He had a weapon out and aimed at her midriff.

They both stood there, growling at one another for a moment.

"Perhaps I can be of service," I said in a light tone. "It seems to me that there should be plenty of status points to go around for all of us. Isn't that the way it works?"

"No," Captain Ursahn said without taking her eyes off the admiral or his wicked-looking weapon. "Not exactly. The trouble here must be that there isn't a direct chain of command to the Secretary. Am I right, Admiral?"

He looked at both of us with hate. "Let go of my throat or I'll gut you, Ursahn," he rasped. "No one will question it. I'll even get a few extra points—not much, but something."

"I don't get it," I said to him. "Why do you care? I came up with a winning plan and we took down the Imperial Fleet. As Ursahn here is my captain, she shares in the glory. As you are her admiral, you get a piece of that too. Isn't that good enough?"

"And what about the Secretary?" Admiral Fex asked. "Is he to be left out in the cold? Shug is his subordinate, which makes you his creature, his discovery. If you'd only followed orders, he'd have gotten the majority of the credit for all this. But no! The military is claiming it all!"

Frowning, I tried to puzzle it through. I gently waved for Captain Ursahn to release the tall bastard, and she did so reluctantly.

"Now," I said reasonably, "why don't you lower that weapon, Admiral? You can always shoot us later."

He did so, fractionally.

"Don't try any of your tricks on me, human," he said, rubbing at his throat. "I was sending arrogant fools like you to their deaths before you were born."

It was a surprising statement, but one I calculated could well be true. I filed it away and continued talking to my two barbarians in calm, low tones.

"Listen," I said, "there has to be a way to work this out. Just tell us what you need, Admiral. Why do you care so much that the Secretary cashes in big?"

"Because he has aspirations to enter public service," Captain Ursahn said.

"You mean you want to become a politician?" I demanded. "You want the Secretary's job?"

Admiral Fex shrugged. "What of it? After the rank of admiral, there's nowhere to go in the Fleet. Worse, now that you ended the war, we're all stuck where we are for the rest of our careers."

I was beginning to catch on. "Basically," I said, "now that the Imperials are gone, you're all turning on one another. It's a dog-eat-dog system, and you all want to be at the top of the food chain."

"Crudely stated, but those are the essentials," the admiral admitted.

I rubbed at my chin for a moment, thinking hard.

Admiral Fex reacted with alarm. He raised his weapon again. "Are you trying to hack my personal equipment?"

"What? No! I'm thinking. Please sir, settle down."

They let me think. I stared at one, then the other. Finally, I had an angle.

"As I see it, the problem here is the Secretary. He's causing all this friction between three military people. That's the core of this conflict."

Captain Ursahn eyed me speculatively. "A bold plan," she said. "But I don't know if I have the guts to follow it through."

"Plan?" I asked. As far as I was concerned, I'd yet to lay out a plan.

"Yes," Admiral Fex said. "Stop hinting around, Blake. You're suggesting we kill the Secretary. That will give all of us rank by opening a slot above me. I see the wisdom of it, but I know there are distinct regulations against outright assassination. And just beating him to a pulp won't do it. That path of advancement is for the military, not—"

"Hold on!" I said, interrupting. "I didn't mean we were supposed to knock off the Secretary. "Captain Ursahn here has something that may help."

I told him then about the recorded vids. That we thought they were proof of illegal practices, and that they could be used to bring down the Secretary politically.

"Huh," Admiral Fex said, eyeing me. "You *are* a schemer. A true brother of the trees. I'll tell you what, if this works, I'll see that Earth is taken off the menu the next time around. The Rebel cause could use a race like yours."

"What menu?" I asked.

He shrugged. "We always try to lead the Imperials toward certain troublesome planets when the next hunting party comes along. That way, we rid ourselves of irritants and sate their bloodlust at the same time."

I almost shivered, but I managed to maintain my composure. These people were ruthless. To them, planets could be won and lost without a qualm. Only their own personal advancement mattered.

"Do we have an agreement?" I asked him. "We take down Thoth, then the military gets all the credit for this victory. That's who really deserves it, anyway."

After some grumbling, they finally agreed.

"Just one question," Admiral Fex asked us afterward. "Who gave you those vid files, Captain?"

She eyed him for a moment. "They appeared in my workspace without a traceable source."

Admiral Fex narrowed his eyes and walked away. We followed him, and I hoped this fragile alliance would last.

* * *

The takedown of Secretary Thoth turned out to be more difficult than expected. He was as slippery as an eel and much better connected.

Nevertheless, new evidence kept appearing to support our case at critical moments. Some of his indiscretions didn't even make sense to me, but they created a firestorm of excitement among the Secretary's peers.

I gathered he wasn't all that well-liked in administrative circles. Either that, or someone really wanted to stomp him flat in the courtroom of bureaucrats.

It wasn't until two months later that I figured out who was behind it all.

We were still docked at the battle station. My role had morphed into one based around the teaching of hacking techniques. I had no doubt the brass would throw me back onto the front lines the second the Imperials showed up again—but so far, the Orion Front had stayed quiet.

After a long day of technical training, I happened to run into Dr. Shug. I had a soft spot for the fuzzy guy, even though he'd pretty much tortured me on the rack when we'd first met.

"Hey Shug!" I shouted, and he spun around to look at me.

He hesitated as I marched toward him. He looked like he wanted to bolt, but then he straightened and stood as tall as he was able.

"Well met, Ensign Blake," he said. "I'm glad to see you're still healthy."

I eyed him for a second. "Any reason I shouldn't be?"

"A man like you has many enemies," he said. "You'll always attract the ambitious, the vengeful. Take care."

He turned to go, but somehow I had a flash of intuition.

"It was you, wasn't it?" I asked him.

He froze then glanced back. "I have no idea what—"

"The secret communications. The vid files. All the incriminating evidence against Secretary Thoth. You helped us take him down. Why?"

Dr. Shug's mouth twitched, and his ears seem to widen on their own. "I'd appreciate it if you would keep such wild speculations to yourself, Human," he said stiffly.

I laughed. "No chance. You did it. I can see it in your face."

He appeared alarmed. "Have you taught your sym to perform facial analysis?"

"No, I can do that on my own."

"Fascinating... I really should have dissected you the first time we met. Perhaps there will be another opportunity in the future."

"No, I don't think so. In fact, talk like that makes a man like me want to expose the ape behind the scenes."

We eyed one another sternly for several seconds. Finally, he showed me his teeth, and I did the same. I hoped he was smiling—it was sometimes hard to be sure.

"Very amusing," he said at last, giving me the hint I needed. "Yes, I provided you with certain details. You did the rest, however."

"As you knew we would. You know, when I first came aboard *Killer*, everyone told me they hated our kind—the primates. They said that we were sneaky and always ended up on top of the organization no matter what anyone else did. Now I can see their point."

He clasped his hands in front of himself. "Someone wise once said that it isn't the deed that counts. What matters is who gets the credit afterwards."

"Right... but you still haven't answered my question. Why take out the Secretary?"

He shrugged. "Perhaps you should look at an organizational chart sometime. There are only so many paths to advancement. I'm on the scientific track, but I've topped out my steps."

"You don't mean—you want to be the new Mr. Secretary? Is that possible?"

"Why not?" he asked me. "I'm just as clever as anyone else at the top, and I've been close to the heart of this project from the beginning."

"Says who?"

He gave me another flickering smile. "You military types aren't the only ones who receive anonymous packages of information now and then."

Shug left me then, standing in the passageway. I watched him go, marveling at how smooth and low-key he'd played it from the very beginning.

I would have to keep my eyes on that guy in the future.

=50=

Shaw came to see me a few weeks after I'd run into Dr. Shug on the station. He was all smiles.

"This is truly a glorious day for both of us, Blake," he told me. "For your entire crew, in fact."

I looked around at my people, and they gathered slowly. We were all wary. Now that we were known as heroes, it was like we had giant "kick-me" signs on our backs. We'd been threatened and attacked several times.

"That's great," I told Shaw, unsure what he was talking about.

"You want to hear my good news?" he asked us.

Samson narrowed his eyes. "You were promoted, is that it? I see new squares on your shoulders."

"It's quite true," he said proudly. "I've been moved up in rank. You will now refer to me as Commander. Note that this reflects well on all of you. I wouldn't have been recognized as an achiever without your help."

Gwen put her hands on her hips, and her expression flinched disdainfully. Shaw wasn't good enough at reading human gestures to catch on.

"You took all the credit, didn't you?" Gwen demanded. "Why hasn't Blake been promoted? Hell, we should all be stepped up in rank!"

Shaw looked at her in surprise. "Your logic is twisted," he said. "I'm in command. You followed my orders, and my plan worked. I hardly see how—"

Samson threw up his hands and took a threatening step toward Shaw. "You mean to tell me we got *nothing* out of this?"

"Far from it," Shaw said. "You've been granted the greatest gift the Fleet could spare. You've been released from your duties!"

He clapped his hands over his head oddly. It was a gesture I'd seen repeated several times before. It was a display of excitement and triumph.

"What a rip-off!" Samson complained. "What do you mean released? Have we been fired?"

Shaw lowered his arms and blinked in confusion. "I thought you'd be pleased. *Killer* will transport you back to Earth, where you can live out your days in peace. All the fighter crews are disbanding."

"Seriously?" I asked, trying to absorb what he was saying. "The war is over? We've won?"

"No, nothing of the kind," he laughed, "the Imperials have merely gone to sleep again—or they've decided to raid another part of the galaxy full of easier prey."

"You're going to dump us back on Earth?" Mia asked. "What about me?"

"You'll go back to Ral, of course."

Mia looked disappointed. She glanced at me, and I realized what she was feeling.

For a brief flash, I considered requesting that she be allowed to accompany me home—but I realized that wasn't going to work. She would be a freak on Earth. She would be one of a kind and probably very unhappy.

"Such warrior hearts," Shaw said, shaking his head. "Most crewmen cheer when they get this news. But you—you can't spit the blood out of your mouths, can you?"

"I'll be happy to go home," Dr. Chang said, "but it is a shock."

"You'll technically still be in the reserves," Shaw continued, "but with your extremely short lifespans I'm sure you'll be dead and gone before the Imperials come here again to hunt."

"The reserves?" I asked. "How does that work?"

"Your syms will keep track of you. They'll live on until you die yourself. At that point, your service requirements will have officially ended."

"Ha," Samson grunted. "Just like the Marines back home. I'm surprised you don't just flush us out the garbage chutes into space."

"That would be a waste of good training," Shaw said seriously.

"What about you?" Gwen asked. "Do you stay on or go home?"

"I'm from the planet that commissioned this ship. *Killer* will return to her home space, and I'll return to my duties in my star system."

"But you'll still be a lieutenant commander?" Gwen pressed. "While Leo here gets nothing?"

"Well, there won't be time to put him through the officer training. You'll be back on Earth before it begins. Recruits from the primitive worlds rarely become officers anyway—but in this case, it *could* have happened if hostilities had continued."

I nodded, and I wasn't entirely sure how I felt about the whole thing. The change was so sudden, so final... It was like I'd been allowed to glimpse another world, and then having it yanked away from me.

But I knew I needed to keep my crewmen happy. They were looking down in the dumps, probably for the same reasons.

I slammed my hands together, making a loud report. They all jumped and looked at me.

"This is fantastic!" I said. "Can you believe it? We're going *home*! Back to our green Earth at last. Can any of you tell me you haven't felt homesick?"

They shook their heads.

"Good enough then," Shaw said. "I wanted to tell the five of you in person, because you helped make all this happen. Now, I'll spread the news. Feel free to tell anyone you meet."

He left us, and we stood in a loose circle.

"You led us home in the end," Samson said, smiling. "And to think I tried so hard to kill you back on Earth."

"Yeah," I said, "that would have screwed up everything."

Our group laughed and broke up. All over the hangar deck, I heard cheering break out. The word was spreading. For us, the war was over.

Dalton found me next. He put out his hand, and I shook it.

"You did good, Blake," he said. "I want to take back every shitty thing I ever said about you. Well, most of them…"

"Same here," I replied.

We both grinned.

"Look me up when we're standing on real dirt again," he said. "I'll be somewhere around Manchester."

"I'll do that."

In a similar fashion, I met with numerous others and discussed our future plans. They were all stunned, relieved, and a little bit sad. We'd been part of something big together. We all had lives to go back to, but there was no way they could be as interesting and unique as serving in the Rebel Fleet.

Mia was among the last to find me. The first bell had rung, calling us to our pods again.

"Once more," she said, pressing her warmth against me. "In the fighter this time."

I didn't have to be convinced. I took her hand and led her aboard *Hammerhead*.

We made love in there until the second bell, when we walked together back to the pod. The crew knew us well enough to know what was up, and they eyed us in amusement.

All except for Gwen, that was. She was curling her lip. Could she be jealous still? I thought she'd gotten over that.

=51=

Returning to Earth took almost a month. By the time we jumped into our home space, we were more than ready to muster out and leave *Killer* behind.

The carrier's deployment system followed a consistent pattern as the crews were disbanded. Each time, a single fighter was shunted out of the lower breach. When it was fired out into open space, it was up to the crew to land safely.

It was a strange way to end our enlistment in the Rebel Fleet. Commander Shaw explained that they had to return us home as soon as the Imperials retreated. We were, after all, not prisoners aboard *Killer*. We had been "volunteered" by our home planets.

Piloting *Hammerhead* for what I assumed was the last time, I steered the tiny ship toward my birthplace.

"You're sure you know how to reenter an atmosphere?" Dr. Chang asked me again.

"As long as I keep our speed down, we'll be fine," I assured him. "This will be a powered landing, not a glide-down or a splashdown. I'll keep the angle fairly shallow, and I won't let the friction build up too much."

"Are you still sure you want to land on the Pentagon's lawn?" Gwen asked nervously. "That seems provocative."

"We're cleared for it," I said. "Shaw said that he talked to the government, and they were agreeable."

"What if they try to shoot us down or something?"

I chuckled. "Samson, look sharp on those countermeasures!"

"I'm on it, Chief."

Dalton was in Mia's place today, as she'd been left behind with her original crew. He stretched out, ignoring the armament controls.

"I'm going to miss weightlessness," he said. "And Hawaii, too. You should land us on those islands, Blake. Let our governments pay if they want to fly us somewhere else."

"He's got a point there," Samson agreed. "They'll probably do a brain-suck on us to get every drop of information they can. No reason to rush it."

"They won't have to," I said, looking around the crew thoughtfully.

"Uh-oh," Dalton said, taking his legs off the trigger mechanism for the main cannon. "I can tell you're going to do something unexpected. What is it?"

"Well… what if we didn't return *Hammerhead* to the Rebels? I mean, what if she had a malfunction and *Killer* had to leave her behind on Earth…?"

They stared at me for a second, then Dalton grinned. He grabbed my shoulder and shook it.

"That's the first smart idea I've heard come out of your mouth in a month! Listen, I know the perfect fence. He can move anything, a Rembrandt, a—"

"Hold on," I said, "I wasn't talking about selling it."

"What then?"

I shook my head and turned to the group. "Listen up. Earth is now in contact with the rest of the wild Kher, but we lack any serious space-going tech. We'll never catch up enough to build a fleet of our own—at least, not in our lifetimes. I intend to help with that. If Earth's engineers can dissect this ship, they can build their own based on this design."

"That's wrong," Gwen said.

I turned to her, a little worried. Her skills were going to be critical in order to implement my idea. I hadn't floated my plans back aboard *Killer* because I knew there were too many recording devices everywhere. But now, I needed the cooperation of everyone aboard.

"I'll need your help, Gwen," I said. "You're our best hacker. We need to use our syms to take this ship for our own. We'll make it look like an accident—a malfunction of some critical system."

"I don't like it," she complained.

"Listen," I said, "this is bigger than we are. We're talking about Earth's future."

"Why can't our government just buy one of these ships, if they need it so badly?" she asked.

Forcing a smile, I lowered my voice and tried to stay calm.

"Listen," I repeated, "we don't have anything to trade. At least, nothing that's worth traveling across interstellar space to get."

"I don't know about that," she said, "they came here to get us."

"Yes, but only because that was a legal requirement for them."

She eyed me for a while then sighed.

"Okay," she said at last. "I'll help you. But if they come after us, I'm telling them it was all *your* idea."

"That's exactly what I'd do if the situation was reversed," I lied. "But don't worry—they won't come after us. We should be good for another thousand years."

We spent the next hour guiding our ungainly bird down into the blue skies and streaky white clouds of Earth. She really was a different-looking planet than I'd realized. Bright colors interlaced and swirled with a frosting of gasses, but they were more muted than I'd seen in books or movies. The ocean was an unexpected shade of blue, almost a gray, and the land was a mottled patchwork of greens and browns.

When we glided down toward the East Coast of North America, none of them objected. Dalton was from the UK, and Dr. Chang had begun his life in China. Even so, they seemed to agree the United States government was the most trusted entity to receive this jewel.

Maybe they would screw it up. Maybe my brothers and sisters on Earth would squander this opportunity, or try to hoard it for their own national gain. But I couldn't control that part. I could only hope the tech would get out, and my home world would grow up.

The universe was so much bigger and more dangerous than it had been just a few short years ago. Instead of random points of light that we theorized about, we'd been allowed to go there.

Just the data logs aboard *Hammerhead* would grant humanity centuries worth of interstellar exploration. We'd been out there, and the sensor data was all in the data core. The storage capacity of even a small, outdated fighter was tremendous by Earth standards.

So, before we touched the mesosphere, Gwen was hard at work hacking *Hammerhead*'s central guidance computer with her sym. We were supposed to set the fighter down, climb out, and stand clear while the ship flew back up to the carrier on automatic—but I planned for events to proceed differently.

"I can't get in," Gwen complained. "They—they changed some parts of the security interface. My old codes have already been locked out."

I was busy piloting *Hammerhead*, but I had a plan for this, too.

"Dalton," I said, slapping his leg. "You're on. Fly this bird down to D. C."

"What?" he said, looking shocked.

Like the others, he'd been busy soaking in the sights of the East Coast below us. We'd pierced the cloud-layer and were beginning our final descent. The view was fantastic.

It was dusk on this part of Earth, and I could see lights and highways. There was a thrill in everyone's gut. We couldn't believe we were really home. It had been many long months since we'd been collected and processed back on Hawaii.

I locked the controls, switching them over to Dalton. Then I climbed out of my harness. Dalton, cursing steadily, took over.

We were still running the anti-grav system, so I floated to Gwen's station in the back.

"Let's do it together," I said.

"I don't think this is going to work."

"Don't worry," I said, giving her my most reassuring grin.

Together, we let our syms out to do their worst. I'd already cut our data-feed channel to *Killer*. No doubt the CAG was annoyed and trying to reconnect—but I didn't care.

This was too important. Today, I was no longer a member of the Rebel Fleet. I was a human helping out my home world.

"I think I've got an angle," I said, "check out Tand's log entries."

"Why?" Gwen asked. "He's dead."

"I know he's dead *now*," I said, "but he had full access to this fighter in the past. Based on how the Kher seem to operate, I'm gambling that they haven't updated his login info yet. It probably hasn't even occurred to them."

Together, we followed that thread of logic. Suddenly, the ship opened up to us. We'd done it. We'd hacked a Rebel fighter with an old passcode.

"We're in," I said.

"It really isn't a crime," Gwen said worriedly. "I mean—this is *our* ship, right? They assigned it to us. We're her crew."

I touched her arm and assured her our former commanders wouldn't mind a bit. I don't think she really bought it, but she gave me a flickering smile to show me she appreciated the effort.

We landed on helipad three, just as we'd been ordered to do. I took pains to alter *Hammerhead's* programming—well, not really. I just blanked the rest of her flight plan.

Outside the landed ship, a throng approached cautiously. I saw uniforms, service trucks—even an ambulance. They weren't taking any chances.

"Now," I said, "drop the fuel pods."

Samson looked at me in surprise. "Me?"

"That sub-system is on your interface, isn't it?"

Grinning, he did as I asked. We heard a clang and a rolling sound. The group outside scrambled back in alarm. I was glad to see no one was crushed.

Outside, the rescue crews retreated and Marines moved in to surround our ship at a safe distance. We could see them standing warily in full dress. They didn't seem to know if they were a color guard or a combat team. They avoided the fuel tanks as if they were dangerous—which they were.

"Edgy, aren't they?" Dalton laughed.

"They probably think we've just laid a pair fusion bombs on them," Gwen said.

"Time to make this real," I told them, and I opened the main hatch.

A few Marines approached us. I kept my hands over my head and waved at the nearest troops.

"I need these fuel tanks rolled off the pad!" I shouted.

"Are they dangerous?" asked the duty commander.

"Yes, of course."

He swallowed, folded up his lips into a tight line and began shouting orders. My request was honored immediately by a dozen men with surprised looks on their faces.

While they worked, Gwen and I edited the ship's logs—by erasing all records from the last shift. No scrap of data since we'd launched from *Killer* was spared.

A squad of brass shouted for my attention, but I ignored them. I pointed up at the sky, indicating I was calling the Rebel Fleet. They shut up, pronto. No one on Earth had the balls to go up against what they considered an alien menace from the skies.

After we rebooted *Hammerhead*'s computer, I made a call to the CAG. He relayed me to Captain Ursahn herself.

"We've got a problem, sir," I said.

"So, human," she said. "You're not infallible after all."

"Afraid not," I said ruefully. "This ship is old—almost falling apart after all the combat she's seen. We had to drop her tanks over the ocean. She's functioning now, but barely."

"A pity…" she said. "What do you suggest that we do?"

"It's all up to you and your time schedule. You can call her scrap, or you can send down a tug to pick her up."

"That will delay our departure by hours," the captain complained.

"Like I said, it's your call."

I waited tensely for her decision. I was hoping she'd just piss-off and go away. It would be the easiest that way.

After a full minute, she called me back.

"We're dispatching a tug. Hold at your position."

I gritted my teeth and sucked in a hissing breath through them. *Killer* wasn't going away.

"You've got it, Captain," I said, as if I didn't care at all.

When she cut the channel, it was my turn to release a long series of curses. A two-star general walked up to me during this tirade and asked what the hell was happening.

I told him quickly, and he caught on right away.

"We need this ship," the general said. "We've been talking about stealing her ever since we were told you were returning."

"I'm glad to know my efforts will be appreciated," I said.

He clapped me on the shoulder and leaned close. "Not by everyone," he said. "Some are terrified it will start some kind of war. What do you think we should do to pull this off cleanly?"

I looked around at the greeting party and my crew. *Hammerhead* stood proudly on her skids, all burnished metal and wicked-looking weapon mounts.

The sun was setting, looking orange through the haze.

"We've *got* to steal her," I said.

The general nodded grimly and smiled. "You've got my attention, Blake. What can we do to help?"

=52=

Sometimes, I think I'm at my best when I'm winging it. That seemed to be true with women, work—and war.

We had to move fast. It was getting dark, and we had maybe forty-five minutes before the tug from *Killer* arrived. I had to make every minute count.

First, I requested a Blackhawk gunship. They complied worriedly, and twenty minutes later it set down on a nearby helipad. The weight and size of the vehicle was pretty close—I hoped it would be close enough to be convincing.

Then, we rolled one of the two big fuel tanks right up against the gunship.

My crew was getting nervous by this time.

"Dammit, Blake," Dalton said, "why don't you just let us go home? I'm itching for some iced whiskey and a warm companion."

I appreciated his state of mind, and I expected a hero's welcome too—but business came first.

"You're still under my command for now, Dalton," I said. "We're part of the Rebel Fleet until Captain Ursahn releases us."

"You're a right bastard, Blake," he muttered. "What can we do?"

"We're blowing that up," I said, pointing at the Blackhawk and the fuel tank. "With you manning the cannon."

"You crazy sod," he laughed. "We'll be hanged—or worse."

"You let me worry about that. Gwen, blank the ship's logs again the second it's done."

"Oh... this is too insane."

"Keep it together," I said, "trust me."

"I don't trust you."

"Well then—trust in America."

She looked at me and shook her head. She sighed. "I'll do it, but I want it noted that I was only following orders."

"So noted."

"That defense always works, Gwen," Dalton cackled. "Don't worry for a moment, my love."

She muttered foul words, hacked into the ship again, and gave me the thumbs up.

Dalton didn't even wait. He blasted the helicopter to fragments. Flaming pieces went cartwheeling into the air. He hooted with joy.

"Right under the Yanks' noses," he said. "Look at them run!"

The marines who'd been ordered to clear the vicinity had been loitering at what they'd thought was a safe distance. But when the air ripped apart, releasing deadly radiation in pulses, they'd all fallen on their faces. Some of them had singed hair and uniforms. I hoped no one was seriously injured.

"Dammit Dalton," I said, "You might have killed someone."

"I had to make it look good," he argued. "If the tug gets down here and—"

He didn't make it any further as the ship lost power. Gwen had blanked everything again, which had shut down *Hammerhead's* systems.

We piled out and I waved for the two-star. He came striding to me, red-faced in anger.

"I've got injuries, Blake!" he shouted. "Why didn't you tell me to clear the area?"

"There wasn't time, sir," I said. "And I need your help again."

"What do you want from me now?" he asked, marveling at the audacity.

I pointed at *Hammerhead*'s hulk. "Get this thing off the pad and hide it," I said. "You've got... nineteen minutes."

Roaring and waving his arms violently, he spun around and began shouting orders.

"What do we do in the meantime?" Gwen asked.

"Maybe we could go inside and get something to eat," Samson said. "I'm hungry."

"We'll stand near that exploded helicopter and wait," I ordered them. "Look sad. When the tug gets here, it has to be convincing."

The next twenty minutes passed by in a whirlwind of activity. First, the Marines tried to lift the ship with a Skycrane, but it was too heavy. Then they tried a bulldozer. I assured them the hull wouldn't dent in. It was tougher than steel.

That got it moving. With an awful screeching sound, they pushed it over the pavement and even a section of grass. The only hiding spot in range was a subway station nearby. They evacuated it and shoved the fighter down the escalators. It was still showing a little—so they parked a set of trucks in front of it.

We watched the skies for the tug coming down from *Killer*. Since we'd powered down *Hammerhead* after pretending to destroy it, there was no data transmission for the tug to lock onto. From their point of view, the fighter had vanished.

When the tug finally landed, the crew aboard wasn't happy to see a pile of smoldering wreckage.

I met them at their hatch.

"Hey guys," I said. "We've had an accident, I'm afraid."

Then I faltered. All my bullshit died on my lips. The tug crew was made up of Terrapinians. I'd forgotten that they'd been reassigned to this duty after it had been decided they were too slow to fly fighters.

"Blake?" asked the chief. "Did someone destroy your vessel?"

I looked from one pitiless set of eyes to the next, and I swallowed hard.

"Nope," I said. "We tried to—"

"We monitored unusual activity on the way down here," he interrupted. "We saw your fighter's cannon fire—but now the vessel appears to be missing."

I had a whole line of crap to feed him, but I could tell it wasn't going to work. My plan had been to claim the ship had blown up when we'd tried to get her flying again on our own. But all of that was out the window now that there were impartial witnesses.

"I'm afraid I'm going to have to arrest you and your crew," the turtle chief told me.

The Marines behind me lifted weapons and pulled back bolts. I waved for them to relax.

"Wait a minute," I said to the big Terrapinian. "Don't you owe me, Chief? Didn't we have a deal? I'm your lord or whatever, right?"

"That service-arrangement has lapsed. You've left the Rebel Fleet."

"No I haven't. Not until you call up to *Killer* and report in. Right now, we're still part of the same service. You owe me, and I'm calling in your debt right now."

He hesitated. "What is it that you wish of me?" he asked slowly.

"Report back the truth, that *Hammerhead* was destroyed, but her crew escaped the accident."

"That's not the truth," he said in a flat tone. His kind were painfully literal.

"You must present it as the truth," I explained. "If you do, your debt will be repaid. You'll be free of my service."

"I don't want to be free."

"Then find yourself a new leader! You'll be discharged on your home world soon. You can find peace there."

He pondered this for what seemed like several long seconds. Finally, he agreed.

"I will dishonor myself with this deception, but this will end our pact.

"That's the deal, buddy," I told him. "Have a nice flight home."

He stared at me for another few heartbeats. Finally, he said a single word: "Primates..." He said this word with disgust, even loathing.

Then he turned around and climbed back into his tug. Minutes later, he flew his ship back up into the sky. I watched the ugly vessel shrink until it vanished. Only then did a smile spread across my face.

The two-star came up and clapped me on the shoulder again.

"That was some grade-A bullshit, Blake," he said. "You've got a lot of stories to tell, I'm sure."

"I do indeed, General."

=53=

The following days were a whirlwind of meeting and greeting. We were heroes—of a sort.

Some people on Earth seemed to believe we were half-alien ourselves. True, due to our syms, we were stronger than normal humans and could do strange things like hack computer systems with minimal equipment. But I rejected the idea we weren't Earth's lost soldiers. I felt everyone on my home planet owed us a "thank you" at the very least.

We did find some who were quite grateful, or at least curious, about us. We enjoyed celebrity and endured debriefings in random order.

After a few months, we became mascots. We did the talk show circuit, had ghostwriters pen tell-all books, and even started our own web-shows. All the while, we weren't allowed out of the sight of government agents.

Those agents shadowed us, guarded us, and picked through our trash. It was like being a suspect and a victim at the same time. The people of Earth didn't quite seem to know if they should arrest us or nominate us for sainthood.

Part of the problem was due to the status of the other humans who'd been affected by the Kher. They were still homicidal. Apparently, when the Kher had rejected them as prospective crew members, they hadn't bothered to shut down their syms. These subjects were still in the same aggressive mode that we had experienced, seeking one another out and trying to kill each other.

Several had succeeded in dying, but not all. Lt Commander Jones was one of the lucky ones, so to speak. He asked for me often from his maximum security cell, and eventually I was given permission to meet him there.

"Jones?" I asked, seeing a large shape at the back of his cell.

It was dark inside his cage—apparently, it calmed him to stay in a cool, dark place. The psychologists who'd briefed me said it was the light of the stars that drove him to madness.

He came forward until his face was splashed with a soft glow from the passageway. His eyes had a haunted cast to them.

"Jones?" I asked. "What have they done to you?"

"The jailors?" he asked. "Nothing. It was the Kher that left me like this—like discarded garbage. I rage every night tearing up my flesh—but by morning, I've healed."

He showed me red gashes on his arms. Apparently, he'd ripped right through the tough fabric of his prison uniform.

"You called for me," I said. "Is there anything I can do for you?"

"Maybe," he said, "but I doubt you'll do it."

"Try me."

He licked his cracked lips as if he was hungry. His eyes were red-rimmed and fixedly staring.

He shuffled closer, to the bars, and I stood my ground.

Then he lunged. He caught hold of my jacket, and he pulled me to the bars.

Surprised, I struggled with him. Two guards sprang forward, jabbing with buzzing sticks through the bars. They stung him over and over. He howled, but he didn't let go.

There was madness in his eyes, and I realized the bloodlust the syms had released into his body was still there, still churning in his brain. He *needed* to kill me with every fiber of his being.

I left behind a clump of my hair, some skin and my jacket before I wrenched myself free. He retreated to the back of his cell with these prizes—and began to chew on them.

Shaken, I retreated from that place and walked the streets of D. C., feeling troubled.

Later that same night, Gwen called me. She used her sym, as we'd figured out how to get them to interface with our cellphones. It was a neat trick that no one else on Earth had yet mastered.

"How did it go?" she asked me.

"Badly," I said, describing Jones' attack.

"That's awful," she said. "What can we do?"

It struck me at that moment that there might be something we could do.

"Will you come see me?" I asked her.

She hesitated. "All right," she said in a quiet voice.

We met at a bar. We talked about a plan. We drank, and one thing led to another.

Since time immemorial, individuals who went through great trials tended to bond. We were no different. Because of our experiences off-world and our biological modification by the syms, we were in a class with very few peers on Earth.

We ended up making love in a hotel room. Afterward, we lay awake for a long time, discussing plans.

"Do you really want to do this?" Gwen asked me sometime before dawn.

"Yes. I think we have to. We owe it to Jones. We owe it to all the survivors."

She didn't answer. Soon, her breathing slowed and deepened. She'd fallen asleep—but I wasn't able to.

* * *

The next day, I returned to the prison to see Jones again. This time, I brought Gwen with me. It was a special facility for very special prisoners in the Appalachian Mountains. We were allowed inside, but we had to get past an army of officials before we could see Jones.

They all told us it was hopeless. Rational appeals had been tried, and they couldn't penetrate the evil haze that clouded his mind.

We asked for a chance. We hinted that we could do things they weren't able to do with mere drugs and counseling.

At last, probably because some general somewhere figured we couldn't make matters worse, we were allowed into Jones' presence.

"Blake?" he called out softly. "Have you brought me dinner?"

Gwen shuddered at my side. She had no doubt in her mind that she was the dinner Jones had in mind.

"We're here to help you," I said. "As you helped me once, on the side of a lonely road."

He laughed. It was a sudden, loud sound and tinged with madness.

"I remember that!" he called. "Did you kill Dalton? I still hate that little frigger."

"I beat him down more than once," I assured him.

"Oh good—good. Now... just let me have the girl. I promise to be quick."

Gwen and I exchanged glances. We stepped forward together.

Jones lunged again, but he did so too early. He couldn't reach us. His face was pressed up against the bars, straining and grunting with effort. His dirty, outstretched fingers clawed the air.

Each of us grabbed a wrist and held on.

Our syms had made us strong—not like him, but close. Together, we could keep him pinned to the bars. He struggled and grunted like a wild animal.

The next part was the most difficult of all. We invaded his mind.

More accurately, the syms in our bodies leeched through our shared blood in crescent pools torn by his fingernails. Our sweat, blood, grime—it all intermingled.

We hacked him. We hacked his mind.

It was a strange thing. It wasn't telepathy, or any other variety of psychic mumbo-jumbo. It was all chemical.

What is a brain other than a collection of cells? How did it communicate with our bodies if not by sending impulses through chains of other cells—the tissue we call nerves?

We used these same pathways. It was just another network to us, different only because it was one made of flesh rather than copper wire.

The symbiotic creatures that resided in all three of us were alike, but Jones' sym had never been switched out of its initial mode. It had gotten worse, in fact, after the blood-trials on the ship.

But we managed to capture his mad sym, to calm it, to get it to modify behavior patterns.

Three long minutes passed, and by the end he was squirming weakly instead of howling. Dry sobs wracked his body when we finally let go of his hands. He sank down onto the floor of his cell, letting his face rest on the stained concrete.

"This feels good," he said in an utterly calm voice.

"You feel better now?" Gwen asked.

"Yes…" he said hoarsely. "Yes, I think so. My rage is gone. I don't need to kill you anymore… Thank you."

"We don't deserve your thanks," Gwen said. She was crying silently, wiping tears from her face.

"You don't owe us anything, Jones," I said. "You served Earth just as much as we did."

We left him to recover, but that wasn't the end for us. There were other survivors in other cells.

We had a long day ahead.

The End

Books by B. V. Larson:

UNDYING MERCENARIES
Steel World
Dust World
Tech World
Machine World
Death World
Home World

STAR FORCE SERIES
Swarm
Extinction
Rebellion
Conquest
Battle Station
Empire
Annihilation
Storm Assault
The Dead Sun
Outcast
Exile
Gauntlet

LOST COLONIES TRILOGY
Battle Cruiser
Dreadnought
Star Carrier

Visit BVLarson.com for more information.

Made in the USA
Columbia, SC
05 September 2017